WORTH OF
A DUKE

A LORDS OF FATE NOVEL, VOLUME 1

K.J. JACKSON

First Edition: June 2015
ISBN: 978-1-940149-10-3
http://www.kjjackson.com

DEDICATION

– AS ALWAYS, FOR MY FAVORITE Ks

– BONUS DEDICATION, TO MY GRANDPARENTS

There is a character in this novel (the grandfather) that embodies such the spirit of my very own grandparents, and I would be remiss if I did not include them in the dedication.

All four of my grandparents were unique, flawed, wonderful, humorous people.

I am fortunate in that I knew them when they were older and they had figured out life, so they were nothing but caring, intelligent, and fun influences on my life—from my Colorado grandpa who used to take us hunting for rattlesnakes (to my mom's horrification), to my Minnesota grandpa who would do headstands just to get us to giggle. Both of my grandmas raised and kept their families together, and left legacies of how truly strong women could be.

So, to them, thank you.

CHAPTER 1

YORKSHIRE, ENGLAND
JANUARY, 1821

He was done rescuing damsels in distress.

Done.

Done with grace. Done with witty conversations. Done with feigned kindness.

Done with women.

Throughout the season, the summer full of house parties, the mini-season—every function, every event, had the same women, the same machinations. A stubbed toe. A spilled drink. A lost direction. Anything to get the attentions of the newest duke—to get him alone.

He'd already expended too much energy—too much time— in the goal of gaining a wife and producing an heir. A goal that wasn't even his own.

He was done.

That resolve did nothing to halt his hand the second he turned the bend in the trail. No, his hand dove for the pistol in his overcoat, instant outrage at the scene down the hill.

Nor did that resolve curb his instincts—instincts that sent his heels into his horse's sides without thought of the vow he had just spent hours brooding about.

Avoid women at all costs. Especially ones that needed saving.

Pistol in hand and horse thundering down the incline, Rowen Lockton, Duke of Letson, squinted. He blinked hard at the scuffle near the bottom of the hill, trying to clear the sleet from his eyelashes.

A woman, black cape swinging and dragging her down, had the bridle of a nag tight in one hand as she jumped and scrambled with her other hand, trying to reach a leather satchel. The satchel was high above her head, held from her grasp by a scrawny man on the nag.

Even from his distance, Rowen could hear her yelling, begging for the bag while the man laughed.

The nag spooked, and the man yanked on the reins. The nag reared, and there was no avoiding the front hoof that nicked the woman's head. She dropped hard at the blow, hand still tangled in the nag's bridle, leaving her hanging.

Fast down the hill, Rowen closed the distance and had his horse blocking the path before the thief could drag the woman any further, trampling her into the mud under the stomping nag. Rowen pulled up on his reins, his pistol pointed at the man.

The nag stilled and the scrawny man looked up from the woman dangling to the ground. Seeing Rowen's pistol, he stuck the satchel under his leg, digging into his pants and pulling out a short knife.

"I would recommend you sheathe your knife, sir," Rowen said, keeping his voice casual.

"I ain't 'fraid o' a stinkin' pistol."

Rowen cocked the hammer, leveling the barrel at the man's chest, shaking his head in pity. "Look at me, man. Do you honestly think the pistol is the only weapon I have with me? I can easily run a bullet through you from this distance. Can you say the same for that butter knife you hold?"

The woman below scrambled to her feet, untangling her left hand from behind the horse's bit ring.

The man clamped his mouth shut, staring at Rowen's pistol. Rowen could see the thief blustering, wanting to argue—wanting to spit in his general direction—but was just smart enough not to.

Rowen gave a nod to the woman below. "It appears I have wandered upon a distinct difference of opinion between the lady below and you, sir, on the ownership of that satchel."

"You ain't come up on nothin', nob."

"Hell and damnation, you ass." The woman had already slipped between the two horses and was after the satchel under the man's leg. "Give me my damn bag back."

The man started to swing the short knife in her direction.

"It will be the last thing you do if that blade even whispers her skin." Rowen's voice was no longer casual. It was death.

The man froze, his eyes darting back and forth to the thick woods that surrounded the trail on either side.

"Do not even think it," Rowen said. "You will get nowhere in these woods on that horse."

The woman reached up, grasping the long leather strap on the bag, and yanked it from under the man's leg. Clutching it to her chest, she skirted out from between the two horses, stopping at the side of the trail.

"I think you would do well to remove yourself from these lands before his lordship learns of this. I believe he would not look kindly upon a thief in his woods—certainly not as generously as I am." Pistol still trained on the man, Rowen nicked his horse to the left, allowing enough room for the man and his nag to pass.

The man glanced at the woman, then at Rowen. Fuming and clearly weighing his options again, he finally shook his head and kicked his horse into movement, eyes shooting daggers at Rowen as he passed.

Rowen did not lower his pistol until the man was well over the hill and out of sight.

When he finally looked down at the woman, she hadn't moved from her spot. She still clutched her bag and still stared at the area on the trail where the thief had disappeared. Sleet had collected on the top strands of her dark blond hair braided to the side, some of it frozen, some of it melted.

Rowen dismounted.

It wasn't until he walked across the trail to her that she looked up at him. The dire set of her mouth instantly disappeared when she met his eyes, a bright smile appearing and turning her whole face into—Rowen could only describe it as—innocent radiance.

Blast it.

Another distressed damsel. And a beautiful one at that.

He needed to extract himself from this situation as quickly as possible.

"Thank you, sir. I was in a bit of a jam there and was not having any success at getting my bag back."

"A jam?" Rowen's eyebrow cocked.

Her hazel eyes turned serious. Big, hazel eyes—blue flecks flashing—that were a direct view into every emotion that flickered through her body. "I had hoped I could hold on long enough that he would tire and give me my satchel back. Silly, now that I think on it. But I did not know what to do."

She lifted up the dark leather flap on the bag and peeked inside. Satisfied, she closed it, retying the leather strings that held it closed.

He studied the bag. "What is it you were fighting so hard for?"

"Oh…I…" A sheepish look overtook her face. "Nothing."

"It was something you almost just died for."

Her bottom lip sucked under her front teeth as she eyed him. "If I do not show you, are you going to try and take it from me as well?"

"No."

"Thank you," she said with a breath of relief. A slight blush began to color her cheeks as she looked at him. "But you are still curious?"

Rowen nodded. The fleeting thought that this was an elaborate trap by this woman and that man went through his mind. Throughout the years, he had not only honed his skill of judging intentions, he had mastered it, and everything about her told him she was not a threat. Misguided, being alone in the thick of these woods. But not a threat.

"Fine. Best to have you not wondering." She untied the flap and opened the bag, holding it up so he could see inside.

"What? Brushes? That is what he stole? Did he know?"

She shook her head. "No, I do not think so. I have nothing else of value on me—I was surprised he took them. I came upon him just as he was grabbing my bag, and he ran."

"Why would you risk your life for them?"

"Why would I not?" She snapped the flap closed, retying it, and then wiped a stream of melted sleet from her forehead before it could drip off her eyebrow. "They are the most important things in the world to me, save for my mother and grandfather."

Rowen laughed.

"Do not laugh at me, sir."

"No. I only laugh at the absurdity of this situation. That I just risked my own life and limb for a few brushes."

"You were hardly at risk, sir. You had a pistol. That man was weak. A weasel. And weasels rarely do damage, unless they are mad or crazy."

Rowen shrugged.

She sighed again. "Do not look at me like that, sir. There must be something you would risk your life for?"

"No. Nothing."

"Nothing?"

Rowen crossed his arms over his chest and shook his head.

"Interesting." She cocked her head, looking at him curiously. "Well, we are of different sorts." She paused, watching him while clutching the bag to her belly. "But I do thank you. You look to be travelling as well. Can I offer you some of my food? I had just snagged a squirrel before I came upon that man at my camp. It is not a lot of meat, but it is something."

"That is not necessary." Rowen glanced back over his shoulder at the hill. He wasn't quite sure that the thief was gone for good, and judging by the man's anger as he left, Rowen didn't like the thought of that man coming back after this woman.

But the more he talked to her, the more Rowen realized he needed to disentangle himself from the current situation. She was too attractive. And her speech pointed to her roots being in the Americas. Not a true Englishwoman. Which made her oddly interesting to Rowen. Interest that did his vow to avoid all women little good.

"Please, sir, I insist. It is the least I can do to thank you. Plus, I need to get back to the squirrel before it goes bad and I am famished."

Rowen gave a quick nod. "I will stay for a short while, at least until you move out of the area. I am not convinced that thief is leaving these lands."

"Excellent. And truly, thank you. I did not mean to interrupt your travels, but I do appreciate your assistance. I do not know where all these odd Englishmen are coming from—" Her mouth pulled back in a cringe. "I apologize. I did not mean to include the present company in the 'odd' part. But these woods—this area has been particularly disconcerting."

"No offense taken."

"Thank you. I am Wynne. And your name, sir?"

"Rowen—Rowe is what I am most accustomed to."

"Very nice. Proper forest introductions are complete." She gave him a bright smile and brushed past him, disappearing into the woods on the opposite side of the trail.

Rowen grabbed his horse's reins and followed her into the trees, clomping through the thick, wet underbrush. Below the tree cover, the sleet yielded, only the occasional drops falling on Rowen's shoulders.

"I did not expect to come across a trail like that," Wynne said over her shoulder to him, still clutching her bag. "And I am not too far inward—I have been following the stream."

Within a few minutes, Wynne stopped in front of a small fire nestled between the thick roots of an oak tree. It sputtered against the dampness. She stuck her head through the long strap of the satchel, slinging the bag to her back.

Rowen tied his horse's reins to a low branch as she moved to a mangled knee-high root. She grabbed the tail of a dead squirrel sitting on top of the root and picked up the sizable knife next to it, pointing the tip to the flickering flames. "You can warm yourself by the fire—what little that is left of it. It has been hard to find dry wood. I have to gut the squirrel, but I would rather not do it here—not with the bears."

Rowen stopped motion and glanced at her, startled. "Bears?"

"Yes. The bears and coyotes can sniff out the slightest blood, and I would rather not invite them to camp. Even if I now have to move on from here, I would rather eat in peace."

Rowen stared at her, mouth agape as she stepped over the tall root and started in the direction of the stream Rowen could hear. Bears? Coyotes? Where the hell did this woman think she was?

A moment passed before he shook his head and followed her. He caught up with her at the stream and watched from a distance, silent, as she knelt by the water and took the large hunting knife, handle wrapped in strips of rough leather, and slid it along the end of the squirrel. Skin removed, she worked the long blade efficiently, and within minutes, the squirrel was gutted and she was separating the meat.

He stepped closer to her. "That is a rather large knife."

"It is. My grandfather's. He hates it when I take it." She smiled up at him with a quick glance. "What is it that brings you this way? You are the first soul I have come across in days—aside from that thief. Why are you in the area?"

"I breed horses. I was in the vicinity to assess a stallion for siring—impeccable lines, I was assured."

"Not as impeccable as touted?" she asked, not looking up from the squirrel.

"No, it was not. It is why I like to make my own determinations on the worth of a horse, rather than send a proxy."

She nodded and leaned forward, flicking innards into the running water, and then dunked the bloody knife into the stream. Blade clean, she set the knife on a rock and scrubbed both hands in the water, shaking her head. "Ouch. That is wicked cold."

She looked up at him as she scrubbed her fingers. "I know you must be new to these parts, but do you know what mountain I am on? I am not quite sure how, but I seem to be off Shiote Mountain and am having a devil of a time orientating myself."

"Which mountain?" Rowen's eyes narrowed at her. Again, where the hell did she think she was? It was quickly becoming clear this woman was possibly a bit addled.

"Shiote. I have been following the stream. I assume I will hit the valley where I can see Shiote Mountain, but I cannot figure out how I strayed off the mountain in the first place. Shiote is my home—with my mother and grandfather."

Her fingers clean of the blood, Rowen noted that several of her fingertips were stained dark, almost black. Whatever that was, it didn't wash off. She quickly rinsed the meat and stood, walking past Rowen back into the woods.

Rowen was close on her heels this time.

"So you are lost?"

"Yes. I do not recall how I moved off the mountain. I was painting, and grandfather was with me. But I sometimes lose time when I am deep into a scene, and he tends to wander away from me to hunt." She stopped to pick up a long stick, swiping the end twice with the knife to make a point, and then started to thread the meat onto the stick as she walked. "And then the next thing I knew, I was alone in these woods."

"How long have you been following the stream?"

"A few days. With no luck of direction except for the stream. That is what my grandfather taught me to do. Follow a stream downward. You will always end up in a valley or a wide clearing to orientate yourself, or come across a travelled path. But I do not think that trail over there counts—aside from the thief—it looks more like a little used cut-through than anything else."

"It is."

She looked over her shoulder to him, relieved, just as they arrived at the fire. "Good—so you know where we are?"

She quickly sat on a thick root, adjusting her satchel on her lower back, and sank the tip of the knife into the dirt, the leather handle sticking upright. Tossing a few scraps of bark by her feet onto the fire, she started to roast the meat, slowly spinning it above the flames.

Rowen stood a distance from her, trying to decide what to do.

On the one hand, he didn't want to leave her vulnerable to the thief coming back. On the other, she was clearly confused about not only her current location, but what land mass her feet were even on—and that meant she was thick in a heaping mound of trouble that she didn't even realize she was in. Trouble he had no desire to embroil himself into.

He pondered her, watching her roast the meat, head cocked to the side as she hummed. She didn't have the slightest inclination she was an ocean away from her mountain. His eyes drifted downward to the hunting knife stuck into the ground.

He stepped to a spot across the fire from her. "Why did you not take the knife to that man?"

The humming stopped. "The knife? Oh, this?" She glanced down at the blade by her leg, then looked up. "I do not know how to use a knife on a man."

"You knew exactly how to use it on a squirrel."

"Truly, sir, a squirrel and a man are hardly the same thing."

"A given. But they both cut the same."

Her face contorted into squeamishness. "Yes, well, my grandfather has never taught me how to use a knife on a man— only on game. I would not know what to do. Perhaps it is a skill I should ask to acquire."

Rowen knelt, balancing on the heels of his black boots as he clasped his fingers in front of him. "It does seem a good skill to have. One never knows what is around the bend. Especially when one is a young female alone in the woods."

"Honestly, sir. This is the first time I have ever encountered a thief in these mountains."

"Your accent, Wynne. I am trying to place it."

She pulled the meat from the fire, jabbing a thumb on the thick of it. "Spongy." She shook her head, sticking the meat above the flames once more, and looked to him. "I am surprised an Englishman could discern regions. I do not have the mountain dialect, do I?"

Rowen shrugged, clueless. "No?"

"I lived in New York until I was thirteen. When my father died, my mother and I came to live on grandfather's mountain. Even after all these years, I know I still do not have the proper twang."

Hell.

There it was. She thought she was on a mountain in America. One mystery solved.

Rowen hid a sigh.

Any way he looked at it, he couldn't leave her. A woman with no notion of where she was, where she was headed to—and as far as he could discern, entirely too innocent.

It was that last part that particularly unnerved him. Depending on whom fate put in her path next, life could go very horribly for her.

Young. Attractive. Innocent. He shuddered. Very horribly.

The last thing he wanted was to be saddled with an addled woman—he had enough problems to deal with here at Notlund.

Wynne pulled the meat to check it again, impatient, and groaned as she stuck it back into the fire, tapping her booted feet under her skirts. He imagined her heavy cloak did her well in this cold but could see the skirt of the dress she was wearing was rather thin.

He would have to take her with him—the very last thing he wanted at the moment. But first, he would have to delicately convince her to come with him.

"You are a painter?"

Her bright smile appeared. "Yes. I was taught in New York from an early age, and since we moved to the mountain, my grandfather has been teaching me. He is not trained like the masters in the city—his strokes, his sense of scene and how he approaches it is very different—but his pieces are breathtaking. He has taught me things I never would have imagined. And he has shown me how to make my own paints from what I can gather from the land." She chuckled. "Which my instructors in

New York would be appalled at. Such a thing is so far beneath
them. But I actually enjoy it."

"You create your own paints?" Rowen asked.

"Yes. Grandfather is nothing if not self-reliant and demands
the same from me. He is happy to take care of mother, though.
We are very alike, he and I, while I am told my mother is very
much as my grandmother was."

"Your grandmother has passed?"

"Yes. I never knew her." Wynne pulled the skewered meat
from the fire, tested it, then smiled and started peeling back strips
of meat and blowing on them. Shaking her fingers from the heat,
she stood and held the stick above the fire to him. "If you do not
grab pieces now, I will gobble it all before you blink."

Rowen held his hand up. "Please, eat. I am not hungry, and
you look ravenous."

The side of her mouth pulled back, perplexed. "I am, but my
mother would be horrified if I did not share. Especially after your
kind help."

"I truthfully want to watch you eat it. I am not hungry."

Eyes narrowed at him, she stepped back, sitting on the tall
root and tearing into the meat. Several pieces swallowed, her
suspicious look only intensified. "Why did you come with me if
you were not hungry?"

She tore off another piece and chewed slowly, staring at him.

At least she had the good sense to question his motives. That
was the first sign of healthy skepticism he had seen from her.

"I do not desire anything from you, Wynne. I know where I
am and would be pleased to help you on your way," Rowen said.
"I would have offered earlier, but it was clear you were famished
and needed to eat. And I did not wish to leave you alone with
that thief still in the vicinity."

Her left eyebrow rose, touching the blond hair that swept
across her brow into the long side braid. "Your intentions are
honorable?"

Rowen nodded. "They are. If you will place your trust in me, I would like you to accompany me for a stretch down the trail we were on."

She fingered a strip of meat hanging from a bone. "Why?"

"I think it will help you get to where you need to go."

"You know where Shiote Mountain is?"

"No. But I can at least get you to a place where you can figure out where you need to go."

She eyed him for a long moment, fingers still rolling the piece of meat back and forth. "My grandfather would not approve."

"Your grandfather is not here."

"But he always told me, no matter what, follow the water. It would get me home."

"That may be, but I think in this instance, he would approve." Rowen stood, hands behind his back in the least threatening manner he could manifest. "If where I bring you does not solve your problem, I will be happy to return you to this stream, and you may go along your way. It is still early afternoon, and at the worst, it will only take away part of your day."

She popped the piece of meat into her mouth, staring at the fire. She looked up at him, her hazel eyes big. "You are an honest man? Honorable?"

"If I were going to steal your brushes or assault you, would I not have already done so?"

"You might just be an odd duck that likes to watch women eat."

Rowen laughed at her solemn look. "That is true. But I think the odds are slim on that account, and you can safely take the chance that I am not one of those."

She stood, fingernails scraping the last remnants of the meat off the bones. "I will go with you, but please, if you are an odd duck, I would prefer you continue to hide it from me."

If *he* was the odd duck?

Rowen shook his head. "I will do my best."

{ CHAPTER 2 }

"You are worried about the oncoming darkness?"

Wynne nodded, peeking out at Rowen from under her wide, black hood. She had it pulled down to her brow and realized he probably couldn't see her nod. The sleet had eased, but the overcast skies had only darkened as they walked. "I am. You said it would only take an hour or so to get to where you wanted to take me."

"Yes. I did. But I did not anticipate that you would refuse to ride on my horse."

Her face went down, eyes on the slushy dirt of the trail for a few steps before she looked at him again. "Sir—Rowe—I realize you have had to walk as well, and I apologize, but as I said at the beginning, I cannot ride on a horse with you. It is much too forward and I do not know you."

"The last four hours have done nothing towards knowing me?"

She smiled and could see he was hiding a chuckle. "You do realize you have only asked me questions and have artfully dodged everything I have asked of you?"

"I have?"

The smile didn't leave her face. "Do not pretend ignorance. You know exactly what you have been doing."

Rowen unwrapped the reins of his horse from his knuckles and re-twisted them around his palm before answering. "I am accustomed to traveling in solitude. And not at all accustomed to talking with another for any length of time."

"Is your solitude a choice or happenstance?"

He shrugged, once more adjusting the reins of his trailing horse in his hand.

She pushed the hood from her forehead, letting it fall to her back, and she scratched the matted hair at her brow. Rowen spoke with a calmness, a smoothness that eased into her ears. That is, when he spoke.

She stole another glance at his profile, wondering if he realized the obnoxious way in which she continued to look at him. The man was handsome. She hadn't realized it at first—she had been so overwhelmed by the thief.

But once she really looked at Rowen, studied him over the fire, she hadn't quite been able to stop. Every time she had dared to flick her eyes onto his face, she was sure she would have gotten used to his looks—that they wouldn't startle her.

Every time, she was wrong.

He was entirely too interesting to look at—his dark hair, strong chin with a light smattering of dark scruff, and eyes that she was still trying to figure out. So deep in color, only the faintest hint of brown kept them from true blackness. He dressed simply—dark buckskin breeches, tall black riding boots, a simple dark overcoat.

But it was something else about him—how the air around him vibrated—that unnerved her more and more the longer they walked. Much like her grandfather, this man was solid, of the earth—he had a raw force that she had to cut through, just to get her eyes on his face.

Wynne gave herself a slight shake and diverted her attention to the trees that were beginning to lessen. The forest was finally thinning out. Hopefully they were close to wherever Rowen was leading her.

She glanced at him. "Well, even if you have shared very little, you have been remarkable in listening to me talk for the last hour about the best ways to sift and grind ochre from my mountain and to then procure it into paint."

He nodded. "I do now know more about ochre pigments than any man ought to have the right to know."

"You are teasing me?"

"Possibly."

She laughed. "If nothing else, I do think you are patient man, if not talkative. And possibly quite bored—but you have maintained the utmost in polite interest."

The trail began to widen noticeably, and they walked a stretch up a long hill in silence.

"Do you think it is much further?" Wynne asked, halfway up the hill.

Rowen pointed ahead. "Just up this hill the forest breaks, and that is where I think you will find an answer about your locale."

Wynne nodded, trying to hold the knot in her stomach down. She hadn't confessed to Rowen the fact that, over the past two days, she had grown increasingly worried that she had strayed so far from home. Her mother would be beyond worry at this point. The opposite, she imagined her grandfather would give her just a slight nod once she walked back into their log house. Wynne had never seen him worried about anything.

Reaching the crest of the hill, her feet suddenly crunched onto loose grey gravel as the woods around them abruptly ended. In front of her, a wide, flat expanse of winter-dormant grass rolled upward.

And then she saw it. Her eyes went impossibly wide in shock, but it didn't halt her feet. Without thought, her feet remained in motion, walking forward.

Ten steps and she stopped, jaw dropped.

"Where are—what is that?" she asked.

A step behind, Rowen moved beside her, looking at her, but Wynne could not shift her eyes to him.

"It is a castle." His voice was far too casual for what was in front of them.

"Yes, but where...how...who built that here? I have never seen anything like it, never heard that this existed here." Wynne gawked at the ancient greying castle. Atop an enormous, open hill, large stones were stacked, the high parapet walls creating a square. A keep rose from inside the walls, and tall, rounded towers—weathered harshly by the years—capped each of the four corners.

Rowen cleared his throat. "It all depends on where you think here is."

Her eyes flashed to him, shrewd. "What? What do you mean, 'where I think here is'?"

"Do you not find it odd that you were near your mountain, and then suddenly, we come upon this castle that you have never seen, never heard of before?"

"Of course I do." Her arms crossed over her chest in a weak attempt to protect herself from the riddle he spoke.

"Look around, Wynne." His arm swept wide across the landscape. "Look around."

Wynne quickly scanned the long flat grounds rolling downward from the enormous grey structure. Her head jerked back to him.

"Turn your body and look around."

"What?" Her eyes cut into him.

"Spin. Turn your body around and look. Truly look around you."

Hesitant to look from his face, Wynne slowly started to turn on the balls of her feet. Her eyes shifted to the landscape around her. It passed by in a blur—the trail, the brown of the trees, the castle.

"Look upward, Wynne, upward."

Wynne spun again, eyes above the treetops into the grey sky. Nothing but high clouds. High clouds as far as the eye could see in every direction.

"No. No. No." She spun around again.

"There are no mountains here, Wynne."

"No—a trick—this is a trick—a trick—it has to be."

"Wynne—" Rowen took a step toward her, but she sprang away before he could get another word out.

Tearing up the long hill to the castle, she ran faster than she ever had in her life. Minutes of running, her thighs burning, her feet lead weights, she didn't stop. Didn't stop until she reached the base of the castle.

Sliding to a halt, the toes of her boots stopped in the mound of dirt hugging the base of the castle. Panting hard, she stared at the grey stone as her hot breath sent droplets to cling in the pockmarked crevices.

Terror shaking her hand, it took will she didn't know she possessed to lift her arm. Her palm flat, it hovered a hair away from the stone as disbelief kept her hand from touching it—from altering the reality she had been so firmly in.

A quick thrust, and her palm hit the dank stone. Cold. Hard. Real.

Her other hand came up, and she ran along the wall, hands dragging on the rough stone until she rounded the corner tower. She looked down the next outside wall.

Still real. Real and there was no telling herself it wasn't.

Breath shallow, she pushed from the stone, spinning again, looking out at the vista around her.

The castle stood on a high hill, and from this spot, she could see land. Just unending stretches of rolling land. Forests. No mountains. The furthest thing from mountains.

She noticed Rowen making his way up the hill, approaching her, his horse still following him. He strolled, not hurried, a cautiously curious look on his face.

"No." She whispered it before he was even near enough to hear. "No. No. No." She repeated herself over and over, her voice only getting louder, head swinging back and forth.

It was when Rowen had almost reached her that she bolted. Bolted as fast as she could back to the trees. Back to the forest. Back to the mountain.

She had to get back to the mountain.

"Wynne—" His shout was low as she blasted past him, her already angry lungs screaming as her speeding legs pushed her muscles past pain and into agony. She wasn't about to stop.

She had to get back to the mountain.

She made it down the length of the brown grass, her feet slipping, her bag slapping wildly on her backside, but she kept her balance.

Five steps into the trees, an arm clamped around her waist, yanking her off the ground, her legs flying forward.

Earth no longer below her boots, she tried to spin in Rowen's hold, shoving at his arm wrapped around her.

She hadn't even heard him behind her.

"No, Rowe. I have to get back. Back to the mountain. Let me go," she screeched.

"There is no mountain, Wynne. None. You are not in America. You are in England."

"No."

"Yes."

"No. Put me down. My mountain. Shiote. It was right there. It was right there. Just let me go. I can get back to it."

"Will you swim? Because that mountain is an ocean away from here, Wynne."

She stilled, craning her neck up to him. "Put me down."

"Are you going to run again?"

"Put me down." She repeated herself, each word punctuated with calm.

Gently, the clamp around her waist loosened. Her toes touched the ground.

Dazed, the weight of her own body heavy, Wynne walked stiffly away from Rowen toward the castle.

Halfway up the hill, the heft of her feet became too much to bear and she crumpled, sinking to the ground.

She sat, her feet folded under her, numbly staring at the top of the corner tower closest to her, the grey clouds swirling above it.

She remembered.

Remembered her grandfather dying. Remembered his weathered hand slipping from her cheek. Remembered standing at the mound of dirt claiming him back to the land. Remembered walking up the plank onto the ship. Remembered days of sickness, wishing for death on the water.

"You are in England, Wynne." Rowen's voice, soft, reached her ears from behind. She hadn't heard him approach this time either.

She could not turn her head to him. Could not move. "I know. I remember."

He knelt next to her, his knee resting on a scrub of brown grass. "Where did you come from, Wynne? There are no towns even remotely near the trail where I found you. How did you get there?"

It took a long moment for Rowen's question to sink into her muddled mind. How had she gotten there? She hadn't the slightest inkling.

Her head swayed back and forth. "I do not know."

"But you do remember traveling across the ocean—traveling to England?"

"I do. My grandfather died. And we boarded the ship."

"I am sorry for your loss. He sounded like a fine man."

She could only nod at his words, her throat constricted.

"Do you remember arriving in England?" Rowen asked.

Wynne swallowed a deep breath, trying to shove her grandfather's last hours out of her mind. "No. The last thing I can place in my mind is the ship. The horror of it."

"Did something happen to you?"

"I was sick. Very sick. My mother was there—my mother—" Her suddenly frantic eyes went to Rowen. "Where is my mother?"

"She was with you on the voyage?"

"Yes. She was the one that wanted to travel here after grandfather died. Where is she?"

Rowen shook his head, his dark eyes somber, telling her he knew even less than she did.

She looked away from Rowen, her eyes running across the castle in front of her. "Where am I?"

"That, I do have an answer for. Are you ready to hear it?"

Wynne closed her eyes. It took seconds for her to afford the slightest nod.

But Rowen said nothing.

She cracked her eyelids to look at him.

"You are in Yorkshire, on the estate of the Duke of Letson." He pointed up the hill. "And that behemoth is Notlund Castle."

{ CHAPTER 3 }

Rowen paused by the castle wall, pretending to look out at the grounds, but kept Wynne in his vision.

She had asked to be alone for a few minutes, and Rowen obliged, fetching his horse from nibbling on a few sprigs of hardy green weeds at the base of the castle.

Right hand clasping the reins of his black stallion, Rowen scratched at the outer stone of the castle with his forefinger. The stone crumbled to sand at his scraping, letting loose the disintegrating layer of the wall. His mouth settled into a frown. The decay was worse than he remembered.

He glanced fully at Wynne. She looked miniscule sitting in middle of the wide-open hill. Taller than average, she was nonetheless slight, and she looked as though she could blow away like a fallen leaf. She hadn't so much as twitched in the minutes since he left her, but he wasn't so sure she wouldn't run again.

He had to keep a wary eye out for that. He could just let her go, let her disappear into the woods—but he already knew he was not about to let her leave this place. Not alone. Not without a destination.

For all that Rowen lacked faith in, there was one thing he did trust—fate. Every time in his life he had listened to fate—done what fate asked of him—he had been richly rewarded. Every time he had fought fate, ignored it, he had been punished.

He already knew that fate had put this woman in his path. That she had appeared on that usually deserted trail, getting robbed at the same time he crossed her path, was too much obvious fate to ignore.

He understood perfectly the message fate was giving him.

And that fate was laughing at Rowen's vow to avoid women.

But what was he supposed to do with her now?

Rowen had been relieved when she had asked to be alone—it was incredibly awkward being near her—he had no idea what to do with her obvious pain. Comfort her? He had not an inkling on how to do that.

The wind whipped up, barreling along the open ground, and it caught loose blond tendrils around her face, whisking them into her eyes. The movement seemed to awaken her from the stupor she was in, and her toes flipped under her as she rocked her body onto her heels.

She was standing by the time Rowen reached her, adjusting her cloak and settling the sling of her bag over her shoulder.

Eyes pensive to him, she waited until he stopped walking before speaking.

"I would like to thank you again, Rowe, for not only assisting me with the thief, but for leading me here. You were correct in that I would not have believed you had you told me where I was while we were in the woods." Her voice wooden, she tucked one of the rogue tendrils of hair behind her ear. "It was a kind thing for you to do. Especially after I interrupted your travels."

Kind was not something that was usually attached to his name. Rowen cleared his throat. "It was not a bother."

"I have nothing to pay you with for your troubles—I thought we were on mountain politeness, where sharing a meal would suffice as gratitude. I can offer you my brushes—"

"No, Wynne. Absolutely not. No payment is expected or accepted. And your brushes—how can you even think of offering those after you nearly died for them?"

She gave a sad half-smile. "I did not truly think you would take them. I know my knife is more valuable, but I need that more than I need my brushes."

"Why?"

"I will be returning to the woods."

Rowen's mouth set into a hard line. "You will? Did you remember where your mother is?"

"No. Nothing since the ship. So I have to find her."

"Where I found you, Wynne—there is nothing for many miles in every direction. This castle is the closest thing. There was no sign of anyone but you at your makeshift camp. You said yourself you had been in the woods for days. You were out there alone, Wynne."

"You do not know that." Her arms crossed over her chest.

"I do. What is your plan? It freezes nightly. There is no shelter. You have no food."

Her eyes narrowed at him. "You do not think I can survive in the woods by myself?"

Rowen shrugged, not wanting to anger her more, but not willing to add fodder to her delusions of surviving in the forest.

She took a step toward him as her arms dropped rigidly straight at her sides, hands balled to fists. "My spine was forged on one of the wildest mountains in my land, Rowe. I think I can handle a simple English forest."

"And then what?" he asked. "Do you plan to wander the woods for years? You may never find your mother. Do you plan on dying alone in the forest?"

She spun, her bag flying and hitting Rowen in the hip as she started away from him.

Before she stomped three steps, Rowen grabbed her wrist, jerking her to a stop. She tugged at his hand, attempting to free herself.

"Please. Just stop a moment," Rowen said, voice calm. "Think, Wynne. Think. You are insisting on madness."

She tried to twist her wrist free of his fingers. His iron clamp didn't allow it. He hadn't seen the slightest crack in her since she had stood, but suddenly, the tiniest tear in her facade. Her back to him, she looked up at the sky, shaking her head. From the angle, he could see her eyes start to water.

"I do not have a choice, Rowe. I have nothing. Nothing but what I wear. What I carry. No memories of this land. Nothing. So I need to go back to where I was and try to figure out what I am even doing here."

"You are right, Wynne. You have nothing. Nothing."

Her head swung to him, a tear slipping down her cheek as her eyes turned to fire. "Rude."

"I do not mean it as it sounded." He dropped her wrist, taking the chance that her anger at him was enough to keep her in place. He did not figure she was one to run from a fight.

"Then you meant it how?" The edge in her voice told him he was right.

"I only mean to express the fact that you are blank right now. And tracking down how you got here and where your mother is will be much easier once you remember some things. Trying to survive in the forest in the cold with little food is going to take all of your energy. Energy that would be better spent trying to remember how you got to the middle of the forest. So do that somewhere where there is a roof and food."

"I have no money, Rowe. I could not afford a place to stay even if you brought me to a comfy tavern."

"So stay here at Notlund."

She looked over his shoulder up to the stone structure. "Here? I do not know the people that live here."

"You do. You know one."

Her eyebrows went impossibly high. "You? You live here?"

"Not so much live, as own."

"Do not talk in riddles to me, Rowe, my mind cannot take it now." She scratched her forehead. "You own this place but do not live here?"

"I do. And there is one other thing I need to tell you."

"What?"

"I am the Duke of Letson."

The words did not faze her. No sudden cowering. No sudden fawning. Entirely peculiar.

"But you said you were a horse breeder."

"I am that as well."

Her arms went wide, palms up to the sky. "So you are a duke, so what?"

"So I own that castle, and you may stay there."

She looked from his face to the structure again. "It looks as cold as the forest."

"It is." Rowen's cheek rose in a half-smile. "But there are fireplaces and tapestries that try very hard to squelch the drafts."

Wynne shook her head, arms folding across her chest. "I cannot take your pity, Rowe."

"I understand—I did not think you would take so easily to the idea."

"You were right."

"So I have a bargain for you."

She took an instant step backward from him, startled, but then she stopped herself, foot in midair. Her heel went to the ground, purposeful, but her eyes wavered between trepidation and curiosity. "My grandfather always said to trust my gut, Rowe, and my gut is suddenly very much wary of you."

He broke into a full smile at her words. "I do believe I would have liked your grandfather, Wynne. He did you well. But believe me, my bargain does not contain anything untoward."

"What does it contain?"

"It contains you painting. I have something—someone for you to paint—you are skilled? You can do a portrait?"

"Art demands that skill is determined by the eye of the beholder." Her words came out carefully. "And yes, I can do a portrait."

"Excellent. So I suggest a trade. Lodging and food in exchange for a portrait. At the very least, it will afford you time to gain your bearings back about you."

Her head cocked as she stared at him. He could see her wavering. "Would I be painting you?"

Rowen chuckled. "No. I will never have a portrait done. The portrait would be of the dowager duchess that lives here."

"A duchess…you have a wife?"

"No. The dowager duchess is the widow of the last Duke of Letson."

"So she is your mother?"

"No. My aunt."

Wynne glanced over her shoulder at the trail into the forest, then her eyes swept to the castle and eventually landed on Rowen. "A trade—that is all?"

"That is all."

"I would need paints. There is nothing growing in the forest right now to create my own."

"Easily remedied."

"And nothing indecent—I have your word?"

Rowen shook his head, smile still on his lips. "Nothing of the kind."

It took her several more long seconds to decide. Seconds Rowen had a hard time believing she had the gall to take. He was offering her an incredibly generous way out of her current situation, and she should know that.

She gave him a curt nod. "Thank you. I will agree to your trade."

She stepped past him, starting the walk up the hill.

Rowen whistled. "Come, Phalos."

His horse trotted to his side. Rowen grabbed the reins.

Wynne looked over her shoulder at him, not stopping her stride. "Alexander's Bucephalos?"

Startled, Rowen chuckled. "Yes."

Her eyes swept over the horse. "He is a handsome stepper."

Rowen started after her, smile on his lips. He watched the back of her head—tawny blonde hair pulled to the side into a thick braid, rogue tendrils still floating about with the wind.

He shook his head.

He couldn't remember the last time a true smile had graced his face.

~ ~ ~

Wynne's initial wariness faded the second she plunked a toe into the warm water of the bath Rowen had ordered for her and then insisted she take.

He had said he did not want to present to the dowager
a woodland nymph with squirrel guts under her nails. And
truthfully, Wynne saw the validity in that statement.

After leading Wynne through an empty maze of cold stone
hallways, Rowen had deposited her into a cavernous bedroom
with a simple four-post bed. A tin tub sat beside the fireplace, and
within a few minutes, the fire was lit and several maids, Julie and
Esther, were hauling in steaming buckets of water. Wynne was
just happy to see other people in the place, as she was beginning
to question whether or not they were actually alone in the
castle—she had neither seen nor heard anyone else on the way to
the room.

Both of the girls were young and had giggled and looked at
her with peculiarity when Wynne offered to help them with the
buckets. But the memory was so distant in her mind of when she
was young and her parents had maids in New York. She assumed
she had made a guffaw with them, but couldn't be sure.

Wynne sank deep into the tub, letting the water lap onto
her chin, and took a deep breath, the steam sinking into her lungs
and fighting the chill deep inside her. A chill she knew was days
old in her body.

How on the Lord's good earth had she gotten to the middle
of the forest? And why? And where was her mother? And why did
she have nothing except for her grandfather's hunting knife and
her brushes?

The questions swirled in her mind, repeating again and
again, but answers never appeared in the brew. It wasn't until
goose bumps pricked the skin on her forearms that she realized
the water had turned cold and she had been frozen in place.

She sighed. Still filthy, and now cold.

Ducking her head below the water, she scrubbed the bar of
soap into her hair and quickly worked down her body. She did
stop at her nails, giving them a longer scrub than usual. Rowen
had been particularly kind in helping her, and if he thought the
absence of squirrel guts from her fingers was appropriate when

meeting a dowager duchess, she wasn't about to blatantly deny the obvious suggestion.

Wynne was already in front of the fire drying off when Julie reappeared, a chemise and a grey muslin dress hanging over her arm.

"We need to hurry, miss. The duchess be madly mad at the duke showin' up. No notice, no nothin' she be harping 'bout. I ain't been here that long, and I rightly know she be liken her dining on time, that one."

Wynne shrugged herself into both the chemise and the dress being tossed over her head, trying to separate out the girl's spitfire words.

"Buggerly boo. I forget the slippers, miss. Ye got shoes?"

Pulling her still-tangled hair into a quick braid, Wynne nodded. "I have boots, will that do?"

"It be havin' to. 'Tween boots and late, best bet be the boots with the duchess."

Before Wynne could get another word in, Julie grabbed her boots, holding them out for her to step into. Wynne tied one while Julie tied the other shin-high boot, and Julie promptly grabbed Wynne's shoulders, shoving her out the door, down a long hallway, and down two flights of stairs. Three more hallways they sped along—one long, two short—and every one of them went by in a blur looking exactly like the last—dark, cold grey stone, empty.

Julie yanked Wynne to a sudden stop in front of a set of heavy wood doors, their vertical planks held together with bars of thick, black iron stretching from the hinges.

"Good luck to ye, miss." Julie dropped her hands from Wynne's shoulders. "She be just as bad as ye be imagin', just so ye be prepared."

Discombobulated by the whirlwind walk and Julie's words, Wynne gave a troubled smile. "Thank you, I think."

Pity crossed Julie's face, and she spun to give three sharp knocks on the wood, then instantly turned and disappeared down the hall.

Wynne wondered for a moment if she was an idiot to not run after the girl, escaping whatever was beyond the door in front of her.

Just as she went to her toes, starting to turn and do just that, the door cracked open, and an impossibly wrinkled man in a dark uniform hobbled backward, drawing the door with him. Wynne could almost feel the shards of pain in his stooped back as he wheezed his way through the motion.

Door ajar just enough for her to enter, the man straightened the best his curved back would allow, running a hand along the lapel on his black jacket. "Please, enter, miss."

She could still run. There was no way this elderly butler could ever catch her. The wild thought hit her, but she squashed it down. Again, Rowen had been entirely too accommodating for her to rudely disappear at this point—her mother would be mortified at her.

Plus, the reality of Rowen's earlier words was beginning to sink in. She had nowhere to go. Nowhere to live. At least not until she remembered where her home was. Where her mother was.

Until Wynne remembered something, she had two choices: wander the forest aimlessly, scavenging squirrels to survive, or stay here and try to get her memory back.

Wynne put on her brightest smile. Best to just face whatever was in the room and get it over with.

She turned sideways, slipping through the slim space the door allowed. She had to squeeze past the elderly man, as he had stopped at the edge of the open door. Wynne didn't have the heart to ask him for more room—it had taken him so long to open the door as it was.

Past the butler, Wynne looked up and realized she was interrupting a heated conversation. Standing by a long, dark table, Rowen faced Wynne's direction, arms crossed over his chest. He stared at the woman in front of him. The woman was in black from her toes to the scarf that had just fallen back off of her head.

"You have no right to do what you propose, L.B.," the woman said in a controlled shriek. Bound in a loose bun, her jet-black hair with streaks of grey bounced in agitation. "No right to come here and destroy this. You are not just an idiot, you are a delusional idiot to think you can."

Wynne instantly took a step sideways back to the door, but the old butler had already closed it. Apparently quicker at closing it than opening it.

Rowen glanced up at that moment, catching Wynne's eye. She saw his dark eyes give an odd flicker, but she wasn't exactly sure what she saw. Embarrassment at the woman's words? Amusement?

The look disappeared before she could pin it, and Rowen looked down at the woman, his countenance neutral.

"We will have to discuss this at another time, Duchess, as the guest I mentioned has arrived."

The woman whipped around, and Wynne was immediately struck with two things. One, the woman was older, but beautiful. And two, she had the saddest eyes Wynne had ever seen. The woman was tortured. And her black dress only exacerbated the despair.

Wynne stood rooted in her spot by the door, and the woman advanced on her. The woman stopped, her toes almost touching Wynne's boots, and she stared at Wynne's face.

Her breath heavy, she used her slight height advantage to lean over Wynne. Wynne took the scrutiny, trying not to shrink backward.

Rowen moved to the side of them, his voice low. "Duchess."

There was clear warning in that one word.

The woman waited a moment before she took one step backward, her almost translucent blue eyes going to Rowen.

"This? This is what you bring? This does not placate me, L.B., if that is what you intended to do. You will have to do entirely better than presenting me with this twit of a girl."

"You hardly know that she is a twit, Duchess. Her name is Wynne Theaton, and she happens to be a very skilled artist. I cannot help it if you have not heard of her works. You have been complaining of the monstrosity that is your portrait since it was delivered twenty years ago." Rowen inclined his head to Wynne. "She is the one to re-do your portrait. I do believe your son would have rectified the situation himself, were he alive."

Her eyes flew to Wynne. "Why are your fingers filthy, girl?"

Wynne refused to look down at her fingertips, instead, meeting the duchess's demanding stare. She couldn't apologize for something she couldn't help. "It is the paint. It stains my fingers."

The duchess tilted her head back, looking down her long, straight nose at Wynne. After a second of silence, she gave a curt nod. "Let us dine."

The first two courses came and went in complete silence. The duchess sat at one end of the long table. Rowen sat at the other. Wynne could not discern which was at the head of the table—appropriate, as she had already figured out the battle for dominance in this castle was raging in full force between the two.

She also realized she had just been unwittingly plunked down into the middle of it.

Wynne stole a sideward glance at Rowen. He had changed his attire and was now in full evening wear, his crisp white cravat a stark contrast against his dark hair. His black jacket—if possible—made his shoulders look even wider. She liked the simplicity of him in the woods better, his casual white linen shirt peeking out from under his black coat, along with the well-worn boots and buckskin breeches.

But she also could not deny that he was just as handsome in polished clothes. The light of the fire opposite her flickered against one side of his face. And she was fascinated by the distinct way he ate. Utterly precise, not allowing a finger out of place, or the slightest morsel of food to tumble to his chin. She wondered at it, as she had not imagined this fastidiousness of him.

"At least she knows which fork to use."

The duchess's voice cut into her thoughts, and Wynne jumped, realizing her sideways glance at Rowen had turned into a full gawking. It sent the bite of fowl on her tongue into her throat, and she tried valiantly to hold in a choking, coughing spasm.

"Where are you from, Miss Theaton?"

Head down and eyes watering, Wynne succumbed to the hacking determined to escape. A quick drink of the wine, and Wynne looked up to the duchess, wiping her wet eyes. "Please, excuse me," she choked out, and had to take another sip of wine.

The duchess waited, perturbed politeness raising her brows.

Wynne glanced at Rowen. He was smirking. Ass.

Throat back to normal, Wynne looked at the duchess, smoothing the napkin in her lap. "America. Both the Blue Ridge Mountains and New York. My mother was very adept at society, and schooled me exhaustively on manners. Which is where my knowledge of proper forks comes from. But the manners rarely came in handy on the mountain."

"You were in polite society in New York?"

Wynne could see the duchess's sudden interest, and nodded. "Yes. My parents were. My mother adored the dinners and galas that they both hosted and attended, and was preparing me for a very similar life. That was also where I was initially trained as an artist. I was thirteen when my father died, and we left the day after his funeral for my grandfather's mountain. I do apologize if I misstep in my manners. It has been some time since I have put them to use at an elaborate table such as yours."

The duchess raised her wine, sipping slowly. "How interesting. And how did you make it from America to Yorkshire?"

Surprised, Wynne looked at Rowen. "You did not tell her, Rowe?"

Rowen opened his mouth, but was instantly cut off by the duchess.

"Rowe?" Horrified, the duchess's hand went flat onto the black lace across her chest. She glared at Wynne. "Pray tell me you did not just call the duke 'Rowe.'"

Confused, Wynne's eyes went from the duchess, to Rowen, and then back to the duchess. "I—I did. Is that not his name?"

"He is a duke, Miss Theaton. You address him as 'your grace.'"

The words of apology formed on her tongue, but Rowen spoke before Wynne could get sound out. "I am rather fond of Miss Theaton calling me Rowe, Duchess."

The duchess leaned forward, eyes slicing into Rowen. "The duke is rolling in his grave."

"I am the duke."

"Unfortunately."

Rowen didn't flinch, didn't rise against the obvious disgust the duchess shot at him.

They stared at each other, Wynne frozen between the two. It was when Wynne could hold her breath no longer that she cleared her throat, leaning forward over the table to try and break the sight line between the two.

She produced a humble smile as she looked at the duchess. "I apologize, Duchess, I did not realize." She turned to Rowen. "I meant no disrespect, Ro—your grace."

"I prefer Rowe, Wynne."

The duchess flew to her feet, arm flying into the air. "Travesty. A grievous insult to all you represent, L.B. Disgusting travesty. I have lost my appetite." In a flash, she stomped to the heavy doors, pushing past the elderly butler as he fumbled with the door for the duchess.

Eyes wide and heart thudding, Wynne looked from the closed doors to Rowen. "I apologize. I did not mean to be the brunt of discord between the two of you."

"You are not the brunt, Wynne," Rowen said calmly, appearing indifferent to the duchess's scene. "Merely a convenient pawn to be used by the dowager against me."

"But I believe I should call you 'your grace'—had I known, I certainly would have done so from the start. Things are much different here from on our mountain."

"No." The one word came fast and hard. But then Rowen blinked, and his voice softened. "No 'your grace'—I do not wish that from you. I would prefer you to call me Rowe. It is how we started."

Unnerved at his insistence, Wynne silently nodded. She already called him Rowe, so it would be easy enough for her—though she made a mental notation to not refer to him as anything in front of the duchess. She did not want to repeat that particular scene.

Smoothing the napkin on her lap, Wynne picked up her knife and fork, slicing her meat, searching her mind for a topic to move past the awkwardness of the last few minutes. "The duchess—she has had a portrait done she is not pleased with?"

"Yes, it hangs in the main hall here, and it is the one thing I agree with her about. It is awful. And she has been terrified for years that the portrait would end up representing her throughout the ages."

"Why not remove it?"

Rowen's eyes stayed on his plate. "Her husband was a stubborn man and oftentimes bitter. He demanded that be her legacy. And since he died, she has not removed it either." He shrugged. "Better to be represented by an atrocity, than not represented at all, I imagine."

"That sounds particularly awful."

"I suppose it depends upon how much one cares about what others think, even generations that have yet to be born." He looked up, his dark eyes focusing on her hands. "All in all, it should not be too difficult for you to improve on the original portrait. I will show it to you after we finish dining."

~ ~ ~

Bellies plump, Rowen grabbed a hanging wall lantern from the dining hall and led Wynne into the labyrinth of stone hallways. Within two turns, Wynne realized the necessity of the lantern and suddenly wished she had her own.

Pitch blackness both in front of them and behind them, Wynne made sure to move slightly behind Rowen and keep her steps close to his. Spooky—and her grandfather had long since cured her of being spooked by the darkness.

But the darkness of an open mountain was very different than the dank, cold darkness they were surrounded by. Wynne started to hum to herself and then realized the echo of it made the hallways even spookier.

She looked up at Rowen's profile, the light of the lantern sending a warm glow across his cheek. "What is it that the duchess does not want you to destroy?"

"The dowager would prefer for me not to tear down half the castle."

Wynne stopped in place. Rowen kept walking, and it took a moment for her to realize she was getting left behind in the dark. She scurried to catch up. "You want to tear down half the castle? Why?"

"It is crumbling, and it would cost five fortunes to repair it." His smooth voice offered calm logic. "The dowager is adamant I fix it instead, as you overheard."

"But what about the history of this place?"

"I am not interested in a history that serves no purpose other than to drain my finances."

"Even crumbling, this is an impressive structure," Wynne said. "Spooky and confusing, but impressive. I can understand her resistance."

"Yes, but it is ridiculous to keep it standing. We do not live in feudal times. This castle was built for defense and knights and wars and surviving sieges. Not for one woman and her team of servants. It is a ridiculous waste in this age."

Rowen stopped, and Wynne bumped into his back—a solid wall against her slight frame.

He turned and handed her the lantern as he used both hands to lift what looked like a heavy black iron latch on a thick wood door. The creaking of ancient iron hinges filled both the hallway behind them and the room in front of them as Rowen pushed the door open.

Taking the lantern from Wynne, he walked into a cavernous hall. High on the stone walls, eerie slits in the stone let what little moonlight there was into the space. Three stories high and wide, this hall had to run at least half the length of one side of the castle, Wynne guessed. On the two levels above, landings and balconies capped the ends, while symmetrical arched alcoves lined the sides.

Rowen walked ahead as Wynne stood and took in the grand hall. He lit several torches leaning out from the stone, illuminating the area he wanted her to see.

Wynne joined him, scanning the stone wall before them that displayed a long row of large portraits.

Moving sideways along the display, she studied the few works she could see in the light of the flames, all of them oils. Men on horses. A beautiful woman with a baby in her arms. A man surrounded by hunting dogs.

She gasped.

Hideous in front of her, a portrait of a woman standing, back hunched, crooked mouth, a nose with an odd lump, frizzy dark hair, and eyes that were mangled, one set higher than the other. Wynne stepped closer to the painting, eyes running over the long-cured globs of paint.

She had seen it immediately, of course, the slight resemblance to the dowager, but couldn't quite believe someone had actually wasted paint on producing this atrocity.

In as much as she had seen and observed of the dowager, Wynne knew she was a hard, demanding woman, but also beautiful. This painting had very few remnants of the woman. Such disparity, that this painting had to have been a vengeful act—there was no other explanation for it.

Rowen cleared his throat. He had been silent as she studied the painting and Wynne had forgotten he was there.

With a shake of disgust, she stepped back from the painting. "I am sorry, was I losing time?"

His eyebrow cocked. "Losing time?"

"It was always a frustration for grandfather." Her cheeks flushed. "I lose time and place when I am thinking. Sometimes minutes, sometimes hours. He was always convinced I would get eaten by a mountain lion, I am so unaware of my surroundings. Was I gone for long?"

A curious smile touched his lips. "No. Only a few minutes."

"I am sorry. I did not mean to be rude." She pointed at the painting. "And that thing is ridiculous."

"You can do better, then?"

"I could do better when I was seven." She shook her head as she gazed at the portrait, wrapping her arms around her ribcage to ward off the cool draft collecting by the wall.

"But the odd thing of it, the painter—whoever it was—knew what he was doing," Wynne said. "Knew about strokes, shadows, light. He knew what he was doing, but chose to create this. So very odd."

"Not so odd, if one considers the past, the history of these people."

"You say it as if they are not your people?"

"They are not."

Wynne looked at Rowen, instantly seeing he would say no more. "More history that does not currently serve a purpose?"

Without answering, Rowen stepped around her, snuffing out one torch, then the other. Wynne watched his profile as he bent to pick up the lantern.

Silent, he started to the door, not glancing back to make sure she was following.

Stifling a sigh, Wynne ran, her boots clomping on the stone floor to catch up to him.

{ CHAPTER 4 }

The thumping was odd. Odd enough that Wynne stopped walking and cocked her head, waiting for it to repeat.

Silence. And then another thump. It started in front of her and echoed twice behind her. Or at least that's what she thought.

She took three steps.

A groan—almost a grunt. But this one seemed to start behind her and echo in the front.

She looked around the hallway she was in. Same grey stone that had been twisting and turning her in circles for hours. For the past two days, bored and waiting for the paints to arrive, she had been trying to make sense of the maze that was this castle.

Wynne knew she was currently on the third level, unless she had counted the landings wrong when she was on the last tight, spiraling staircase. Possible, for how dizzy it had made her.

A grunt. A true grunt. A grunt like someone was in trouble.

She took a guess and turned around, walking back along the hallway she had just started down. Passing the staircase that had delivered her to this level, she heard another thump. Louder in front of her this time, and the echo now seemed to be more of a whisper behind her.

Passing by an arched wooden door, Wynne stopped to open it. The door stuck, so she kicked it. Once. Twice. It cleared the jam, but she still had to lean on the wood to get the door to swing inward.

Peeking her head past the door, she was surprised to see a mostly empty room. Warped plank floors. An old wooden bureau leaning crooked with a missing foot. An enormous tapestry lining the far wall, the scene of wine and women faded to almost blankness. One wooden chair, its tall back carved with scrolling leaves. But no noise. No thumping.

A low growl brought her back into the hallway.

Two more doors forced open, and Wynne still had not found the source of the sound. But she was getting closer. The thumping was louder.

The hall turned in front of her, and at the corner, another arched door sat in the middle of a rounded wall. It looked like it led to a corner tower of the castle.

This door opened with ease.

She gasped. "Hell and damnation."

Rowen turned his head to her, his shaking arms straining at the movement. His head, shoulders, and arms sticking straight out were the only things she could see of him.

The rest of his body disappeared through a gaping hole torn in the wood floor.

"Stop. No. Stay back." The order was barked harshly, even as Rowen shook with the strain of holding his body from falling through the floors.

"I can help." She made one step into the circular room.

"No, Wynne. Stop. The floors are rotted. You'll break through." His mouth pulled back as he sucked in a hard gasp.

"But Rowe, you cannot get out. I have to help." Taking a step back, Wynne gripped the doorframe, going to her toes as she leaned in, trying to see down the hole past Rowen's body. "What is below?"

"Nothing. Nothing for three levels." His left hand slipped, and he sank a notch, grunting as he stopped the fall. Only sheer arm muscle kept him from dropping through. "I am trying to swing my legs up without crashing down. I can't reach the beam below. Get help. Get help now."

"But—"

"Now, Wynne. Go."

Frantic, Wynne stepped away from the door, looking down both hallways she could see. Barren. Just like everywhere else she had been. She turned back into the room. "No, Rowe. There is no one. I have not seen a soul in the past three hours. And I do not know how I got here or how to get back."

A half growl, half yell from Rowen made her jump.

"Just go, Wynne. Go. Now. Quick." His arms shook with even more intensity.

Wynne slapped the stone next to the doorframe in frustration. She couldn't leave him. There was no way she could find her way back to the main living area, get help, and be back before Rowen fell through that hole—and plunged three stories.

She looked around, searching. Searching for any way to help him, to get him out of the hole. Nothing in the room. She stepped back into the hall, spinning. Empty. No way to help.

It hit her in a flash, and she ran back down the hallway she had just come from, stopping at the first room she had looked in. The door still ajar since she couldn't re-wedge it closed, she kicked it open and ran straight to the tapestry on the far wall, yanking free her grandfather's knife from the rope sheath she had fashioned around her waist and buried in her skirts. Thank goodness her life was still in such unrest that she felt the need to keep it on her person.

Wynne grabbed the bottom edge of the tapestry, stabbing the tip of the blade into the fabric, and ran the length of the room, cutting loose a wide, long strip. Running before the last threads separated, she yanked the strip free as she escaped out the door.

Breathless, she almost skidded into the tower room as she bolted back to Rowen. Still holding on, his head was down, chin on his chest, and his fingertips curled on the wood, nails digging in.

"Rowe—here—watch. I'm going to throw this to your left hand."

His head swiveled to her. Sweat covered his brow as he winced with the movement. "Dammit, Wynne. You cannot pull me out of here—I will drag you in."

"I can. Trust me. I will try to get it on your hand." She balled the end and threw it at his fingers. It missed by a wide swath. She re-gathered the strip and whipped it back into the room, and it landed on the back of Rowen's hand. "Grab it, Rowe. Grab it and give me just one moment."

"No. I am not dragging you down, Wynne."

"Trust me. Rowe, look at me."

His dark eyes met hers.

"Grab it. Trust me. You will not pull me down."

It took an agonizing moment, but Rowen finally flipped his hand, his wrist holding him up, and he awkwardly wrapped the fabric around his palm.

"Wait." She stepped back, twisting the fabric for strength, then wrapped it behind her hips and threaded it around both of her forearms.

Sitting, she wedged her feet onto the stone on either side of the doorframe and locked her legs straight. She leaned slightly forward, her arms wide to place her palms on the stone and brace her upper body.

"I am ready. Put your weight on it slowly and pull yourself up."

"No, Wynne." He grunted, slipping another notch. "Are you sure?"

"Yes. My legs are locked and I will lean back as weight is added. But do not look up my skirts."

A grimaced smile overtook the strain on his face. "I will resist."

Achingly slow, he wrapped the fabric further around his left hand and then his wrist. The weight pulled her, and Wynne leaned back, letting the angle of her body take the pressure. It worked. She was able to hold steady against half of his mass.

"You will not fall? You are sure?"

"Yes. Go. Grab it and pull yourself over here."

Rowen nodded, and in a quick move, his body dropped as he swung his right hand over to grip the fabric. It jerked Wynne forward, the line digging into her hip bones and arms, but she held her anchor.

At that moment, the wood splintered and cracked beneath Rowen, rough planks dropping to the depths of the tower. Rowen fell fully through the floor, swinging on the tapestry rope.

For an instant, he was weightless, and Wynne thought she lost him. But then a harsh yank pulled her forward, and she had to fight to straighten her legs, grunting, and leaned back even further. The fabric cut into her arms until bone felt like it was cracking, but she managed to keep her elbows locked straight.

Rowen dangled below her. Safe for the moment, but she knew, even with her leverage, she could not hold his weight much longer.

"Climb, Rowe. Climb, dammit."

The first tug came. Then the second. Hands moving up the fabric. She could not see him past the ripped wood of the floor in front of her, but she felt every notch he made up the rope, his weight ripping her muscles.

And then his right hand made it to the line above the wood, his fingers scraping underneath the strained fabric for grip. Another intense growl, and he yanked himself up over the lip of the wood.

Hand over hand, he pulled himself to Wynne, not stopping until he was between her legs and his chest was on the hallway floor.

Finally—thankfully—the line went slack and Wynne fell backward, her head hitting the stone wall behind her.

She quickly unwrapped the tapestry rope cutting into her arms, letting blood flow back into them, and then rolled over, trying to remove her legs and skirts from around Rowen's head.

Landing flat on her back, she panted as she swung her head to look over at Rowen. He was still on his belly, not moving, his head turned away from her on the floor.

"Rowe?" She propped herself up on her elbows and poked him with the toe of her boot. "Are you injured?"

His body did not move, but he managed to flop his head so he could see her. It looked like it took immense effort. White sleeves rolled up, she could still see the lines of muscles on his forearms quivering.

"How the hell did you know to do that?" His voice was ragged, breathless.

She chuckled at the sheer disbelief on his face, still trying to catch her own breath. "A pig."

"What?"

She took a moment to get air deep into her lungs. "My grandfather made me save a pig like that once. It had gotten out of the pen and fell down the side of a cliff," Wynne said, rubbing the sweat from her brow. "The nearest trees were too big for how much rope we had, so he wedged me between two boulders with a rope around me, like I just was, and he went down after it."

"Did you save it?"

"We did. It squealed the whole time. And I figured if I could hold a pig up like that, I could hold you up like that."

A full smile came to his lips, crinkling his dark eyes. "Are you comparing me to a pig?"

She laughed. "I suppose I am. Your weight is similar."

Rowen groaned. But this was a laughing groan, not the desperate, struggling-for-life groan of a few minutes ago. "So your grandfather did not yield to possible death or injury merely to save a pig?"

Wynne chuckled. "My grandfather did not yield to anything. Plus, he liked his pork meat. He was not about to give up a pig if he could help it. Especially one already fattened for winter."

Head still on the floor, Rowen smiled, his eyes focused on her face. "You miss him."

"I do." Wynne nodded. "I know it has been a while since he passed, and that I have already grieved, but in my mind, not but three days ago, I thought he was alive. So it is hard."

"I am trying to imagine him. What did he look like?"

"He was huge, and one never knew what he really looked like because he had a burly, crazy, mountain man beard." She smiled, shaking her head. "He was so very different from my father. My father was refined—dignified. Grandfather was the opposite. I was afraid of him for a long time when we moved to the mountain."

"Afraid he would hurt you?"

"Oh, no. Goodness no. He would never hurt me—he would die before harm came to me." She pushed herself to sitting and scooted back to lean against the wall. "No, I was afraid because I came to him on the mountain very much like my mother. Docile and sweet. Fragile. Needing to be taken care of. He had raised her like that. But that was not to be my fate."

"No?"

"No. He saw more in me. Grit—that was the word he liked to use. He saw that I could be more—and he expected it of me. Would not let me cower from all he needed to teach me. He demanded that I be much more than what my mother was. That I knew how to survive."

"Then I now have an enormous debt to your grandfather— no ordinary woman could have done what you just did." Grunting, Rowen rolled onto his back, bringing up his knees and kicking himself backward so his body was fully on the hall floor. He arms still stayed limp at his sides.

"Rowe—your leg." Wynne knelt forward in full alarm.

Rowen's dark buckskin breeches were ripped wide open on the side of his thigh and quickly turning a bright red from what looked like a deep gash in his leg.

Lifting his thigh to see the wound, he shrugged. "Not too deep. It will be fine."

His leg went down and he looked at her. "Wynne?" His eyes went wide. "Wynne, you are turning pale."

She could feel her head start to float away from her. She tried to grasp it, bring it back down to her body, but she could not catch it. "Blood—it is just the blood...I cannot..."

Her head started to sway, spin, and she slapped both her hands to her forehead to try and gain solidity. Solidity that fleeted away.

"Wynne..."

Rowen's voice faded. She tried one last time to fight against it, but lost.

Rowen and the hallway disappeared into the abyss of blackness.

~ ~ ~

Wynne cracked her eyes. Something hard underneath her, but not the floor. A bench? The smell of wet wool hit her nostrils, and she realized a musty blanket was on her body.

Rowen's voice, low, greeted her immediately. "You passed out when you saw the blood, Wynne."

She opened her eyes fully, only to see Rowen leaning over her, worry creasing his brow.

Instant hot embarrassment flooded her cheeks. "I do that."

He nodded, solemn. "I will remember that."

"You carried me in here?"

"I did."

"Then I am embarrassed you needed to do so."

Rowen straightened, giving her space as she pulled her hand from under the scratchiness of the wool blanket, rubbing her forehead with her fingertips.

"You will be fine?" The worry on his brow had not eased.

"I will be. I am." Just to prove it and to erase his worry, she sat up, her palms resting on the wooden bench. "It does not affect me past the initial blackness, and I will be fine as long as I do not look at your leg again." Her eyes unwittingly flickered down his torso.

"Then you need to not look down at my leg." He turned his body so the blood on his buckskin breeches wasn't visible to her. His arms were motionless, limp, at his sides. "I find it entirely odd that you can stomach squirrel guts but not the blood of man."

"They are very different things. I have always been this way around human blood."

"Which is truly why you did not go after that thief with your knife?"

"Possibly." She pointed at his arm. "I am sorry you had to carry me into here—you did not know, but I would have woken in short order. Your muscles must be torn into a thousand pieces."

"No apologies. You just saved me from what could have been a slow, torturous death with a broken neck at the bottom of that tower. So I was not about to leave you in that cold hallway." He let a half-smirk slide onto his face. "Besides, I tossed you over my shoulder, so it was not so difficult. You are light."

"Aaah," Wynne said, rubbing her middle as she looked down. "That explains why my ribs hurt. I thought it was from the rope."

"I have hurt you?"

She shook her head, pushing the blanket from her lap. "No. I am fine."

"Wynne, look at me."

She tilted her chin up to him. The worry had reappeared on his brow.

"Have I hurt you?"

"No, Rowe. Truly, I am just sore. It is of no consequence."

He stared at her for a moment, judging whether to believe her words. His face relaxed slightly, but Wynne could still see the concern around his eyes.

"Even if it is of no consequence, I would never wish to injure you, Wynne. I will take care to carry you properly the next time you faint."

Wynne's breath caught, her chest tightening at his earnest words. She had to be very careful around this man. His dark eyes were still watching her intently, and Wynne started to squirm under his gaze. She wasn't quite sure it was just concern in his eyes. Curiosity? That would make sense. She was the curious sort.

Even under his scrutiny, she had a hard time looking from his striking eyes. Long dark lashes, flecks of silver light in the almost black of his eyes. Dark and haunting, they looked like they just barely kept bridled a power he was not about to let her see— like they could steal her soul and hold it captive for all eternity.

Careful. Very careful, lest she lose her soul.

Rowen looked into her mind too easily with those eyes—she already knew that about him. And she also already knew she didn't mind so much that he looked into her so easily.

If only he could see what she couldn't remember. What happened to her. Where her mother was.

Wynne wasn't quite ready for it, but she stood, just to avoid squirming more under Rowen's continued stare. "Thank you, but I do not plan on fainting again in the near future."

She immediately swayed, and his arm went around her instantly, his hand supporting the small of her back as he set her down on the bench.

"Too soon," he said, his eyes still searching her face.

She forced a light chuckle. "My plan did not work so well."

"No." He shook his head, the right side of his face holding a smirk. "Sit for a moment. Get your legs about you."

"Only if you will sit with me. Your body must still be exhausted as well—more so. How long were you holding yourself up?"

"Too long." With a sigh, Rowen sank to the bench beside her, his arms having gone back to limp jelly.

Wynne looked about the room. It also looked like a long-abandoned room—cobwebs in the corners, a few stray pieces of marred furniture, two small tables, a plain wooden chair, and this bench. "Where are we?"

"Not too far from that tower. This was as far as I could take you without collapsing myself."

"We are a pair of messes, are we not?"

He laughed. "That is an apt description, yes."

His smile came so easy it surprised Wynne. She had not thought it of him the other day. She shifted, turning more to him on the bench. "I know I was lost, so just wandering aimlessly in these hallways, but what were you doing in the tower?"

"Checking out one of the areas I would like to tear down."

"Why do you want to tear it down?"

His head cocked at her. "Have you been speaking to the duchess?"

"No, I have not seen her since that dinner. Why?"

"It is nothing."

"It is something or you would not have asked."

He shrugged. "She is dead-set against me. Against my plan. I would not put it past her to try to convince you to convince me to leave it be."

"Leave the castle be?"

"Yes. But I am doing this only for the very reason you saved me from. Floors are rotted. Stone is crumbling." His gaze went to the stone wall above the door to the room, his face weary. "I would rather not have anyone dying in this monstrosity because holding onto the past is too blasted important for one person."

Wynne watched his profile with interest. "Do you think the castle is fighting you?"

"What?" His eyes swung to her.

"Maybe it is not just the duchess. Maybe it is the castle fighting you as well? Maybe the floor dropped out because the castle would prefer not to be torn down."

His eyes swung to her, his look incredulous. "You speak of ghosts?"

Wynne shrugged. "I speak of things that happen that I cannot explain."

"I have enough ghosts to contend with, without adding in the demons of this place." A heavy sigh expanded his chest, and his gaze went to the floor in front of them. "The floor boards were rotted, Wynne. Nothing more."

She nodded, silent for a moment. "You said the duchess had a son? But he died?"

"He did. At the same time as his father. Typhoid fever—they both went to London and came back with it. The duke, my uncle, died fairly quickly. Their son held on for a week more before he died."

"That is why the duchess is dressed in black? How long ago was it?"

"More than two years ago. My father would have been next in line, but he died years ago. The duchess held out for months, claiming pregnancy in a desperate attempt to delay the inevitable. But it happened—I inherited the title and the estate. Much to the horror of the duchess."

"Horror? Why would she be horrified? I would think she would be happy to have you as the duke, save for you wanting to tear down this castle, of course."

"The duchess and I have always had a strained relationship." Rowen's jaw line started to throb.

"But you seem very agreeable to me."

Rowen looked from the stone to Wynne, his mouth hard. "My past is not agreeable to her."

A vague comment, and Wynne could sense she was stepping into prickly seas. "I do not know your past, but what I do know is that you have been quite kind to me. And generous. You have given me a place to stay and food to eat. I would still be wandering aimlessly, trapping squirrels, frozen to the bone were it not for you, and I am grateful."

"Have you remembered anything more?"

"No. And the fact remains—you did not need to do any of those things to help me. But you did. So whatever issues the duchess has with you, I imagine I would tend to disagree with her."

"You do not know the waters you wade into with her, Wynne," Rowen said carefully. Too carefully. "You will do her portrait, as I need that from you since it is how she is accepting your presence as a guest in this place. But be forewarned—your presence will shift her attention from me, to you. And she can work tirelessly to destroy a soul when she so desires."

His words hung in the air, in the silence of the ancient room. Rowen was clearly speaking of things he would rather not.

Wynne studied his face, studied the dark scruff on his jaw, the slight age around his eyes, the hardness that had been etched into his forehead.

She took a deep breath. She wanted answers, but answers rarely came without questions.

Her voice was soft. "Your soul?"

Rowen shook his head, suddenly standing. "Forget I said anything, Wynne. I do not know how you do so, but you pull more words from me than I am accustomed to sharing. Can you stand? Walk?"

Wynne exhaled. She would get no answers today from this man. "Yes. My head is firmly upon my body once more." She stood, folding the blanket. "But can I ask you to show me the way back to the main living quarters of the castle? I was lost on this end of the castle for quite some time before I stumbled upon you."

His eyebrow rose at her. "Your questions will cease?"

"They will." She put on a bright smile as she set the neatly folded blanket on the bench. "But then you will have to listen to me wax poetic on the fine attributes of the pigments made from cochineal insects—the most beautiful scarlet one has ever seen."

Rowen chuckled as he walked to the doorway, his left limp arm rising slightly to usher her out the door. "It is something I have never been curious about until this very moment."

{ CHAPTER 5 }

Wynne thrust her tongue onto the roof of her mouth, concentrating on the canvas before her. She had redone the base of the backdrop, deep reds swirling with blacks—dark, just as she had discovered the duchess's spirit was.

Ten days ago, the paints and canvas had arrived, shipped from London. Antsy and ready to start the portrait, Wynne had spent the next four days, hour after hour, with the duchess just trying to convince her to decide on a setting and clothing. Four days of listening to the duchess complain about everything from the cold dampness permeating the castle, to the sunlight shining through a window too strong and overheating her.

But it didn't deter Wynne. She had always had a lot of patience—her mother often complemented her on that trait— and Wynne had nothing else to do. So she sat, listening to everything the duchess could invent to complain about. Including thinly veiled barbs aimed at Wynne's hair, clothes, and general appearance.

For all that the duchess wanted a new portrait done, her resistance to actually sitting for it was stubborn—she hated that Rowen was blatantly trying to bribe her with the portrait, and she had bluntly complained of that very thing to Wynne.

It was on day four that Wynne realized she had one small window of opportunity—the duchess's dog, Pepe. The small terrier was always nipping at the duchess's skirts, hoping to gain her lap, and the duchess almost always complied.

Once Wynne got the dowager talking about Pepe, Wynne knew she had finally stumbled upon the one thing that made the duchess happy. Or at least somewhat pliable. So when Wynne suggested putting the terrier in a prominent spot in the portrait, the smallest glimmer of interest finally touched the duchess's eyes.

Wynne sketched the dog, and the duchess was so pleased with the likeness, she finally agreed to move forth with sitting for the portrait.

A success. But now Wynne was stuck.

Six days, of pondering, of alternating back and forth with the backdrop—adding, replacing, tweaking. The duchess's likeness had come together nicely, although her eyes were still missing. But the canvas had filled, getting increasingly complex the more time Wynne spent with the duchess.

Wynne clucked her tongue, leaning back in the hard wooden chair she usually sat at the edge of or stood in front of.

The sadness she had initially seen in the duchess was true—but it wasn't just sadness—it was a lifetime of angry despair, and this woman held onto every last shred of it. Wynne wondered how the duchess even managed to eat with all that angst in her stomach.

Staring at the silver-slippered toes peeking out from under the duchess's royal blue gown on the painting, Wynne contemplated the latest thing the duchess had just spent the last hour telling her.

"Good. You are still in here."

Rowen's voice echoed into the empty room and it made Wynne jump and look over the top of the portrait to the doorway.

She sprang to her feet, grabbing the long white cloth bunched atop the easel, and unfurled it, draping it in front of the portrait.

In a simple white linen shirt with sleeves rolled to his elbows and buckskin breeches, Rowen walked toward her. He swallowed the room with too much ease when he entered, his presence overtaking any thoughts Wynne was having about the duchess.

She had seen very little of Rowen since he helped her set up the large easel and paints nearly a fortnight ago, and at the sight of him, she realized she missed his company.

Wynne stepped to the side the canvas, almost as tall as her. "I am. The duchess said she was done for the day just a few minutes ago. Did she need something else from me?"

"No. But she did need something from me." Rowen stopped in front of Wynne, looking down at her. "I need to see it."

Her eyes flickered sideways to the covered canvas. "See what?"

"The portrait. Your progress. I need to see it. The duchess cornered me and demanded I come in here. She is not convinced that you are doing anything she would be pleased with, and since you will not allow her to see the work, I agreed to view it—she thinks you are abusing my hospitality."

"She does?" Panic set into Wynne's voice. "But I am not. And there is no reason for you to see it in this stage. Do you think I am abusing your hospitality? Because I can leave—"

"No, Wynne—stop. What she believes and what I believe have never been the same thing—and our beliefs have not miraculously aligned. But I do need to see the work to sate her."

Wynne crossed her arms over her stomach, shaking her head. "No—not until it is complete."

"Wynne, I will not judge. I just need to see the work, to be able to tell her something of what is on that canvas."

"No."

Rowen tried to step around her, but Wynne jumped to her side, blocking his path.

He stopped, looking down at her with one raised brow. Not angry, slightly amused if anything. "Wynne, I must insist. I am not expecting a masterpiece—I only need to see that something has been done—I am sure whatever you have created thus far will more than satisfy what I need to tell the duchess."

"I do not let people see my unfinished work."

Rowen stared at her, silent, waiting patiently.

Seconds slid by until Wynne exhaled a deep breath in a drawn-out sigh. "Fine. As long as you do not judge—it is nowhere near finished."

"I promise."

She moved in front of the canvas and rolled up the white drape, tucking it on top of the two protruding arms she had devised at the top of the easel.

Rowen moved behind her. She could feel his stare over the top of her head, feel the heat of his body on her backside.

He stood for a long minute behind her, not saying a word, not moving. Agony, for she truly never did let anyone see her unfinished works—save her teachers and her grandfather—and the fact that Rowen was seeing it in progress was torture.

Torture because she was positive he was judging her skill. Judging her vision.

Her eyes on a specific stroke of green at the bottom left corner of the canvas—one she needed to change—Wynne could not bear to turn around to him. Could not bear to break the silence. Hear the judgment.

A low whistle fell from his lips to her ears.

"Wynne…that…that…"

Rowen's words—his thought—unfinished, hung in the air, and Wynne could feel her ears burning red. She jumped forward, ripping the white cloth from the top and draping it downward, hiding her work.

"No, Wynne. Do not do that. Pull that back up."

"But you think it is hideous."

"I never said that. Pull it back up."

Slowly, Wynne bent, her arms wooden, and bundled the cloth to the top.

"I do not think it is hideous, Wynne. I think…I think…I think it is…interesting."

She whipped around to him. "Which is the word one uses to describe hideousness."

A smile touched his lips as his dark eyes refused to look at her, instead remaining glued to the canvas. "No. I will come up with better words, I promise. I just…" He shook his head. "I just have never seen anything quite like it, and I am trying to study the nuances of it—in-between your curtain calls on it. Give me a moment to take it in."

"I already have. You have seen what you need to see." She moved to grab the white cloth once more, but he snatched her arm, jerking her to a stop.

She didn't bother to hide the fire in her eyes when she looked at him.

This time, he met her gaze. And he opened his mouth, his voice soft. "Please. Just a moment."

The few words hit her, and she recognized the genuineness of them. With a silent nod, she moved a step backward to the side of the portrait, letting him have full view of the canvas.

She watched him, breath held, as his dark eyes moved across the painting, stopping and staring at different areas, one by one.

His stare did not leave the portrait. "What is this? What am I looking at, Wynne?"

Wynne's breath exhaled slightly. Had she truly thought she would not have to explain herself—especially to Rowen? Foolish.

Her arms came up, wrapping herself. "It is what I have always done. People, animals—it does not matter what I am painting—if it is profound in their lives—what makes them whole, what makes them react, think like they do—then I paint it into the backdrop. Especially with people, my paintings have never been about the veneer they put before me. I will paint the veneer, because it is what I am supposed to do. But I do their likeness—and myself—a disservice if I stop there. The backdrop—the memories I include in it—creates the vividness of the whole."

"But how do you know so much about the duchess?"

"She talks, just like all the others." Wynne shrugged, the hold on her stomach tightening. "It started when I was young—seven, maybe eight. It was incredibly awkward for me to sit with someone and stare at them for a portrait—it still is. I am much more comfortable when my subjects talk to me. So I ask them questions. A lot of questions. I spend hours and days with them. And they tell me things. And the deeper I can move into their memories, their thoughts, the more complete I can make their portraits."

"I am amazed you got her to talk to you at length."

Wynne took a deep breath. "It has always been like this. The longer people sit for a portrait, the more secrets they share. It always starts small—something they loved but told no one about, something they did that caused them shame. And I just listen, and then the secrets snowball. Affairs. Death. Betrayals. Incest. Lost loves. Illegitimate children. Everything a seven-year-old should never have heard."

His eyes left the canvas to look at her, and he stared at her. "Has that been hard?"

Wynne paused, her eyes dropping from him. He was seeing too much of her again. "Yes—no. It was at first, but at this point, this many years later, I have heard enough about the madness of men that very little surprises me. I learned to channel the worst of the worst into the paintings so they do not rest in my mind."

"That works?"

"Yes—too much so. Now I find it necessary. All of the secrets, each and every one tells a story about a life that could never be fully captured by clothes, by the trimmings around a person. The secrets give me much to work with—the lines on a face—the hollowness in an eye."

Her gaze came up to him. "But it is not all dire. I have also heard of much beauty in life, the fine that can be humanity— the first time a mother looks at her newborn babe, the kindness a stranger can give, the dignity of dying well, love so deep it transcends time and space. For all of the bad I have heard of, I have also learned of the true grace of the human spirit and what it can overcome. Those…those are the stories I keep tiny pieces of for myself."

Rowen nodded, his gaze going back to the portrait. He stayed silent for a long stretch. "It is extraordinary."

The rest of Wynne's held breath escaped.

"What is this?" He pointed to the upper right corner where Wynne had started an imagined fresco on the ceiling behind the dowager duchess. A white dove, blood staining its chest centered the miniature scene.

Wynne cleared her throat. "If I tell you, I must have your utmost discretion. Even though it is never spoken of, there is an inherent trust that people who sit for me give me. The secrets are not mine to keep."

"You have it. I swear. I just want to understand."

Wynne nodded, one arm pulling from her belly to point at the fresco. "The duchess started that tale flippantly—she was talking about her early childhood, her mother's skill at molding her into the epitome of a well-bred lady of the aristocracy. She is so proud of her mother—how she instilled backbone into her."

"What does a bloody dove have to do with that?"

"When the duchess was a small child—she did not say how old, but I would guess maybe five or six—she found a baby bird, a dove, injured on her family's estate. She brought it home and kept it hidden in her room in a cage she had a maid steal from the groundskeeper. She managed to raise the bird, feeding it from her fingertips. Months went by, and she eventually let it live outside of the cage in her room, which was fine, as only her maid and her nanny ever came in."

Wynne paused, knowing she was betraying confidence by retelling the story. But then she reminded herself it was the duchess that had demanded Rowen look at her work. So this was her work, and the work needed explanation.

"Until?" Rowen prompted her.

"Until her mother came into her room one day and discovered the bird. It was obvious the bird had become a pet when the dove landed on the duchess's shoulder. And her mother believed it was not of good breeding to care about anything. Anything."

Wynne stepped next to Rowen, her eyes centered on the dove, solemnly shaking her head. "So her mother silently left the room. The duchess tried to get the dove to fly out the window, but it would not leave the windowsill. Would not leave her. By the time her mother returned, knife in hand, the duchess was desperate. But she was not tall enough to push the bird off the sill. Her mother, on the other hand, easily caught the bird and then, without a word, promptly stabbed it in the chest and tossed it out the window."

Wynne's voice caught and she had to wipe a tear from her lower lashes. Out the corner of her eye, she saw Rowen watching her intently. She rushed on. "And by the end of that story, the duchess—her eyes—it was the heartbreak of crushed innocence. That the world could be cruel, and move on, and not acknowledge her despair. I believe it was when she first realized that what she wanted—what she loved—was insignificant. And that is something she has obsessed about—battled against her entire life."

"Yes, well, we were all innocent once." Rowen's words came out clipped and cold.

Wynne blinked at the harshness in his voice and looked up at him, only to see his face had set hard, his eyes on the canvas.

She knew she was close enough to him that he couldn't help but notice she was staring at him, but he refused to meet her gaze.

Her brow creased. This land, these people were so very different than the mountain folk she had known—even what she remembered of New York. People who said what they wanted to without reservation. She was quickly finding out that polite society was not so polite here in England, if this household was any indication.

"Some of this is very...dark," Rowen said, his voice softening. "It would be jarring to the unprepared eye."

"Yes, well the duchess is dark. It is all around her. There are a few spots of happiness, but not many." Wynne looked at the portrait, her eyes scanning the edges around the duchess. The face of her newborn son swirled into the dark black-reds of drapery. The ship she had dreamt of seeing the world in. The corset that stole a child from her womb. The grave of her mother she refused to see buried.

Wynne shook her head, washing her mind free of the duchess's memories. "My instructors in New York would always paint over my backdrops before they were delivered. They never

believed people would want to look inside themselves that
deeply."

"Was that difficult—watching your work destroyed?"

Wynne shrugged. "It should have been, but it was not. I
never minded—so many secrets need to remain secrets."

She stepped forward, pulling the white cloth forward to
drop before the portrait. Rowen did not stop her this time. "But
my grandfather would never allow me to paint over what I had
created—he was steadfast in his belief that more people needed
to acknowledge what makes them what they are—both the good
and bad."

"Where do you fall in your belief?" Rowen asked.

"I honestly do not know. I understand both sides. I am just
a conduit, trying to represent these souls in the best way I can."
She looked up at him, startled by his eyes boring into her again.
"How about you—where does your belief land?"

"You will never paint me, Wynne. That is where my belief
falls."

"To live the unexamined life?"

"As you said yourself, some secrets should remain secrets.
And some memories should remain untouched. That does not
mean it is unexamined."

Her eyebrows arched as she turned from him, going to a
simple wooden table with a bowl of water on it. She started to
scrub the tips of her fingers, matted with dried paint.

Rowen followed, stopping by the table, knuckles resting on
the wood. "You disagree?"

"I do not know how one can find peace in the present,
without finding peace with the past. That is all."

"Are you sure about that, Wynne? You yourself have
memories your mind will not even allow you to acknowledge
right now," Rowen said. "Yet you seem at peace. Do you honestly
think you cannot remember what happened to you because it
was something good? You cannot remember how you got in that
forest for a reason, Wynne."

"Stop." She slammed her hand in the bowl, sending water flying. Breath suddenly hard, she glared up at him. "Do not make the mistake of thinking I am at peace, Rowe. I have no idea where my mother is. What happened to her. What happened to me to send me into a barren forest."

She stepped closer to him, craning her neck upward to still meet his eyes. "So do not make that mistake. You have no idea…" She took a deep breath, shaking. "No idea how lost I am. How I am pretending."

His hand came up, landing on her cheek, his fingers wrapping along her chin. She expected harshness in return from him, but it was the gentlest touch, and she couldn't pull away from it.

"You will remember, Wynne." Rowen's voice was just above a whisper. "I forgot. I forgot how desperate you are. You will remember. I know it."

His words, so soft, so sure, took all her sudden angst, blowing it to the winds. The only thing Wynne could do was nod her head.

Nod, and pray he was right.

~~~

Rowen stood, staring up at the high stone wall before him. He looked down at the list on the paper he had set by his feet, then back up at the three stories high wall. He was supposed to be calculating how much work it would take to re-mortar the wall and fix the crumbling stone, or if it would be better to tear this room and this part of the castle down as well.

He would like to keep it intact, for if he took this wall, he would have to remove this entire section of the castle up to the tower. And his plans already included tearing down more than half the castle—not that he had shared that with the dowager duchess yet.

But his mind wandered to Wynne again, just as it had
insisted on doing repeatedly in the last day and a half since he had
seen her in what he had begun to think of as the painting room.

He was impressed with her skill, but more than that, he
was impressed with the depth of her thoughts. And unnerved by
them.

She took way too much in, saw too much, heard too much—
and that could only be doing her mind harm. Harm when she
should be concentrating on getting her memory back.

More than once in the last week, he had walked by the
painting room deep in the night, only to see a flickering light
from within. Once, Wynne was scrunched up sideways on a short
bench, sleeping. Another, she was slumped over the table, her face
on a sketch and her hand still gripping charcoal.

She had a perfectly comfortable bedroom two doors away,
but the woman didn't understand the concept of walking ten
steps to sleep properly on a bed.

Rowen closed his eyes from the stone, only to have the image
that had been haunting him flash in his mind.

The utter despair on Wynne's face when he had inadvertently
pushed her too far sat heavy on his conscience. Heavy, for he had
caused it. She had acclimated so easily to life in the castle and to
painting the duchess—and he hadn't seen her for more than a few
minutes here and there—that he hadn't realized how much she
had been covering up.

He heard her boot steps, echoing light on the stone floor
behind him, before he heard her voice.

"Does this room come down as well?"

He turned to her. A simple mauve muslin dress swished
around her legs, her shoulders and arms draped with a black
shawl that she held tightly to her chest. Her dark blond hair was
pulled into a singular thick braid that came over her left shoulder.

"Taking a break from the duchess?"

Wynne smiled as she came to a stop next to him, looking
down at the paper on the floor. "She sat for a few hours with me
early this afternoon, but was not feeling well. Even Pepe could

not draw a smile from her. So she retreated to her rooms, and I needed to escape the paints for a stretch."

"It is good to know you can remove yourself on occasion from your work."

"You have noticed I have trouble doing so? I am like that—I especially lose time in the middle of a painting like this."

She looked up at the stone wall before them, reaching out and rubbing her paint-stained forefinger on the mortar between the stones. It crumbled at her touch, chunks falling to the ground.

"Why do you want to tear down the castle, Rowe? Truly?"

"So the duchess has gotten to you?"

She looked up at him, her hazel eyes showing strikes of blue in the sunlight coming from the windows opposite them. "This place has a lot of history. History that is important to the title, or so I have gathered."

Rowen swallowed an outward sigh, his spine straightening. "Or so you have been told. I do appreciate the fact that you have kept the duchess very busy, and for the most part, out of my affairs here at the castle. But do not insert yourself into this, Wynne."

Her eyes narrowed at him. "That is the true reason you have me doing her portrait? To keep her away from haranguing you?"

"Partially, yes."

"And the other part?"

"To give you a purpose that does not involve wandering the woods lost and prey to the unscrupulous. I admit your painting of the duchess solved two of my problems."

Her fingers gripped her wrap, pulling it taut across her shoulders as she clasped her arms. Her bottom lip was very close to jutting out in a pout. "I did not know you saw me as a problem."

"No, Wynne. You are not the problem—but your current situation is—that, you cannot deny."

She shrugged. Her eyes left him and went to the window over his shoulder. "You have not answered the question. Why do you truly want to tear down the castle? Is it revenge?"

Rowen almost sputtered. "Revenge?" He shook his head. "Do not believe everything she tells you, Wynne."

"Why not? She is the only one that has told me anything of this place, of the family."

"Can you not see when you are being manipulated, Wynne?"

Her hazel eyes fixated on him. "I know the duchess has told me things to try to convince me to convince you not to tear it down. But you are the one that has put me in the middle of whatever warfare you have going on with the duchess. And you are not above manipulation as well, Rowe. You have used me to keep the duchess away from you. At least she has been honest about what she would like me to do."

"Honest in her lies? What has she told you, Wynne?"

"She believes you have no regard for the title, for all that it has produced over the past three hundred years. That the history of this place—what your lineage has meant to England—is more important than the coins it would cost to repair the structure. That this place deserves respect. That you are doing this to spite her for past deeds done." Wynne's head tilted as she looked at him. "This is her home, and she sees herself as safeguarding the castle for future generations—not just to fight you or to cause you grief. Which is what you seem to be intent on doing to her."

Rowen held in a growl. "So you believe it should stand as well? That I should put lives at risk?"

"Lives at risk? Of course not. But there are other ways. And the duchess has spent her life devoted to preserving the history of the title, of this place, for her son."

"Exactly—for her son." His words came out biting. "Not for a near-bastard child she has hated from birth."

"What?" Shock vibrated across Wynne's features. "Near-bastard? What are you talking about Rowe?"

"No." He stepped away from her, picking up the paper and ink and quill from the stone floor. "I will not give you fodder to use against me."

"What? Fodder to use against you? What? Rowe—I would never—"

He stood straight, whipping to her. "Never what Wynne? Disagree with me? Side against me? You would not? What are you doing right now, Wynne? Questioning decisions I have made. Decisions I have every right to make, and you have no right to question."

Her brow furrowed in compete confusion. "But the duchess—"

"Dammit, Wynne. I do not want to hear another word about the damn dowager. I do not want to hear another word from you. I have had this argument with the dowager too many times, and I sure as hell am not going to have it with you, Wynne. Not with you."

"But—"

"Do not do this, Wynne." He shook his head, sighing as he looked upward to the ceiling. "You. You I thought…"

"You thought what, Rowe?"

His eyes dropped to her. He saw the confusion—genuine concern—clear on Wynne's face.

But he was not about to explain.

Not about to explain the years of maliciousness he had suffered under the duchess.

Not about to explain that, in Wynne, he thought he had finally come across a person that he did not have to explain himself to—to validate himself to. That Wynne just liked him for him—trusted him for him.

No, he was not about to explain that to her.

He shook his head, his voice defeated. "It is of no concern, Wynne. What I thought does not matter. I was wrong. Excuse me."

Ignoring her open mouth about to speak, Rowen walked past her and out the door.

{ CHAPTER 6 }

Wynne stared at the shadows under the dark canopy above her. Flat on her back, her hand sat on her belly, holding it, as it had not been right since her encounter with Rowen hours ago. Even if his last words to her were soft, he had left angry—that much she knew.

What she didn't know was how she had managed to bungle so completely what was supposed to be just a gentle conversation about the castle. She wanted to hear his side of the story, but instead, it had turned into an argument before she even knew what was happening.

She had always been so good at walking a line with people, skirting up to anger, but always able to back off and placate someone before they exploded.

But not with Rowen. With Rowen she didn't have a sense of when to stop. When to leave him be. She wanted to know him, but he continued to be mystery upon mystery—and she pushed too hard for it. It drove her to madness that she would see tiny snippets of who he really was, but then he would erect a guard and she never saw a full picture of him.

She turned over in bed, trying once more to fall asleep. Trying to push Rowen out of her mind. To push his eyes, the low sound of his voice, the heat of him when he was near her, out of her mind. She hadn't slept in the bed for a few nights, and the luxury of not having a cricked neck in the morning was something she knew she shouldn't pass on.

The knock on the door startled her, and Wynne sat upright just before her bedroom door swung open.

"Good, you are awake."

"Duchess?" Wynne swung her legs from under the covers and stood up. She could see in the moonlight the duchess was terrified. "What is wrong?"

"Pepe—Pepe is gone. It is the full moon. He scratched at my bedroom door for too long, so I took him down, thinking he just wanted to run for a moment." Her voice shook. "But he ran. He ran and he has not come back."

Wynne grabbed the duchess's flailing hands. "Where did he run to? Has he done this before?"

"Yes, he runs, but he always comes back within a few minutes. Always." Her hands captured, the duchess still jerked them in agitation. "I am so frightened. He is all I have and I cannot lose him."

"How long has he been gone for?"

"Two hours. I have been waiting downstairs. I do not know what to do. No one here would care. No one would help. No one knows how much he means to me."

"I know." Wynne squeezed her hands. "I know, and I will go look for him."

The relief in the duchess was so palpable she almost crumbled to her knees. "Truly? Thank…thank you."

Wynne guided the duchess to sit on the edge of the bed. She dropped the duchess's hands and went to the closest dress, slipping it over her head, and then swung her black cape over her shoulders before getting her boots on. Without thought, she grabbed her grandfather's hunting knife, sliding it into place in its inside pocket in her cape.

The duchess sat, agitated and wringing her hands as Wynne got ready.

Wynne gave her a bright smile. "I am sure Pepe has not gone too far. Let us stop by the kitchens for some meat, and then bring me to where you let him out. He loves the treats, so I am sure his nose will find me long before I find him."

~~~

The hand on Rowen's bare shoulder squeezed tightly, shaking him. Shaking him so hard he thought for a split second he was on the continent, years ago, needing to wake and move from enemy lines once more.

"LB. Wake up. L.B."

Pulling him from the deep of sleep, the last voice in the world he wanted to hear was in his ear. A nightmare.

"L.B." A slap on his face. "Wake up."

Rowen jerked upright.

The dowager hovered over him. "I need your help, L.B. For heaven's sake put a proper shirt on and get out of bed." She turned on her heel and walked out of his room.

Rowen rubbed his eyes, looking around the room. Still the middle of the night. He hadn't drawn his drapes, and the full moon that had been high in the sky hours ago now sat above the treetops.

Was he awake? Had the duchess just been in here?

His door opened, and the dowager stuck her head into the room. "No time to waste, L.B. Clothes." The door snapped shut.

Rowen shook his head, swinging his legs off the bed and standing. What the hell did the dowager need from him in the middle of the night? She had never in her entire life needed his help, and now she suddenly needed him under the light of the moon? And why in the world would she even think he would help her with anything? Bizarre.

Against his gut telling him to get back into bed, Rowen rose and put his clothes on. Better to just find out what she needed than to have her pestering him until morning.

Quickly dressed in a white shirt, buckskin breeches and boots, Rowen opened the door.

The moonlight from his room illuminated the duchess, standing in her robe, her arms crossed and foot tapping as she glared up at him. "That was not with haste, L.B."

"What do you want, Duchess?"

"Miss Theaton is gone."

Rowen's eyes popped wide awake. "What? What do you mean she is gone?" He and Wynne had argued, sure, but she wouldn't leave over something so simple, would she?

"She went after Pepe. He ran off into the woods hours ago, and I was worried. So she went after him. She should have been back by now."

"Which woods?"

The duchess shook her head, not willing to answer him.

"Which woods, Duchess?" Rowen asked, his voice hard.

"The north woods." Her voice was meek.

Rowen stepped back to grab an overcoat he had slung on a chair by the door, and then pushed past the duchess, sending her stumbling as he started down the hallway. "You sent her into the north woods? How could you do that? In the dark, no less."

The duchess scurried after him. "It was Pepe—she offered, and I could not leave Pepe out there by himself. I am so worried about him, and—"

Rowen stopped, whipping to face the duchess. "He's a damn dog, Duchess. Wynne is a goddamn person—a person, Duchess."

"I—I thought—I did not mean—"

"I do not care what you meant to do, Duchess." He started down the hall again, reaching the stairs and descending them two at a time, still yelling at the woman behind him. "You sent Wynne into the woods when you know full well what might happen—she has not a clue as to what can happen to her up there."

The duchess caught up to him by the library, only a step behind. "You will find her?"

"How long has she been out there?"

"Three hours. Maybe more."

"And you just got me now? Dammit." His open palm slammed on the stone wall of the hallway.

"You will find her?"

Rowen flung the door to the north side of the estate open and stopped. The cold wind whipped into the long hall. He looked down at the duchess. "I damn well hope so. Or you will have an excruciating hell to pay, Duchess."

Rowen ran in full sprint across the open ground sloping from the castle, his speed slowing as he made it deeper into the woods.

The full moon shed only spotty light through the canopy of the forest, so gave few clues as to Wynne's path. He searched as he moved, looking for broken twigs, trampled underbrush, but found none.

And he needed to get to the area he feared she was in as fast as possible.

Halfway into the thickest part of the forest, Rowen heard barking echoing through the trees. Definitely in front of him. Still quite a distance. He pushed harder.

The barking guided him. Frantic. A dog that was either injured or excited. Heaving for breath, Rowen pushed on, even though he had been running solid for more than a half hour. As the trees started to clear, the barking got louder.

He was close now. Close, and the barking hadn't ceased. That wasn't good.

Reaching the clearing line of the woods, Rowen stopped, trying to force air into his chest as he surveyed the wide-open area in the moonlight.

It was at this line that the land turned drastically from forest to peat bog.

A bog that could suck one down to death before one even knew a foot had been captured.

Rowen cocked his ear upward. The barking had gone silent, and the barking had been his only guide. He squinted, his eyes running across the low mounding vegetation.

No movement.

And then another bark.

His eyes whipped to the sound.

A distance away, Pepe stood, four feet firmly on the ground. The dog barked again, all his attention on the ground in front of him. Whatever it was, Rowen could not see past Pepe on the short mound.

Rowen squinted harder. What was that sticking straight out of the ground next to Pepe?

Shit. A knife.

Wynne's knife.

Rowen jumped back into the woods, quickly finding a sturdy long stick, just as tall as him.

He ran back to the edge of the peat bog, stick moving and diving into the ground in front of him, guiding him to solid land and past the sinking muck of the bog.

The progress across the bog was agonizingly slow. And Pepe had started jumping, agitated, the closer Rowen got. But Rowen could not afford to get stuck himself. Not if Pepe was barking at what Rowen feared he was.

Pepe went silent for a moment, and Rowen knew he was now close enough.

"Wynne?"

No answer.

Pepe looked at him and barked.

"Wynne?" He repeated the yell.

"Rowe?" It was a faint whisper, exhausted.

Relief swept through him. "Wynne. I'm coming."

"Rowe? I'm almost under. I have tried. God—I'm going—"

"Stop moving, Wynne. Stop talking. Stop everything." Yelling, Rowen's foot slipped into muck as he stepped forward too quickly. "Dammit."

"Rowe?"

"Silent, Wynne." He yanked his foot out of the sucking muck. "Stay still. I will get to you. Just hold on."

Precious minutes passed, and Rowen moved forward, swearing at himself with every swipe of the stick before him. Every painstaking step.

Why had he not told her of this place? How had he ever let the duchess near Wynne? Of course something like this was bound to happen. No one ever got near the duchess without pain.

Pepe kept up a vigil of barks, and Rowen finally leapt onto the mound Pepe was perched on.

Hell.

Up to her chin.

One hand still stretched upward above the muck to her right, oddly removed from her body. Tears soaking her face, her eyes moved upward when Rowen's feet got near her.

"Rowe."

She sank down another notch. Terrorized, her mouth opened but no sound came out.

"Stop, Wynne—no sounds—no moves. Trust me, Wynne. I will get you out."

Ripping off his overcoat, Rowen went to his belly, stretching his body out as wide as he could in every direction while staying on the mound of solid ground. Pepe went to his ear, licking, and Rowen had to shove the dog away.

He scooted forward on his belly, his outstretched hand reaching what remained of her fingers above the bog. He sank his hand into the muck below her fingers, finding her wrist.

Slowly, moving through the suction of the bog, but not fighting it, he began to pull her wrist toward him. Progress crept along, and notch by notch, her arm moved closer to him.

And then a loud crack and a pop came from the muck.

Wynne screamed. It sent her downward, mud and water choking off the sound. Her head tilted back, sputtering.

"Stop moving, Wynne." The order was harsh, not to be denied.

She stilled.

"That was your shoulder pulling out of place. And I am damn sure it hurt to no end. But look at me, Wynne."

Her eyes found his, now not only terrorized, but pain vibrating through them as well.

"I can fix your shoulder." Rowen forced his voice calm. "This is the only way to get you out, Wynne, and it is going to hurt like a blasted hell hole the rest of the way out. But you cannot scream. You cannot fight it. You have to go limp. You have to let the muck move around you. This is going to be agonizing. And slow. But you have to trust me, Wynne. Trust me."

She gave the slightest nod, a tear sliding from her left eye.

He started to pull again, and Wynne's face cringed in a wicked wince. But Rowen could not stop. Not now. No matter how harsh her wince against him.

Her eyes closed, and he could see her head shaking, her hand trembling in pain as he pulled her, slow and even.

He scooted himself back on the mound.

It was working. Agonizingly slow, but she was moving in the muck toward him.

She gasped hard, her mouth opening.

"Don't break on me, Wynne. Don't break. I have you."

Her jaw closed against her scream, but the smallest whimper came out. A whimper that tore at him, tempted him to stop. But he knew this was the only way. He couldn't reach her body yet without getting sucked in himself.

His muscles straining, he ignored her quivering arm. Ignored the fresh tears streaming down her face. Second by second, he dragged her closer, closer, until she was just on the border of where he could reach her.

Ignoring caution, he dug into the bog with his free hand, aiming at her body. His knuckles ran into her chest, and he moved his hand around her ribs, wrapping his fingers under her arm and around her body.

Finally, a solid hold, and he afforded no delicacy against the suck of the bog and yanked hard. His arm flexed, the muscles twanging, but he could feel her body move. Real movement against the muck.

The pain eased on her face, her out-of-place shoulder finding relief from Rowen's dragging.

It still took excruciating minutes, but Rowen had her now, solidly pulling her from the bog. Close to the hard mound he lay on, her chest finally broke free. Rowen dropped her hand, both of his arms going around her torso, and he pulled her forward, freeing her far enough to rest her chest on the mound.

She stayed limp, her arms splayed, her cheek on the ground, as Rowen went to the edge, gathering her skirts from the bog until he could reach one leg and free it, and then the other.

Clearing her from the suction of the bog, Rowen rolled Wynne as gently as he could onto her back, wiping free as much mud from her face and head as he could. Her eyes were still closed, pain etched in her brow. And she was listless. Limp.

Rowen's hand went full along her cheek.

Freezing. Blast it.

"Wynne." His other hand framed her face. "Wynne."

The softest moan came from her.

"Wynne," he said again, not quite hiding the desperation in his voice.

Her eyelids fluttered open, but it was clear she could not focus on him.

"Am I out?"

Rowen exhaled. "Yes. Yes. You are on the ground. I have you."

"Cold." Her eyes closed. "Cold."

Pepe started to lick her neck as Rowen dropped his hands to her body. Her chest, her arms, her stomach. Every bit of her sopping in freezing water.

"Dammit." He leaned away to snatch his jacket and draped it over the front of her.

Pulling her knife from the cold ground, Rowen shoved it alongside his calf into his boot. He picked up the long stick and slid his arms under Wynne in one motion, picking her up and trying to not jar her wrecked shoulder.

He lifted her high, and her head draped onto the crook of his neck as he shifted her weight into one arm. He turned and started jabbing at the ground with the stick.

A quick low whistle and Pepe caught up to them.

The dog stayed at his heels.

{ CHAPTER 7 }

Her shivering had turned into violent spasms before Rowen reached the end of the bog. So violent, that Rowen had to reassess getting her back to the castle.

Carrying her and picking his way through the forest would take at least two hours. Two hours he doubted she had.

So when his stick hit solid ground along the edge of the forest, Rowen dropped it and turned west, going to the nearest place he could think of, an old shack carved into the woods at the far end of the line between the moors and the forest.

In use when the estate used to keep watch over the harvesting of peat for fuel, the place hadn't had a caretaker in years. Not since Rowen was a boy and the grumpy old man, George, had died.

Rowen just hoped it still stood. Still had a few scraps of wood for a fire.

The door was slightly askew on its hinges, and Rowen had to both wedge open the iron latch and kick the wood to gain entrance. The jerking sent Wynne into painful spasms, her shoulder hitting Rowen hard.

Leaving the door open for light, Rowen went into the shack, scanning the small room in what little moonlight was left beyond the trees. Completely empty, except for one old wooden table and a few logs of peat by the fire. It would have to do.

He went in front of the fireplace and laid Wynne down on the stone floor, moving his jacket to her backside and wrapping her the best he could. She looked at him, eyes still unfocused, but seemed to know it was him. Her shaking hand went out to him, but no words came through her chattering teeth.

He grabbed her hand, shocked at how cold it still was. "I will be right here, Wynne. I am just going to start a fire."

Turning, Rowen knelt and stuck his head into the fireplace, looking upward. He thought he could see moonlight, and could hear wind whipping above the stack. Hopefully it was clear of nests and animals—he would have to take his chances. Setting the few peat logs into the fireplace, he went to the table, turning it on its side and slamming it into the stone floor.

Pepe skittered across the room as the brittle wood shattered apart. The dog had remained only a step away from Rowen, but was now happy to eye Rowen from far across the room. Rowen snapped apart the weak planks with his hands as he set them to kindle the fire.

He had to lift Wynne, who was still convulsing, to dive into his jacket for a flint box—a favor that he had thought to grab his usual traveling jacket. He laid her back down, and within minutes, Rowen was nursing a small fire, fanning it until the logs caught aflame.

Heat finally started to roll out into the room, and Rowen turned around to see Wynne had curled into a ball on her side, shaking while trying to hold her limp arm to her side.

Rowen took a deep breath for fortitude, going to the door to close it and buy himself a moment. Before anything else, he had to wedge Wynne's shoulder back into place. She would be in agonizing pain until that happened.

Without telling Wynne what he was going to do—he doubted she would understand him at the moment—Rowen went over to her and set his feet on either side of her, straddling her torso.

As gently as possible, he pulled her wrist free from under his jacket. He bent slightly, putting a knee on the side of her ribs to both capture her and hold her stable, and then straightened her arm.

A scream was his instant reward.

She thrashed, but Rowen held fast, stretching her arm slowly, pulling it hard, but smoothly away from her shoulder.

The sound of a pop and he could feel her shoulder lock back into place. Her thrashing yielded.

Gently, he bent over her, his face above hers, and he laid her arm back to her body.

"I am sorry, Wynne. I could not prepare you for that." He smoothed wet hair away from her temple, his hand calm against her shudders. "But the pain should ease now."

Damn. Even her hair was freezing. She was not warming up.

Rowen swallowed hard, resigning himself to what he was about to do. But it had to be done—the wood he had available to burn would be gone before the warmth breached her soaked clothing. And he doubted she would be able to fight him on it.

He pulled her knife from his boot, went to the fire and poked the wood to renew the flames. Waving the blade in the air to cool it, he ran his fingers along the steel to test the temperature before he went to his knees behind Wynne's back.

Still on her side, she faced the fireplace, her shaking violent.

He bent over her, his mouth near her ear as he pulled his overcoat off of her body and out from under her. He pushed her wet hair from her neck. "I cannot get you warm with these wet clothes blocking the fire. They have to come off, Wynne."

She shook her head as he laid his jacket out flat on the ground, driest side up, in front of Wynne.

Rowen cleared his throat. "I will be as delicate as possible to your sensibilities, Wynne. But they have to come off."

Eyes closed, she nodded.

He lifted her, shifting her forward onto his jacket, then picked up the knife. Quickly, he slid the blade under the top seam of her dress and ran the edge down the back of the cloth, splitting it to her waist.

Taking his own shirt off—the sleeves were still wet, but the back of it was mostly dry—he draped the fabric over her chest before wedging the dress down, removing it to her hips.

He paused, wondering if he should continue. But then another wicked spasm racked her body, answering his silent question.

Shaking his head and cursing fate, he yanked the dress downward as he pulled his white shirt with it so that it covered her down to the top of her thighs.

He stood, hanging her dismantled dress from an old peg next to the fireplace.

A few more pokes at the fire, and Rowen turned to Wynne. Shivering on her side, her skin had turned a ghostly white, and her lips were decidedly blue.

It was not enough.

And now she was naked except for his thin shirt draped from her chest to her thighs.

Rowen sighed, steeling himself, and walked around her.

Dropping to his side on the cold stone floor, he tried to wedge a scrap of his jacket under his bare skin. He slid his left arm under Wynne's neck, lifting her head from the hard floor, and then wrapped his forearm across her upper chest, bringing his body close to her.

His right arm went over her waist and he pulled her entire backside onto his bare skin, tucking her into a cocoon. It was as if an enormous piece of ice had landed on his chest, hardening all muscles against the cold. He couldn't imagine the torture it was to be in her body right now.

Eventually, with Rowen shielding her backside from the cold and capturing the warmth of the fire, her spasms petered into shaking. And then the shaking petered into shivers. Until finally, her body went still, her breathing even.

Rowen felt the moment she slipped into sleep, her body letting go, and he exhaled the anxiety that had held half of his breath captive since he had found her.

He closed his eyes himself, though he was nowhere near sleep.

Not with what had just happened. And not with a mostly naked Wynne in front of him—her skin against his.

And not with the anger that had taken a hold of him. Anger at her. At her stupidity to go after a dog in the middle of the night. That he had almost lost her to a blasted bog, of all things.

It was that very thought that ran around, madcap, in his mind.

He almost lost her.

And it shook him to his core.

He searched his mind for the moment—when had she come to mean so much to him? After she saved him from the tower, and she opened her eyes on that bench and just expected to see him—not at all frightened, only complete trust in her eyes? When they were looking at the duchess's portrait, and her body was so close to his that he could feel the passion she possessed over her art? Or was it back to the beginning, when she smiled at him over the fire, offering him squirrel meat?

Did it matter, the moment? Or only that it was. Only that this woman had entered his life, and without asking had become all that he thought about. All that he dreamt about.

And he had almost just lost her. Damn.

A quiver ran through her body, and Rowen was acutely reminded that she was naked in his arms.

For one brief second, he imagined. Imagined what really holding her, naked in his arms, would be like. He clamped down on his imagination the second his body began to react to that very thought.

He heaved a sigh. The last thing he needed was to be hard as a rock behind her.

He looked at Pepe, sleeping soundly by the fire. The dog had barely twitched since they had made it here. Rowen's anger came back full force.

He let it take him over. Better anger than where his mind was headed.

It was just when his anger had reached a peak that Wynne jerked and moaned. He glanced down at what he could see of her profile, and her long lashes started to flutter open.

He stilled, not moving as her eyes opened fully. She stared at the low fire for a long minute, not shifting from him, not turning her head to look at him.

"I am naked." Her words came out ragged.

"Yes. But my shirt is covering some of you."

She nodded, her cheek rubbing on his arm. "The important parts. And you are warm. And naked as well."

"I have breeches on." Rowen tried to keep the smile out of his voice. "Do you want me to move away?"

It took her a few seconds to decide. "No. You are warm and my bones are still cold. As long as you are all right with the position."

"I will survive."

Pepe's brown and white head popped up at the conversation. Interested, but not interested enough to move from his lazy spot by the fire.

Rowen gave a slight head shake at the dog, his anger stoked. "Why the hell did you go after a dog—a damn dog, Wynne— into a damn bog?"

She turned her head, eyes stretching to see him. "Is that what that was? We do not have those on the mountain. I did not know. And Pepe was in the middle of it. I got stuck a couple of times but pulled myself out."

"Blast it, Wynne—you got stuck, yet you kept on?"

She let her cheek fall back onto his arm, face to the fire. "Yes."

His arms tightened around her. "So why keep going, Wynne? Idiocy. It is not hard to figure out the danger of it."

"Ouch—my shoulder, Rowe."

He forced his arms to relax around her, biting off his next words.

"I did not know, Rowe." Her voice was tired, meek. "I thought the muck could get my feet. Nothing more. And Pepe was stuck, yelping. I did not imagine..."

"But a damn dog, Wynne. It was the middle of the night. You should not have gone to begin with."

She was silent at his words, and Rowen watched as she closed her eyes, bowing her chin to her chest.

They both stilled, neither moving for long moments.

"How can I get you to understand this, Rowe?" She opened her eyes and craned her face to him again, looking for his eyes. "When you see someone drowning, Rowe, do you let them sink?"

Drowning? What the hell was she talking about?

"Do you let them sink, Rowe?" Her voice demanded he answer.

He shook his head.

She pushed herself upright, her left hand clutching his shirt in front of her chest as she turned to him. "No—exactly—you go after them. You dive in and try to help them—you give them everything you have in order to save them. You do not think about it, you just do."

Her head angled to Pepe, still by the fire. "That dog is the last thing keeping the dowager afloat. The dowager is drowning, Rowe. Drowning. In grief. In a life that has cut her at the knees at every turn. And Pepe is her last line to staying in the land of the living." Her voice turned vehement. "So yes. Hell, yes, I go after the damn dog."

"She does not deserve for you to gamble your life for a dog's."

"And I do not get to judge her. I offered to go after Pepe. That was me."

"But she came to you, Wynne—that in itself was her asking."

"Possibly. But you cannot understand what she has lost, Rowe—it is grief so deep, so visceral, and it has not dulled in the slightest since her son died. And that dog has been her salvation."

Rowen looked away, staring at the embers of the fire.

"You dive in like you did with me tonight, Rowe. Like you did that first day." She gingerly eased her right arm up to hold the shirt, and her left hand went to his face, touching his cheek, pulling it so he would look at her. "The first day you met me, Rowe. I was drowning and you dove in and saved me. You did that, and you did not think. You just did. You did not judge whether or not I deserved it. It is the same that I do with the duchess."

Rowen could stand it no longer. He leaned forward, capturing her face, his thumbs landing on her cheekbones. It cut off her words, as intended.

And now Rowen wanted more.

She hadn't jerked away from his touch, her hazel eyes holding his. Surprise in her eyes, curiosity, but not worry.

He moved in on her, his lips meeting hers. Soft. No resistance to his mouth.

Lust had urged him to do it, and now that he made contact, his chest tightened. He needed more. Much more.

He deepened the kiss, tilting her head, slipping his tongue between her parted lips. She gave over to it willingly, and the softest moan came from her, vibrating through Rowen.

Damn. He shouldn't have touched her. Shouldn't have tasted what his body now demanded to have. Demanded so insistently, it made him pull away.

Cheeks flushed, her eyes opened to him. "That...what was that?"

His hands did not drop from her face. "You. You are beyond...beyond compare."

"I did not realize." Confusion set into her hazel eyes. "Is that bad?"

"You care too much, Wynne. Too insanely much—you have no regard for your own safety when it comes to saving others. Me. The dog. It is something that is wholly unique unto you."

"How could I not want to help, Rowe? To help others find peace? For the duchess." Her fingers went up to touch his jaw. "For you?"

"And that is exactly why I kissed you, Wynne."

"So kiss me again."

He groaned. "I have never needed to be an honorable man, Wynne, and you are suddenly testing me like I never imagined I would be tested."

Reluctantly, his hands dropped from her face and he leaned away, but he could not stop his eyes from dropping down her body. Her bare arms. Naked legs folded under her. The line on her thighs where his shirt hung, hiding her skin from him.

He swore to himself. What he wouldn't give for a gust of wind to move that fabric. He looked away to the fire. "You have no clothes on, Wynne. And I do not possess enough willpower to stop this if I kiss you again."

She looked crestfallen. "So that is it? You will never?"

Rowen smiled, pushing himself up to his feet. He needed to extract himself before he did something they would both regret.

Hell—truth was, he would not regret it in the slightest. He would revel in it—in her—and feel no remorse.

Rowen stood. "I never said never, Wynne. This is not the right place. Right time."

Her hazel eyes huge, she looked up at him. Even more beautiful than a moment ago, her lips still raw from his kiss, the shirt lowered ever so slightly. But still incredibly innocent. "When is the right time?"

He chuckled. "When you have had a hot bath. When your shoulder has healed enough to move your arm properly. When you are not covered only by one thin shirt."

She nodded.

"I do not think you should try to make the way back through the woods with bare feet," Rowen said, changing the topic. "Will you be fine here while I get Phalos and come back for you? I believe the sun will be showing soon."

"Yes. But you need your shirt, and I…" Her eyes darted around the room. "I cannot move without…"

"Without dropping the shirt?" Rowen could not hide a smirk.

"Yes. And do not laugh. I am quite stuck down here."

Rowen bowed his head to her. "I will wait outside. Your dress is wrecked down the back, so use my jacket to wrap yourself against the chill."

She nodded, and Rowen stepped out into the early morning darkness.

The coolness hit him, clearing his senses. But it did nothing for his desire.

He sighed.

Fate was laughing at him—that he knew.

{ CHAPTER 8 }

Wynne stared at the white piece of vellum resting on the flat board sitting on her lap. Charcoal darkening her thumb and forefinger, her hand was motionless above the newly started sketch of Pepe.

She had nearly completed the dog on the portrait, him proudly sitting in the dowager's lap. But Wynne had now rethought his entire countenance in the painting. After last night, she wanted him, at the very least, impish.

She couldn't fault him for running off. He was a dog chasing a full moon and that was what dogs did. That he had gotten stuck in the moors wasn't his fault.

Since getting the quirk of Pepe's head just right, Wynne had been motionless, losing time as the image of Rowen, half-naked in front of her, kept filling her mind. His chest. The hard lines of his muscles. No matter how valiantly she tried to shove the image to the back of her brain, he kept appearing.

Half naked and kissing her.

Half naked, kissing her, with his hands on her bare skin.

And she had loved it. For how she should feel shame at the moment, she felt nothing but warmth. Nothing but right. Nothing but wanting it to continue.

She had kissed more than one boy from the mountains—but that was what they were: boys. So clearly boys when compared to Rowen. And none of them had ever come close to creating the fire deep inside of her that Rowen did.

How could she think of anything else?

A knock on the door made her jump, the charcoal dropping from her fingers. It took her a second to remember that no one could see into her mind, and she cleared her throat.

"Enter."

The door opened and Rowen stepped into the room. He wore a fresh white linen shirt, rolled up at the sleeves per usual, and buckskin breeches that disappeared into his tall boots. His eyes swept the room.

"You are alone?"

"Yes. The duchess was tired after waiting up all night for Pepe. And physically exhausted. She near drooped when she came in here."

"It serves her well."

Wynne's eyes went to coffered ceiling. "It was not her fault, Rowe."

"I disagree." He stopped in front of her, looking down, watching her face. "But I did not come in here to argue."

Her head cocked, curious. "No?"

"No. Did the dowager procure new boots for you? A cloak?"

"She did."

"Are you tired?"

She should be—she hadn't slept since they arrived back at the castle in the early morning light, but Wynne was nothing close to tired at the moment. Not since Rowen walked in the door. "No. Near-death apparently makes me want to be awake."

"Would you like fresh air? I have to walk down to the stables."

Wynne blinked, momentarily stupefied.

The offer came random and was completely unexpected. But time with Rowen. This man that had just kissed her hours earlier. She wasn't about to pass on the opportunity.

She set the charcoal, vellum, and board onto the table next to her and stood up. "Yes. I am not producing much of anything right now."

He glanced at the sketch as she moved it and a smile crossed his face. "Good. It shows the bugger's naughtiness." He looked to her. "Boots and overcoat first. It is sunny, but still chilly out."

Within a few minutes, Wynne found an overcoat and boots in the wardrobe the dowager had cobbled together for her, and

Rowen was ushering her through the maze of hallways to an old wooden door.

She stepped into the sunshine, squinting until her eyes adjusted to the light. It had been days of mostly grey since she had arrived, and the sun instantly warmed her cheeks.

Slowing until Rowen fell in step beside her, Wynne took in this side of the castle. It had the same empty, downward slope that surrounded the outer walls, but she could see a break in the tree line with a graveled drive going into it. Wynne assumed the drive led to the stables.

"How is your arm—your shoulder?" Rowen pointed to her right shoulder as they walked.

"Sore. But it does not pain too much. How did you know what to do to fix it?"

"Working around horses—breaking them in—I have had to wrangle more than a few shoulders back into place. But I will admit the first few times I did it were not nearly as successful as yours last night. Your shoulder slipped back into place fairly easily. It helped that you did not fight me."

"I did not know that I had a choice." She looked up at his profile. "You manhandle me without much effort."

He chuckled, but did not argue her point as they reached the drive and his boots crunched onto the crushed gravel of the path.

"I would like to paint you, Rowe. I truly would."

His eyes went to the ground without looking her way. "Why?"

"I like to paint interesting things. And you, Rowen, are interesting."

His cheek, grizzled with dark stubble, rose in a soft smile as he looked down at her. "Again, I would never allow it. I know your methods."

She laughed. "True. It would unearth more of you than I would guess you are willing to let see the light of day."

His smile slid away. "I am trying hard to not let you see much of me, Wynne. Things you can never know of me."

His words, soft and earnest, made her breath catch in her throat. They walked in silence a few steps.

But Wynne could not let it go that easily. Not if it could be her way into his mind.

She looked up at him. "But that does not mean I should not do it. That is exactly what I want to see of you. To know the things you do not tell me. To know you."

The smile returned to his lips, his eyes on the path, no words in his mouth.

She bit the inside of her lip. Rowen was stepping very carefully against being drawn into an argument. Suspicious.

The trees parted in front of them, and Wynne sped up. An enormous clearing, as far as the eye could see, met them, with rolling pastures dotted with horses. Some were in groups, some alone, distant spots in the pastures. Right in front of Wynne stood three long stables lined up, with a two-story brick house off to her left, snugged to the woods.

She looked up at Rowen. "This has been down here the whole time? This is where you disappear to? I thought you were spending all that time planning the destruction of the castle."

"I have more to do with my time than to aggravate the duchess, Wynne. This is the reason that I plan on keeping any of the castle in place—it needs to welcome visitors—horsemen."

Wynne stopped walking, taking in the scope of the area in front of her. "Are all of those stables filled? I know you said you dealt in horses. But there must be one hundred stalls here."

"One-hundred-and-sixty-eight, as of right now. And yes, most of them are full. I plan on building at least two more structures, probably bigger, on the estate."

"The dowager allows this?"

Rowen's head snapped to her, but his voice stayed even. "She does not have a say. The estate is mine to do with as I wish, Wynne."

Wynne nodded, regretting her blurt. Rowen was actually walking with her, talking with her, showing her something that clearly meant a tremendous amount to him, and she had brought up the duchess. The one thing that she knew, without fail, raised his ire.

"Please, show me inside. Is Phalos in there? I expected you to come back with him this morning."

"He is. But he looked slightly slow so early in the morning, and I did not want him carrying your extra weight—as light as you are."

They walked down a slight slope to the first stable. The middle stable looked to be the oldest; the adjacent ones looked quite new.

Stepping aside as a stable boy led a white speckled horse out from the main door, Rowen gave him a wave. Wynne's eyes had to adjust as she moved from the sun into the dark stable, following Rowen to the fifth stall on the right.

Rowen opened the waist-high stall door and went in, pulling an apple from his pocket as he patted Phalos's neck.

Wynne followed him into the stall, stopping in front of the dark horse. Her palm went onto the spot on his nose where his hair thinned, his hot breath coming from his nostril and warming her wrist. Rowen fed him the apple.

"He is a beautiful horse, Rowe. Older, but I imagine in his prime he was a sight to behold. He has more of a wise, noble dignity now. How did you come about him?"

"He was a war horse. He was not on the list, but he was more than worth saving."

"A war horse?" Wynne looked to him. "You were in a war? Which war?"

Rowen's attention went to her. "Even with your American accent, Wynne, I do forget sometimes that you do not know of England. The Napoleonic wars—with France. Six years ago."

"Did you participate in much fighting?"

"I did."

His eyes did not leave hers, but she could tell his answer was not inviting deeper questions.

Wynne rubbed Phalos's nose, leaning in and rubbing her cheek on his smooth hair. "What did you mean, Phalos was not on the list?"

"It was what I was charged to do during the wars. Save the most important horses, the ones with lineage, the ones that, were they to be lost, would be a disgrace to the world."

Rowen's hand went under Phalos's mane, scratching. "The innocents that are ensnared in the folly of man are a sin. Too many innocents—horses, women, children—were caught in those wars. But we managed to save a number of horses—horses that were worth risking all for."

"Are many of them here?"

Rowen gave a half nod, moving back along Phalos, his hand trailing just below the horse's spine. "Some. Some have since died of old age. The younger ones we have spread out to where they can be bred, and many were returned to the original owners—no matter their nationality—when we could. Our mission was solely to keep them safe."

He patted the horse's side. "Phalos I kept, though. He was mine from the moment I saw his eyes on that battlefield. Standing his ground against the exploding gunpowder, the gunfire, the death around him. It was remarkable—he was remarkable."

Wynne stayed silent, afraid to move, watching Rowen out of the corner of her eye as she stroked the horse's dark nose. Rowen was telling her something real, something of him, and she didn't want it to end, didn't want to risk the slightest movement to interrupt him.

"We got him out of the battle, and he has not left my side since." Rowen moved forward, his hand going up to rub the odd white ring around the horse's left ear, admiration clear on his face. "But you are right about his age. I have tried to leave him to the fields to age in comfort, but he refuses it. He becomes overly jealous of any other horse I use. So much so that he torments them if he gets close. And he gets away with it. He has never not been in charge of his kind."

"Did he see you this morning?"

"No." A sheepish smile crossed Rowen's face. "I snuck that steed from the far stable. And then I took a bath when we got back to rid myself of the other horse's scent."

Wynne laughed. "Afraid of your own horse. I would not have thought it of you."

Rowen shrugged. "Anything to avoid his jealousy. Every other horse here knows he is in charge. He does not have to prove it, but that would not stop him from going after that poor horse. Phalos is just too proud to not want to be working."

Wynne looked up at Phalos's black eyes, taking in the size of him. "I cannot imagine any horse wanting to be on his bad side."

"One would not think it to look at him—his size and stature are intimidating—but he is especially good at putting nervous mares at ease," Rowen said. "Gentle. He nuzzles them and they are jelly—will follow him anywhere. It was especially helpful when we had to move the horses silently in the cover of night."

Wynne looked from Phalos to Rowen. "You two seem to have that in common."

"Sneaking along in the cover of night?"

"Putting women—at least me—at ease. It is one thing about you—I have never been nervous when I am with you. For all that I do not remember. For how you found me in the woods—in the moors. I have never been afraid when you are near me—even though I should have been, a thousand times over."

Rowen cleared his throat with a slight nod, stepping away from Phalos. "Come. I would like to show you the other stables."

She had meant it as a compliment, Rowen's innate ability to calm her, to make her feel safe. But his abrupt change of subject threw Wynne, and she thought she misstepped her words with Rowen.

In the next few steps through the stable, though, his light chatter as they moved past the other stalls reassured her. She may have made him uncomfortable, but it wasn't so grievous that she got sent back to the castle.

They stepped out into the daylight just as a man on a tall, spirited, white horse came to a rearing halt at the entrance of the stable.

"Blast it." Rowen yanked Wynne to the side of the entrance to avoid the flying hooves.

Wynne watched as Rowen's annoyance at almost getting trampled turned into an easy smile once the horse calmed and he could see the rider.

"Seb, you arse. Learn how to ride a horse," Rowen scolded good-naturedly.

The man swung his leg over the mare, dropping down in front of Rowen and Wynne, the reins in his hand. He was tall, taller than Rowen, dark brown hair, solid build with a handsome face that looked like a pinch of the devil sat on the edges of his mouth.

"It took all of my wiles during the past two days just to get this one here, for all her angst." The man patted the mare's sweaty neck, and she turned to nip at his arm. "Is Phalos in here? I want to get her next to him to see if she can be calmed."

Rowen nodded. "Yes, but hold for a moment." Rowen turned to Wynne. "This man, I would like you to meet. Miss Theaton, may I introduce Lord Luhaunt. He is friend from years ago. Sebastian, this is Miss Theaton."

Wynne gave Luhaunt a bright smile. "And I thought the afternoon could not get any better, Rowe showing me the stables—and then to meet a friend of his."

"I am pleased—" The mare reared, kicking away from Luhaunt.

She watched Luhaunt scramble to get in front of the horse's nose, trying to calm the mare.

Wynne stole a glance at Rowen and he caught her eye, his amusement plain. "We were in the war together. Luhaunt has a sixth sense when it comes to finding horses of merit, so he was particularly handy for our work on the continent. He still is."

The horse semi-calm, Rowen turned his attention to Luhaunt. "I did not expect you for a few weeks."

Luhaunt shrugged. "I am just passing through—I thought to take this one up to Lanark. But she got spooked a half day back and has not recovered. I do not think we could make the trip without killing each other, so I veered here to switch her out."

Rowen looked to Wynne. "Luhaunt is on his way to pick up several horses in the north. If he approves of them, of course. He has as much of a stake in this breeding farm as I do."

"Yes, plus, Rowe needs me to find the good breeds," Luhaunt said. "He is much too particular with how his horses measure up—this place would be near empty without me."

Wynne nodded. "I imagine Phalos has done that to him."

Luhaunt chuckled. "Yes, Phalos does set a high bar to match." He looked to Rowen, his eyebrow arched. "Miss Theaton is a discerning one. I look forward to chatting with her further when I return."

Rowen stepped forward, slapping Luhaunt on the shoulder, ushering him into the stable. "I can see you are anxious to be along—drop the mare by Phalos. I will check on her in a few minutes. Stall sixty-eight has a nice mare—fresh—for the rest of your journey. Are you sure you do not wish to stay the night?"

"No. I had hoped to be to the border by nightfall, so best to stay on the move. I will stay for a spell on my return."

Rowen gave him a nod. "God-speed."

Luhaunt looked to Wynne. "It has been a pleasure—short— but a pleasure."

"The same for me," Wynne said.

Luhaunt moved from Rowen and Wynne into the stable. Rowen watched him for just a moment before turning to Wynne, holding his hand forward for them to walk.

"He is the wind, that one. Loves the travel. Loves the people everywhere he is. Loves not having anything permanent in his life."

"But I understand he is a good friend to you?"

"The best."

For the next two hours, Rowen walked Wynne through the other stables, showing her some of the horses from the war, some of their descendants, some that were here for breeding, some that were currently being trained for racing, some that were here to live out their elderly years in peace.

It was when they were walking up the hill from the edge of the stone-lined pastures that Rowen stopped, turning back to survey the stables and expansive land.

Wynne turned with him, though her eyes were drawn more to his profile than the vista before them. His jawline looked settled, more peaceful than she had ever seen him.

"I did want you to see this, Wynne. To know that there is another purpose to my being here, other than to destroy the castle—other than to drive the dowager into utter madness. All of these horses now have a home where they are well cared for and can be bred appropriately."

His hand swept around him. "Notlund has the perfect land and the location—England, Ireland, Scotland, the continent—horsemen have started to come from far and wide to buy, sell, and breed horses here. Which is why the castle is so important—I need a place to host the most discerning of those men. Decisions about what lines to breed are not taken lightly."

Transfixed, Wynne's eyes could not leave his face. "It is amazing. And these horses—you pamper them. It almost makes me wish I were one of your mares."

He smiled, giving her a sideways glance. "I doubt you would let me pamper you, Wynne."

"What? Why?"

"You are far too spirited to be owned by pampering. If you were a horse I would have to take great pains to take care of you, without you knowing I was doing so."

She laughed, acknowledging the truth of it. "Blame my grandfather. I am sure if my father had not died, I would have reached adulthood like my mother—gentle, kind, demure—but always needing someone to take care of me. It was the way of my early years, and it was jarring at first, living with my grandfather."

Wynne turned, her gaze on a far-off hill with one lone horse atop. "He expected so much more of me—demanded so much more. How to survive off the land with only a knife. How to take care of myself and my mother. And I loved that life." A smirk lined her lips as her gaze went back to Rowen. "But that does not mean I have not, on occasion, looked longingly at the pampered life."

"I will remember that."

She turned fully to him just as a waft of smoke drifted by. It stopped her movement and her nose turned up.

"What?" Rowen asked.

Wynne tilted her head, unsure as she took a deep inhale. "That smell. It was in that shack by the bog, as well."

Rowen lifted his nose to the air, sniffing. He looked at her. "Peat?"

"Peat? What is peat?"

"It is cut out of the bog—the moors. Many people burn it instead of wood. It makes for a good fire, but there is an odor to it." He pointed to the smoke coming from the chimney of the two-story building by the woods. "The workers are burning it in their quarters."

"Tanloon…" The word came out of Wynne's mouth as a whisper and her eyebrows arched.

Rowen shook his head, forehead collapsed in confusion. "Tanloon? What?"

Wynne took another sniff of the air. "I do not know. That smell. That word came to my mind last night when the smell from the fire you lit drifted to me, but I lost it before I could say it out loud. Tanloon. What is that?"

Rowen's eyes went to the sky, pondering. "There is a town, Tanloon, up in northern Yorkshire."

Her eyes widened. "It is a town? Where? How far away?"

"A half day by fast horse, maybe more. Why? Did the dowager say something about it?"

"No. I know that name. That place."

"What?" Rowen grabbed her shoulders. "Wynne, are you remembering something?"

"I..." She rubbed her forehead. "It is just the name. The smell and then that name. It is all I can pull out. Nothing else—nothing..."

"Try, Wynne. Tanloon. Try to dig it out. Tanloon. Did you live there?"

"I do not know. I—there is nothing. Just that name. I am trying. Tanloon. Tanloon." She hit her forehead with her palm repeatedly, a low, frustrated scream tearing from her lungs.

Rowen grabbed her wrist, stilling it before she could continue the onslaught. "We will go there, Wynne. If it will help you remember. We will go there and search. Your mother could be there."

Her face whipped up to his, her eyes huge. "My mother..."

Nodding, he lowered her wrist to her side and released it.

She seized his forearm, fingernails digging into his bare skin. "Rowe, I have to go. I have to go now. She could be there. She could be there and waiting for me. She would be frantic."

"It is too late in the day, Wynne. We will go first thing in the morning."

"No, Rowe, I have to go now."

"Wynne, you do not know what is there. Much less where the town is. I will bring you there as quickly as possible and we will find answers. But we have to leave tomorrow—before dawn breaks, we will go. I promise."

She searched his dark eyes, desperate against his logic, but she knew he was right. Her fingers still digging into his arm, she had to force herself to nod agreement.

Her mother. She truly could find her mother again.

And with that, her memories.

{ CHAPTER 9 }

The moment they saw the edge of the small village from a far-off hill, Wynne dug her heel into her horse, pushing it as hard as she could toward the town. They had left before dawn and had made it to the area by late morning—much faster than Rowen had expected.

Rowen hustled Phalos after Wynne, but gave her healthy space. He didn't want to be between her and her memories if she recognized anything.

The town was snugged into a narrow valley, mostly made up of tiny houses and buildings, some two or three rows deep into the surrounding hills. The whole of it—small.

Rowen had only been through this town once, late at night and years ago. He had stopped at a tavern for a quick meal, but then had been on his way, not noting anything of importance about the village.

In front of him, Wynne slowed, her head swinging back and forth with frantic eyes on every building. Rowen kept Phalos back a few horse's lengths, vigilantly watching her study the houses. He could tell she had yet to recognize anything.

Though small, the town still supported at least the three taverns that they had already passed, a church, a bakery, a blacksmith, one boarding house, and a butcher, and Rowen could see a tall water wheel spinning at a mill on the far edge of the town.

Wynne curbed her honey-colored mare to an almost crawl. A moment later, she yanked on the reins, flying off the horse.

"There." She was pointing, on the run before Rowen caught up to her. He dismounted, grabbing the reins of both horses before following Wynne up a path between two houses. There were two small, square shacks stacked up the hill behind the bigger house on the main street.

"This." Wynne looked back over her shoulder at him. "This. I know this house, Rowe. I know it." The sheer excitement on her face made her cheeks glow. Rowen just hoped it was warranted.

"Eh. Ye. Where ye be goin', sir?"

A gruff voice from behind made Rowen turn around, looking around Phalos's head to see a girthy woman wiping her hands on a stained apron. She stood in the doorway of the bigger house they had just passed.

"Hello. I apologize for the intrusion. Do you know who lives here?" Rowen half-turned, pointing at the two houses. Wynne was already jiggling the door latch on the far house.

He moved to block Wynne from the woman's view.

"Boon send ye from the tavern? Ye be needin' a room ta rent?"

"Is that what these are? Both of them?"

"Just the back one, sir. Front one be rented. Back one be open now."

"Who rents the front one?"

The woman's hands went on her wide hips, thrusting her left hip higher as her eyes narrowed at him. "Why ye be needin' to know that?"

"I am just curious if it is a loud neighbor," Rowen said.

"It be ole Jack that lives there. He ain't too loud." She leaned further out from her doorway, stretching to see past Rowen. "What yer lady be doin'?"

Rowen re-angled himself in front of the woman. "She is tired. We have been traveling a distance, and she is anxious to rest."

"Oh. Well, ye cin take a look inside and see if it be to yer likin'. Ye be stayin' a stretch? There be a post out back for the horses."

"Thank you. We will take a look around."

She gave him a nod, spinning back in through her doorway.

By the time Rowen walked up the short hill, Wynne had already disappeared into the confines of the small shack.

She left the door open, and Rowen looked in to see Wynne in the middle of the main living space, her back to him. She looked rooted to the spot, not moving.

He gave her a moment, going around to the back of the shack to tie the horses to the post. Foot creaking the wooden floorboards, he stepped into the house tentatively, not wanting to disturb her, but intensely curious as to what was going through her mind.

The place was dark, only one small window in the back where he could see Phalos's tail swishing. It was sparse—a fireplace, a wooden table with two chairs, a black iron pot on the floor by the hearth, a fire poker, and beyond that, a doorway into another room with a grey curtain hanging for privacy. Dusty wood shavings littered the floor. Not large, but comfortable enough for two people to live there.

Wynne had yet to move.

Rowen stayed by the doorway, wanting to block the landlady if she came up to check on them. "Have you remembered anything?"

Wynne nodded, without a word, and then her head dropped forward. Rowen closed the door behind him and went over to her.

Tears streaming down her face, dropping, she didn't look up as he rounded her.

"You were here?"

Wet droplets splattered onto the floor, darkening the dusty boards. "We lived here. I remember living here...Painting over in that corner." She inclined her head to the spot between the table and the fireplace. "My paintings..." Her arm swung around her. "They lined the walls—filled them."

"Why were you here?"

Wynne shook her head, her fingers going to her temples, rubbing as she closed her eyes. "She wanted to...mother...after grandfather died...she thought she could find my father's family. His cousins. She did not think we could survive on the mountain without grandfather. I tried to convince her to stay. I knew we could. I tried. She would not listen—would not see. And this... this is where she thought they lived."

"The cousins? In Tanloon?"

"Yes...but my mother—she is not here. I do not remember..."

Her head dropped again.

"Do not give up, Wynne." Rowen's hand went to her upper arm, rubbing against the dark wool cloak draped over her. "Look around. You have only been in here for a few minutes. If you have started to remember, the rest will come."

It took a few seconds, but she nodded numbly at his words, her movements wooden as she walked around the small room, her hand trailing across the table, stopping to look out the window, bending over at the hearth to look into the fireplace.

"Where did it all go?" Her head wobbling, she stood straight. "I remember it all, Rowe. I remember all of this. But I do not remember why we left. Our possessions are not here. My paints. My easel. My portraits. It was a home. We had a home. But all of it is gone."

Rowen was at a loss. He didn't want to give Wynne hope against what her mind was determined to keep secret. But he held back his pessimism. "Keep walking. Keep remembering."

She took a deep breath and moved past him, her eyes on the floor. Stopping at the entrance to the back room, she drew aside the curtain.

The instant she looked up, she gasped, her body doubling over. But instead of stepping backward, where her body leaned to escape, her feet took her forward into the room.

Rowen was at her heels in an instant, ready to catch her, and looking over her head into the room.

Empty.

A worn bed. A dresser. That was all.

But Wynne's body had begun to shake. Shake violently.

Her hand was solid over her mouth, and it looked like she was holding back a heave.

She spun, frantic, and Rowen caught sight of her eyes. Terrified. Terrified and horrified.

"No, Rowe. No." The words barely formed.

"What is it?"

"He beat her here. I was in the forest and I came in…" She spun slowly in a circle, her eyes glazed. "The blood…I tried to stop him—I went between them and bent to cover her—but he picked me off and threw me into the wall and it all went black… And when I woke, that—"

She pushed Rowen aside, running past him into the main room. He quickly followed.

Her steps halted in the middle of the floor, sending her slipping toward the fireplace. She fell onto her butt. "The poker…"

Scrambling backward on her feet and hands, terrorized, she only stopped when she hit the wall opposite the fireplace. But her feet still moved, pushing her into the wall, toes fighting against the floor—against the horror.

"Tell me, Wynne. Tell me."

She shook her head violently, the back of her head banging on the wall. But she opened her mouth. "He beat her—with that." She pointed across the room. "The poker. The poker. And the blood flew. The blood…I went weak. And then he saw me awake."

Her hand flew across her mouth, her eyes shut hard against the scene in her mind.

"I tried to get my knife out, but I lost it in my bag. And he swung. I rolled. And he swung again. I got past him. And I ran. I ran."

Her breath heaving, her words stopped.

Rowen looked around the room. Everything seemed somewhat clean and orderly. Whatever had happened here had long since been removed. He took a step backward to look into the bedroom again. Neat and unused.

Just as he leaned forward, his eyes caught sight of a large dark spot on the planks of the wood floor. It wasn't much, the wood was dark to begin with, but it was noticeable, even under the wood shavings and dust covering the floor.

He moved into the small bedroom, dragging the toe of his boot across the floor to scrape it down to the plank. Noticeably dark. Blood? Long dried, but cleaned up blood?

Stepping back into the main room, Rowen's gaze fell down to Wynne. Sitting, her back propped against the wall with her arms wrapping herself, her breathing had slowed.

Her eyes opened to him.

Torture, down to the depths of her soul, shook in her eyes. He recognized it instantly, and it twisted his chest. Stole his breath.

"I left her, Rowe." She whispered the words. "I ran and I left her."

Rowen took a small step toward her. "Was she alive, Wynne?"

Her eyes closed again, her head hitting the wood behind her, fresh tears streaming down her cheeks. "It does not matter whether she was alive, Rowe. I left. I god-damned left her. I never...I never should have left her."

Rowen took another step, bending to one knee next to her.

"You had to stay alive, Wynne. It would have been death if you stayed."

"No, I had to take care of her. That was the one thing I was supposed to do—take care of her. I had the knife, but I ran...I ran."

"Wynne." His hand went lightly to her shoulder.

She jerked away, scrambling to her feet. "Don't touch me."

Standing, Rowen reached for her again. "Wynne."

"Do not touch me, Rowe. Do not touch me."

Her words vicious at him, Rowen stopped, hands hanging in midair as she backed out of the door.

Rowen gave her a few seconds, then followed. It was just in time to see her skirts turn the back corner of the building. He stopped, cocking his head to listen.

Her footsteps went around the small house and then stopped.

He went to the back post, rubbing the noses of the horses. He could hear her, muffled sobs just loud enough to reach him.

His heart breaking for her, what he truly wanted to do in that moment was scoop her up and take her away from this place as fast as he could. Make this right for her somehow.

But he knew he couldn't. He would have to give her this time, as much as it curdled his stomach to have to hear her sobs. As much as it wedged a heavy brick onto his chest that refused to move.

If he couldn't touch her, he would listen. Even from afar.

It was all he could do.

{ CHAPTER 10 }

She was drowning. Drowning into depths she didn't know existed.

Looking around, the world blurred—the forest starting up at the crest of the hill, the backsides of the houses on this end of the village, a slew of chickens pecking at the cold ground.

Wynne wasn't quite sure how she got to this side of the house.

She sank, sobbing, losing all strength to stand, her back scraping down along the grey wood planks on the house. Chills invaded her body, ravaging all of her nerve endings, pain in every muscle.

She had abandoned her mother.

Ran.

A coward.

Her mother had had such hope for this land. And it—their life here—had descended into depravity so quickly. Her beautiful, kind, mother—the one that had always made the world bright for Wynne—had become the cautionary tale whispered about in the corners of the polite houses.

Her mother had turned into a whore.

The word echoed in Wynne's head.

Whore.

Whispered behind them, again and again, along the paths of the village.

Wynne crumpled even farther. Her legs curled into her chest, her face deep in her arms, the wall still supporting her back.

Her body started to shake again—the chills fighting her sobs for control of her body.

How had Wynne let this happen? Failed everyone so miserably? Her mother. Her grandfather. She was supposed to protect her mother. Take care of her.

She'd failed.

The vicious ache in her muscles intensified, and thoughts disappeared, tears disappeared. Just pain. Pain was all she felt, all she could think.

Minutes…hours…lifetimes passed, she had drowned so deep in time. And just when she was about to lie down—lie down on that cold ground and pray for death to take pity on her—a warm force appeared next to her.

Rowen.

Even with her eyes closed and her body so excruciatingly weak she could not look up, she knew it was him.

Next to her, but not touching. Not speaking. Just there.

There and solid and alive.

A barricade against what she wanted to do—give up.

A long stretch of time went by—Wynne wasn't sure if it was ten minutes or an hour, she was so fully lost—before the shaking eased enough that she felt strong enough to raise her head.

"I abandoned her." Eyes closed, the words tore from her throat. The last time she saw her mother—beaten, lifeless—haunted her mind.

"Who was the man, Wynne?" Ever so slowly, she felt Rowen's arm go behind her, gently wrapping her shoulders.

She couldn't jerk away. Not at this moment.

"I do not know. She…" She lost strength and crumbled into him.

His hold on her tightened, and Rowen's hand went to her temple, tucking her onto his chest. "What, Wynne? She what?" he whispered, his chin on the top of her head.

"We did not find the cousins. We had very little money. I knew it, but she would not tell me how much. Enough to rent this place for a month…maybe two…but then…"

"Then what?"

Another chill ravaged her body, and she trembled violently for a minute. Rowen held her solid, waiting for it to subside.

Wynne took a steadying breath. "She had to make money. So men—she started to entertain men. She tried to hide it from me. She said we were fine, but I knew. I knew. I would see them leaving. Hear things."

His hand moved softly against her hair. "Whatever she did, Wynne, she did to survive. To take care of you."

"A whore, Rowe. She became a whore."

He stiffened around her. "Wynne—"

"It was what it was, Rowe—I let her turn into a whore. She turned into a whore for me. It—"

"You did not turn her into a whore." His chest vibrated under her, and even in his deep whisper, his voice was harder than she had ever heard it. "Do not take that on, Wynne."

"I let her do it. I was supposed to take care of her—that was what grandfather was preparing me for—for the day he would die and I was to take care of her. But I failed her. I failed him. I let her do that—become a whore."

She tried for a moment to sit up, but Rowen wouldn't let her escape his hold. The small movement depleted her energy, and she relented, sinking further into him, her voice haunted. "She was sophisticated, Rowe. Beautiful, and mannered, and a lady, and I…I let her do it. And then when she needed me most, I ran."

Wynne drew in a quivering breath. "I ran and now I do not even know where her body…" The words left her, not able to say out loud what she had caused.

Rowen's hand went deep into her hair at her neck. "We will find out."

"Eh, there ye be. I seen yer horses, but not ye."

Wynne wiped her eyes clear, looking up from the cave Rowen had her in to see a robust woman rounding the back corner of the house, her hands on her hips.

"What ye be doin' back here?" she asked.

Wynne blinked hard at her. "Mrs. Pemperton?"

The woman stopped for a second, looking around her and then narrowing her eyes at Wynne. "Mrs. Pemperton, duckie? Who be that?"

Wynne pushed up off of Rowen, and this time, he let her escape. Her eyes didn't leave the woman. "You are Mrs. Pemperton."

The woman shook her head. "Not me name, duckie. I be Mrs. Dewgerd."

"What? No. Mrs. Pemperton—you know me—I lived here with my mother. My mother—Violet—Violet Theaton."

"I don't be knowin' ye, duckie. Never had no mother and her daughter livin' here."

Wynne scrambled to her feet, going over to the woman and grabbing her arm. "It was just weeks ago, Mrs. Pemperton—we lived here for a year."

The woman grabbed Wynne's wrist, twisting it as she removed it from her arm. She leaned her girth in on Wynne. "Ye be mistak'n, duckie. There ain't been no ladies livin' here—last one in this house be a young gentleman, in town fer work in the fields. Five months he be here."

"But it was just weeks ago, Mrs. Pemperton." Frantic, Wynne grabbed Mrs. Pemperton's other arm with her free hand. "I am Wynne, and my mother is Violet. I paint—I painted you. You have to remember that. On your front stoop—I painted you."

"I ain't got time fer this. Get yer hands off me and stop callin' me Pemperton, duckie. Ye best be gone with ye." The threat was real in her voice.

Rowen grabbed Wynne's shoulders, pulling her against her will a step away from Mrs. Pemperton.

"I apologize, Mrs. Dewgerd, there must be some misunderstanding," Rowen said. "Do you mind if we take one more look around the house? That may help us."

The landlady's hands went back onto her wide hips, her face now red. "No. No. Ye be gone. The both of ye. I don't want no crazies 'round me. A drunkard be enough to handle. Get gone."

Wynne tried to step toward Mrs. Pemperton again, hands out to grab her, to shake her, to get her to see that she knew full well both Wynne and her mother.

Rowen held her back.

Struggling against him, Wynne shouted, desperate. "But our possessions—my mother—my paintings—where are they? What did you do with them? What did you do with my mother? You have to tell me, Mrs. Pemperton. You have to tell me."

The woman took a step backward, her eyes on the house next to her. "Get gone, or I be gettin' the musket from next door. They be comin' if I yell. Get ye gone."

"But—"

"Wynne, come." Rowen's voice was low in her ear. "She says she does not know you, and we need to leave."

Her head whipped over her shoulder to him. "But, Rowe, we—"

"We have to leave, Wynne. Leave now."

"Good. Yer man's got some sense. Now get gone."

"But—"

Rowen started to push her, but Wynne wouldn't move her feet. She needed answers. She needed to find her mother, and Mrs. Pemperton was her only chance at that. Wynne leaned back against his hands, her feet solid.

So he picked her up.

Picked her up and started walking.

Shock held her still for a moment, and then she realized Rowen was manhandling her away from the one person that knew what happened to her mother.

"Rowe—stop." Wynne's arms were clasped to her sides under Rowen's hold, so she started kicking and squirming, yelling. "Stop, Rowe. Let me go, dammit. Rowe. Stop."

Not the slightest hiccup in his stride.

They got to the horses, and he set her to her feet, one arm still holding her captive, as he untied the reins from the post.

Rowen went to her honey-colored horse, giving a slight grunt against her struggling as he hoisted her straight up to her saddle.

She waited until he stepped away to Phalos before she jumped off her horse, running.

Nine steps, and the arm around her waist jerked her to a stop, her feet slipping, sending dust into the air.

"Dammit, Wynne. This is not the way. I am getting you out of here."

Wynne didn't bother to struggle against him, as his hold around her belly was so tight it was cutting into her breath.

This time, he stomped straight to Phalos. Without setting her down, his boot went into the stirrup, hand on the saddle, and he pulled both of them onto the horse.

Rowen plopped her sideways in front of him. He grabbed the reins, his arms on either side of her torso, holding her captive.

She stole a look at his face. He was not pleased.

But neither was she. The man was insufferable, picking her up like a sack of grain and throwing her onto his horse. Did he not see she needed to find answers here—answers that lived back with Mrs. Pemperton?

"I can ride my own horse, Rowen," she seethed.

"Not a chance. You have already proven what you will do." Annoyance overrode the usual smoothness in his voice.

"But my horse."

"She will follow." Rowen clicked his heels into Phalos, and Phalos nosed Wynne's horse as he started to move. The mare fell into line behind them as they went down the lane between the houses and back to the main road through the village.

Wynne sat, arms crossed high over her chest, steaming in silence as she suffered the humiliation of the curious looks from a few residents. The spectacle they were making apparently didn't bother Rowen in the slightest, as his face stayed calm with his silence.

The only indication that he was still perturbed with her was in his stiff arms, muscles flexing repeatedly on either side of her.

It wasn't until they were up the hill, well into the forest with the village long behind them, that Wynne was able to control herself enough to speak without screaming at him.

But she could not look at him.

"She knew something. You took me away and she knew something, Rowe." Her hands balled into fists. "After running I woke up in the forest not remembering a thing. I do not know what happened to my mother. That woman does."

Rowen shook his head, sighing. "It does not matter if she knew something or not, Wynne. She was not going to admit to knowing you or your mother. And we were in a town I do not know, and all I have on me is a pistol and a dagger. Against that woman, against three or four more, I could protect you, but beyond that—if more came to her aid—that could have gone very badly for us. If she was lying—"

"If she was lying?" Wynne's eyes flew from the trees to him. "You do not believe me?"

His dark eyes on hers, he took a deep breath, his chest squishing her upper arm into her body. "I saw enough in that shack to believe you, Wynne. What happened was very real. What happened to you, what you saw—that was real. But there is no proof. There was nothing in that house that gave evidence to you or your mother. And that woman was not going to help us. That woman was, in fact, very set against helping us. She wanted us to leave as quickly as possible."

Wynne watched his dark eyes, searching for something to hold onto. His words were sensible, she knew that, but all she had now were new memories, more mysteries—and no mother.

What happened to her mother's body? What happened to the rows of paintings? What happened to their clothes, all her paints? It all couldn't just disappear like that.

A shudder ran through her body. She was getting very tired—exhausted—and weak.

"Am I crazy?" Wynne's words came out frail, defeated. She didn't want to ask the question, but she had to. It was a very real possibility.

Rowen's eyes swept over her face, searching every corner, searching her eyes.

His right hand came up from the reins and he grabbed the back of her head, holding it still from bobbing with the gait of Phalos.

"No. You are not crazy, Wynne. You are very much sane." His voice stayed low, raw with the words as his fingers curled into her hair. "I do not ever want to hear you doubt yourself like that again. You have been through a hell. That does not make you crazy. Do you understand?"

Closing her eyes, fighting for breath, she could only nod.

"Good." He pushed her head to his chest, wrapping his arm around her body. "Good."

It was the last word she heard before surrendering to the dark exhaustion calling for her.

{ CHAPTER 11 }

Darkness had just settled when Phalos's hooves slowed to a halt before the main entry of the castle. Rowen hadn't pushed him too hard to get back.

Nearly impossible with Phalos's heavy gait, Wynne had managed to fall into a deep sleep. So Rowen had given her the time in silence and tried to slow Phalos. Time for her to sleep and get over the shock of the day was more important than getting her to the castle in a hurry.

Rowen looked at the hefty oak door to the castle. Wynne's body still limp on his chest, he rubbed her upper arm to rouse her. She fought it, nuzzling her head deeper between the folds on his overcoat.

"Wynne," he whispered. "We are at the castle. Wynne."

A soft moan. And then she jerked upright. Fast, her head swiveling, she almost slipped forward off the horse. "What? Where?" Her eyes settled on Rowen, and for an instant, he could see her confusion. Her lack of knowing time and place.

In the next second, it hit her, and her face, her world, crumpled right in front of Rowen.

She gave him a numb nod and slipped off the horse, not waiting for Rowen to dismount and help her down. Hitting the ground with a thud, her legs straightened, but her head stayed down, her shoulders slumped.

Rowen tied both Phalos and the mare to the front post as Wynne trudged to the front door, opening it and disappearing into the darkness. The dowager's voice floated out past the open door, but Rowen could not hear her words.

By the time he turned to follow Wynne in, the duchess had made it out into the darkness. Her black dress and shawl disappeared into the night, making her look like a floating head bearing down at him.

"You took her out without a companion?" the duchess hissed.

Rowen tried to sidestep her, but the dowager hopped in front of him.

He stopped, his eyes to the dark sky. "Not now, Duchess."

"What did you do to her, L.B.? She could not speak, could not look at me."

His chin dropped as he glanced through the doorway. Wynne was long gone from the entry hall. He looked at the duchess. "It is not your concern, Duchess."

"You may refuse to bow to the standards of polite society, L.B., but this is my home and that—taking her—was not in the realm of propriety." Her finger poked into his chest. "I will not allow it."

"You do not have a say in it, Duchess. Wynne is a grown woman."

Her finger did not stop. "Are you trying to ruin her, L.B.? Trying to make Miss Theaton into a whore? Like your mother? I will not allow it—"

Hand instantly around the dowager's neck, cutting her words, Rowen pushed her back onto the outside wall. "I said, not now, Duchess. And I will never hear you say the word 'whore' near Wynne's name again. Or so help me, my hold on your neck will not be as gentle as it is in this moment." He leaned into her face. "Do you understand?"

Refusing his words, the duchess fought his hand on her neck, her fingernails scratching his skin.

And then the fight ran out.

She nodded, her face twisted in bitter disgust.

Rowen released her.

What he wanted to do in that moment was to check on Wynne. But he wasn't about to do so with the dowager hovering at his heels. So Rowen stalked over to the horses, grabbing the reins.

A long walk to the stables would do him well.

~ ~ ~

"I want her back the way she was, L.B."

Rowen closed his eyes to the hoof he was bent over, scraping. He took a deep breath. To his knowledge, the dowager had never been to the new stables. For her to even step foot into the structure meant something dire. And he wasn't in the mood for whatever she was about to say.

He looked back over his shoulder. The dowager stood over him, just inside the stall, her arms crossed over her chest, middle finger tapping incessantly on her elbow.

"What did you do to her, L.B.? You have destroyed her and I want her back to being her."

Rowen's attention went back to the hoof, and he flicked free one last embedded rock with the hoof pick before setting it down.

He stood, patting the Arabian mare's neck. "I did not do anything to her, Duchess." Voice dry, he turned fully to her, kicking hay off his boots.

"Do not lie to me, L.B. You must have done something to her. Miss Theaton has sat in that dark room for four days now. Four days. She does not come out. She does not speak. She eats very little. She just sits, L.B. Sits. It is not right."

Rowen stared down at her. The black shawl that always covered her hair was missing. He hadn't seen the full of her dark hair—now half grey—since before her son and husband had died.

The duchess actually sounded sincere. Sincerely worried about Wynne. It was the first time Rowen had ever seen sincerity from the duchess, and he wasn't sure he trusted it.

Rowen evened his voice. "Again, I did nothing to her, Duchess, and I am offended you think I did. Besides, I do not know what you imagine I can do to help her."

It was true. Rowen had already racked his brain, visited with Wynne, day after day, all to no avail. Wynne was stuck solid in the darkness that her world had become, and Rowen had no idea how to pull her out of it.

Stepping around the duchess, he moved out of the stall. He waited until she removed herself as well, then latched the gate.

The duchess's arms stayed solidly crossed. "Well, you need to think of something, L.B. The only thing you have ever done of value was to bring Miss Theaton into this castle. The only good thing. Do not make a mess of it now. Make her right again. I want her back. Talking to me. Smiling. Laughing. I want my portrait."

"Selfish." Rowen's ire reared and the word escaped him before he could stop it. No matter that it was true. Whereas Rowen wanted Wynne in the land of living because he hated seeing her without life, without energy—the duchess wanted Wynne back in the land of living for her own amusement.

The duchess's jaw jutted out, and Rowen waited for the tongue lashing to unfurl.

But it didn't come. Instead, the dowager just shook her head. "What happened that day, L.B.? Let us pretend for a moment you were not the cause of her current state. Did she remember something drastic? Tell me. I cannot help Miss Theaton if I do not know."

Rowen bit his tongue, contemplating the duchess. She had never failed to make his life miserable, he recognized that. But with Wynne, the duchess was very different. He had to acknowledge he had seen that much. The duchess adored her— actually seemed happy when Wynne was around.

Was it possible that the dowager could surprise him? Truly help Wynne?

Rowen sighed, running his hand through his hair.

Going against every fiber in his being, he opened his mouth.

"She did remember something. A town—Tanloon. But that was all, just the name. So I took her there."

The dowager's lips pursed. "You should have told me, I would have accompanied her. Or, at the least, sent a maid."

"It was all I could do to keep her from leaving right when she remembered—to at least have her wait overnight. She wanted to leave for the town right before dusk. And she would have gone off on her own had I not promised I would get her there quickly. It would have taken a full day in a carriage."

"Yes." The duchess's eyes went to the roof of the stable. "I suppose she would have. She is far too independent." Her gaze dropped to him. "What did you find in Tanloon?"

"The house she lived in with her mother."

"Her mother?"

"Yes. And something happened to her mother, something dire. She was attacked, and Wynne witnessed it."

The dowager's hand flew to her chest. "Is the woman alive?"

Rowen shook his head.

"Who did it?"

"Wynne did not recognize him."

"A robber?"

Rowen stopped, staring at the duchess. Her ice blue eyes looked nothing but sympathetic. Again, he shook his head. "She entertained."

"Do not speak in riddles, L.B. What does that mean—she entertained?"

"She entertained men to survive, Duchess. To keep her and Wynne in a home with food on the table."

The dowager stiffened. "Unfortunate."

Instant judgment.

The sympathy he had seen in her eyes vanished. A mistake. Rowen knew instantly it had been a mistake to tell her.

Why had he expected any different from her? Because it was Wynne? Preposterous. This was the duchess, and what little humanity he had thought he saw in her had been his imagination.

"Duchess, whatever you are thinking, you need to stop," Rowen said, warning clear in his voice. "Wynne is a very different person from her mother."

The duchess's eyes narrowed at him. "I know that, L.B. Do not insult me. And do not let this wallowing of Miss Theaton's go on. It is not proper." Her voice dropped. "Fix her, L.B. Fix her."

Before Rowen could reply, the dowager spun, arms still at her sides, and walked out of the stable.

Rowen stared at the back of her black skirt, frowning in disgust.

Not proper? Wynne's grief was not proper?

A large breath stuck in his chest, forming into a rock.

Only the dowager would see Wynne's grief as unbecoming—inconvenient.

The breath hissed out between his gritted teeth.

Why had he expected more?

~ ~ ~

Rowen stood at Wynne's door, staring at the dark walnut wood, waiting. He rapped his knuckles once more on the wood. He always gave her three solid knocks, three times—three opportunities to respond. She never did, but it at least gave her a chance to prepare herself before he entered.

Continued silence.

He turned the handle on the door slowly, bracing himself. He still had no idea what he was going to tell her. The duchess seemed to think he would know what to say, but he hadn't been successful in moving Wynne's eyes from darkness to light in the last four days, and he wasn't sure what else he had to offer her.

He did know he would give anything to take away the pain she was wallowing in. And in that, he knew he needed to at least try again with her.

Cracking the door, he stepped into the room. Long draperies were drawn tight against the bright day. Dark, even though it was in the middle of the afternoon.

His eyes scanned the room. Wynne sat, despondent, on the one chair in the room. It had an upholstered seat that butted into a tall, straight back and had wooden armrests. It was a chair for sitting for only a few minutes—completely uncomfortable—but there she sat. He had seen her in no other spot, no other position in days.

She looked tiny, her feet tucked up under her, disappearing under her skirts. Holding herself tight across her belly, she lifted her head slightly, her eyes meeting his.

Dark circles lined her hazel eyes. Eyes that still looked dead.

"Have you eaten today?" He inclined his head to the tray holding bread and cheese on a side table next to her.

She gave one slow shake of her head, her eyes dropping down to her lap.

"Have you looked outside? It is a beautiful day."

No response.

This was the point where he usually prattled on for a few minutes about the horses and the latest happenings in the stables, and then exited, leaving her because he thought that was what she wanted.

He scratched the back of his neck.

Stepping forward, each foot soft against making noise, Rowen stopped in front of her, his boots almost touching the front legs of the chair.

He knelt before her, balancing on his heels, his knees touching the chair. At this angle, he could see her downward-angled face perfectly.

She closed her eyes to his presence.

"Wynne. I have no idea what you are going through. My imagination does not do justice to what you must have witnessed. But you are starving yourself."

His hand went lightly on her knee. "Not only starving your body. You are starving your soul. You are punishing yourself and it is not right."

Her eyes cracked open to him. Vacant. But at least she was looking at him. It was progress.

"I do not know what to say, Wynne. I am at a loss." His fingers tightened on her leg. "I have racked my brain a thousand times over. I cannot say anything to take this away, to make this right, to lessen your pain. But you must understand, Wynne, this was not your fault."

A tear slipped off her lower lashes, forging a line down her cheek.

Rowen waited, silent for a long moment.

"Maybe you need to paint, Wynne. The dowager misses you. Maybe you need to get out of that chair and get a brush in your hand and paint. Lose yourself in it so you can bring yourself out of this."

A sudden gasp swallowed a sob, and Wynne exhaled, words whispering out. "I cannot paint. I cannot paint her."

Her words choked off, and she shook her head, her forehead etched in pain. "I never should have listened to her."

"The duchess?"

"My mother. I should have made us stay on the mountain. Never boarded that ship. She said it would be a new start. We would be fine. An adventure."

"You could not have known what was to happen, Wynne. She could not have known."

Wynne shook her head, suddenly vehement. "You do not understand. I failed her. It was me. I was supposed to take care of her—it was what grandfather trained me to do, expected me to do—and I failed her. I failed him. I did not take care of her and she turned into a whore because of me."

"Wynne, no. Do not do that to yourself." His other hand went to her knee as well. "You did not make her do anything."

Her fingers untangled from her arm and went to her forehead, rubbing it. "You do not understand, Rowe. It was not just that she turned into a whore to support us—it was that I let her. I knew. Deep down, I knew exactly what was happening, what she was doing. And I did nothing to stop it."

"You saw her with men?"

"No, just them leaving. But I did not need to see her with them. I wanted to paint. I wanted to keep living like I wanted, so I pretended not to notice. She did not want me to know…so I pretended. It was easier. And I did not say anything."

The tears streamed as her bottom lip went under her teeth. Rowen could see her fighting for control.

"I could see it in her eyes, Rowe, how hollow she was becoming." Wynne's look glassed over. "She used to be vivacious—the mirth in her eyes. She made me happy every single morning—just opening my eyes and seeing her and I was happy. She was so proud of me. Of my talent. I was special just because she thought so. And...and she just degraded. Fell into nothingness. Every day. Right before my eyes."

Her head dropped again, the tears landing on the back of Rowen's hands.

"And I did nothing. Nothing to stop her, nothing to help her. I just painted. I let her tell me that my painting was the most important thing, and I believed her because I wanted to deny the truth—that she was trading her body so I could continue to paint."

She shuddered and opened her eyes to Rowen, the hazel depths haunted.

"How can I forgive myself for that? For what I did? For what I did not do? And then at the end—it should have been me under the poker. Under the fists. After everything, I owed her that."

For all the words that had not come to him before—this—this Rowen knew something about. A mother that would give limb and life for her child.

His hand wrapped around the fingers at her forehead, peeling them away. Settling her cold hand under his, he pulled from his own depths, his own memories. "She never would have allowed it, Wynne. From all you have said of her, she never would have allowed it. And you may have thought she was weak. But she was not. She was a mother. Your mother, Wynne. You were her baby. And some mothers will do everything to protect their children. Endure anything. No matter the harm that comes."

Her eyes searched him, searched for the truth of his words. Searched for absolution she could not give herself.

Rowen doubted she would ever find that absolution. He never had.

Wynne took a deep breath, shaking her head again. "I cannot paint. I cannot paint her—the duchess. Not now. I look at her and all I can see is my mother."

"So do not paint her. Paint anything. Paint Pepe. Paint the stable master. Paint a bird. Just paint."

Her head bowed, swinging back and forth. "I do not think I can." Her voice cracked. "I cannot. Please, Rowe. Please, just leave me."

"Wynne…"

"Please. Please just leave."

His legs stiff, Rowen slowly stood, fingertips reluctant to leave her hands. But he took a soft step backward, spinning to the door, trying to exit as silently as he had come in.

A step outside the room, Rowen paused. His hand stayed on the doorknob as he weighed what he knew instinctively was right—Wynne painting, creating as fate intended her to—against the woman sitting behind him, steadfast in her self-punishment and torturing herself.

Wynne may not see it—how important it was for her to paint again—but he did.

Rowen turned back into the room, striding to Wynne with intent, and stopped in front of her. The clip of his boots on the wood floor was harsh, but he reached forward gently, grabbing her chin, lifting her eyes to him.

She fought him for only a second before her watery eyes met his.

"Paint me."

"What?" Her hazel eyes clouded in confusion.

"If it will get a brush back in your hand, get you out of that chair—paint me." His fingers did not move from her chin.

"But you said—"

"I do not give a damn about what I said. Paint me."

She stared at him for a long moment, questioning it—reading his intentions.

"You will answer my questions?" she asked, her voice hesitant. "It is the only way I know how."

His hand dropped slowly from her skin, but he fixed his gaze on her, unflinching. "I will. I will answer any blasted question you have if it will move you from this room, from this darkness."

It took her another long moment before she offered one small nod.

"Good." Rowen took a step back. "I will set the room. An hour?"

She nodded once more.

A grim smile came to his lips. It would do. For now, it would do.

{ CHAPTER 12 }

Situated on the wooden chair behind a large, blank canvas, Wynne busied herself with mixing a dark brown on the makeshift palette in her arm. Weeks ago, she had fashioned the palette from a thin board she had found in a refuse pile on the other side of the castle. Cracked, it had just the right curve to fit along her wrist—all she had needed to do was smooth the splinters.

Not that she had used it at all in the last three days.

She didn't know how Rowen had sat in this room with her for three days—three days that she had sat, crying, unable to move, unable to talk.

Every day she had come into the room with intentions to put paint to canvas. Every day, the second the bristles had touched the paint, she had crumbled.

And Rowen had sat through it all. Sat on that hard wooden chair across from her. Sat for hours. He never asked her to stop, never left. Just busied himself with his papers or watched her, concerned, waiting patiently. A silent comfort.

Three days, and not a drop of paint had made it to canvas.

But when she had woken up this morning, she had felt stronger. Maybe it was that she had no tears left. Maybe it was the food that Rowen kept insistently pushing her way.

Whatever it was—breath held—she made it past the first touch of the bristles to the paint on the palette.

Though paint had yet to touch canvas, Wynne felt, deep within, that she could do it. Today she could do it.

Her head came up so she could study Rowen.

He sat, relaxed, leaning back, his hands clasped over his belly, one boot-clad foot up and resting on his knee. His usual white linen shirt was slightly rumpled, the sleeves rolled up to just below his elbows. When her eyes made it up to his face, she realized he was watching her intently, curious.

Understandable after the past few days—she would usually be crying by now. It was curious to herself as well, and just to prove that she wasn't about to break again, she lifted her thin brush to the canvas, setting the deep brown paint to the white canvas.

Success.

She didn't crack, didn't heave, didn't become instantly consumed with guilt and grief. The grief was more numb now, a raw constant presence, rather than the violent consumption it had been. She wasn't healed—far from it—but she could function. And functioning—even numbly—felt good.

Her eyes went from the canvas, back to Rowen. She had had no goal in mind with the brown paint, had merely wanted to make sure she could do the motion without cracking.

But now she was faced with the actual process of painting Rowen.

Thinking of him. Learning of him.

She needed to start with what she knew. What he had let her see of him. She leaned to her left, her eyes meeting his look. "When did you become so passionate about horses?"

"This is where it begins?" Rowen asked.

"I can think of no other place than the thing that is most important to you."

She straightened, her eyes going back to the blank canvas. People were usually more apt to share when she was not staring directly at them. But she already knew she was going to have a hard time keeping her eyes off of Rowen.

"So tell me," she said. "Did you know it for as long as you can remember, or was there a moment?"

"A moment." His voice was soft.

So soft, that Wynne had to steal a glance at him. A small smile played on his lips, a memory of long ago lighting his features.

"I was schooled at Eton, and I did not…" His face turned dark. "I was quiet. I was not in the direct line for the title, and I did not easily find my way there with the other boys. I preferred my time in the stables."

His eyes eased from troubled to relaxed. "And by the nature of the refugee, I found myself in the good graces of the stable master, Freddie. He was crusty, old—liked very few people. But I was always around. I pitched hay, cleaned stables—just to be doing something—and he eventually took to me, as did the rest of stable hands. Freddie was the one that woke me in the middle of the night to watch a mare foaling."

Rowen's head tilted back as he paused, his eyes in far-off memory. "That was the moment. A little black foal. A star-shaped white splotch on his nose. Wobbly legs. That…that was the moment."

Rowen's eyes stayed on the ceiling for a long moment in silence.

It wasn't until Rowen's look dropped to her, that Wynne realized she was leaning far out from behind the canvas, arm resting on the table next to her and staring at him, fully entranced at the genuineness of the tale.

It took her a breath to recover, and she cleared her throat, sitting up right.

"And that was it? That became your life?"

"Yes. I became rather good at getting my schoolwork done as quickly as possible. I made Freddie into my de facto tutor, and I learned everything I possibly could from him. He had seen thousands of the most well-bred horses in England come through the stables at school. And he came from a long line of horsemen. He had family, connections all over the continent to the best breeders."

Rowen nodded to himself. "As hard of a nut as he was, he was generous in introducing me to his connections. Which was why I was recruited during the wars to save the important lines—I not only knew how to recognize the essential horses, but I knew the right people to navigate me to them. Many of those people just did not have the means to get the horses to safety. I did."

Wynne blinked, realizing Rowen was done talking. Blast it. She was leaning on the table again, transfixed by his story. She was going to get nothing done on this painting if he continued to draw her in so.

She set her paints and brush on the table, picking up a piece of thin paper and a nub of charcoal. Rubbing the edge of the charcoal into a point with her nail, she glanced up at Rowen.

"I have not heard of it, but I presume Eton is a prestigious school?"

A wry smile appeared. "Yes. One could say that. I forget sometimes that you do not have the English history."

"And did you live there?" Wynne asked without looking up as she arched a line down the side of the paper, the exact cut of Rowen's jaw. "What about your family?"

"Yes, I lived there. It was after my mother died. I was eleven. The last duke, my uncle, sent me there along with his son. My cousin found it a befitting place for himself. I did not."

"You did not ask to be removed?"

He shook his head. "It was better than the alternative."

"Which was?"

"Live here."

The answer was short. Clipped. Wynne wasn't yet ready to delve further into that history.

"Tell me about your family."

"I would rather not."

She glanced up from the outline of the right side of his face she had sketched. "You do not wish to continue?"

The sudden thought that he did not want this, would not sit for her, unsettled her. She needed him here. Needed him to help her through this. She didn't think she could do it on her own.

He opened his mouth, about to say something, but then he swallowed the words. A relenting sigh. "What do you want to know?"

Relieved, her gaze went down to the paper before her. "Anything. Everything. Your father. What was he like?"

"Dead."

Her eyes went huge to him.

Another sigh. "He died when I was four. I never truly knew him."

"How about your mother? What was she like?"

"She…she was a gentle soul. We came here to live after my father died. And her gentle soul did not survive well in a home such as this."

"What does that mean, Rowe? A home such as this?"

"It means she endured things here that no person should have to. It means I know exactly what a mother would do to save her child." He stopped speaking as he leaned forward, his eyes intent on her.

Her breath had sped at his words, panic setting into her chest. She could feel the blood draining from her face, her cheeks tingling.

She shouldn't have asked him about his mother. Stupid. All it did was to explode that gnawing pain in her heart once more. Explode it until it reached every nerve on her body.

Rowen stood, moving to the doorway. "We need to stop for today, Wynne. I have to get down to the stables."

Wynne tossed her paper and charcoal onto the table. She didn't want him to leave her. Not now. Not when she was about to break again.

"Stop, Rowe." She ran over to him as he went to the door, sliding in front of him before he could reach the doorknob. "Stop. Do not leave."

"We can continue this tomorrow, Wynne."

"No. Please." Desperate, her hands went on his chest. She needed him to stay. She needed to not break. How could she get him to stay? "Kiss me."

"What?"

"Kiss me." Her fingers went up, circling his neck. "Kiss me."

Slowly, he raised his hands, settling his palms along her jaw, cupping her face. His dark eyes searched her features, her gaze, until he exhaled slightly, his voice rough. "You are not ready."

Shocked, she blinked, but her body remained frozen. "I…"

"You are not ready, Wynne." He shook his head. "Do not misinterpret. I want you, Wynne. I want to kiss you in this very moment. Your breath on mine. Your hands around my neck. Your body brushing up to me."

His fingertips swept across her cheeks. "I will kiss you when you are ready. You are not ready now."

He dropped his hands from her face, taking a step backward.

It effectively removed her fingers from his neck, and when she didn't move, still stuck to the spot she was in, Rowen gently grabbed her shoulders and shifted her to the left. Just enough room to get past her and out the door.

A full minute passed before Wynne could tear her eyes away from the door. Her legs moved without conscious thought, bringing her to the chair Rowen had sat in. She sank onto it, drawing her legs up under her as she curled into a ball.

She expected tears. But they did not come.

She expected anger. But it did not come.

It was then she realized her body, her mind, had nowhere to go. Confusion so thick, she was at a standstill.

If she was to ever be anything again, she was going to have to fight.

Fight for a path away from this grief. Away from what she had done—what she had not done.

Her grandfather would have demanded of her.

Fight.

~ ~ ~

Wynne stared at the likeness of Rowen on the canvas in front of her. It was still just an outline—details, shading not present, but it was there.

True to his words, they did not stop—Rowen would not allow her to. And over the past week they had covered a gamut of topics—what it was like to fight in the wars and to have a friend die in one's arms; Rowen's favorite foods; why he didn't care for cats, save for the rats they caught; what he knew about the stars; where he had travelled.

For every tiny piece of information she got from him, she wanted ten more. And he humored her through all of it. But of all the many topics, both of them had skirted far away from any talk of family.

She knew Rowen did not want to set her off again. She realized that now. On that day she had first started asking him questions, he had immediately realized her reaction to his talking about his mother—before she even did—and he was trying to cut the session short just so she wouldn't break, wouldn't regress into wallowing again.

Wynne's eyes swept over the canvas. The light wasn't as bright as it was in the middle of the afternoon, but during the past few days Rowen was needed down at the stables. His friend, Lord Luhaunt had returned from Scotland with three mares they were adding to the stables, and they were testing temperaments and deciding on breeding—so the painting sessions had switched to after dinner. At least the moonlight was pretty, pouring in the far window to lend a glowing light to the yellow from the lanterns and fire.

She had begun creating Phalos in the upper left corner, charging—bold and snorting—but retaining gentleness in his eyes. She liked how he was coming along, but she needed to get Rowen to take her to see him running. She wanted to study his form in full gallop to get it right.

She ducked her head around the canvas to look at Rowen. He was sitting, head down, reading The Times. He had held true to answering her every question, never bothered when his reading was interrupted.

"Have you ever been in love?"

Without moving his head, Rowen's eyes shifted up to her. "Is that one necessary?"

Wynne could already feel pink burning her cheeks, but she smiled. "It is for the art. The most complete picture of you, all in all. Love is a part of that."

He stared at her, his dark eyes burning into her.

Her smile widened. "Fine. Also for me. My own curiosity would like to be sated as well."

He smirked, shaking his head in a chuckle. "You are the only one who would ever dare to try to charm something like that out of me."

"Did it work?"

"Your honesty did." He set the paper down on his lap, his full attention to her.

"So?"

"I thought I was in love once. At the time it seemed real. At this point though, I know it was not true. I believe I mistook my own pride for something more serious."

"What happened?" She fiddled with the brush in her fingers. "If I can ask that?"

Rowen shrugged. "I was younger—she was younger still. She was from this area and I first knew her when we were children. She was gentle bred, from a wealthy, but not titled, family. Her name was Victoria, and I courted her years before I came into the title. I was truly never to have one, but I was wealthy, which she liked. We were near to engaged."

"But then?"

Rowen's hands clasped in his lap. "But then a man with both a title and wealth came sniffing about—and she liked the option of the title even more than what I could offer her. She was willing to trade herself for that title. And the man, Lord Vutton, was worthless as a human being."

"You disliked the man?" She rolled her eyes. "Silly question—of course you disliked him."

"Yes. But beyond Victoria, I disliked him even more for the beating I saw him give his horse. He has an estate about two days from here and was participating in a local horse race. The beating told me everything I ever needed to know of the man. I tried to buy the horse from him—a beautiful brown mare—but Vutton refused."

"The horse caused you more alarm than losing the woman you were to marry?"

"No…Yes. The horse had no say in the matter. Victoria did. I tried to convince her of Vutton's nature—whether she stayed with me or not, I did not care—I just wanted her safely away from him. But she made the choice—she was not to be swayed from Vutton."

"What happened to her?"

"She married him. Got her title. Lady Vutton." Rowen's arm went onto the wooden table next to him, fingers tapping. "Any occasion I ran into her after that, she was always dressed in the finest, her red hair impeccably coifed. And she would end up cornering me, crying, professing what a mistake she made leaving me. But there was nothing I could do at that point. She had made her choice. A year later, she died in childbirth. The baby as well."

Wynne frowned. "It is very tragic for her. I am sorry for your loss."

"She was not mine to lose."

Frown still in place, her head shook. "It is hard for me to understand why any woman would choose a title over you."

Rowen's head cocked, sideways grin lifting his mouth. "No? Tell me more."

She laughed. "You would like that, would you not? Be careful, or this is how I will paint you—cocky smirk, begging for compliments."

"Begging?"

"Shamelessly."

Rowen's laugh kept a smile on her face as her head went down to her paint board, and she started mixing yellow and brown to a skin color. "These paints—they are of such high quality. I am not used to such luxury. The pigments I had grown accustomed to using took so many layers just to get proper saturation. But these remind me of the ones I used in New York when I was young. I have been meaning to tell you they are a delight, so thank you."

"I cannot take credit—I just asked for the best they had, and those were what they sent."

Wynne could feel Rowen's eyes on her as she got the skin shade just right. Satisfied with the color, she looked up to him, only to be startled by how intense his gaze was.

"What?" she asked, suddenly on guard.

He gave a contrite smile. "I apologize, I was just wondering what happened to your father—your family was obviously wealthy when you lived in New York."

Wynne set down the brush, fingers moving unconsciously from one wooden handle to the next on the row of her brushes. "We were wealthy. Even young, I knew we had much more than most. But it was all lost right before my father died—or at least that is what I believe happened."

"You do not know?"

She shrugged. "I asked many times, but my mother never told me. I do not know if she was trying to protect him—his memory for me. The day before he died, I heard them arguing— it was something about him losing everything. It was the only time I ever heard my mother yell at him—the one and only time I had ever heard her yell at anything. The next day he died. Trampled by a horse and carriage. And the day after his burial, we left for the mountain."

Her fingers found the brush she wanted and picked it up. "We brought nothing with us. Not our clothes. Not my paints. Not my brushes. Nothing. We left it all behind."

"Which is why you believe everything was lost?"

"Yes." Wynne ducked behind the canvas, out of Rowen's sight. Closing her eyes, she took a steadying breath. Even after the many years, the pain of her father's death—of leaving her home in New York, her friends, her life—still stung. Still made her heart feel like it was going to pound out of her chest.

Rowen fell into silence, letting her hide for the moment, and she was grateful for it. She worked on the line of his jaw in silence for a few minutes, her mind wandering through thoughts of the dead.

"I want to go back there." The words came out of Wynne's mouth before she realized they hadn't stayed in own her mind as intended.

"New York?" Rowen asked.

Wynne took a breath. Now that she had said it, she might as well finish the thought. "Tanloon."

Seconds of uncomfortable silence came from Rowen. She pulled her brush from the canvas, leaning to look at him. His jaw had gone hard.

At her look, he cleared his throat. "Why? There is nothing for you there, Wynne."

"There is my mother. I need to know what happened to her, Rowe."

"No. That landlady is dangerous, Wynne. She was lying for a reason, and she would only do that if she knew something."

"Which is exactly why I have to see her again—to get her to tell me something."

"She is not going to tell you anything, Wynne."

"Well, then, someone else in the town will remember me. Someone else has to know something. The neighbors. They would know."

"No, Wynne, no. You will not go back there."

She blinked, her head snapping back at his harsh words. "You are deciding where I will or will not go?"

Rowen opened his mouth, then clamped it shut, half shaking his head. "I do not want you in that danger, Wynne. Whatever happened to your mother—it was evil. And evil spreads—it does not exist as a singular entity. The landlady is already involved, and who knows who else. And those same people that you know may be the exact people that are dangerous."

She closed her eyes against his words. He did not understand. Did not understand how important this was to her. "I have to go." She opened her eyes to him. "I have to know. You do not understand the hole I have in my heart from this, Rowe. What happened to her—I need to know. I owe her that."

"I will go. You will stay here, and I will go," he said. "They will not know me in that village."

"But you are a duke—would they recognize you?"

"They may have possibly recognized my cousin—he was heir. But my estate does not stretch that far in that direction. No one will know me. I will go and search for the answer. And I will take Luhaunt with me as another pair of ears."

Rowen leaned forward in the chair. "Tell me that will suffice. Tell me you will not disappear from here and put yourself in that danger, Wynne."

Wynne bit her lip. Rowen was pleading with her—in his demanding way, but yet, pleading.

Against her better judgment, against what her heart wanted her to do, Wynne nodded.

Unsettled, she picked up a new brush and disappeared from Rowen's view, hiding behind the canvas.

He had just overridden her.

And she had let him.

{ CHAPTER 13 }

Rubbing his ribcage, Rowen walked out of the stable into the descending twilight. Five steps, and he sank onto a sagging plank bench that lined the front of the stable.

Luhaunt collapsed next to him. "I do not even recall the last time you got me into trouble like that, Rowe."

"Too many years." Rowen shook his head, his left forefinger probing the corner of his split lower lip. "You have grown weak, Seb."

"I did not see you faring much better, my friend."

Rowen grimaced, easing himself onto the wall behind them. His fingernail went across the cut on his eyebrow, splitting open the crusty scab that had formed. "I was not expecting that—the town looked benign when we were there the other day."

"There you are."

The shout made both men look up, only to see Wynne in a full run coming down the path from the woods. She did not stop until she reached them, holding her side and panting. "I saw you come up the lawn, but you did not come into the castle."

Rowen thumbed over his shoulder. "Getting the horses settled."

"What happened?" She bent over to be at eye level with them, her eyes flickering between Rowen's face and Luhaunt's. She stood straight. "Wait. Hold your words."

She left them, disappearing into the stable. Rowen could hear fabric ripping and water sloshing. A few minutes passed before she came out of the stable, hauling a bucket full of water.

She plopped it on the ground in front of the men and dipped what looked like a strip of white linen from her chemise into the water.

Her eyes went back and forth between the two, her mouth grim. Decided, she went in front of Luhaunt, holding the wet cloth up. "Do you mind?"

Luhaunt gave a quick sideways smirk to Rowen. "Not at all."

Wynne nodded, starting to dab on the long cut from Luhaunt's left eye to his jaw.

Rowen watched her fingers move across Luhaunt's wound. A drip of blood dropped into his own eye from a cut lining his eyebrow. Jealousy pricked—it did not matter that Luhaunt was his friend and the guest—Wynne should not be touching another man like that.

It only took a moment for her to start swaying. Rowen had to give her credit—she tried. But within seconds, she went pale and her eyes dropped closed.

Rowen grabbed her elbow, pulling and spinning her to the bench between him and Luhaunt just before she passed out. She slumped onto Rowen's chest, the cloth dropping from her fingers to the dirt. He wrapped his arm around her, propping up her limp body.

Luhaunt gave him a questioning look over Wynne's head.

Rowen pointed to the blood dripping from his own eyebrow. "The blood."

Luhaunt nodded, picking up the cloth from the ground and dunking it in the bucket. He rang it out and tended to his own wound. "Will she be out long?"

"I do not imagine so." Rowen tilted her face up so he could see it. Still out cold. He settled her back onto his chest. "It has happened before, and it was just a few minutes."

"Why would she even bother getting near the blood if that is what happens?" Luhaunt asked as he cringed, his own rubbing on the cut sending fresh blood onto the cloth.

"I imagine she feels responsible for our current states. She has an unusual sense of duty."

Wynne jerked upright, gasping. Confusion set on her face as she looked at Luhaunt, but disappeared once she saw Rowen had her. Her hand flew to her mouth. "I—I am mortified. Lord Luhaunt, forgive me."

"It is nothing, Miss Theaton."

She untangled herself from Rowen's arm, but did not try to stand. "I am sorry. I just feel so horrible that you went to Tanloon and this…"

Her gaze drifted to the red-stained cloth in Luhaunt's hand, then snapped away to the dirt in front of her boots. She leaned forward, resting her forearms on her thighs. "That this is how you returned. I did not wish for harm to come to either of you, and I would not have allowed you to go had I known."

Rowen leaned forward to see Wynne's face.

Her hand went up, blocking him. "Do not come into my view, Rowe. I can barely look at Lord Luhaunt, and he is mostly clean. I truly cannot look at you, or I will be in blackness for the rest of the day."

Rowen moved back to lean against the stable wall. "You have not asked what we learned in Tanloon."

"I have been afraid to ask."

"We did not learn anything."

Wynne didn't move, didn't react.

Rowen set his fingers lightly on her shoulder. At that, her head dropped in her hands. He could tell she was not crying, just trying to collect herself.

Abruptly, she stood. "I have to get some fresh cloth for you…ones that are not bloody."

She started to walk into the stables, but then spun and changed direction, trudging away from them toward the path back to the castle.

Rowen could see she was discombobulated, but walking a straight line, so he let her go. Better to not stop her, only to have her pass out from watching blood drip down his face.

He and Luhaunt watched her in silence until she was out of view.

"She is entrancing."

Rowen's eyes did not leave the spot in the trees where Wynne disappeared. "No. She is not—not for you."

Luhaunt chuckled. "Point taken. And that saves me my next question." He cocked an eyebrow at Rowen. "Unless there is the possibility when you are done with her?"

Rowen's head whipped to Luhaunt, glaring. "I do not plan on being done with Wynne."

"You are not saying?"

"Yes."

"She is a commoner." Luhaunt shook his head, his face incredulous as he dunked the cloth in the bucket.

"As I was not but two years ago." Rowen's look went pointedly to his friend. "As you were five years ago. Have you forgotten your own past so quickly, Seb?"

"But the lineage—"

"Do not talk to me of lineage. You have embraced the aristocratic way of thinking far more fully than I thought you would, Seb."

"It has its finer points." Luhaunt handed the rinsed cloth to Rowen.

"Yes, and a lot of stale blood in the lines." Rowen wiped the blood from his eye, dotting the cut on his eyebrow. "The peerage would do well to have new blood in its heirs."

"But you are not just talking about new blood, Rowe. You are talking about plopping an American—with no connection to this land—right into a dukedom. Lunacy—there is no argument for it. She is scandal in the making."

Rowen's dagger glare deepened at Luhaunt. "You speak of things I could care less about, Seb. Let the old bats think she is a rich heiress. That should suffice the tongues."

Luhaunt sighed. "And you still do not know what happened to her—what happened after her mother was beaten—who that man was—he could have some claim on her."

"I highly doubt it. Wynne saw him and did not recognize him. And that mystery is exactly why I brought you to Tanloon, to see if answers could be found. I would prefer to deal with surprises connected to Wynne sooner, rather than later."

"But we found nothing except bruised ribs and bloody faces." Luhaunt made a fist, looking at his cracked, bloody knuckles before he dunked them into the bucket. "Are you going to tell her about the drunk—what he said?"

Rowen sighed. They had found the drunk that lived in the house next to Wynne's, but he had been beyond foxed. "If he had made sense, maybe, but, 'The town loses a whore it celebrates—but it loses a teat it has hell to pay.' What the blast is that supposed to mean?"

Luhaunt shrugged, checking his cleaned knuckles.

"And I will not repeat such nonsense when the words about her mother would only hurt Wynne."

"For all of your cynicism, Rowe, you are surprisingly un-cynical about this woman."

"You mean the cynicism that managed to keep you alive on the continent?"

Luhaunt shrugged good-naturedly. "That aside, it is something I have never seen in you—actual belief in another."

Rowen shook his head. "I do not know—I see…I see her… deep inside…who she is."

"What you see in her may be clouding your vision. Rowe, how the rest of the town reacted—all I am saying is, be careful." Luhaunt leaned back on the wall. "There was something very wrong with that town, with those people—I understand being wary of strangers with questions, but that was beyond normal. One question and they practically ran us out of town on stakes."

"Yes, and that only convinces me more than ever that she truly does remember what happened to her and her mother in that house. But instead of an answer, it only raises more questions. Especially when there is not a trace of Wynne's life there."

Rowen wiped the wet cloth across his split lip, the motion stinging. "And Wynne does not have the sense to realize the danger she was in—is still in. I do not want to imagine what would have happened if she set foot into those taverns."

"So do not imagine it, my friend. And just make sure she does not visit that town ever again." Luhaunt slapped his hand on Rowen's shoulder. "But if you do change your mind about Miss Theaton—I may just have a go with her if you are not."

Rowen's chuckle leaned more towards threat than laughter. "Prowl elsewhere, Seb. Although I do admire your taste. You always knew how to find the best horses, so why should women be any different? How is it you have not married yet—or gotten yourself trapped?"

"My searching has not delivered for me yet." Luhaunt shrugged. "I will know her when I see her—that has just not happened yet."

"Pure instinct?" Rowen stood, dropping the cloth into the bucket.

"Pure instinct. Just like the horses. I will know." Luhaunt joined Rowen and they started walking to the castle path. "And from what I have witnessed, my instincts tell me you should lock down Miss Theaton sooner rather than later. Her hands on me were short-lived—"

"Are you trying to get another black eye?"

Luhaunt smirked. "All I am saying is that a woman with hands as soft and gentle as that—who can also skin a squirrel—who is also an artist—they do not come more interesting than that."

Rowen shook his head, his eyes on the gravel. "Or as complicated."

~ ~ ~

Wynne had escaped directly into the painting room when she reached the castle. The duchess had intercepted her and requested Wynne dine with her, but Wynne could not stomach the thought of food.

So instead, she had come into the room and gone through the motions of getting the paints and her brushes ready, but then had sat numbly, brush in her hand, staring at the rising moon for hours.

The knock on the door made her jump, and she popped to her feet, dropping the brush before the door swung open.

Rowen.

Afraid to look, she forced her eyes to nudge upward to his face. The bloody cut above his left eye was now a thin scab. She said silent thanks. A scab she could look at. Free flowing blood, not as much.

Rowen had another long scab across his right cheek, a bottom lip that was slightly puffy, and she could tell by the stiff way he moved into the room that his ribs were hurting him.

Wynne frowned, still mortified at her earlier reaction at the stables. "Rowe, I apologize. Lord Luhaunt must think I am a goose. I made a spectacle of myself—I saw the injuries and I thought, at the least, I could help Lord Luhaunt."

Rowen stepped into the room, closing the door behind him. "Not me?"

"You? Preposterous. No." She waved the thought away. "I had no illusions about you—I already know I cannot see blood on you—especially not blood that I am the cause of."

She was surprised to see a slight smirk cross his face, but it disappeared quickly, somberness darkening his eyes. "I wanted to have news for you from Tanloon, Wynne. Something tangible. At least a lead to follow. But I have nothing. We only made it through two taverns with no luck before we were politely escorted from town."

"Politely escorted?" She shook her head. "I would have never let you go if I had known it was dangerous. I never suspected. When we lived there—I would not have guessed it of those people. I feel terrible that both of you suffered for my sake."

He shrugged. "We fared well enough for what we faced."

"Still…" She shook her head, turning from him. The moon was fat in the window now.

Rowen stepped in front of her, blocking the window, the moonlight glowing behind his head. "Tell me you are not thinking of returning there yourself, Wynne."

Startled at his words, her head cocked to the side. "I am not stupid, Rowe. I saw how you and Lord Luhaunt came back. I am not arrogant enough to think I would fare better. To find answers you could not."

Relief crossed his face. "So you are accepting of not knowing what happened to your mother?"

Accepting? Wynne focused on the word. Could she truly accept that her mother just disappeared—no body, no final resting place, no answers? She was not sure she could.

Yet she had no plan. No next steps to take. She had remembered what had happened, but nothing had changed. Her life was in the exact spot it was before the memories.

Wynne's eyes dropped from his face, not answering his question.

"What are you thinking, Wynne?"

Her voice soft, she couldn't look up at him. "That this is my punishment. Punishment for being weak—for leaving her."

His fingers went under her chin, lifting her head to him. "If you had not escaped, Wynne, you could very well be dead right now."

"Or I could be alive. She could be alive."

"Wynne—"

She shook her head, cutting him off. "Would you have left your mother, Rowe?"

"Not a fair question, Wynne."

"Why am I not to be held to the same standard as you, Rowe?" She sighed. "I know you do not understand this, but my grandfather would have expected so much more of me." Her head dropped again, voice a whisper. "I expected so much more of me."

"Just tell me you can accept this, Wynne. Tell me you will lay this to rest."

"I do not know. I do not know what to think in this moment." She looked up at him. "Can you stay? I need to paint, but I do not want to be alone, I—"

"I will stay."

Grateful, she exhaled, turning and walking past the easel, settling herself to hide behind the canvas. She was fighting hard against breaking again, and Rowen was key to that. She needed him not to leave, yet she could not endure his eyes on her. His wondering of her, his trying to read what was in her mind.

So she disappeared. Disappeared into her painting, into the world where she only had to create. Create and not think of things that could break her. Would break her.

Two hours passed in silence, Wynne working, Rowen sitting patiently across the room from her, paper in his lap that he had not bothered to read.

The moonlight moved across the room, and as late as it had gotten, she still didn't want him to leave, was not ready to be left alone with her rambling thoughts when she knew she could not sleep.

It was when her brush was filling in the shadows of Rowen's neck, making her way down to the line of his collarbone, that her earlier avoidance had waned enough to look at him. Plus, she needed to see him in order to get the nuance of his collarbone right.

Wynne leaned from behind the canvas, her eyes trained on the points where his white shirt met bare skin.

"Why do you hate the duchess?" She asked the question without thought—merely to fill the room with something other than silence—and went back to the canvas, recording the gentle slope of the hard line of his collarbone.

That particular question harbored the one thing she still could not place in Rowen—his hatred for the duchess. For all of his generosity, his kindness to Wynne, he continued to show none of that to the duchess.

The one flaw—the one thing in Rowen that she was having a hard time coming to terms with. Had she never seen the two of them together, sniping at each other, Wynne wouldn't even think Rowen capable of treating an older woman like the duchess with such disrespect.

It took her a few minutes of painting to realize Rowen hadn't answered her question.

She scooted left to look at him.

His face had changed from just a moment ago.

Harder. Closed off.

Not what she had intended. And she had thought they were past pretending that Rowen didn't openly loathe the duchess.

Before Wynne could retract her question, Rowen opened his mouth.

"I think the better question may be why does the duchess hate me? Maybe she should answer that for you. Life has brought both of us disappointments in how we wanted our destinies to unfold. And we have handled our disappointments very differently."

"In what way?" Wynne did not stop her painting.

"The duchess's way eats away at her."

"And your way does not eat away at you?"

"I do not feel the need to try to destroy others to soothe myself. That is her particular way, and I have suffered the brunt of it since I was born."

Wynne went silent. The clip in his voice was just harsh enough that she realized she had to stop this particular discussion before Rowen stormed out on her.

That was the last thing she wanted at the moment.

Swapping brushes, she swiveled on her chair to the canvas. She made the cut of the V of his shirt, the white paint contrasting with the skin of his chest. She had suggested days ago Rowen wear full dress—coat, vest, cravat, trousers—but he had just laughed and refused. If the portrait was to be the true him, he wasn't going to show up uncomfortable, putting on airs.

Wynne leaned forward to study the shadow and began to realize the silence was weighing even heavier in the room.

A pop and a crack from the fireplace, and Wynne sighed. She wanted to keep hearing Rowen's voice—it helped her paint, and that was rarely the case with subjects.

So she grasped onto the first neutral question that popped into her mind. "Do you believe in fate?"

"No."

The answer came so quickly that Wynne paused, leaning to look at him. "Truly—for all you have done, for being in the right places at the right time to save all those horses, for not getting killed, for becoming a duke—you do not credit fate with a hand in it?"

Rowen sighed. "Fine. I do. It is just that we have had a difficult relationship, fate and I."

She smirked at his flip. "Why so difficult?"

"Fate was overruled when I was born—I never should have existed." He folded up the paper that had been sitting on his lap and set it onto the table. "Fate then doled out harsh retributions for my birth—retributions that lasted years."

"What does that mean—you never should have existed? Why?"

He waved his hand. "It does not matter—I was born, so it bears no consequence. History cannot be changed."

Wynne cocked her head at the canvas. Rowen was talking in riddles again. "And fate regards you well now?"

"I think fate has accepted the fact that I exist and begrudgingly decided that I may be useful on occasion. But that does not mean fate looks kindly upon me."

Wynne nodded to herself, concentrating on the arch of a stroke. "Meeting me. Was that an instance of you being useful? You did save me. I appreciated it. Fate was more than generous with me that day."

Rowen stood, silent, and began to walk over to her. It took Wynne a moment to see him and she jumped to her feet, dropping her palette and brush on the table and scooting around the canvas to intercept him before he could glimpse her work. She was not about to let him see this portrait.

A slight smile played on his lips as he stopped right in front of her.

Without a word, he settled his right hand on her cheek, his fingertips reaching her neck and sending shivers sparking from his touch. "I have begun to think fate had much more in mind than me just being useful when we crossed paths."

Wynne near swayed with the sudden heat in his voice. The heat in his dark eyes. Her chin tilted up on its own accord and without thought, a whisper came from deep within her. "Kiss me."

His smile turned serious, and like before, he studied her face, searching her soul.

And then judgment.

"You are not ready."

She didn't step away, didn't look from the silver in his dark eyes. "Do not tell me I am not ready, Rowe."

"I will not push this, Wynne. I will not take advantage."

"You are not taking advantage if I want it." She took a heavy breath, trying to stave off the suffocation in her chest. "Do you not see that I am lost, Rowe? That this—that you are the only thing keeping me sane? I do not have anything else to hold onto. And I need something to hold onto."

"You are not ready, Wynne." His hand dropped from her face as he shook his head, but he did not move from her. "You do not know what you are asking."

"You think I am too fragile?"

"Yes."

"I am not." She stepped into him and raised both of her hands, her fingers going along the line of his jaw. "I had hoped you would find answers in Tanloon."

She searched his face. "Maybe if you had...I...I am more lost than ever, Rowe." Her fingers moved up to lightly trace the scab above his eyebrow. "That you would do this for me. I am lost, Rowe—floating, except for you. You I know. You I can feel. You are the only thing I know that is true. In the storm of all that

has—is happening to me—you are there in the middle…solid…
real. Since the moment we met."

"Wynne—"

"No—you do not get to tell me I do not know what I want,
Rowe. I damn well know what I want. And I want you."

He closed his eyes to her, but she could still see the battle
in his mind reflected in his face. He wanted her. She knew it.
He was trying to deny it, trying to save her from herself, but he
wanted her.

And she wanted him.

If she knew nothing else in life right now, she knew that one
fact. She wanted Rowen. Needed him.

Hell—she loved him and there was no denying it.

And she needed his hands on her skin. His mouth on hers.
She needed to be his. Needed to hold onto the rock he was.

Her hands tightened on his face. "I want you, Rowe. You.
Even if I was back on my mountain—if my mother was alive, if
my grandfather was alive, if everything was different—I would
still want you, Rowe. You. Deep in my soul—it is you."

The growl surfaced from deep in his chest before he opened
his eyes.

When his dark gaze cracked to her, the depth of the fire in
his eyes made her gasp. A gasp that was swallowed in the next
instant, his lips covering hers, his hands instantly behind her
head, molding her into him.

The kiss deepened, Rowen tugging on her bottom lip,
gaining entrance to her mouth, exploring. Wynne's fingers went
upward, getting lost in his dark hair, her palm scraping along the
stubble on his jaw.

She felt pins fall from her hair, freeing her head to Rowen's
roaming hand. His fingers twisting in her hair, he tugged her head
back and left her mouth, his lips trailing down her neck. Hot
breath on her skin, his tongue tasted her, sending the core of her
body twisting, aching for more.

His fingers traced a line down her neck and his thumb
slipped behind the fabric on her chest, reaching downward to

find nipple. His forefinger joined in, and rolled the nub, plying pleasure from her.

Rowen's lips still on her neck, Wynne's head fell backward, gasping at the sensation. The sound only urged Rowen on, and he shoved her dress further down, freeing her skin to the air. His mouth followed his hands, travelling down the slope of her chest, landing on her nipple.

The shock of his wet mouth, of his flickering tongue, sent her legs shaking and she lost her footing. Rowen's arm went around her back instantly, supporting her.

He moved her backward, lifting her and setting her on the table, her legs hanging off the side. Her knees a barrier, his hands went down, grabbing them and spreading her thighs wide as he both stepped forward and pulled her body to meet him.

Settled solidly between her legs, the heat of him warming every part of her, his left hand came up to the back of her head, clasping it. He pulled his mouth away from her nipple.

He waited, not moving, until she opened her eyes to him.

"Wynne. Make me stop." His voice so rough she wondered how the words made it from his throat. "I will stop. Heaven help me, I will stop."

His body already covering hers, she arched her hips up into him, tighter, the simple movement creating friction that sent deep vibrations into her body.

Her hands went to his temples, clasping, her fingers curling into his hair as she tried to catch her breath. "I do not want you to stop, Rowe. I want this. All of what you are doing to me. Please. All of it."

It was what he needed.

His mouth came down on hers again. Claiming her. Claiming what he was about to do. One hand holding her head, his right hand went down, tugging her skirts upward as his fingers ran along the back of her calf, behind her knee, and along her inner thigh.

Without warning, his thumb reached her core, spreading her folds. Wynne jerked at the touch, gulping a scream as she pulled herself up onto Rowen at the spasm it caused. She hadn't known—hadn't expected this—to be aching so harshly for what Rowen drew from her.

His mouth on her neck, a heated chuckle escaped him. "Damn, Wynne. You are already ready for me." His thumb flickered again, this time moving along her slickness until his finger entered her. "Damn ready."

A raspy scream tore from her throat and she clawed further onto his back, desperate for more of what he was doing to her. His shirt pushed halfway up his torso, he stopped to grab the back of it with his free hand, yanking it off his body.

The quick movement left her abandoned, gasping, and the second he was free, Wynne grabbed his right wrist, placing his hand back on her bare thigh.

Another satisfied chuckle, and Rowen traced his tongue along her neck as his fingers went up her leg, finding her core again. He kept his fingers deep in her, teasing her. Making her body pitch against him. Hands wrapped to his shoulder blades for stability, Wynne didn't know what she needed, but she knew Rowen could give it to her.

His right hand suddenly left her skirts again and it took a moment for Wynne to realize he was unbuttoning the front flap of his buckskin breeches. Too slow. Her hands dropped from his back and she pushed his hand aside as she worked the rows of buttons.

Fabric loose, he spilled out hard and throbbing into her hands. Startled at the size, her hands moved away, but Rowen caught the back of her right hand immediately, entwining his fingers into hers. He pressed her hand forward, wrapping her palm, her fingers around his member. The groaning shudder that overtook his body at the touch sent her eyes wide.

Every muscle in his arms, in his chest, in his neck strained as she moved her hand. It only took a moment before Wynne instinctively took over, stroking, watching in amazement as her every slight movement sent ripples along his skin.

Just when she could sense he could take no more, he grabbed her wrist, pulling her hand from him and setting it on his shoulder.

Confusion flooded her face for a moment, until he pushed her skirts further up her waist, fully exposing her legs, her core to him.

With a deep-chested rumble, he grabbed her hips, lifting her to the edge of the table. He set the tip of him shallow into her, and then he stopped, his eyes on her face.

His thumbs moved inward along her thighs, reaching into her folds. It sent her body writhing once again and she dropped her chin, her forehead on his bare chest and her fingernails in his shoulders.

"Look up. Open your eyes, Wynne."

His voice reached through the pounding, fiery haze in her mind.

"I need to see your eyes, Wynne. See what this does to you."

She tilted her head upward as her eyes flew open.

Rowen met her look, his dark eyes holding hers, their breath heavy and mingling. He plunged. Sharp pain cut across her core. She gasped. But she could not close her eyes to him.

His grip on her hips held her solid against him as he settled deep within her. Slowly, he withdrew, and new, exquisite sensations replaced the pain. His thumbs moved inward again, slow and fast in her folds, nudging her even further to the depths.

She pitched against him, her legs wrapping around him, demanding more. Demanding he release her from the exquisite torture he was creating.

"Rowe—" She couldn't get more than the one breathless word out.

"Trust what is happening, Wynne. Trust it. Trust me."

His thumb sped in a mad circle as he dove deep into her again.

She let go, screaming.

Rowen's mouth captured hers, silencing the sound. But it didn't stop her body from shattering, twisting against him as agonizing release reverberated from her core.

Even through the ebbing shocks, through his strokes, she could feel Rowen expand even larger within her. With every plunge he reached deeper, until he pulled from her lips. Burying his head into her neck, a ragged groan ripped through his body. Every muscle in him went hard under Wynne's hands.

He collapsed on her, sending them both flat onto the table.

On her, but holding his full weight back from crushing her, Wynne could feel his wild heart against her chest.

It wasn't until they both had regained control of breathing that Rowen untangled his arms, and withdrew from deep within her. He pushed himself upright from Wynne and the table.

"That was not right," he mumbled, voice gruff.

Wynne sat up, immediately yanking her muslin dress up to cover her breasts and pulling her skirts over her lap. Her body was still quivering—did regret truly come that quickly?

Her eyes went to the floor. "Did I not do something correctly? I…I thought it…I mean it felt right…"

He grabbed her chin, forcing her gaze upward. "Hell, yes, it felt right." His voice still thick, he grabbed the back of her head, leaning down to kiss her hard. The intensity of it made her toes curl under the table. When he pulled away, his face had softened. "It is not you, Wynne. It is me. I did not intend for that to happen."

"You did not? Ever?"

"No—well, yes, I did mean for that to happen—eventually. But not on a table. Not rushed. Not without care."

She exhaled, relieved. "I feel very well cared for, Rowe, if it makes any difference."

That brought the smallest smile to his face. "It does." He slipped a finger under the top of her dress, righting into place the bit of lace that lined the top.

Wynne watched his face, concentration on even this smallest task evident. Very well cared for, indeed.

A brown spot of paint from her ring finger, the one she smudged colors with, had made its way onto his cheek. She licked her thumb, reaching up and rubbing it clear.

"Paint." She smiled at his questioning look. "It was still wet on my finger."

He nodded, stepping closer to her again, winding a lock of her hair along his forefinger. "I like your hair like this."

"Down? Mussed?"

"Yes. And in the pins instead of your braid—it is easier to set free that way."

"I will be sure to continue the habit, then. It is how my mother always liked—" She cut herself off mid-sentence and could instantly feel the blood draining from her face.

Her mother.

She had forced herself to not to think about her mother when she was with Rowen.

But at that moment—that moment clarity hit her.

This was what her mother did.

Allow men to touch her. Allow men to…

Wynne jumped to her feet, scooting out along the table past Rowen.

He grabbed her arm before she took two steps, spinning her back to him. He held her still, staring into her eyes.

Seconds slipped by.

And then he grabbed her other arm, pulling her into him. He engulfed her, tucking her head onto his chest.

"You are not your mother, Wynne."

Her head whipped up. The exact thing she was thinking.

This man saw too deeply into her.

She drew a shaky breath, setting her chin on his bare chest to look up at him. She couldn't force the tiniest word out.

"This is just the beginning, Wynne. Hell, this is well past the beginning." His hand came up, brushing back the hair from her forehead. "You have to trust me, Wynne. Trust me."

It was the exact thing she needed to hear. She nodded.

She would trust him.

She had to.

{ CHAPTER 14 }

Rowen pushed his horse, an Iberian Peninsula Barb, down through the cold creek and up the muddy bank to the long stretch of land where he could truly set this horse free.

Mud flew up at him, splattering onto his face, his chest. Phalos would be persnickety about it, but Rowen wasn't about to take Phalos out on a ride like this.

Hard. Punishing—at least to himself. Never to the horse. And this young one could take it—wanted it like no other. Hooves pounded the ground.

Rowen had thought he could stop it at just a kiss.

But then Wynne's skin. So soft. Offering herself up to him. Blast it—not just offering, demanding he take her.

All he had wanted to do was take her pain away. Take her pain and turn it into something raw and beautiful and life-affirming.

And then he had convinced himself he could stop after freeing just one nipple.

He was wrong.

So damn wrong. And hell. Even with the bruising of the saddle, he was hard again.

He pulled up on the stallion, standing in the stirrups.

Hard just thinking of Wynne's skin, of her body writhing under his touch. Of him stretching deep within her. He hadn't even found the sense to pull out before he came—hadn't had any notion at the time it would be the proper thing to do. Too consumed. Too absorbed in the woman under him.

It was her very reaction at the end of last night that he had dreaded, had tried to avoid.

For all that Wynne had convinced herself she wanted him—Rowen wasn't sure she was in her right mind yet.

And he damn well wanted her in her right mind.

He did not want half love from this woman. He wanted all of her. Every breath. Every word. Every thought. He couldn't accept less. Not from Wynne.

He had thought his standard, what he wanted in a mate, was impossible. Impossible until he met Wynne.

Rowen looked out across the long field, the openness stretching until it disappeared past a far-off hill. The cold brown ground shimmered with early morning frost.

What was he to do now? Wait? Pretend last night never happened? Hover until he was sure Wynne was done grieving for her mother? Wasn't looking to him solely to escape?

That was going to be damn hard, as all he wanted to do was strip her down and claim every last spec of her skin. Run his hands along her bare stomach, the muscles on her legs. Make her writhe under him. Watch her come. Again and again.

The horse kicked, demanding to be unleashed once more.

Rowen heaved a sigh. This was getting him nowhere.

And there weren't enough horses in the stables to ride out of his body what he really needed to be doing.

Taking Wynne to his bed.

"Sorry, young fellow." Rowen patted the neck of the black horse. "I will ride this stretch out with you, but it will not be the exhaustion you were hoping for."

~ ~ ~

Boots crunching along the gravel on the path from the stables, Rowen watched the ground in front of him, still lost in thoughts about Wynne. Only a few shards of late evening sun filtered in through the trees above him.

While he had thought to find Wynne soon after he arrived back to the stables, his architect and stable master had caught him, and he had found himself for most of the afternoon refereeing aesthetics versus function for the newest stable to be built. It was to be the show stable, the one meant to impress

future visitors at Notlund arriving to trade, breed, or buy.
Between that, and seeing Luhaunt off, the day had quickly
slipped away from him.

Rowen looked up as he cleared the line of trees at the edge
of the woods, only to see, of all people, the dowager pacing along
the path outside the outer wall of the castle. Rowen sighed, his
gait slowing.

She was waiting for him. And of the many things she could
lambast him for, he just truly hoped, down to his soul, that the
duchess hadn't found out what he and Wynne did last night.

He wasn't about to apologize for it, but he also didn't want to
battle with the dowager about his relationship with Wynne.

Closer to the castle, the duchess grew tired of Rowen's slow
pace and came down the trail, intercepting him.

"You do not walk that slowly, L.B. Entirely rude." She
yanked her black shall tighter around her shoulders.

"Just enjoying the day, Duchess." Rowen stopped in front of
her. "What is it that you need?"

"I asked Wynne today if she was ready to paint me again. She
was in the painting room, just staring out the window. But she
looked different—happier. I thought it the right time to start up
again. But she just jumped—like she did not even know I was in
the room—and then mumbled something about it not being the
right time yet."

"What am I to do about that, Duchess? I cannot make her
paint."

"What is happening with her, L.B.? You are supposed to
be making her well again." She leaned forward, pointing her
finger at his chest. "That is the only reason I have allowed you
such a breach of propriety. The only reason I have allowed you
unfettered access to her—trusted in your status as a gentleman
when you are alone with her."

Rowen's eyebrow arched. "You have allowed it? I think you
forget, Duchess, that I am the one that does or does not allow
who is present at this castle. And I do find your sudden increased
expectation of my honor somewhat laughable."

"Do not push me, L.B. Wynne is a young, unmarried woman in the unchaperoned presence of a man. Even you should understand that it is her reputation that you do harm to, were word to get out."

"Are you truly threatening her at the same time as demanding she be back by your side? That is low, even for you, Duchess." Rowen shook his head, trying to ignore the madness of this woman. "I have done as you asked, Duchess. I have been trying to pull her out of her grief. It is working. She paints me. She converses."

The duchess's arm swung wide. "You have done nothing. She is no closer to being back to me than she was. She will paint you, but not me. She talks to you, but not me."

"I cannot control her grief, Duchess. Cannot control what she will or will not do. You are too akin to her mother. She just needs more time."

"Time? I am through giving you time." The duchess leaned in at him, her words biting. "Your time is now short, L.B. Short. Do not test me."

She spun, stomping away from him.

Rowen could only stand, staring at the back of her black skirts swishing, letting the ball of rage in his gut dissipate before he moved forth.

{ CHAPTER 15 }

"I did not know if you would appear or not." Wynne leaned away from the canvas in front of her to look at him.

Rowen instantly recognized the tentativeness in her gaze as she watched him step past the arched doorway into the painting room. "You were worried?"

"No—" She stopped herself, then nodded her head.

"Worried that I would show, or worried that I would not?" Rowen asked.

She stood from her chair, setting down the paintbrush and her board of paints and walked over to him. Feet stopping right before him, she looked up at him inquisitively. The faint smell of honey—always around her to keep the paints malleable, a trick she had learned from her grandfather—wafted up to his nose.

"Why would that even be a question?" She grabbed the apron about her waist and twisted her ring finger in it, wiping away wet grey paint. Even after last night, innocence still sparkled in the blue flecks in her eyes.

"I was worried you would not come," she said. "But that was silly—I should not have questioned you. I just have not seen you all day, and that is unusual."

"I was stuck down at the stables." Rowen stepped away from her, if only to stop inhaling her scent, and closed the door to the room.

It took him a long moment to steel himself and turn to face her. Heaven help him, he wanted to kiss her. Yank the pins from her hair. Pick her up and carry her back to his room.

Rowen took a step toward her, stopping with plenty of distance between them.

"Wynne, we cannot repeat what we did last night. I will not have you reacting…"

"Like I did?" She crossed her arms over her chest. "Will not have me wallowing in my own choices? Will not let me take responsibility for my own actions?" Her chest rose in a deep sigh. "I needed you Rowe. And I was not wrong about it."

"No, you were not wrong. You knew what you could handle." He eyed her, watching her eyes flicker between ire and longing. "It is that you take too much responsibility for your actions—put too much pressure upon yourself—that is what worries me, Wynne. What it can do to your soul."

"That is it? You are worried about my soul so you will not touch me?"

He couldn't resist another step toward her. Close enough to feel her breath as she looked up at him, challenging. He met her heat. "I want you in my bed, Wynne. God help me, I do. Right now. But I fear…"

"What?"

He shook his head, unable to say more. "Paint." He stepped around her, going to the wooden chair by the table and sat. "Let us sit. You paint. Let us just do this for now."

Her gaze followed him, her bottom lip going under her teeth, biting hard. She wanted to argue, he could see that, but she held back.

Quiet, she walked over to her table of paints, picking up her paint board and disappearing behind the canvas.

Silence filled the room for minutes, and Rowen stared at the lines of the wooden easel supporting the canvas. He needed to get Wynne another one so that she could set the canvas even higher. She hunched over far too much with this one.

"I saw you outside with the duchess." Wynne's voice popped out from behind the canvas. "What were you talking about? She looked distressed."

"She always looks distressed."

Wynne's head appeared, her eyes scolding. "Not with me, Rowe. She can be quite docile." Her voice softened. "But it was not just her. It was you as well. Usually you are calm around her.

Clipped, but steady, not letting her affect you. But your face. I could tell she struck a bad chord with you."

Rowen's mouth clamped closed.

"You are not going to tell me?"

He sighed, scratching the back of his head. "We were talking about you, Wynne."

"Me? Why?"

"The duchess misses you. Misses your company. You have managed to reach her like no one ever has. Not since her son. And he only partially cared for her."

"I know I have been distant to her." A frown lined her lips. "And when she came in here today, she looked hopeful. But I was thinking of other things…"

"Us?"

She nodded. "Unfortunately. And I must have been rude— distracted at the very least. I did not intend to be so. It is still hard for me to look at her and not be reminded of my mother. But why would she come to you about it?"

"She thought I could help. That is all."

Wynne's eyes narrowed. "That is all?"

"Yes."

She gave a slight nod and busied herself with plopping fresh dollops of paint onto her board. She gave him a quick glance. "Why does the duchess call you L.B., Rowe? I would think Lockton or Rowen, given your history. But 'L.B.'—I have been trying to figure it out for weeks. And every time she says it, you blink and an instant of something I cannot grasp goes across your face."

Rowen forced his face neutral. "She has always called me L.B., Wynne. It is the way it is."

"Little boy?"

"No, that is not it."

"Lockton baby?"

"Stop, Wynne." His jaw tightened, and he attempted to relax it. "What the duchess does, and why she does it, only she knows. Everyone I know has stopped questioning her behavior long ago."

Wynne nodded, a quick apologetic smile coming to her face. Her head dropped and she set about mixing colors on her board, softly humming to herself.

Minutes passed, and Rowen thought her lost in thought, and was just about to relax, happy to avoid the topic of the duchess, when Wynne's voice startled him.

"What happened to your mother here, Rowe? Here in the castle?"

"No, Wynne." His head was shaking before the words came out.

"I can hear it now, Rowe. Truly. I can hear it. I want to know. And I want to know from you."

"Wynne, it is not necessary, it is past."

She pointedly pushed the paint board away from her, even though a brush thick with paint stayed in her fingers. She looked up at him. "Past that still, to this very day, puts daggers in your eyes when you even think about the duchess. For all of your forced politeness, Rowe, it is there. I see it. And I want to know why."

"I will not knowingly share a story that is going to lead you to dwell upon your own mother, Wynne."

She shook her head. "Not fair. Whatever the tale is, it does not mean I will not be sad, but I can handle it. I can hear this now, Rowe, and I want to know. I need to understand."

Rowen leaned back in the wooden chair, running a hand through his hair as he looked upward at the thick dark beams of the coffered ceiling. How to even begin this story?

His eyes dropped to Wynne. "You do recall my father died early in my life?"

"Yes. You said you were four."

He nodded. "After my father died, my uncle—the duke— brought my mother and me to live here at Notlund."

"That was generous."

A harsh, forced chuckle escaped Rowen. "Yes, well, so generous, that it was not long before my mother became his mistress."

Wynne gasped, as Rowen expected. What he did not expect was for Wynne to drop the brush in her hand, sending it to flop paint onto her apron, skirts, and then floor.

Her face turning pink, she quickly fumbled to pick it up. "My apologies."

"It is nothing."

She smoothed the hair back from her temple, settling herself. "I presume the duchess knew of the affair?"

"Yes. The duke produced very little effort in hiding it from the duchess. And even less of an effort in protecting my mother from the duchess. And by default, I became a convenient target for the duchess's hatred as well. Almost from the moment we stepped foot in Notlund."

"You were four."

"Yes, and I was told daily that I was lower than dirt. That I did not deserve to be alive. That the best place for me was the dung heap."

Rowen shook his head. It had been a very long time since he had allowed the memories to flood him. And they were still visceral. His eyes drifted back to the ceiling.

"But it was not just that she was vicious with her words. It was the way the duchess would set me up. She would entice me in, coddle me with kindness for just a few, fleeting moments, and I would believe things were different, that she did not hate me. And then she would lambast me. Rip treats from my hands and hand them to her son. Slap me when I reached for a toy of his. Juicy meat on a fork to my mouth, knocked to the floor for the dogs. And her laugh. Vicious. Her words…I was a waste. I should have never been born. The devil did not even want me."

Rowen took a steadying breath. "I was four. Four. I had no defense of it. I did not understand any of it—just that I was somehow unworthy. Ugly. Dumb. I did not know. The only thing I knew was that I should not exist. Every single day was like that. And I learned to never trust anything in front of me. That any high—any comfort would be rewarded with cruelty."

His arms folded over his chest as his eyes dropped to Wynne. "And I soon just accepted the fact that they—my cousin, the duke and duchess—were much better than I could ever hope to be. That I was lucky just to be breathing. Lucky to be alive, even if it was in the duchess's concocted hell. It was not long before I truly believed that I was worthless."

His words yielded, and Wynne stood, grabbing her wooden chair and walking over to him. She set the chair down right in front of him and sat, leaning forward as her hands went gently on his knees.

Wet, her eyes glistened in the light from the lamp on the table. "And your mother?"

Rowen took a deep breath, his eyes shifting to the fireplace across the room. "My mother… when she could, she tried to protect me. Tried to take the brunt of the duchess's viciousness. Took the threats. The hate. Would step in front of the slaps. The kicks. But the duchess knew—she knew it was far worse for my mother to have to watch her only child suffer. So that is what she did. And my mother suffered. The older I got, the more I understood how much she suffered just to protect me what little she could."

"Why did your mother stay—not take you both away?"

"I do not know. I would wonder that every day. I begged her. Every day I would beg her to leave this place. But she had no power. The duke controlled my father's fortune until I was of age. Maybe he threatened to cut her off. Maybe it was because of that. Maybe it was because she knew she couldn't survive on her own. Couldn't feed or house me. Maybe it was because she loved him. I do not know."

"And then she died and you got to leave this place?"

He nodded, his eyes closing. "Slowly, at the end, she starved herself, day after day. She became bones right before me. Just before she died, she told me it was the best thing she could do for me—the only way she could still protect me. I told her she was wrong. I was old enough then. I was strong. I begged. But maybe she was trying to escape her own hell. Again, I do not know. Still to this day, I do not know."

She gave him long seconds. Long seconds Rowen used, eyes closed, to chase the long-ago demons back to the depths of his mind.

That Wynne had even gotten him to speak the words, to talk about it.

Hell.

Then the hands on his knees tightened.

He opened his eyes to her.

Tears were in her eyes, pain for him or for herself, he could not tell. But he could see it—the tears that shone in her eyes brought forth sadness from deep in her soul.

"I know…I know you are not vulnerable like you once were, Rowe. That you know who you are and you do not need me to say this. But I need to say it for me." Her voice rough, it cracked. She took a moment, head down, to re-gather her words.

Then she leaned further forward, her hands slipping onto his thighs. Her hazel eyes came to his face. "I have never met a man with more worth than you, Rowe. Never. Who you are. What you stand for. What you have done. Every breath you take has integrity that cannot be broken. I see that. I see you. The whole of you is what I love."

Her thumbs tightened on his legs, drifting into dangerous territory. "And what you have done for me—all you have ever wanted to do since we met was protect me. Protect my innocence. You are good, Rowe. From your mind, to deep in your soul. Good. Every heartbeat. Every breath."

Rowen closed his eyes, dragging air into his tight chest.

She was wrong. So very wrong. Those were the exact words he needed to hear. From anyone else, it would mean nothing. But from Wynne…from Wynne it meant the world.

"And you are still trying to protect my innocence, Rowe. But that innocence was gone—shattered—before you ever laid eyes on me. It is not something you can protect anymore."

She stood, straddling his legs and the chair. Rowen opened
his eyes to her.

Moving forward, she pulled her skirts upward, bunching
them until she could lower herself onto his lap, her thighs bare to
the world.

Wynne's hands went to either side of his face, forcing his gaze
to meet hers. "I needed you last night, Rowe, and you knew—you
knew exactly what I needed. You gave it to me."

Her lips came down to his, sweet softness brushing his skin.
"And now you need me, Rowe. You need me." Her lips moved
against his, whispering. "Let me give you what you need."

She curled her body forward, her hips rotating on his lap as
she took his mouth fully, her tongue slipping in, her teeth teasing
his skin.

The vague thoughts of resistance, of honor, floated from
his mind. She was right. He did need this. Need her in the most
basic, human way. Her body giving over to him.

He let it happen. Let her deepen her assault, let her move her
body against his until there was no turning back. No argument
against what they both knew he needed.

He needed her.

And she wasn't going to let him choose otherwise.

Wynne's hands slid down his body, her fingers running over
his chest, pulling up his linen shirt until she could lift it off his
frame.

His torso naked to her, she bent, her lips running along his
neck as her hands dove downward, unbuttoning his breeches. The
motion, so simple, and with every brush of her knuckles, Rowen
grew harder.

Freed from the leather, he groaned, arching into her hands,
begging for tightness in her touch.

Wynne obliged, taking him full in her fingers, stroking, as
her teeth ran along a line from his shoulder to the back of his
neck.

"Tell me I am doing this right, Rowe."

Instinct sent his hands around her, popping buttons on her dress and dragging it off her body. For a moment he thought she would cower from her nakedness, but she didn't hesitate, instead wrapping her body even closer to his, skin on skin. Her nipples dragged across his chest.

Rowen's mouth went to her ear, tugging on her earlobe. "You are torture and heaven in one, Wynne. Hell, yes, you are doing this right."

His palms dragged up her body, fingers stretched across her back as his palms, his thumbs explored her curves—reveled in the smoothness of her skin, the way her body leaned into his touch, skin prickling.

When he hit the moment he was straining, holding onto the last shreds of control, he dipped his hands inward, thumbs going to her core, finding her nubbin, waking it, owning it.

Her body already moving in rhythm against his hand, Rowen grabbed her hips, lifting her and sliding into her body. Letting her sink onto him. Slow. Torturous.

He filled her—claiming every part of her body that was open to him, and then he lifted her again. Dropping her with sweet agony, he repeated, fighting against her whimpered begs, her thrusting hips. She wanted him fast, straining herself to reach peak, and Rowen was enjoying the rawness in her need, in her mouth on his skin, in her hands ravaging his body.

She started to beg, swearing, and Rowen grimaced against coming, his thumbs attacking her folds as he let her take over the pace on top of him. She came, arching backward, breasts in his face, and in the next instant, curled into him, fingernails digging into his back, tethering herself to him.

It turned Rowen savage, holding no bars against what he needed to unleash in her. How he needed to take her. Fill her. Deep and hard, again and again.

She held fast to him, her body trembling, the throes of her orgasm jerking through her muscles. Softly screaming his name in his ear.

It only took moments, and Rowen came, brutally, his body shuddering under her.

Emptying into her, lost in her body, in all the woman above him was, the click of the door only partially made it into his consciousness.

Only partially, and he did not bother to convince himself it was real.

His imagination.

Only his imagination.

{ Chapter 16 }

Rowen propped his ankle onto his knee, leaning back in the leather chair. Gaze lost on the fire in the study, he took another sip of brandy.

He had hoped the brandy would numb the urge he was having to go up to Wynne's bedroom, to wake her up, to take her.

No matter that it was the middle of the night. No matter that it was only a few hours since they left the painting room.

But it was already a precarious precipice they were balancing on. He still had serious concerns about Wynne's state of mind. About her grief. About his own state of mind. About the demons she managed to drag from the depths of his mind. About the fact that he was very quickly coming to the point where he was consumed with her.

All he wanted to do was be with Wynne. Talk to her. Laugh with her. Take her to his bed and keep her there until the need for her was sated—sated for at least a few hours.

He needed to get a license and find a minister, and soon. He was done sneaking around with Wynne.

Rowen took another slow sip, still hoping it would help—but also disgusted that the brandy had done very little against easing the turmoil going on in his mind.

"I saw you."

The words came into the room, harsh, accusing. And then the duchess appeared out of the darkness, stepping in front of him and blocking his line to the fire.

Rowen's eyes fell closed with an inhale. He could not take the duchess right now. Not tonight. Not after what he had told Wynne. Not when all he wanted to do was curl up with Wynne tight to his body.

"Let me be more specific, L.B." He heard the duchess's skirts swish. "I saw you in the painting room, not but a few hours ago."

Shit.

Rowen's eyes opened slowly to the duchess, fury palpitating.

"You have compromised her, L.B."

"What do you want, Duchess?"

She took a step closer, lording over him. "I want Wynne back. You have taken her away from me, and I want her back as mine."

"She is not a pet, Duchess."

"I am aware. She was my friend, and you took her away." Her voice turned wicked. "Just as you have always taken everything from me, L.B. But you will not have her as well."

"Wynne is a grown woman who can make her own decisions. And be very careful with your next words, Duchess. Do not dare to threaten her again."

"No. Do not worry on that, L.B. I have decided that would not be fair." The duchess's arms came up slowly, crossing over her ribcage. She tilted her head slightly toward him, her voice suddenly sweet honey. "You are right—Wynne should not be the one to suffer because you cannot keep your breeches buttoned."

Rowen's eyes narrowed, wary. "What are you planning, Duchess?"

"I believe it is time to share our secret, little bastard."

The glass shattered in his hand.

She had not been bold enough to utter those words since he was six—not since she had conveniently replaced them with "L.B."

Rowen threw the shards to the floor, blood drops splattering, and jumped to his feet, stance threatening. "You would not dare."

"No?" She looked up at him with wicked coolness. "It will remove you from Wynne, and she would remain unharmed, her reputation intact."

"You talk gibberish, old woman. How would that remove me from Wynne?"

She shook her head, pitying. "L.B., do you honestly think she wants a man who has been stripped of a dukedom? Who has nothing?" She stepped closer, her folded arms touching him as she sneered up at him. "I removed Victoria from your grasp rather easily. And I did not even need to tell her of your lineage."

"You? Victoria?" Rowen froze, shock vibrating through his body.

She nodded, vicious smile on her lips.

He blinked, shaking himself free of the blow. "Whatever you did, Dowager, it has no bearing. Wynne cannot be manipulated as easily as Victoria was."

"But do you want Wynne to know you are a bastard? A worthless little bastard? Who your real father is? I will do it, L.B., and I will do it with great satisfaction."

Rowen had to physically fight his own hands to keep them from wrapping around the duchess's neck. He seethed down at her. "You would not dare. The line ends with me, Duchess."

"It ended with my son."

He forced a chuckle. "Yes. But do remember it is this very secret that keeps you in this place. That keeps you an army of servants. Clothes to wear. Food to eat. Your own holdings are not enough for any of that—your husband made very well sure of it."

"Something my son would have corrected, had he the chance to do so."

"But he did not get the chance, Duchess. And you enjoy your comforts too much. Your power. Power that disappears the second the duchy is dissolved."

She took a deep breath, a bright smile appearing on her face. "I am willing to sacrifice. If for nothing else, than to see you destroyed, once and for all. And Wynne will be at my side once again."

"Do not do this, Dowager."

The smile slipped from her face. "You go. You leave Notlund. Or I tell her the truth. She will be the first to know. The first to know you are a bastard, living a life, owning a title you do not deserve. Can you imagine how she will look at you, L.B.? The disgust on her face? For her to know you are lower than dirt? I can imagine it. I can imagine it very well."

Rowen glared down at her, her words filling his head, wrapping around his neck, setting free the demons from his childhood.

Demons choking him.

She wouldn't. She had never even dared to suggest this move in the past. She would lose too much.

But then Rowen saw it in her eyes. She would. She would do it just to see him suffer. Just to plunge the knife of revenge into him. The revenge she always needed.

A lifetime of warfare against him would not be enough for her. No—she had waited, waited until this very moment. This moment when he actually had something to lose. She waited until she could make him lose the very thing that meant the most to him.

Wynne.

She had recognized it before he even did—how much Wynne meant to him. That Wynne was the very thing that could destroy him.

Losing the title—he could handle that. The estate—he could care less. He had never wanted the blasted dukedom anyway.

But Wynne knowing. Knowing he was a bastard. How she would look at him once she knew. A bastard baby. Worthless.

He truly was worthless.

If he was lucky, it would just be pity in Wynne's eyes. If he was unlucky, disdain—scorn—revulsion.

And he could not take Wynne looking at him like that. He could not.

Rowen pushed past the duchess, storming to the door.

"Be gone by morning, L.B."

~ ~ ~

He had asked her to trust him. Yet in all of it, he had omitted that one truth. Kept that one lie hidden from Wynne.

Hell, his whole damn life was a lie.

Every morning. Every evening. It was the one thought that sent him to sleep. The one thought that greeted him when he woke.

Who he really was. A bastard.

For as far from his childhood as he had come, that one fact remained with him. He was a bastard. Born a bastard. Would always be a bastard. The one fact he could not escape, could not forget.

Rowen exhaled, his breath crystallizing in the cold morning air. Phalos had been faster along the trail than Rowen would have liked.

He wanted to drag out his exit from Notlund. Drag out putting more distance between him and Wynne. But Phalos was feeling spry legs and happy to be tromping through the forest.

Three hours since he had disappeared from the castle at the sun's first rays. Three hours of torture he could only hope would ebb once he made it to London.

But he was not about to give up on the slight sliver of hope he had left—that Wynne would choose to come after him on her own accord. Rowen had left Notlund to satisfy the duchess's demand, but the one thing the dowager forgot was that she could not control Wynne.

Wynne would come after him. She had to.

He had left her the horse. The note. The money. She would come.

And Rowen was taking the roundabout way to the main road to London—the trail Wynne knew—just in case. The same trail that had first brought Wynne to Notlund.

A squirrel flitted down a tree and scampered across the muddy trail in front of Phalos. The image of the first time he had met Wynne flickered into Rowen's mind. Of her gutting the squirrel. Offering the meat up to him.

Earthy. Genuine. Trusting.

It was who she was. All of those things, to her core.

It hit him.

She wouldn't care. She wouldn't care who his father was. How he was born. If he had a title or not. If he had money.

It was him—without the title, without money, without land—him that she had first smiled at. First offered half a squirrel to. She didn't know who he was then, she just knew she liked him. Knew he had helped her, and wanted to repay him.

She was living in a damn forest—and more than content to do so. And he was worried about how she would react to his lineage? That she would leave him—deny him if she knew the truth?

He had asked Wynne to trust him, yet he had not given her the very same.

Pure stupidity.

Rowen yanked up on the reins, stopping Phalos.

Wynne was the exact opposite of everyone he had ever known. The trappings of wealth and a title were nowhere near important to her.

Take away her painting, she would care.

Not enough food to eat, she would care.

Beyond those two things, she was happy.

Just happy to be in his life.

Rowen curled over, head bowed. Physically disgusted at his own stupidity. Disgusted that he had let the duchess into his head. Disgusted that he had doubted himself—doubted Wynne.

He had just made the decision for her—decided how she would react to his lineage.

Except he was wrong, and he knew it. Completely and utterly wrong.

And he had left her with a note.

Bloody hell.

He spun Phalos, heels digging in. He needed to get back. Back to Wynne before she found his note.

{ CHAPTER 17 }

The feel of Rowen's lips, his body encasing her, ebbed away as lucidity pulled Wynne away from the darkness of dream and into the morning. Too exhausted by Rowen the previous night, she hadn't bothered to pull the heavy drapes against the window, and sunlight streamed in, calling her to the day.

She rolled to her side, eyes closed and lips still pulsating. She needed to fall back asleep. Fall back into the deliciousness of her memories—of Rowen.

Her eyes flew open. Even better than the memory of Rowen would be finding him and tagging along with him down to the stables. She could get him to take Phalos out so she could study the muscle tone of the horse. Plus—she smirked to herself—then she could study the muscle lines of Rowen as well.

The sun would be warming the air, and if she was fast, she might catch Rowen before he headed out of the castle for the day.

She was dressed, sitting on the side of the bed and tying up her tall boots when she noticed a cream envelope with her name scrawled across it on the table next to the bed.

Had that been there last night and she missed it?

Boots tied, she stood, picking up the envelope and opening it.

A small notecard inside, it had just a few words on it.

Wynne—
Please visit stall 39 in the stables.
—Rowe

A smile spread wide across her face. Rowen had a surprise waiting for her. She sprang over to the bureau and pulled out a dark wool cloak, wrapping it around her as she went out the door.

Braiding her hair along the way, fifteen minutes later, Wynne had greeted several of the stable hands on the way into the center stable, and was watching the brass numbers on each stall tick upward as she made it deep into the structure…34…35…36…37…38…39.

She stopped, seeing immediately a gleaming new side saddle, a motif of ivy etched into the deep brown leather, draped over the short wall at the front of the stall. The horse she had ridden to Tanloon, the beautiful honey-colored mare with a creamy white nose, stepped forward at noticing her, sniffing at the saddle and watching Wynne with interest.

She glanced into the stall and then looked around. No one was nearby. And Rowen was nowhere to be seen.

Opening the gate of the stall, Wynne moved in and stroked the bridge of the horse's nose. "Here I am, sweetheart. Stall 39. Do you know why I am here, girl?"

The horse whinnied, shaking her mane, then nudged Wynne's still outstretched hand for another stroke. The smell of fresh hay wafted up and Wynne had to hold her nose against a sneeze. Mindlessly, Wynne rubbed the horse's nose, looking around.

It was then that she saw the corner of a cream envelope sticking out of the leather pouch on the sidesaddle. The same cream envelope as in her room.

She looked about once more. Still no one around.

Lifting the flap on the pouch, she pulled the envelope free. It, too, had her name across the front of it. This envelope was sealed with a splotch of thick red wax. She hadn't thought of Rowen as the romantic-surprise sort, but the mystery of this was fun, she had to admit.

Smile playing on her lips, she cracked through the wax and pulled out a lighter, folded sheet of vellum.

Wynne—
This horse. You know her, and she is now yours. Her name is Sandy. She comes from a fine line of horses—direct from the

Godolphin Arabian. She will take you wherever you decide to go. She is honorable and smart. She likes you, and I pray she will be as loyal a friend to you as Phalos has been to me.

The sidesaddle has a special satchel attached to it that will hold your brushes, and has a few containers for paints that should hold steady enough not to break.

I have had to leave Notlund, Wynne, and will not be back.

The horse, the side saddle, and the money you will find in the bottom of this satchel should be able to take you wherever you would like to go, give you the opportunity to do whatever you wish. It should give you freedom to live your life how you most desire.

I wish you nothing but happiness, Wynne. You are a remarkable soul, and I am a better man for knowing you.

Thank you for coming into my life.

Please know that I will be in London, should you ever need assistance. For anything.

You are never alone, Wynne. Never.

Love,

Rowen

Her eyes narrowed in on the words at the bottom of the letter.

Love.

Love, Rowen.

Love.

Her eyes went over the last two words again and again.

Rowen was telling her he had left—never to return—then wrote "Love"?

What type of vicious cruelty was that?

Her mind could not immediately comprehend the note. He had left, but he loved her? Gone, but it was nice to know her?

Without thinking, her left hand dove into the satchel, reaching to the bottom. A leather bag. She picked it up, heavy in her hands, and could hear the coins clinking within.

She dropped it, fire in her hand.

He had just paid her.

Paid her like a whore. Money, a horse.

A whore.

She was a whore.

A whore like her mother.

The paper fell from her hand as her legs crumpled beneath her, dropping her into a scattering of hay.

A whore.

Just a damn whore.

~ ~ ~

Six hours into the woods, and Wynne knew she should think about trapping a squirrel or a rabbit, but the anger in her belly had not eased in the slightest, and she knew she wouldn't be able to eat anything anyway.

Not that she could even see straight enough to trap anything right now. The whole of her leaving Notlund—of grabbing her brushes and her grandfather's knife—had been done in a blinding haze.

She had kept the clothes she had on. They were from the duchess, so she gave herself margin in taking them—but beyond that, she walked out of the stone keep with exactly what she had walked in with.

Less, as she already realized how very much of her soul would forever be lost to that place.

She had started off in the only direction she knew—the way she and Rowen had first walked into the estate. But as soon as she had seen a trail veering, she took it, and within a few hours, she came upon the stream she remembered and she turned south.

Wynne didn't know how she was going to manage it, but she was going to get to the coast. Get to the seaport at Liverpool where she and her mother had landed in this blasted country. And then she was going to figure out a way to get on a ship back to America.

Back to the only place she knew was a home. The only place she could trust as a home.

It didn't matter what she had felt at Notlund—how very much that had started to feel like a real home. It didn't matter because all of that had been a lie.

A cruel, crushing lie.

For hours, the trees, the woods, the stream had all drifted by out of focus, her eyes only able to see to the next step in front of her.

Until, unexpectedly—with the woods surrounding her, the cold water flowing next to her—her grandfather's voice entered her head. Her feet stopped.

"Keep your soul alive, little bear, and that will keep your body alive. Food always needs to be a part of that. Do not forget that. Food keeps the mind on a goal. On living." His words, his voice drifted through her head, focusing her thoughts, straightening her spine.

Survival. That was what mattered most right now. Survival.

Wynne lifted her chin, looking around her. Tightening the wool cloak around her shoulders, fighting the cold she hadn't realized had taken hold, Wynne took a deep breath. The first real breath she had taken since the stable.

Her eyes went to the tree-filtered sky. Still enough daylight to at least find or concoct shelter.

Tomorrow. Tomorrow she would find food. But right now, she needed a fire. A lean-to. If she could concentrate on those things, on her grandfather's voice, she could push the pain from her mind. Push Rowen from her mind.

She kept walking, veering away from the stream into the brush, searching for a large, fallen tree with an upended root system. Dirty, but a huge clump of roots made for a nice start to cobble together a quick shelter—earth soft from being torn up, and a natural depression that could be turned into a warm little cave with some work.

It wasn't long before Wynne found what she was looking for: a beastly old oak so girthy that, even fallen on its side, it was taller than her. After poking about, she found the small hollow uninhabited by any creatures. Perfect.

Wynne started working her way around the fallen tree, gathering long branches and piling them near what would be her little shelter.

A twig cracked behind her.

Sound that shouldn't be there.

She dropped the wood in her arms, whipping out her knife from her bag as she spun.

Rowen.

Phalos ten paces behind him, Rowen stood, panting, face terrified, sweat full on his brow. Nothing against the cold. No overcoat. Just his white shirt soaked through like he had been running for miles.

Her fingers tightened around the blade's handle.

"Wynne." Even with no breath, he got the word out.

Her head instantly started to shake at him. "No. No, Rowe."

He took a step toward her, hands up with palms open to her, swallowing hard as he tried to catch his breath. "Wynne, you—"

"No. Stop. Stop right there. You left me, Rowe."

"I did not mean to leave you."

"But you did." Her voice raised into a yell. "You left me money. A damn horse. A damn note. That is what you left me with."

He took another step. "I could not leave you destitute, Wynne. I did not—"

"You left me with money like a damn whore."

He stopped his advance, caution overtaking his eyes. "What?"

"A damn whore—the money—the horse. You paid me. You turned me into a blasted whore, Rowe."

"Wynne—no. That was not what I intended."

"What did you intend?" Her hand with the knife started flailing wildly about. "For me to follow you and be your mistress while you went and married a proper lady? To use me and discard me when I no longer pleased your eye? You said it was the damn beginning, Rowe. The beginning. I was a stupid fool to let you become so much more to me. But I now see how excruciatingly evident it was that I was nothing more than a common prostitute to you."

"No, Wynne, no." He advanced closer, palms still up to her. "I did not want to leave you at the mercy of the dowager. I did not know what she would do after I left."

"So instead you turned me into my mother? A whore?"

"Wynne, just stop. Listen." Close enough, Rowen tried to grab her wrist.

Not fast enough. She had the blade on his neck before he could clamp her down.

"Do not touch me, Rowe." The words hissed from her mouth.

"Wynne." He stilled, but didn't step away, only leaning slightly backward from the knife.

She pressed forward. "I will fight you with every breath I have, Rowe. Leave me the hell alone."

"Wynne, you are overreacting."

"Your grace, do not make me do this." Her voice turned to cold viciousness. "Just step away. Leave me. Get Phalos and go. You will not touch my body again."

"You cannot hurt me, Wynne. I know that."

"Do you? Maybe I can." Her eyebrows cocked. "Maybe I finally figured out exactly what you are. Exactly who I am to you. And that has given me a brutality I did not know I had."

"Wynne—"

She pushed the blade into his skin. He didn't move away and a thin line of blood started to appear. She swallowed hard, her head already spinning.

"Wynne. Stop this."

The blade went harder into his neck. The blood came thicker.

She just had to hold on. Hold on until he left. Then she could pass out. Then she could vomit.

She had to get rid of him.

She leaned in, her lips curling around words that spat from her tongue. "You are worthless, your grace. Worthless."

Rowen's eyes snapped wide open at her, and she could see the instant pain she caused.

Her hand started to shake. No time left. She pressed harder. "Leave. Me. Alone."

His eyes pleaded with hers, and Wynne focused through the dizziness, her eyebrows collapsing hard against him.

He took a sudden step backward.

His hands came up again, slowly, palms to her. "If it is what you wish, Wynne, I will leave."

"So leave."

Not turning from her, he backed away slowly, grabbing Phalos's reins as he passed the horse. Phalos looked back at Wynne, tugging against Rowen, until Rowen yanked the leather. With a nicker, Phalos turned and reluctantly followed his master.

It took long moments after they were out of view, their steps fading into the forest, before Wynne dared to take a breath.

As soon as it hit her lungs, bile chased its way up through her throat. She bent over, vomiting, what little was left in her stomach landing on the forest floor.

Tears streaming from her face, she sank to her heels, balancing for several minutes, trying to steady herself.

When she dared to finally look up, the forest was quiet.

Time to find new shelter.

{ CHAPTER 18 }

On the main trail, Rowen sat on Phalos, staring at the woods he had just tromped through. She wasn't too far in—but she may as well be an ocean away.

He could not leave her.

But he could not go after her.

Ruined.

He had ruined everything.

Wynne would never look at him the same way again. He saw it at the end, with the blade against his neck.

The trust that had always beamed in her eyes when she looked at him. Gone. Gone and replaced with harshness. With hate. With a hurt so deep, so bitter, that it could never be overcome.

He had done that in one stupid move. One momentary break in his confidence, and the duchess had finally beaten him. Finally recognized and exploited the one crack in the impenetrable facade that he had created against her—Wynne.

And now he was stuck.

He could not follow Wynne, but he could not leave her to the woods by herself—to danger.

There was only one thing he could do.

He gave a low whistle, turning Phalos in the direction of Notlund.

His face to the sky, he asked for grace for himself and strength for his horse. He had already pushed Phalos far past what he should have, and now he was going to have to push Phalos just a bit more.

~~~

Rowen stepped into the lavender drawing room, finding the duchess with needlepoint in her fingers and sunlight beaming onto her lap.

"She is yours, Duchess."

The dowager looked up from her thread. She didn't look surprised to see him, just annoyed. "I thought we were agreed that you would leave Notlund, L.B."

He moved further into the room to stand in front of her. "You do not know, do you?"

"Know what?"

"That Wynne is gone."

"Gone? No. I saw her a few hours ago come back from the stables. She looked distraught. I was giving her some time alone."

"She left."

The duchess stood, her eyes turned into daggers at him. "You made her leave? That was not our bargain, L.B."

"She left on her own, Duchess. With just her brushes and her knife. That was all. She is already hours away in the east forest."

"No. Why would she do that?"

Rowen stared at her, holding back his very intense need to strangle her.

He forced a deep breath into his lungs, swallowing every bit of pride he had.

"You said I took Wynne away from you. This is your chance, Duchess. She is yours if you go after her and convince her to come back to Notlund."

"You want me to go into the woods? I will get dirty."

"You are the only one that can convince Wynne to come back, Duchess." The words grated from his chest, a putrescent stew he forced himself to endure.

"I am?" Her head tilted at him, eyes narrowing, understanding dawning. "But why would I want to do that?"

Rowen shook his head. The woman would not let an opportunity pass. "If it means Wynne's safety, she is yours, Duchess. I will not approach her. Not contact her. I will leave. Never put myself in the same room with her again. All of that if it means you will find her and keep her safe. I just need to know she is safe."

"You will leave Notlund forever?"

"Yes."

"And your plans for the castle—you will cease them?"

"I will leave this damn castle alone. I will rebuild it. Just find Wynne. Keep her safe."

The duchess stared at him, deciding.

Rowen took her assessment, not flinching. For all he had hoped to do with the estate and the land, he would halt it all. Wynne was the most important thing.

"I accept." She gave a crisp nod of her head. "Do not dare to go back on your word, L.B."

Rowen exhaled, relief flooding his chest. "I will tell the stable master where she is, which path she took. He will accompany you, and it should be easy enough to catch up to her on my fastest horses."

~~~

Wynne heard the brush breaking behind her, this time, not quiet in the slightest. At least Rowen was announcing himself this time rather than scaring her half to death.

Kindness in approach—but it still did not soften her heart to him. To what he did to her.

Pulling her knife, she turned, waiting for him to appear in the moving brush.

Two figures, high on horses, soon appeared between two thick evergreens. She recognized Tom, the stable master, first. He had an additional horse with no rider following him, attached to a lead. And behind him—Wynne's jaw dropped.

The duchess.

The duchess on a horse, in the middle of the woods. Wynne never would have thought the woman even knew how to ride. Much less owned the full regalia of a fine red velvet riding habit that fit her body perfectly. It was the first time Wynne had seen her in anything but black.

The dowager spied Wynne. "Boy—leave us now. But do not go far."

Tom nodded to both Wynne and the duchess, then moved his horse and the trailing mare past the clearing by Wynne, turning them to the stream. It left the duchess and Wynne in relative privacy.

Wynne flipped up the flap on her bag, putting her knife back in place, and then looked up at the duchess. "Why are you here, your grace? I cannot believe the duke convinced you to come after me."

"Please, dear, L.B. cannot make me do anything." She stacked her leather-gloved hands on the horn of the saddle. "I presume he treated you like a harlot?"

Wynne blinked, stunned at the duchess. "How did you know?"

"He nearly said as much, after he told me about your mother."

Her stun exploded. "He...he told you about my mother?"

Wynne's eyes dropped to the forest floor, staring at the decaying leaves by her feet. He couldn't have. He couldn't have betrayed her like that. Not only told the duchess about them, but about her mother as well. No. Impossible.

She looked up to the dowager. "No. The duke would not have told you."

"He did, child." Her matter-of-fact words rained down on Wynne. "That was why he thought it would be appropriate, your affair. He thought you would find it amicable, what with how your mother was. I think he misjudged your reaction."

Numb, Wynne nodded. "Yes. Yes, he did."

"Do not bother your energy on it, dear. You could not have known." Her hand flipped dismissively into the air. "It is the way with dukes. They do as they please with little regard to what they destroy in pursuit of their own pleasure."

Wynne had to give herself a little shake. Still reeling from the duchess's words, all she wanted in that moment was to be alone. "What do you want from me, Duchess?"

"I would like it if you would reconsider leaving Notlund. If you will become my companion."

"Companion?"

"I do need to rectify your general lack of knowledge, Wynne. A companion is a paid position, and is exactly as it sounds. Although I do hope you will finish my portrait. You may leave the position at any time, and you will have plenty of time for your painting. I believe it will be fun, as well, to introduce you to my connections that would appreciate having their portraits done."

Wynne was already shaking her head. "I cannot be around the duke, your grace."

"Nonsense." The duchess shook her head. "There will be no seeing him. I have sent him away. You need never be in the same room with him again."

Wynne's head cocked, wary. "He is gone?"

"Yes. Come, my dear. I have not been off the main grounds of Notlund in years, and I am finding it overwhelming. There is a definite chill and I would like to be home by nightfall."

Wynne studied the duchess, deciding. The woman offered employment. A way to save enough money to buy passage back to America. And most important, no Rowen.

Wynne nodded.

She would be stupid not to accept.

{ CHAPTER 19 }

Rowen slid the window closed in his study, staring at the crisp, green hedges of the gardens. The brisk wind had picked up, blowing papers off his desk.

The recent cold had been a welcome respite after the warm summer, but at the same time, Rowen didn't want to spend the afternoon picking up and organizing papers strewn about his study.

He knew he could easily have his solicitor taking care of the bulk of the affairs of the duchy, but it had kept his mind occupied. Occupied in a realm far away from one where he thought of Wynne. The realm where he would try to drink her memory away. Three months of that had left him nowhere except angry and exhausted.

Even though Wynne was safely ensconced at Notlund, Rowen had hoped against hope that she would have a change of heart. That she could find a way to forgive him. Find her way to him.

But it had not happened. Months had passed, and there was only the occasional short note from the duchess that Wynne was there and safe.

At the very least, Rowen was happy for that. He had no right to ask for more.

Latching the window closed, he crumpled further in his hand the already half-crushed letter that had just arrived from Notlund. Tom, Notlund's stable master, had verified what the duchess had written a month ago. That Wynne was set to become betrothed to a physician in the area.

Rowen wasn't going to believe the duchess alone on that particular message, so he had actually stooped to inquiring about Wynne from Tom. As distasteful as it was to have to skulk about the shadows for news on Wynne, Rowen had to do it.

And man that Tom was, he had written back just the facts, with no judgment. Rowen was grateful for it, even if it wasn't the news he had wanted to face.

Wynne had apparently done the physician's portrait during the late spring, soon after the duchess had started to entertain at Notlund again. Tom knew every horse in and out of the estate and had verified the physician's ongoing visits to the Notlund— long after the man's portrait had been finished, as Tom had seen it shipped off to the physician's house himself.

Rowen crushed the letter into an even tinier ball. Preposterous. Wynne could never be around a man with constant blood on his clothes.

His eyes drifted out to the evergreen hedges. Planted long ago by his grandfather, they were now tall enough to be level with the bottom of the study window. A group of three rogue leaves flew by in the wind, spinning together.

Rowen shook his head.

He had to face it. October first—eight months since he had seen Wynne. Eight months without word from her. Without the slightest indication she would ever allow him back into her life.

He had been a fool to wait this long.

It was time to concentrate on an heir.

~ ~ ~

"You should be ready, dear, not in here, paint still thick on your nails."

Wynne's gaze drifted from the canvas in front of her to the doorway. In a deep blue gown, the duchess stood, her dark hair coifed to perfection and ready for the grandest ball, even though it was just a few people coming to Notlund to dine.

The duchess's eyes went to Wynne's fingernails, and Wynne started flicking away dried paint. "What time does he arrive?"

"You have lost time again? He is already here, Wynne." The duchess walked into the room, stopping at the opposite end of the paint table. "Mr. Rookton said he was most content to wait for you, but you are at least an hour away from cleaning up properly. You will have to rush, now."

"I cannot do it, your grace." Her voice a whisper, Wynne couldn't look up at the duchess.

"Do what, dear?"

"Mr. Rookton."

The dowager sighed, clasping her white-gloved fingers together. "But Mr. Rookton is so well respected, kind, from a wealthy family, and might I mention, pleasing to the eye, Wynne. He adores you and I have spent such care in producing this match."

The dowager came around the table to stand next to Wynne without giving her a chance to drop a cloth in front of her painting.

The duchess glanced at the canvas and her nose wrinkled. "And this does nothing to help your state of mind, dear."

Wynne looked at the canvas. Rowen's dark eyes stared back at her. All of his strength. All of his fire.

The rest of the portrait still sat unfinished.

Wynne wasn't sure what had possessed her, but in the weeks after Rowen had left, she had been fanatical about capturing his eyes on the canvas before memory failed her.

And then she had put it away, covered, in the dark corner for months. Through spring breezes wafting the smell of lilacs into the room. Through summer birds tweeting outside the window. Through the first brisk wind that heralded the chill of fall.

Wynne's eyes stayed stuck on the canvas. "I am trying, your grace. But I have not been able to erase him. His presence…it lingers in this castle. On the grounds. His voice still echoes in the stables. He haunts me everywhere." She shook her head, sucking in a breath. "And his face when the blade hit his neck. He hates me."

The duchess's gloved hand landed lightly on Wynne's shoulder. "All the more reason to move on with Mr. Rookton, Wynne. Continuing to keep the duke in your thoughts does nothing but keep you in turmoil."

"And that is exactly why I cannot continue on with Mr. Rookton. It is not honest." She forced her eyes from the canvas to look up at the dowager. "You know what it is to deny your heart and marry another, your grace. Were you to go back in time—"

The duchess stiffened. "One cannot, so it does not need to be discussed, Wynne."

"But do you understand?"

"I do, dear." The duchess softened and patted her shoulder. "Would you like me to excuse your presence this evening?"

"No. I will talk to Mr. Rookton. He is a fine man, and it is my responsibility."

The duchess nodded, moving to the door, then paused. "Maybe a change of scenery would do you well, my dear? Give you a fresh start? I have been pondering going to London for the mini-season. I had thought to never go to London again. But I do feel stronger these days, Wynne. It is atrocious in the city with the heat, but the land is cooling now. It would be nice to show you London, and I have so many more connections there that would adore having their portraits done in your style."

Wynne's eyes flickered to the canvas. "London—is that where the duke is?"

"Yes. But there is no chance that you will cross paths. London is a very large city, my dear, and I will ensure it. The duke is quite busy running the holdings of the estate and, I am sure, with his horses. Will you accompany me?"

Did she want to be in the same city as Rowen? No.

But would she be one step closer to a ship headed for America? Yes.

And she truly needed to be far from this place. Far from the memories. Far from what happened to her mother. Far from this land that only sought to bring Rowen to her mind. Far from the stone walls that only kept a raw ache in her heart.

If she was to ever move on with her life, she needed first to leave Notlund. And then to leave England.

Slowly, Wynne nodded her head.

London it would be.

~~~

"I know this is the way of it, but I do find this disconcerting, how you have to stare at me."

Wynne laughed, leaning forward to smudge a purple with the knuckle of her pinky. "I am aware, my lady. But you are one of the first here in England to admit to such a thing. Most are quite happy to be gazed upon."

Lady Southfork chuckled. "I can imagine. This does seem quite enticing for a certain sort. But I would not be doing this were it not for the insistence of my husband."

"Your husband is quite right to want to capture you, Lady Southfork. You are beautiful." Wynne looked at Lady Southfork, only to see a deep blush had filled her face. Well, that wasn't natural. Wynne frowned. She couldn't paint the marchioness like that.

Wynne made a mental note—no more compliments for this one, even if they were true.

Wynne moved on to capturing the marchioness's dark glossy hair, pinned up, and trailing in a long curl over her bare shoulder. "Tell me about the children—that was why you had to exit our first session, correct? Children at an orphanage?"

The embarrassment instantly left Lady Southfork's face, leaving only an excited glow on her cheeks. Clearly this was a topic that the woman was passionate about. "It was. I do apologize I had to cut our first session so short. I oversee an orphanage, just a block away. The most precious children. Also the most precocious." She smiled with clear love in her eyes.

"There is far too often an injury that needs tending to. And I am the designated soother when I can be."

"I would like to visit the children with you, if you would show me?" Wynne asked.

The marchioness's hands clasped. "That would be wonderful. I have several little artists that would be so excited to meet you. But I warn you, they will have so many questions for you. I have not seen your work, but my husband has, and he was so impressed he requested this be done right away. So you must have extraordinary talent to create such enthusiasm in him."

It was Wynne's turn for a hot flush to fill her face. She took compliments no better than Lady Southfork. Her eyes dodged to the canvas.

It truly had been remarkable. She and the duchess had only been in London for three weeks, and Wynne was already juggling twelve separate portraits, so her days had been quite full, sitting with as many as three subjects on some days.

Part of Wynne knew it was too much, too many stories to keep track of, too many nuances that she would lose in the artwork. But the other part of her was eternally grateful for the extremely full schedule. It kept her mind centered on an area far away from Rowen.

Of all the twelve clients she currently had, she liked Lady Southfork the most. Not only was the woman a gorgeous subject to paint, but she also had depth of spirit that enhanced her beauty, rather than detracted from it. Wynne had already determined that Lady Southfork was an exception to the rest of the gentry that she had been introduced to so far.

Bristles sweeping the swoop of Lady Southfork's dark hair to Wynne's liking, she didn't notice the knock or the person that came into the drawing room until a woman's voice broke through her concentration.

"The milliner just finished them. I think they are fabulous."

Wynne looked up at the words, only to see a well-dressed woman holding an incredibly ornate mask in front of her face. Curved around the eyes, it exaggerated out wide, turning into a plume of tall, dark blue feathers. The woman handed a different mask to Lady Southfork.

"They are. Outrageous—and so much fun." Lady Southfork held up the mask to her face. "Does it work?"

The woman that had come in with the masks dropped hers from her face, assessing Lady Southfork. "It does."

Lady Southfork turned to Wynne. "Miss Theaton. Thoughts?"

Wynne chuckled. A splash of deep red feathers smoothed into Lady Southfork's dark hair. "Outrageous is an appropriate word. I imagine that is the goal? The red does an admirable job at setting off your features and dark hair. Whatever are they for?"

Lady Southfork pulled the mask from her face, flipping the front of it toward her and smoothing the feathers high. "It is a masquerade ball tonight. We hide behind masks. Such ridiculous pomp involved." She looked up to the woman standing next to her. "Duchess, may I introduce Miss Theaton? She is the incredibly talented artist my husband has been raving about. Miss Theaton, this is the Duchess of Dunway."

The Duchess of Dunway turned and gave Wynne the warmest smile. "I am honored to meet you, Miss Theaton. You have a number of advocates outside of this household as well— your name has come up in more than one conversation I have been privy to in the past few weeks. So you must have made some remarkable impressions."

Wynne shrugged, the blush returning to her face. "Thank you. I do not know that it is warranted, but I appreciate that it has kept my hands busy."

"It is a fickle crowd judging your skill, so your talent must be genuine," the duchess said. "I must add my husband to your list as well. If I can get him to sit still long enough for it, that is."

"I would be delighted, your grace," Wynne said.

"Duchess, do you have Miss Dewitt's mask as well?" Lady Southfork asked.

"I do." The duchess turned and unwrapped the white cloth she had placed on the settee next to Lady Southfork. She extracted another one of the feathered masks. "I thought to keep hers simpler, and that the multi-colors of it would set off the many shades of her hair. But I did ask to have the eyeholes larger with hers, so she could converse with the Duke of Letson in a more appropriate manner. She is so very close to a prop—"

Wynne's palette clattered to the floor, paint splattering everywhere.

Frozen, it took Wynne a moment to react to the two women staring at her in confusion. Wynne dropped to her knees, grabbing a rag to wipe the mess. She kept her head down, hiding her face. "I am so sorry. I have made such a mess. Please forgive me."

Wynne picked up the paint board, setting it on the small table next to her, and went back to wiping the floor. Never mind all the paint that had hit her own skirts, she was mortified at the mess on Lady Southfork's floor.

"It is not a bother, Miss Theaton. Accidents happen." Lady Southfork stood, ringing a bell, and then walked over to grab a rag as well, bending to help wipe the floors. "A maid will be here in moments. Do not look so frazzled. Truly, Miss Theaton. Your hands are shaking. It is just a little spilled paint, and certainly not the worst thing that has ever been dropped on these floors— especially with the troops of children so often running through here."

Wynne couldn't control her hands. Couldn't control her wild thoughts. "I—it is just that I have made such a mess. I apologize. Would it be possible to continue this in a few days' time? I have to—I must excuse myself."

"Of course." Lady Southfork grabbed her wrist. "Are you all right, Miss Theaton? Your hands are shaking even harder, and you have turned very pale."

Wynne shook her head, pulling her wrist free as she tried to wipe a wide streak of paint from the wood floor. "I will be fine. The paints just overwhelm at times. I will be fine with fresh air."

The concern didn't leave Lady Southfork's face. A maid appeared, quickly snatching the rags from both Lady Southfork and Wynne's hands, and taking over the cleaning.

Wynne stood, grabbing her leather satchel and her brushes. "Truly. Fresh air and I will be well. Please, send word when you will next be available and I will schedule all the others around it."

"Of course." Lady Southfork trailed her to the doorway. "Do feel better, Miss Theaton. I enjoyed our time today. And we will visit the children next time."

Once through the front door of the townhouse, Wynne leaned back on the door, taking a deep breath to fight her shaking body.

The dowager had said their paths would not cross.

She had promised.

Yet out of the blue. The Duke of Letson. Rowen.

Rowen courting a woman named Miss Dewitt.

Wynne did not think it possible, but in that moment, the remaining intact pieces of her battered heart shattered.

Maybe she hadn't been honest with herself. Maybe she had been nursing the smallest hope that in time, Rowen would come for her. Find her. Forgive her for what she did to him.

Her pride that had been so steadfast was waning. Her resolve against him—vanishing. No matter what he had done to her. No matter that he wanted her in his bed and nothing more.

Damn her wavering defenses. But she could not lie to herself. She still wanted him.

But he had moved on.

Ready to propose to a Miss Dewitt.

The possibility of Rowen—of someday—gone. Just like that. Gone.

A passerby at street level, cane twirling, stopped and looked up at her. Wynne realized she had been leaning on the Southfork's door, shaking, for some time.

Ignoring the stranger, Wynne hurried down the stairs to the sidewalk, her feet walking without thought. No destination, just as far away as possible from what she had just heard.

Three hours later, she looked up from her daze and saw the angle of the sun. She had long since missed her last appointment. More profuse apologies would be necessary.

In only three weeks, Wynne realized she had been lulled into this fascinating lifestyle here in London. The duchess had not only given her full rein to paint as much as she wanted to, but had introduced her to half of her current clients.

So Wynne got to paint daily. And she had met so many interesting, quirky people. She lived in the duchess's elegant townhouse. Had all of her basic needs met with the dowager's high standards for food and drink and clothes. The duchess had also taken Wynne to quite a few events—the theater, the opera, several dinners—always excited to show her artist-in-residence off to her friends.

Wynne had been lulled into luxury that wasn't hers. Not truly.

She needed to reset her mind to her goal. Getting on a ship to America. Removing herself from the slightest possibility that Rowen's name would be mentioned in front of her. Removing herself from repeating the suffering of the current chasm of pain in her chest.

Wynne looked around. She was in an area she wasn't familiar with. A variety of shops surrounded her—a bakery, tailor, milliner, furniture store, seamstress—all very elegant. Peeking into windows as she walked, Wynne knew she was still in an expensive area of the city. At least as far as the goods in the stores told her.

She walked several more blocks, searching the streets for something she recognized. The duchess always offered Wynne the carriage, but Wynne preferred walking to and from client's homes and had crossed many of the areas around this part of the city. So she knew it was only a matter of time before she recognized a familiar location.

It was then she saw it.

Wynne's feet jerked to a stop. Her heart, her breath, stolen. Staring out of the window right in front of her, those eyes. Her grandfather's eyes.

His portrait.

The first one she had done when she and her mother had settled into the house in Tanloon. She had missed him so much, and it was the best thing she could do to ease the sadness in her soul—paint him.

His face, larger than life, swallowing the canvas. His mountain behind him. The thin stick he was always chewing on. His beard, grey and bushy and out of control. The deep lines on his face. The smirk of mischief on his lips when he looked at her with a new challenge in mind.

The very portrait that had hung in their little Tanloon house. One of the portraits that had just disappeared. Disappeared just like her life. Just like her mother.

Her grandfather's portrait, now hanging in a window shop in London.

How in the triple-blasted hell had that happened?

Heart thundering, she took a step backward, desperate eyes taking in the shop. It looked to be a small art gallery.

Wynne rushed through the door.

The only one in the store, a clerk, quickly approached Wynne, the pretty lady's bosom half-hanging out of a tight corset with only a touch of lace keeping her modest. "Hello. I saw you admiring the art from outside. It is to your liking?"

Wynne barely heard the woman's words, as Wynne's attention had gone to the wall of paintings on her right. The weary lady doing laundry with four children hanging off her skirts. The burly blacksmith slamming a hammer, sparks flying and burning his skin. The weathered old man, drunk and half asleep at the tavern bar, ready to slip from the stool under him. The bar keep watching him with resigned pity.

Up and down the wall they went.

All paintings she had done, purely for her own pleasure, purely to capture the nuance of life in Tanloon.

All the paintings that had vanished.

Wynne turned to the clerk. "Who buys these?"

The lady smiled. "All sorts, miss. They have—"

Wynne shook her head, cutting the woman off. "I am sorry, I meant where do they come from?" She swept her hand along the wall in front of her paintings.

"Oh, as most of our paintings are, these particular ones are on discreet consignment."

"What does that mean?"

"It means they are being sold for a gentleman that I cannot name."

"A gentleman? Are you sure it is not a woman?"

The clerk tilted her head at Wynne, apologetic. "I am not at liberty to say."

"Why not?"

The clerk's smile had turned awkward, but stayed glued on her face. "Paintings that come through our shop are usually being sold for financial reasons—the owners need the money more than they need the art. I am sure you can understand why that would be devastating for reputations. Why do you ask, miss?"

Wynne nodded, more in control of herself after the initial shock had a moment to subside. "I apologize. That was rude of me to ask about others' affairs. It is just that I appreciate the form and collect."

"You must also partake?" The clerk pointed at Wynne's skirts.

Wynne looked down at her paint-splattered dress and apron. She hadn't even had the sense to remove her apron upon leaving Lady Southfork's home. "Yes. But I am just an amateur. It makes me appreciate the works of others even more."

Wynne turned from the woman and stepped closer to the wall that showcased much of her own art. Walking along the wall, her eyes flickered from one memory to another.

She stopped, her nose almost touching a painting. She knew this one well. It was from memory, also of her grandfather. Now it sat in a fine, fancy, gold-gilded frame.

Her grandfather sat next to the stream that ran a stone's throw from their house on the mountain. Whittling. Eyes downward, concentrating on the task.

Wynne reached out, tracing the air above the deep lines she had set along his face. She had to force herself to keep her fingers off the canvas.

"This one. When did this one come in?"

The clerk sidled Wynne, looking at the painting. "Yes, the Americas. The style is very much from there. This collection has been popular. I have sold five of them in the last month."

Wynne's head whipped to the lady, and then just as quickly back to the painting, trying to cover her reaction. She cleared her throat. "It is very interesting. I would like to tell my husband of it."

"Do you think your husband would be interested in purchasing it?"

Stepping away from the wall, Wynne nodded at the clerk. "I do. I will be sure to bring my husband in here soon."

"Splendid. I do look forward to working with you and your husband."

Offering up a weak smile, Wynne nodded and exited the shop, squashing her instinct that wanted to rip all of her paintings from the wall and run off with them.

Doing that would not get her any closer to the person who brought them here.

The person who would know what happened to her mother.

Blinded with rage, with shock, with disbelief, Wynne made her way down the street, stopping at the first stairs she could find.

She sank onto a step, trying to control the welling panic in her chest.

Her mother's blood flashed through her mind.

The swinging fire poker.

The terror.

Her cowardice.

Wynne's eyes squeezed tight against the fear that was about to overwhelm her.

Hell.

She needed to find Rowen.

{ CHAPTER 20 }

Past an iron fence she had to awkwardly pull herself over, Wynne slipped through the shrubbery at the back side of the deep gardens. Through the dark, she could see a ballroom glowing above the hedges, and now she just needed to work her way inconspicuously toward the bright building.

It hadn't been hard to find where the masquerade ball was to be held. The event was on everyone's lips—two of the duchess's friends had talked of nothing else during an earlier short visit—as masked balls apparently happened rarely in the mini-season.

Wynne brushed the twigs from the midnight blue silk of the gown she had borrowed from the dowager's wardrobe. Luckily, the duchess had an opera to attend that night, so that had left Wynne free for the evening.

Free to find Rowen.

But as Wynne looked at the many couples strolling about the gardens, and the many bobbing heads inside the ballroom, she was beginning to realize how impossible a task it was going to be to find Rowen in this mess.

She took a breath for fortitude. She still had to try.

Eyes demure on the brick path, gloved hands clasped in front of her, Wynne walked leisurely toward the ballroom, hoping this was the most direct path through the maze of evergreens.

She passed numerous couples coming and going, and she quickly realized her assumption that only half of the women would be wearing masks—and that she could blend right in—was terribly wrong. Everyone she encountered had masks firmly in place. Some were attached with ribbons behind the head, some were held up on little sticks.

So when she passed a stone bench with a rogue black mask attached to a stick just sitting there, forgotten, Wynne quickly glanced around, looking for an obvious owner. None around her were mask-less, and none seemed to take note of her.

Wynne decided stealing would have to be forgivable in this instance, and she did a slight dip by the bench. She slipped the stick into her fingers and buried it along her skirts until she was well removed from the bench.

Approaching the building, she saw identical marble staircases capping both ends of a long veranda and curving downward to the gardens. Wynne reached the shadows of the building and stopped by the right set of marble stairs leading upward, her stolen mask now firmly in place and covering the top half of her face.

A deep breath for courage, and Wynne started up.

Three steps up, and a dark figure on the other end of the gardens stormed out of the evergreen maze and caught Wynne's eye. She stopped, fingers gripping the gold gilded railing.

Hands balled into fists, the man was heaving, and had no mask on. It wasn't until he stopped at the bottom of the left stairs, turning around and crossing his arms over his chest that Wynne could clearly see his face.

Rowen.

Out of nowhere. Amongst hundreds of people. Rowen.

Her knees went weak and her grip tightened on the railing.

His darkness blended into the night—his dark hair, dark coat and trousers—the white cravat the only thing drawing attention. So fully the picture of an aristocrat. So completely not how she was used to seeing him in his simple white shirt, buckskin breeches, and well-worn tall black boots.

But he still held the rough handsomeness that had made her breath catch, time and again.

A man not to be approached. Everything about him screamed that.

Had he always been like that, and she had just never seen it?

Rowen's head went up, his eyes to the moon for a long moment. Then his chin dropped, his glare going to the evergreen hedge in front of him, his head shaking. But he did not move from his spot.

Whatever he was waiting for clearly had him vexed.

She couldn't possibly approach him now. He was already beyond annoyed, and the little painter from a half-a-year ago was not something he would want to deal with at the moment.

This was a mistake. She shouldn't have come.

The mask over her eyes bumped hard onto her nose, and Wynne realized her hand holding the stick was shaking uncontrollably.

Instantly irritated with herself, she sucked in a deep breath. Rowen was exactly why she had come here. And by the crazy grace of fate, he had appeared.

And now she was cowering? Questioning herself?

She was here for his help. He had said that would always be the case. Rowen would help her if she needed it. She had never thought she would need it, but she was wrong.

Time to swallow her pride and ask for that very thing.

Not trusting her legs, her hand tightened on the railing, and she took three backward steps down the staircase, her slippers landing on the cobblestone walk.

Just when she was about to release her death grip on the railing, a couple stepped out onto the veranda above Rowen and quickly descended the stairs. They stopped in front of Rowen, chatting with him. Wynne recognized the woman, the Duchess of Dunway, from earlier in the day, but could not hear what they talked about.

What started out as a pleasant chat soon turned animated, arms gesturing into the hedges and fingers pointing around the building.

Wynne stepped sideways into the deep shadows below the veranda, hopefully putting herself out of sight. She couldn't approach him with others around. She realized that now.

So what to do? Hide? Try to follow him? Knocking on the door of a bachelor was strictly off-limits according to the dowager—there was no surer way to ruin Wynne's reputation. Not that Wynne even knew where Rowen lived.

At that moment, a woman appeared from the same area of the hedges that Rowen had been in and approached the small group. Wynne couldn't see half of her face for the mask covering her eyes, but the half Wynne could see was beautiful.

Red-blond hair in an artful upsweep, she was lean with ample, creamy bosom floating above a deep scarlet gown. The woman chatted with the group, elegantly poised.

The way the woman smiled at Rowen, she could only be the Miss Dewitt that Lady Southfork had talked about.

A rush of wicked jealousy ran through Wynne. Rowen was hers to be smiling at. To be laughing with. And Wynne was having a hard time not running at the woman and knocking her down to the ground.

Wynne dropped her chin to her bare chest. She had to get a hold of herself. Rowen had moved on from her. Forgotten about her. She needed his help and knew she could ask for no more. Not after what she did to him. Not after calling him worthless.

She could have called him anything—called him the devil himself, swore at him up and down—and it wouldn't have mattered. But she had called him worthless. The one thing—the only thing—that was guaranteed to destroy any affection he did have for her.

Within a minute, Miss Dewitt, the Duchess of Dunway, and the man beside her left Rowen, walking off and skirting around the building. Rowen watched them leave, still standing at the base of the far-left stairs.

Alone again.

Wynne knew fate would not be granting her another chance at Rowen alone.

She stepped from the shadows, moving toward him in the glow of the light casting downward from the ballroom.

The movement caught Rowen's eye, and his head swiveled to her.

Scowl still on his face, Wynne braced herself and took several more steps toward him.

He just looked straight at her, scowl not budging. No reaction.

Wynne's heart sank. She had not dared hope for a smile, but she had hoped for at least the slightest eye crinkle of recognition.

The mask. The blasted mask still covered her face.

Her hand holding the mask dropped. The stick slipped from her fingers, falling to the ground.

Instant recognition, then disbelief flooded Rowen's features. "Wynne…"

Wynne stood, unable to move another step forward. Unable to do anything except open her mouth, a whisper escaping.

"I need you."

The three words reaching him, Rowen's eyes went from shock to burning heat. In the next instant he was to her, not stopping his stride as his arm wrapped around her body and he half picked her up, pushing her to the shadow of the veranda.

Before she could take a breath, Rowen's lips were on hers, harsh, crushing, demanding every nerve in her body submit to him.

Wynne's back hit the cold stone wall. Rowen did not stop, his hands running along her body, taking in every curve, his mouth taking possession of every sense she had.

It wasn't until she was drugged hazy by his touch, her body limp in his arms, that he pulled slightly back from her face. Supporting her lower back with his left arm, his right hand came up, capturing her face, his thumb under her chin, palm and fingers along her cheek.

"Do not leave me again, Wynne. Ever. I will do anything. Anything. Give you anything. Go anywhere. Do anything you need. Just do not leave me again."

Stunned, Wynne could only stare into his dark eyes. Eyes that were begging her. Eyes that needed her.

"Wynne."

Her mouth moved. "I need your help." The rehearsed words spilled out, for she had nothing else to draw upon.

It took a moment, and then realization set onto Rowen's features. His hand dropped from her face and he extracted his arm from behind her. Wynne fell backward, only the stone supporting her.

"You are...you are not here for...you did not find me for..." His voice came rough, forced.

The words, the pain in them, snapped Wynne's mind into working again.

"No." She shoved herself off the stone before he could turn away from her, grabbing his face in both of her hands, clasping him so he could look nowhere but at her. "Rowe, I have not caught up. I never imagined—I did not know that seeing you—"

Tears started to slide down her cheeks, the emotion so thick in her chest it overwhelmed. "After what I did to you. How I hurt you. My blade. My words. I was...I just needed to get away and I...I never meant..."

His arms went around her, grabbing her again, hard steel against all her regret.

Mouth on her ear, his breath sent shivers down her spine. "I know. I know you did not mean it, Wynne. I know. I ruined it—us—I only wanted to take care of you, and I did not think on what I was doing. What it would mean to you."

She turned her head, finding his mouth again. She needed him, needed him kissing her again, feeling her again—possessing her again—for this to be real.

Rowen needed no encouragement, and he opened his mouth to her, tongue diving, tasting her. Wynne instantly lost herself in him.

And the brutal truth hit her with a force she could not deny.

She had thought she was strong. Thought she was steadfast in her pride, even if it was waning. Steadfast in what she would not do for this man.

She was wrong. Wrong on all accounts.

It was painfully—gloriously—clear to her in that second. She would not deny him anything. Anything he asked, she would do.

She didn't hear the footsteps until Rowen drew up slightly from her, stopping the kiss. His breath still mingled with hers as he sheltered her from sight. The footsteps came closer, went past them, and receded.

He shook his head, his voice a ragged whisper. "Not here. This is impossible. There is too much to say."

He drew back further and Wynne opened her eyes to him. He stared at her, intensity still burning in his eyes.

"My home is only three blocks from here. We do not need my carriage. Come with me, Wynne. Please."

"Yes." She nodded before he finished, and his eyes closed in relief.

He grabbed her hand, moving them quickly along the pathway to the side street.

Within minutes, Rowen was ushering her up the back stairs to an enormous brick townhouse. Several lanterns were lit in the hallways, just enough to make it up the main staircase without stubbing a toe.

Hand still tightly gripping hers, Rowen glanced over his shoulder at her. "I do not keep the staff up late. I actually have little use of them, but they still need to be employed. So everything I can dream up they take care of in the daytime— which means this place is mostly empty at the moment, but I do not want to chance any gossip. I want you in my chambers— none would dare enter without my permission."

Wynne nodded, her eyes set so firmly on Rowen's profile they were not even noticing the surroundings.

Into a room near the top of the stairs, Rowen dropped her hand and went behind her, closing the door and locking it.

His hands slid over her shoulders from behind, his lips attacking the base of her neck. Skin tingling from scalp to toes, Wynne's hand went over her shoulder, grabbing Rowen head, holding him to her. She didn't want this to end. Didn't want any space, any air between them.

"I need to tell you things, Wynne." His words floated up to her as his hands slipped down to her breasts, his thumbs diving under the front of the gown to gain access to her nipples. "Things you need to know about me."

His thumbs circled her nipples in unison, and Wynne gasped for air, her body curling as shocks rippled down to her core.

She spun in his arms, her fingers fumbling free his jacket and cravat. "The only thing I need right now is you, Rowe. We will set all of this right. But I need you, now. I need you to make this real." She went to her toes, her eyes closer to his. "Now."

With a groan, his hands went behind her, working down the row of buttons on the back of the silk dress, slowly moving her backward. By the time they reached the bed, her gown, stays, and chemise had slipped off, and Rowen was dropping his trousers.

Naked, except for stockings held up by blue ribbons and her slippers, Wynne stood, breathless, staring at Rowen's chest, his body, just as he stared at her—hungry. Hungry and wanting nothing more than the taste of his skin under her tongue, the feel of his heartbeat on her chest.

Hands at his sides, fingers twitching, his dark eyes met hers, the silver flecks glowing. "Are you sure, Wynne? Sure of me? Trust me?"

"Blindly."

He winced.

"With my eyes wide open." Her heart twisted—that he even had to ask her that. That he even had to wonder if she still trusted him.

Her hands went to his chest, fingertips curling along his warm skin. "I am yours, Rowe. I never stopped. Yours. I will never leave you again."

His mouth found hers, and he sent them to the bed, legs tangled, his hands roaming her body, finding her core. His fingers deep in her flesh, he flickered, readying her.

She didn't need it. Already more than open for him and straining for release, she caught his face in her hands. "Now, Rowe. Now."

He slammed into her, discovering all that had been lost, and all Wynne had thought never to have again. Within minutes—too soon—she was pitching under him, writhing, begging for release.

She tried to slow, attempted to relish the feel of him deep within her, his fingers on her body, his mouth on her chest. But this was too necessary, too guttural for anything other than Rowe in her hard and fast and making her his.

Fighting her own body, she shuddered with force, screaming, nails digging into his back as her legs clenched around him. She refused to release him, keeping him throbbing far within her as her body spasmed around him.

Shocks still vibrating through her muscles, she embraced each twitch of her body, holding tight to the blinding blackness.

"More."

Her eyes fluttered open to his chest, still unfocused, still reeling from the aftershock. "Hmmm?"

She looked up, only to see Rowen still hovering over her, still straining against release.

His eyes focused in on her.

"You have more in you, Wynne."

"What?"

"You have more in you." His lips went to her ear, his breath hot on her skin. "You will come for me again, Wynne. Now."

She could not answer him, only nod her head.

She didn't think it possible to even move in that moment. But if Rowen said she could, she believed him.

He pulled almost out of her, flipping them on the bed. Pushing her shoulders upright, Rowen grabbed her knees and set her in full straddle above him. His palms went to her hips, and he lifted her, sliding her slowly onto him.

Thrusting from below, Rowen held her steady against the blows, and she rode, fingertips going to his chest, grasping muscles for stability.

Within moments her body reawakened, turning to fire, and she took over the gyrations, drawing Rowen long and slow, then fast, not letting him escape from her depths.

Growling against her onslaught, against his body demanding release, Rowen held on, his thumb sliding into Wynne's folds, plying her until her body pitched against him with desperate violence.

Unable to hold on, she could feel him expand, filling her completely as he exploded deep within her. It sent her over the edge of sanity, releasing a current so powerful it ripped through her body, driving her past screaming.

She collapsed onto him, weak, lost in darkness with flashes of light flickering through her mind.

His arms wrapped her, holding her to this world.

Holding her to the reality she had never thought to have again.

{ CHAPTER 21 }

On top of him, Wynne's skin still twitched, and Rowen's hand trailed up and down her spine, counting the bumps, relishing the feel of her under his fingers. Her full weight on his body.

He could stay this way for a thousand years. Sweaty and sated and wrapped up in this woman that could wreck him with the merest breath.

Without any effort, most of her blond hair had fallen from the pins holding it up, a now wondrous haphazard crown that tickled his chest. Wynne turned her head, nuzzling her nose into his neck.

"Your skin—the smell, the feel of it—I had held onto the memory of it, but my memory did not do it justice," she murmured into his neck. "I tried so hard, but I was never able to convince myself I did not need this. Need you."

He turned his head, kissing the top of her head, inhaling. Still sweet honey. "Wynne, do you realize you should not trust anyone like that?"

"Like what?"

"Blindly."

He could feel her smile into his neck. "Not even you?"

Rowen's hold tightened around her back. "I know how much I could hurt you. Did hurt you. You should not give that power to anyone, Wynne."

"Do you not know by now that you cannot control my emotions, Rowe?" Her head popped up, and she pushed herself to hover over him, her face above his. "You ask for my trust, but then tell me I should not trust you? I love you, Rowe, and I have to trust you to do that. I have to give up all that power. Give it to you. I give you my trust, because you asked, and I believe to the depths of my soul that you will not hurt me." She shook her head in awe. "I did not know that very fact until I saw you tonight."

"You did not?"

"Part of me did, I am sure. But I refused to acknowledge it fully. I knew my heart never healed—knew that you would always haunt my dreams. But I did not know upon seeing you that it would be so raw—that I would give up anything to be with you again. Anything. I would. Mistress or not. My soul going to hell or not. At Notlund, I did not know about your world—I did not know that this was how it was done here in England. My grandfather taught me how to survive in the woods—on a mountain. Not how to survive in a society like yours."

He brushed a blond tendril free from her left eye. "What are you talking about, Wynne? How what was done?"

"That you cannot marry a commoner. I must be your mistress. And you must marry and have children solely for the title."

Rowen shot upright and Wynne slid down, landing on his thighs. He grabbed her shoulders. "What? What on earth? Who told you that?" He growled. "Wait. I know exactly who told you that."

Wynne's eyes went wide. "What do you mean?"

"I mean it is not usual for a duke to marry a commoner—but I am not usual, and neither are you." His hands moved up, cupping her face. "I mean to marry you as soon as humanly possible, Wynne. I am not going to ever give you the chance to leave me again."

"What? You can? You are?"

Rowen could see her mind reeling.

"But what about the woman—Miss Dewitt? Lady Southfork said you were to propose, and I saw her tonight, and she is beautiful."

"You know Lady Southfork?"

"I am painting her. That is how I knew where to find you."

"And you saw Miss Dewitt? What did you hear?"

"Nothing. I saw her by the stairs with you. I was watching you while you were waiting there—is that why—did you propose and then she spurned you?" Wynne pushed away at his chest. "Oh no—am I consolation, Rowe? I saw how mad you were."

He grabbed her wrists, pulling her back toward him. "What you saw was me questioning what the hell I was doing. Everything was wrong about it. So very right on the surface, the veneer of it. I did not want to move on from you, Wynne, but I knew I had to, no matter how hollow. And she reminded me of you. And I was lying to myself."

"So you did ask her?"

"Yes. But she, luckily, did not commit, so I can end it with minimal drama."

"Do you like her?"

"Yes. She is a good woman."

A flicker of fear ran through Wynne's hazel eyes. "More than me?"

"No. Hell, no. I like her because she is a good soul. A friend." His hands went down to her backside, lifting her toward him until her chest was touching him. "Make no mistake, she is not you, Wynne. You are the only one I want."

"Truly?"

"Do not vex me, Wynne. I never want you to question me again on this particular topic. It is you. You and only you. And I will not let you change the topic from marriage." He kissed her, tasting her lips, still plump from his earlier onslaught. "That is, if you will have me as your husband. I should have demanded this that day at Notlund. I never should have left. Never should have left you that note."

"So why did you?"

Rowen sighed. "I have some things to tell you, Wynne. Things that could ruin me. Ruin what you think of me." He paused, not wanting to continue. But Wynne deserved to know the truth. The truth about what could happen. "You should know before we marry. You may…"

"What? Change my mind? Not want you? Not love you? Impossible."

Half in avoidance, half because goose bumps still dotted Wynne's arms, Rowen lifted her, moving forward until his legs dropped off the bed, and then he set Wynne beside him. "Let me stoke the fire."

She did not let him escape that easily and pulled the coverlet free from the bed to wrap it around her as she trailed him to the fireplace. She sat on the arm of a leather chair by the hearth, her now bare legs dangling.

"What is it, Rowe? Tell me."

Rowen poked at the embers and flipped a log, contemplating.

Wynne could very well decide to walk out of his life after this, and he had to prepare himself for that real possibility. Could he really let her go if that was what she chose to do—if she looked at him with disgust?

A few more embers nudged, and Rowen set the heavy iron poker next to the fireplace and faced Wynne.

It was back in her eyes. Complete trust.

He swallowed hard.

"Do you recall, long ago, when I made mention that I never should have existed?" he asked, voice heavy.

Wynne nodded.

"I am a bastard, Wynne."

"What?" She went to her feet, her face growing pale.

"The man who truly sired me was the duke. My mother was his mistress for many years, even before he married the dowager. The duke convinced his younger brother to marry my mother to give me a legitimate lineage. But even with that, the marriage happened a day too late. I was already born. Born a bastard. So they lied. Everyone lied."

Rowen took a deep breath, trying to force the words quickly, hoping it would be less painful that way. "But I know the truth, who my true father is. How I was born. The dowager knows the truth. It is why I left. She threatened to tell you if I stayed, and

I could not face that. How you would look at me if you knew the truth. I am as the duchess has always said. Worthless. If the world knew, I would lose everything—no claim to the title, to the estates, to the holdings. Everything."

Wynne's hand flew over her mouth and her head dropped, her face hidden.

Rowen watched in silence as her shoulders started to shake, tears dropping from her eyes and soaking into the coverlet wrapped about her chest.

Rowen hardened. "Do not hide from me, Wynne."

He stepped forward, grabbing her shoulders. "Show me your damn eyes, Wynne. You will not hide from me."

Her face whipped up to him, head shaking and voice bitter. "How could you even think…even think I would care, Rowe? I never wanted a duke. Never wanted a title. I wanted you, Rowe. I wanted the man. The man who owns my heart. Never anyone—anything more."

"Wynne—"

She jerked her shoulders away from his grasp, jumping up and stepping backward. "Dammit, Rowe—I trusted you with everything—everything of me, and you could not trust me with this. You left me instead of trusting me."

He didn't afford her any space, closing the gap between them. "I did not trust myself, Wynne. I did not trust what I knew of you—who you are. Not until it was too late."

The tears stained her cheeks, not yielding. "Do you not understand how this hurts me?"

He could see. He saw very well the pain in her eyes. Pain he put there. "I never wanted you to know, Wynne. Never wanted to take the chance that you would look at me like that. Like you are. With disgust."

"Hell, yes, I'm disgusted, Rowe. But I do not care a wit about who your father was. You did not trust me with the truth—I gave you all of me—every damn piece of me—and you could not do the same."

The realization of her words sank in. Rowen took another step forward, trapping her to the chair. No escape. "You do not care?"

"What?"

"I am a bastard, Wynne. I could lose everything if it was revealed. The title. The homes. The money. All respect."

Unable to move past him, her arms crossed over her chest as a last line of defense. "Yes, I heard—you already said that."

"And you do not care? You do not care that I am a bastard?"

"No." Her chin jutted out at him, her eyes rolling. "Dammit, Rowe, listen to me. I am furious with you. Beyond angry with you. And you are asking me if I care about your parents? Hell, no. I will say it again and maybe you will hear it. Hell, no."

Rowen wrapped his arms around her, his mouth finding hers. She did nothing but struggle against the kiss. His head pulled back, but he kept her captive in his arms.

"I am still mad at you."

Rowen covered her lips again, taking all of her rage. Gladly taking all of it.

He gave her room for a breath.

She squirmed in his arms, glaring up at him. "Still mad."

"I know." He kissed her again, smiling to himself. She struggled less this time.

He stopped, meeting her livid look.

"Still. Mad." The glare did not leave her eyes.

"I do not care, Wynne. Be mad at me all you want. You do not have a knife to my neck. I know you are not going to leave me."

"My knife on your neck—that is the bar of how you judge my anger?"

Rowen shrugged. "It preceded the worst thing that has ever happened to me—you leaving—so yes, as long as your knife stays off my body, I am happy to have your glare on me. Just as long as your eyes are on me."

She harrumphed. "Did you consider that it is just that I do not have my knife with me?"

Rowen laughed, brushing back a wild curl from her forehead. "I love you, Wynne."

Her arms loosened in front of her, her face softening. "Do not misunderstand—I am going to be mad at you for a stretch of time." She stared at him, a devilish twinkle taking hold over the ire in her eyes. He could tell it was begrudgingly, but her arms slipped around him.

"But that—those words—are so much better from your lips, Rowe, than in a damn note. Say it again."

"I love you, Wynne."

~ ~ ~

The polite rap on the door made Rowen tear his eyes away from Wynne's sleeping face. He had kept her up far too long last night—hell, she had kept him up far too long last night, and now it was late morning.

Good thing the door was still locked.

The rap sounded again, this time more insistent.

Wynne flopped sideways on the bed, throwing her arm over his chest and her leg over his thighs. No need to keep quiet at this point, since the knocking wasn't about to disappear.

"Yes?" Rowen bellowed in the general direction of the door.

"I am sorry to wake you, your grace, but there is a young lady, a Miss Dewitt, who is in the front drawing room," Rowen's steward said, his voice muffled by the heavy oak door. "She has a chaperone, of course, and has insisted on seeing you. She has refused to leave until doing so. What shall I do with her, your grace?"

Blast it.

Miss Dewitt. He had to break it off with her. He just hadn't planned on doing so this very moment. Not when his plans had been to ravage Wynne again the second her eyes opened.

Instead, Wynne sat up, her palm flat on the divot in his chest and a worried look on her face. "Miss Dewitt—she is the one you were to marry?" Wynne asked in a whisper.

"Possibly marry, yes. And you can remove the worry from your eyes. You need to trust me, Wynne." Rowen kept his own voice low—no need for anyone but him to know Wynne was in here. "The first thing I had planned to do today was visit the offices of the Archbishop to arrange for a special license. We can marry with that within a few days, but you will need to stay with the duchess until then so there is no scandal—that is, did you actually agree to marry me last night? Now that I think on it, I never received an answer from you."

She thwapped his chest, smirking. "Yes. More than happily. And considering where my lips were on your body last night, I had better marry you."

Rowen chuckled, grabbing her wrist and bringing it to his mouth. A simple kiss on her palm turned into her forefinger slipping into his mouth, and he sucked, wicked gaze on Wynne.

"Your grace?"

A muttered blasphemy, and Rowen turned his head to the door. "Tell Miss Dewitt I will be down in five minutes." He sat up, setting Wynne's hand in her lap as his voice dropped. "And you will not move. I plan on finishing that thought I just put into your mind when I return. Then I will need to sneak you out of here so your reputation remains intact."

"Devil."

"Yes, well, I lived nothing but an upstanding life before I met you, my dear Wynne."

{ CHAPTER 22 }

Never had Wynne endured such an excruciating hour as the one spent in Rowen's bedroom, waiting for him to return from his almost-betrothed.

She felt awful for Miss Dewitt—Wynne had already lived through her heart being crushed when Rowen left her, so she could easily imagine what was happening in the drawing room. But the woman was beautiful, and from what Rowen had said, she was a good person, so Wynne was certain Miss Dewitt would move on successfully and lead a wonderful life—with someone other than Rowen.

But the longer the seconds ticked by, Wynne's pity for Miss Dewitt could not help but mix with a touch of jealousy—and doubt. During the past weeks, it had been Miss Dewitt smiling at Rowen, laughing with him, staring at his face—his eyes.

Wynne paced Rowen's room, the dark blue sheet from the bed draped around her. He had made the decision to move on with his life—move on with Miss Dewitt. What if in merely talking to her, he was having misgivings? What if he looked at her beauty and decided he would rather look at that face for the remainder of his life, instead of Wynne's? What if she demanded he not retract his proposal, and he had to marry her? She scanned her mind—was that what the duchess had said often happens in the peerage? Scandal and then marriage? The duchess had told her so much of this world Rowen lived in, but Wynne now realized the dowager's truths were somewhat suspect.

Her feet wore an even quicker path on the bedroom boards. She was quickly finding that the trust Rowen asked of her was difficult when the devil awoke and wormed around in her mind.

The doorknob turned and Wynne flew to the leather chair by the fireplace, landing and tucking her feet under her before Rowen had the door ajar.

Breathless, she feigned calm patience, but Rowen took one look into her eyes, and laughed. He closed the door, locking it.

"You can remove the worry from your eyes. I told you to trust me." Holding what looked like a tan muslin dress draped over his forearm, he looked about the room. "What have you been doing, pacing?"

Wynne's eyes narrowed at him. The man still saw far, far too deep into her mind, which wasn't particularly fair. "How did your meeting with Miss Dewitt go?"

"Amusing, actually."

Her eyebrow arched.

Rowen stared at her, silent.

She jumped to her feet, grumbling. "And you are drawing this out merely to get my hackles askew."

"Punishment for not trusting me."

"Tell me this instant." She poked the bit of his bare chest that showed in the V of his shirt. "How was it amusing? And do not tell me that you find breaking hearts amusing—you are a far better man than that."

"Amusing, because she was here only to tell me that we are to part ways. She is to marry the Earl of Clapinshire in a few days."

"Truly? So you broke no heart?" Wynne shifted the sheet around her, clasping it with one hand, while her free hand went to her hip. "You did not mention me at all, did you? You just let her suffer through all the unseemliness of it."

Rowen shrugged. "I was gracious in my acceptance of her rebuff of me."

"What a weasel, you are."

He smirked. "It was fortunate—I will not deny that. And Miss Dewitt started in right away, so by the time I could interject, it would have just mucked up the conversation. She will find out soon enough that we are to marry."

"I like that she is to marry another," Wynne said. "It takes away my guilt."

"If anyone should feel guilt it is me. I pursued her when I had no business doing so—and I see that so clearly now. I cannot imagine if I had married her and then you suddenly appeared. A torture like no other. I owe fate unending gratitude for not allowing that to happen."

He shook his head, dismissing the thought. "Here, I brought you one of the duchess's dresses that were still in her wardrobe. It should fit you fine and will get you through the streets without suspicion. You do not need the attention that gown from last night would garner at this time of day."

Sighing, Wynne took the dress from his arm, walking over to the bed to drop the sheet and gather her chemise. She knew Rowen was politely ushering her to the door—it was now late morning, and she knew as well as he that if she didn't show up at the dowager's house soon, her whereabouts would be questioned.

She could feel Rowen's eyes burning into her naked body, but he stayed by the door. A gentleman, even if Wynne wanted him very much not to be so.

"Does the dowager note your whereabouts?"

The shift dropped over her head. "No, and I am often away at clients' homes in the morning when she wakes up. So if I arrive there soon, I do not think there will be any suspicion. You will have to give me directions from here to there, though."

"I hate that you have to go back to her, even if it is only for a few days. You will have to keep our wedding a secret from her until the day of."

"Why?"

Rowen shrugged. "I guarantee she would find a way to ruin us."

Wynne picked up the dress, pausing to look at Rowen. "Why did you even take the title, Rowen? For all the angst that comes with it—why?"

"Revenge." He did not flinch with the word. "I will not hide that fact. And it was easier to take the title than come up with an explanation to deny it that did not involve discussions of my birth. But truly, it was revenge. At least at first."

"Against the duchess?"

"Yes."

"So why do you not just leave it all? You do know I will go with you anywhere, live however you would like, if you wish to abandon the title. It does not matter to me." She smirked at him. "I would be happy to teach you how to live on a mountain—live off the land."

Rowen chuckled. "That may be interesting, someday. But the title, since it has become mine, it has evolved into so much more than revenge to me. I am the last in the line. The last."

"What does that mean?"

"It means the duchy dissolves—the title, the estate, goes back to the crown without me. And even though I never respected the duke, my father, I do respect the history of the title, no matter what the duchess has told you. It has become important to me to continue it—to change the trajectory of the power—I can do such good with it. Good that can change the legacy of the title. What it stands for. Even if the duchess would prefer that I fail miserably."

Wynne sighed as she slinked into the dress. Rowen still thought the worst of the dowager. Moving to him and turning, she lifted her hair so he could help her with the buttons. The muslin dress was serviceable—she would benefit from proper stays, but it would have to do for the moment.

"Rowe, did you know the dowager was in love with your father—the man that married your mother? But as the younger brother, he did not have high enough status, and her family demanded she marry the duke instead?"

Rowen's hands paused, his knuckles brushing her spine.

She looked over her shoulder at him. His jaw was clenched, but Wynne continued on—Rowen needed to know this story, needed to understand. "So she married the duke for the title, even though she loved his younger brother."

"Why are you telling me this, Wynne?"

"So you know why I do not hate her. That there is more to who she is."

Rowen's hands were still not moving, so she turned to him.

"It became so clear to me last night. Did you know the duchess lost her second baby just weeks before you were born? That you—her husband's child—lived, but her own baby did not? She was beyond devastated and grieved for years, Rowe. You were the child that should have been hers. And then, not only did your mother first marry the man the duchess truly loved, but after he died your mother came into Notlund and continued to be the duke's mistress. Right in front of the duchess. The duke never touched the duchess again after she lost the baby."

"Do not make excuses for the dowager, Wynne." Rowen's voice stayed in check, but there was clear anger in it.

"You were innocent, Rowe. I know that. And so young, you were caught in the frays of vicious anger and injustice when the duchess could not control herself. I do not defend that—what she did to you, how she treated you was so very wrong—deplorable."

Wynne grabbed both of his upper arms. "But I can imagine. I can imagine if I had to watch you marry another. I would hate the woman. I would—to the depths of my soul. I felt a modicum of it moments ago when you were downstairs with Miss Dewitt— and that was just my imagination running wild. And then if that woman came into my house and I knew she was my husband's mistress. That she could have his baby where I could not. I would have difficulty with that, whether I liked my husband or not. To lose a baby. I would go a little insane. Do things that I would never dream of doing."

"Like crush a little boy."

Wynne's chest clenched. Even in Rowen's few words, his pain reverberated from a deep trough within, and it broke her heart. "Yes. She did that. And for that part of her life—what she did to you—I will always hate her for those actions. But she was also there for me these many months, Rowe. Exceedingly generous with her time, with her home, with her love. After my

grandfather, mother, and then you—I was alone, Rowe. Alone.
And she helped me through all of that brutal, searing loneliness."

Jaw throbbing, Rowen's eyes swung from her face to stare at
the fireplace. Long moments passed before he looked back to her.
"It should have been me that got you through that, Wynne."

"But it was not. It was her." Her hands dropped from his
arms. "The duchess did that for me. Can you understand why
I cannot hate her like you do? I know a completely different
person."

He shook his head. "Can we stop? I do not wish to hear
about the virtues of the dowager."

Wynne studied his face. He was trying very hard not to
explode. That, she could see.

She turned around, lifting her hair once more. "Will you
finish buttoning me, please?"

His fingers worked the buttons upwards.

"Wynne..."

"Hmm?"

"You are mad."

"No." She took a deep breath. "Just sad. I do not want you to
have to harbor that anger. I do not want your body to tighten at
her name. I do not want your thoughts consumed with destroying
her. Her bitterness—she shoved it upon you, and it became yours.
And I just want you to be free of it."

He finished the buttons and she dropped her hair, turning to
him again. Her hand went softly to his cheek. "Rowe, you are a
man that is so much more. The man I love. I only want for you to
have peace with something you had no way to control."

"You ask too much of me, Wynne."

Her head shook gently. "No, I do not ask it of you—I only
wish it for you. I did not suffer what you did, so I cannot truly
understand. And I do not wish to take any of your anger at her
away—only you can decide that."

His hand went over the back of hers, and he turned his head,
kissing her palm.

With the simple motion, Wynne recognized Rowen's limit had been reached, and the conversation was done for the moment.

Her hand slid from his face, and she went to get her slippers. Hopefully, she could get into the dowager's townhouse and change before the duchess caught sight of her.

Rowen stayed in his spot, watching her. "When I was talking with Miss Dewitt, it reminded me of what you said last night when I first saw you—that you needed me—what was that about?"

Wynne gasped, hand over her mouth. "I—all of this—I forgot to tell you. My paintings."

"Your paintings?"

Slippers secure, she went back to Rowen, her words tumbling. "Yes. I saw them—the ones that were in my home in Tanloon. Ones I painted here in England. They are here in a shop—a gallery. They are for sale. I saw them yesterday—it was why I found you. Why I needed you."

"Are you sure they are yours?"

"Of course, yes." Her eyes rolled. "I know my own paintings, Rowe. Two are of my grandfather."

"So you inquired about them?" Rowen's voice was cautious.

"Yes. The clerk—a woman—did not share the name of who they came from. She said they are all consignment and that the sellers need to remain discreet." Wynne couldn't keep her voice from being frantic. "It is a trail Rowe—a trail. She would not tell me anything, but I hoped you could help—help me figure out a way. The gallery is on Bond Street. If we went back there together and if we could find out who is selling them, then maybe…"

"Maybe you will find you mother's killer?"

"Yes." Wynne flipped away the thought with her hand, her voice turning excited. "Or what if I was crazy and I did have the wrong town? The wrong house? And my mother is alive, and she could not find me, and she brought them here, and she is selling them? What if she is alive?"

Rowen's face darkened. "Wynne—"

"No. Do not say it." Her arms crossed over her chest. "It is possible. Possible that she is here. I was addled—my memory knocked out of me—what if she is alive and is here?"

He moved a step closer, his hands clamping down on her shoulders.

She stilled at his touch, then squirmed, trying to get out of his hold. She didn't want to hear what he was going to say. Didn't want him to crush her hope. Not hope that she needed.

His grasp tightened on her.

No escape.

But she didn't need to look at him.

"Wynne, that was the right town. When we went back there—Luhaunt and I—those people were hiding something, protecting someone. There was no doubt, Wynne. Your mother…" His hands moved upward, cupping her face and forcing her gaze to his. "This is dangerous, Wynne. I did not tell you before at Notlund, but this is dangerous. And even more dangerous now that your paintings have appeared. I do not want you going back into that shop."

"But if she is alive—"

"No." The word came out sharp, biting. "She is not alive, Wynne. I will go. Alone. I will find out all I can. But I cannot protect you like I need to until we are married. So I will find out everything I can, and I will tell you everything I learn. But you need to stay away from that shop. Trust me, Wynne."

"I do trust you. But she could be alive, Rowe—you have to see possibility of it. Who else would have my paintings? I told the clerk—"

"I do not care what you told the clerk." His hands dropped down to her shoulders, fingers squeezing. "Your mother is not alive, Wynne. Do not go in there again."

"But if she is alive—I cannot abandon her again, Rowe." She grabbed his wrists, pleading. "You have to understand. I left her once—I will not be weak again."

"No. She is gone, Wynne."

Frustrated tears welled. "Is this what marriage will be like—you will disregard me, not believe me?"

"If it means your safety, Wynne, then yes, this is exactly what it will be like."

She shook her head, eyes narrowing at him. He didn't believe her mother could be alive—and if he didn't believe in that possibility, how could he truly follow a trail to her?

"Swear to me you will not go in there, Wynne."

She twisted out of his hands, moving backward. "I need to get back to the dowager's home. Can you tell me the general direction?"

"Wynne—"

She stepped around him, going for the door. Not quick enough, he grabbed her wrist. Her other hand on the doorknob, she looked over her shoulder at him.

Glaring at her, Rowen said nothing, but she could feel his anger throbbing in his hand.

Wynne met his glare with her own, rage exploding.

Stare at her all he wanted, she wasn't going to swear a thing about her future actions.

If Rowen didn't believe her mother could be alive, then he was not the person to go into that shop. Of that, she was certain.

Muttering an incoherent blasphemy, she yanked her wrist free, opening the door. "I will figure how to get home myself, then."

Down the stairs and out the front door in a fury, she didn't care if she was seen by his staff. Didn't care if there was a scandal. She just needed to leave his presence before she spewed something she would regret.

Into the sunlight, her head swiveled, looking for direction. Nothing familiar, so she randomly turned left and stomped down the street.

Dammit.

Rowen asked for her to believe in him, to trust him. And she did.

So why couldn't he do the same for her?

{ CHAPTER 23 }

Wynne fingered the folded note in her apron. Walking down the sidewalk, her eyes stayed trained on the ground.

She had just left Lady Southfork's home after a cancelled sitting appointment. Lady Southfork had been entirely gracious, apologizing profusely for not getting word to Wynne sooner that she had a surprise wedding to attend to that day and would not have time for a sitting.

Not that Wynne was in much of a mood for painting. For two days she had heard nothing from Rowen—not one word—until this note appeared in her leather satchel with her paintbrushes.

How he had gotten the note in there without her knowing was annoying, and then the actual note—hastily scribbled—was beyond frustrating.

Wynne—
The ceremony will take place tomorrow at 11 in the morning. I will come for you at the dowager's home. —Rowen

That was all. No news about the art gallery—if he even visited the place. No endearments. No love. Just another order.

An emotionless order.

This was the man she was going to marry? For all that he had been everything she ever needed him to be the night of the masquerade ball, his actions since then left a lot to be desired.

Toe stubbing hard on a cobblestone as she crossed the street, she hopped, shaking the pain from her foot and swearing at herself. She stopped at an iron fence lining the front of a townhouse, leaning on it as she lifted her foot to rub her big toe through her boot.

She shook her head, taking a deep breath.

Of course she was going to marry Rowen. She loved him. Down to her blasted toe that was throbbing. Even if his current actions were driving her mad. Even if he was still so clearly mad at her as well.

But for two days—even though it had irked her to do so— she had stayed away from the gallery that held her paintings. Solely to appease Rowen's request, whether he knew it or not.

But this note—no information on the shop, no information on if he had even gone there himself, on if he had even seen her paintings or questioned anyone.

Not a word.

And her mother could very well be here, in London. Still alive and still missing her daughter. Alive and able to see her daughter wed.

Wynne sighed, eyes closed and face to the sky. A mistake, as Rowen's face instantly popped into her mind. His face when he demanded she stay out of that shop. The exact same look as was on his face when he was pulling Wynne away from her landlady in Tanloon.

She had seen it in his eyes in Tanloon, and she saw it again that morning in his bedroom—it was a look that questioned her sanity. A look of trying to protect Wynne from herself.

But why shouldn't he question her sanity? She still couldn't remember what happened during the days in the woods. The landlady didn't recognize her. There was no evidence of her living in that Tanloon home. So why should Rowen look at her like she was sane?

Maybe she wasn't.

Ever since Tanloon, she could not help but question her own sanity—her own memories at every turn.

Maybe she had imagined her paintings in that shop. Maybe that was what Rowen was trying to protect her from. Herself.

Eyes opening, she squinted in the midday sun, hazy behind a bank of clouds. She looked around. She was only six blocks from the art gallery. She could walk by. Quickly. Just to prove to herself

she wasn't crazy. Walk by and not go in. Rowen had asked—
demanded—she not go into the shop. He had said absolutely
nothing about walking by the shop.

She started off.

Minutes later, her footsteps slowed as she approached the
gallery. She could see it before she was even in front of the shop,
the empty space where the painting of her grandfather had been.

Hell. She was crazy.

Her steps quickened.

She had planned just a casual walk-by. Just a glance. But the
glaring empty spot in the window made her stop right in front of
the store, staring inward, searching.

Maybe they had just moved the painting. Her eyes scanned
the interior walls.

None of her paintings were hanging. Lots of empty wall
spaces, but not a single one of her paintings. There were at least
twenty displayed the other day, and now, none.

She pressed her nose on the glass, cupping her hands around
her eyes to cut the glare of the day on the glass.

Nothing. Not one painting from the other day.

Her chest tightened in panic. She hadn't truly believed she
was crazy. But now. Now everything she had thought she'd seen
had disappeared.

Maybe she was mistaken about the shop. She stepped back
from the window, looking at the storefront—it was the same as
she remembered.

Nose to the window again, she scanned the interior, looking
for the clerk from the other day. Had she imagined her as well?
Wynne didn't see her inside, only two men standing, facing the
now mostly empty wall of paintings.

In discussion, one of the men kept motioning to the empty
spots on the wall, pointing.

Wynne could only see their profiles, but it was quite clear
one of them was of lower class, his clothes a mess and slightly
dirty around a round belly, with long, stringy hair pulled back
in a low ponytail. The other man was dressed impeccably, fine

tailored coat, crisp cravat, and neat trousers. The man's neat brown hair did not move as he talked, frozen into place somehow.

Watching them for a moment, Wynne debated about going into the shop to ask them about the clerk. Maybe she was on a short errand, and would be back soon. If Wynne could talk to her, maybe the clerk could tell her what she really had seen the other day. Maybe she could calm Wynne's panic.

The finely tailored gentlemen glanced out the window, and his eye caught sight of Wynne. He paused for a moment, staring at her.

His full face to her, it took Wynne a long second to place that she knew him.

But then recognition hit her, and Wynne's legs almost buckled.

The man from Tanloon.

The poker. The man that had chased her. Killed her mother.

Wynne pushed back from the window, stumbling, her satchel falling forward across her chest. Staggering down the street, she fumbled to open the flap on her bag. Her hand went in, searching for her knife.

A quick glance over her shoulder. He was behind her, running after her, pushing people out of his way.

Wynne swallowed a scream and sped, knife in hand.

Two blocks she sprinted, dodging people in the street, and then she spied a cross street that led to Carnaby Street. If she got there, her paint supplier had a shop just up the block. Safety. Wynne cut the corner, running up the side street.

She could see it in front of her, the busy thoroughfare, people to put between her and that man. Just a few steps further.

Fingertips ripped into her shoulder, yanking her backward at that moment and spinning her sideways into an alleyway she hadn't even seen.

She slammed into a brick wall, her upper arm taking the brute force of her momentum. It sent her to her knees, but she managed to keep a grip on the knife.

Shit. An empty alley.

Grasping the brick, she righted herself, feet running before her balance came back.

She wasn't fast enough.

A forearm wrapped around her neck, jerking her to a stop. Her feet flew out from under her.

Clamped against his chest, Wynne flailed the knife backward over her shoulder, trying to hit flesh. He snatched her wrist before she could make contact and then shoved her forward, hammering her hand against the brick wall.

Her blade dropped.

A grunt in her ear, and his palm gripped the back of her head, tearing her hair. One brutal slam, and her forehead met brick.

Blackness.

~ ~ ~

Rowen watched Wynne disappear into the Southfork residence, her leather satchel bumping along her backside. The red double-doors closed and he turned. If he hurried, he could get to his townhouse to oversee the delivery of all of Wynne's paintings from that art gallery, and be back before she was done with Lady Southfork for the day.

Trailing after Wynne the last two days had given him precious little time to arrange a wedding and investigate the lead at the art gallery.

But Wynne's safety was more important, and Rowen refused to let her tromp about London on her own. Not when her paintings had mysteriously appeared out of nowhere.

He wasn't about to allow a possible threat on his future wife to manifest. So if that meant following her at a discreet distance everywhere she went for a few days, so be it. He could investigate the paintings more fully once they were married and Wynne was safely protected inside his house.

To his surprise, Wynne had not visited the art gallery in the last two days. She had never promised she wouldn't do so, so Rowen had assumed it would be the first thing she did.

Instead, she had gone about her business, visiting clients for sittings. Staying with the dowager in the evenings. She had not made one step in the direction of the shop.

Adhering to his request, even if she was not about to admit it to him. Stubborn one.

Rowen, on the other hand, had visited the shop the first moment Wynne was safely ensconced with a client—even before going to get the special marriage license.

He recognized all of her works the second he saw them at the gallery—her style was so unique—and immediately bought all of them, playing the part of an enthusiastic collector.

Now it was time to revisit the gallery and start interrogating that clerk for more information on the origins of the paintings. But he first wanted to see Wynne's artwork secure at his townhouse.

Several hours later, Rowen hurried back to his spot down the street from the Southfork home, eyes on the front door. He figured he had another half hour to spare, but he didn't want to chance missing Wynne on her way out of the Southfork residence.

Leaning on a railing, he waited.

Pocket watch checked six times, he waited, eyes not veering from the door.

An hour passed, and he waited.

Another half-hour, and Rowen stood, starting to the home. Damn trying to keep himself hidden from Wynne. Trying to avoid raising her ire even further. She should have been out of the Southfork residence by now.

He was just about to cross the street when a carriage pulled up in front of the Southfork home. Rowen stopped. Stairs came down and the carriage door opened, and Lord and Lady Southfork stepped from the coach, going up their front stairs.

Blast it.

Rowen ran across the street. "Southfork."

His hand on his wife's waist, Lord Southfork turned just before he entered his house. "Duke, what can I do for you?"

"It is your wife, actually, that I need," Rowen said, stopping at the bottom of the stairs.

"And why would that be?" Lord Southfork said.

"Stop." Lady Southfork put her hand on her husband's shoulder, rolling her eyes as she stepped in front of him. "Do not mind my ridiculously over-protective husband, your grace. What can I do for you?"

"Miss Theaton—you had a sitting for your portrait with her today?"

"Oh." She looked back at her husband, then back to Rowen. "Yes, I had one scheduled earlier, but I had to cancel. I did not know you knew Miss Theaton."

"I do. Have you seen her since you cancelled?"

Lady Southfork arched her eyebrows, perplexed. She shook her head. "No. She left after I talked with her."

Dammit.

Rowen inclined his head, trying to hide the grimace crossing his face. "Thank you."

He spun, breaking into a run, leaving the Southforks to their bewilderment.

Wynne had been free for hours.

Rowen racked his brain. Where had the dowager's footman said Wynne was going after Lady Southfork? Lady Pogelten's home next?

Rowen veered left, scampering between passing coaches as he took off down the closest side street.

{ CHAPTER 24 }

Five hours later, darkness had set.

Rowen stood on the doorstep, wishing he was anywhere but where he stood. This was the last place he wanted to show himself, but he was out of options, out of ideas.

Wynne had not shown up at Lady Pogelten's home at their appointed time, nor sent word to her. Hearing that, Rowen had gone straight to the dowager's back door to talk to the footman, Thomas—the one he had been utilizing to trail Wynne when Rowen couldn't. But Thomas hadn't seen Wynne since earlier when Rowen took over Wynne-watching duties. Rowen had even waited while Thomas searched every room in the dowager's house.

But no Wynne.

By the time Rowen got to the art gallery, it was dark inside, door locked. Nothing new had appeared yet in the spots where Wynne's paintings had hung. No one to even interrogate.

So Rowen had continued on to every one of Wynne's current clients. She had not visited any of them that day. He had even stopped by his own home on the off-chance she had appeared there. Nothing.

So that left Rowen with one option. One despicable option. The dowager.

His hand heavy, he lifted the brass knocker, letting it fall.

The dowager made him wait, as expected, a full hour before she appeared in the front drawing room. At least there was proper brandy available, and Rowen helped himself to several large splashes to help ease his pacing.

She appeared silently, one moment an empty room, the next, Rowen turned to see her standing inside the doorway. Her face was already set to criticize.

"I see your manners still lack." She pointed to the glass in his hand. "I would have expected better from a man who has become a duke. Except that I know you, L.B."

Rowen had to stop his hand from throwing the glass in the duchess's general direction. He didn't have time for the dowager's barbs.

"Is Wynne here?" He already knew the answer from checking in with the footman again, but wanted to appease his sliver of hope that the footman was wrong.

The dowager's eyes narrowed to slits at him. "You swore you would stay away."

"She found me, Dowager."

"Bastard."

"We say it openly now?"

"Yes, you bastard." Her lip sneered at him. "You did it again."

Rowen's guard flew up. "I did what?"

"Wynne—you made her leave me again. I can see it in your eyes. You saw her and you made her leave me. Why must you ruin absolutely everything, L.B.? Once more, you have stolen Wynne away from me."

Rowen's stomach sank, his last hope slipping away. "So she is not here?"

"No, she is not. She should have been back hours ago. Lady Pogelten sometimes talks her to death, but Wynne is always back by nightfall to accompany me to functions. So where is she, L.B.?"

She stared at him, waiting for an answer, until understanding dawned on her face. True worry suddenly set into the duchess's eyes. "You do not know where she is, do you?"

"No. No one has seen her since this morning."

The dowager's worry flipped to fury. "What did you do to her, L.B.? On your honor you said you would stay away—but why should I have ever believed that?"

Her arm swung wide in his general direction. "You have no honor. It is not possible. A bastard like you. What did you do?

Did you ask her to be your mistress? She is too proud for that, L.B. Or did you rape her? Beat—"

The glass cracked in his hand, shards digging into his palm. He dropped the pieces to the floor. "Another word, duchess, and I will finish you."

The duchess's eyes flickered down to the broken glass on the floor, drops of blood splattering into the fallen brandy. Her gaze made it back up to Rowen's face.

Clearly recognizing she had gone too far, she still stared at him, not willing to back down.

Seconds passed.

The duchess heaved a sigh, acquiescing. "I apologize. But if Wynne is missing, and she is not with you, L.B., then the only explanation is that you have driven her away. You have crushed her once more, I imagine—do you know she suffered for months after you left? That you destroyed everything she thought she was?" Her words spit out at him. "It is no surprise she disappeared—it is the only way to avoid you. And who would not want to avoid you—you are nothing but poison to those you touch, L.B."

Bloody hand wiping across his buckskin breeches, Rowen held back words that fought to escape. Respect the duchess. The one thing his mother always demanded of him.

Even on her deathbed—respect the damn duchess. If his mother had known this was what would come to pass, would she still have demanded this of him? That this would be his fate to bear—bear the duchess and her vileness for far too many years?

Rowen's head tilted down, his eyes pinning the duchess, voice livid. "You do not know what you speak of, Duchess."

"I do not? Are you sure?" Her hands folded in front of her. Demure in posture, if not in words. "You did not see Wynne these many months, L.B. You did not see how she railed against your memory. How she forced herself to lay you to waste—to forget you even existed. If she found you, if she talked to you, then she had another reason other than be with you.

Her head shook. "I know Wynne—for how hard she fought to forget you, she would not go down that path again—not without dire reason."

The duchess's words sliced into Rowen. Far too close to the truth. Far too close to why Wynne found him.

Wynne needed his help. That was why she had found him. Not because she wanted him.

Rowen's mind raced. Was he wrong? Had he imagined all of it? Had he forced Wynne into compromising herself in order to gain his help? Could she actually have left him? Decided to leave London?

The pit in his stomach—the one that he always had to hold at bay around the duchess—expanded, a burning blaze suffocating his breath, choking his throat.

Without a word, Rowen stepped around the duchess, striding to the front door.

The pit in his stomach swelled. Blast it. Wynne could be on a ship at this moment headed to the Americas. And he would have been the one to send her there.

His hand opening the door, his right foot on the threshold, Rowen stopped. Froze. And the fire consuming him exploded.

He whipped around. "No."

The brutality of that one word made the duchess flinch, and go still, standing just outside the drawing room door.

Slamming the door shut, Rowen stalked over to her, his chest nearly touching her face as he stared down at her.

"No. You will not do this to me again, Duchess."

Her nose wrinkled. "Do what?"

"Make me doubt. Make me question my own worth. Make me question the man that I am. The man Wynne wants." He managed to move even closer, and she took a step backward, running into the wall.

"I am not a little boy under your heel, dowager. I have not been for a very long time. But still, I allowed you to worm into my mind at Notlund, and I lost her." His voice growled. "It will not happen again."

Rowen closed in on the shred of space she had gained.

"Wynne knows, Dowager. She knows everything about me—everything. And she does not care."

"So she knows you that you are a bastard?"

Rowen glared at her, offering one slow nod.

"You fight for her now, L.B.?" A wry smile came across the duchess's face as she shook her head. "Of course Wynne did not care. I knew she never would."

His fist hit the wall above her head. "Damn you. This was a game to you? You knew how she would react to the truth?"

"She is a woman of substance, L.B. If you could not see that—if you could not fight for her at Notlund—then you were the idiot."

"I will throttle you where you stand, Dowager."

She pushed his shoulder. Rowen did not let it move him, so she shuffled to the side, stepping past him. "Do or do not, L.B., I do not care. To protect her, I was testing your worth at Notlund. A test you failed, and that is not my fault. I could not let her suffer my same fate—marry a duke who would toss her aside. Marry a man who was not willing to fight—to give up everything for her. I adore Miss Theaton far too much for that. She is too good for you, L.B. She still is."

Rowen did not let the duchess escape so easily, blocking her path. "That may be, Duchess, but she wants me. For some godforsaken reason, she wants me. And I want her. I plan on marrying her tomorrow. Something she was quite surprised by since you told her I could not marry a commoner."

The dowager waved his words aside. "I only told her that to ease the truth of you abandoning her."

Rowen paused. "That is what she thought? That I abandoned her?"

"What was it but that?"

Rowen shook his head, jaw clenched. He could not argue it. He had left because of his own doubt—his own insecurities. He had left Wynne in the dowager's clutches. Left Wynne on her own, instead of making her his, protecting her.

And now she was gone.

His voice went raw. "I need your help, Duchess. Where could she be?"

"I honestly do not know, L.B." Her own voice softened. "What were the last words she said to you and when?"

"It was two days ago, she saw her paintings from her home in Tanloon hanging in a gallery on Bond Street. How they arrived there is a mystery. She asked for my help in finding who brought them to the gallery. I told her I would find out, but that we needed to wait until we were married."

"So you could protect her?"

"Yes. And she left mad."

"Your method was sound, L.B., but Miss Theaton would not understand that. She still does not understand how powerless women can be."

"Unfortunately."

The dowager tapped her finger on her dark skirts, her gaze upward. "So Miss Theaton is either in danger, or you have made her mad enough that she is on a ship back to America."

Her eyes fell to Rowen. "It was what she wanted after you left. She has been saving for that very purpose. I could have given her the money outright, but I did not want her to leave me."

Rowen sighed. "If I have nothing else to thank you for, Duchess, I thank you for that."

She gave him the tiniest smile, painful though it looked.

"I will visit the docks, use some favors to go through the manifests," Rowen said. "Will you search her belongings—maybe there will be some clue?"

"I will do so."

"I will stop back in early morning before the gallery opens. It is the next avenue to search."

The duchess nodded, face solemn.

It was then that Rowen realized how worried the duchess was as well. Other than spite and grief, he had never seen another emotion on the dowager's face.

But there it was—worry, unmistakable.

It did not help Rowen's own deepening fear that all of their worry was justified.

~ ~ ~

With consciousness, two things hit Wynne instantly—first, an exploding head, and second, a heavy, cold metal surrounding her ankle, weighing her down.

She opened her eyes, mind racing back in time trying to place where she was and why. The last thing she remembered— knife in her hand, the blade dropping, her head slamming into a brick wall.

The man.

She sat up, making her world spin. Closing her eyes, she grabbed her head, fighting nausea as she tried to quiet the waves of pain vibrating down from her head into her body.

The spinning stilled, and Wynne opened her eyes again. The first thing she saw was the heavy iron chain that led from the clamp around her left ankle to a square plate bolted to the floor.

Where had her boots gone? All of her clothes were intact, except for her missing boots. She lifted her bare foot, pulling on the chain just to prove she really was chained to the floor.

The thick metal clinked on the floorboards as she scooted backward until it was taut. Solid. She jerked against it a couple of times.

The links didn't budge. She would not be escaping so easily.

Wynne's head swiveled, looking around the dark room she was in. Not a large space, rafters angled down sharply across it, making it even smaller. A small rectangular window with the glass half broken out of it—not within her reach and high on the wall—let what little light there was from the grey sky into the room. But that was all she saw—grey sky.

And then her eyes caught it. An easel in the corner. An easel with a blank canvas on it.

Her leather satchel sat on the floor, propped against a leg of the easel.

What in the hell?

She crawled over to the easel, dragging the chain with her. Reaching her bag, she flipped it open, dumping it. Brushes fell out. A few scraps of paper with her sketches on them. But no knife. Why had she even hoped it would be in there?

Wynne's fingers clenched around the leather strap. The man had knocked her out and was now holding her captive? Why in the world? Why not just kill her? Clearly, they both knew she recognized him as her mother's killer.

Wynne shook her throbbing head. None of that mattered. What mattered was getting out of the damn shackle and escaping this room.

Pulling her ankle onto her thigh, she looked at the thick iron clamp held tight around her skin with a lock. Wynne fingered the clamp, twisting it awkwardly so she could see into the lock's keyhole. She grumbled a sigh. One of the few skills her grandfather never taught her—how to pick a lock.

A few unsuccessful tugs at the lock, and she dropped her ankle, crawling over to the plate on the floor. Four fat, black nails went through the flat iron plate, securing it to the floor. This was her best chance, if she could wedge the nails up somehow.

Stretching backward, she grabbed her thickest brush and then went to work on wiggling it under the edge of one of the nails. The wood cracked in half.

Swearing, she grabbed another brush. She went slower this time, using all of her muscles to shove the wood without breaking it. Struggling with it at length, sweat dripped from her pounding forehead into her eyes.

Finally, she got the thin edge of the brush wedged under the nail head, and she strained the wood stick upward.

The brush splintered in half.

One more brush.

One more cracked in half.

Tears of frustration squeezed out of Wynne's eyes, and she pounded on the plate with her fist.

A minute later, she heard the door open behind her.

Wynne whipped around.

The man.

Grabbing a wooden shard from a broken paintbrush, she scrambled to her feet.

He stood by the door, watching her with curious amusement.

"What did you do to my mother?"

"So I did not mistake the recognition in your eyes." He took a step forward. In his hand, he held a small wooden crate.

His jacket, his trousers were perfectly tailored. His face, perfectly handsome. The whole of him, perfectly docile. All of it did not fool Wynne. She had seen the ugliness inside of this man. She knew.

Her mind raced back to the art gallery. He looked like he was in the same clothes as before, but Wynne could not be sure. If that was true, it gave her some solace—she hadn't been knocked out for long. Small favor.

"You look like your mother. But younger. More virile. You make me regret that I like my whores willing." His voice was perfectly pleasant—like he was at a formal dinner. "But I may make an exception in your case."

"What did you do to my mother?" Wynne's voice came out much stronger this time.

"I took care of her as I needed to."

Wynne doubled over, not prepared for the punch in her gut the words caused.

To actually hear him say he killed her mother.

To take away her hope.

She had known these many months her mother was dead, but to actually hear it…devastating.

She struggled for breath.

Arms wrapped over her belly, it took several seconds for her to look up at him. "Why did you not just kill me?"

He didn't answer her right away; instead, he walked over to the canvas in the corner of the room under the highest part of the rafters. He set the crate down under the canvas and turned to her.

"You are too valuable."

Wynne pulled herself upright. "What?"

"Those paintings you did. They brought me a small fortune. Fortune I need. I want more."

Wynne's eyes dropped from him to the canvas. Slowly, they crept back up to his face. Her words came out slowly, disbelief cracking them. "You want...you want me to paint for you?"

The man was crazy. Pure crazy.

He clasped his hands in front of him, a smile on his face like he thought it was the most splendid idea ever. "Yes."

"No."

"No?" The smile slid from his face and he took a step toward her.

"I will do no such thing."

Before her words finished, he was to her, the back of his hand whipping across her face.

It sent her flailing to the ground, stick dropping from her grasp.

Before she could even get her hands under her, his boot came up, kicking her in the stomach.

It flattened Wynne, leaving her gasping for breath on her side. Gasping for breath that would not come.

"You will not?" he asked.

Wynne stared at the black boot in front of her face, the blood in her mouth sucking into her throat, choking her.

"You will not?" he asked again, voice pleasant once more.

A trickle of air finally made it to her lungs. She shook her head.

His boot slammed into her stomach again.

"What?"

Wynne shook her head.

He reached down, fingers grasping her hair and ripping her head upward.

Then he slammed her forehead to floor.

Blackness once more.

{ CHAPTER 25 }

They waited near the buildings across from the art gallery for the clerk to appear. Rowen stood on the edge of the cobblestone street, ready to pounce. Luhaunt leaned against a wall, relaxed, twiddling with his pocket watch as he watched the early morning traffic in the street.

When the woman finally appeared, opening the front door and disappearing inside, Luhaunt pushed off from the wall, joining his friend.

"You think she will run?" Luhaunt asked.

"I do not know." Rowen did not look to his friend. "She does not seem the skittish type, or at least she did not the other day when I was in there. Too canny. That is why we are waiting until she is comfortable inside."

Rowen rubbed the dryness from his eyes. Once he had enlisted Luhaunt for help, they had spent the night waking up everyone they could to go through the manifests of the recent ships at the docks. The only ships that had left for the Americas in the last day had no "Wynne," no "Theaton," or any variation of those names or initials in their passenger lists.

Not that Rowen had truly believed they would find anything. Wynne would not leave him again. He knew that in his gut, but he had to set aside his gut for logic's sake and still search for her there. He wasn't going to leave any possibility unexplored.

Which left him here for the past hour, waiting impatiently for the clerk to show. It was his only lead. The duchess had found nothing in Wynne's belongings to indicate she went out for anything other than to paint a few clients the day before. Nothing missing. All her savings intact in a satchel. All her clothes.

Rowen glanced at his friend. Even with no sleep, Luhaunt still looked as fresh as the morning dew. He had always been like that. Three days in muddy warfare with no sleep, and he still looked like he just tumbled from a ten-hour sleep with boundless energy.

Rowen's concentration went back to the shop. "Long enough."

He hustled across the street, leaving Luhaunt to dodge horses and carriages behind him.

Into the store, and the clerk looked up from behind a back counter. Recognizing Rowen—the biggest sale the woman had most likely ever had—she stepped around the counter, smile beaming.

"Mr. Peters, it is delightful to see you again."

Luhaunt's eyebrows arched at Rowen's false name, smirk playing on his lips.

She stopped in front of Rowen. "I trust that every item was delivered properly yesterday?"

Rowen nodded. "It was."

"Excellent." Her hands clasped in front of her. "Then you must have another painting you are interested in if you are here this early? Maybe something that caught your eye the other day?"

Her look flickered to Luhaunt. Rowen could see the near drool in her eyes. Her upper arms pushed inward, squeezing her breasts even higher above the cut of her dress. "And you have brought a companion. You are also interested in the arts, sir?"

Luhaunt inclined his head. He was more than accustomed to breasts plumping up before him. "Indeed, I am."

"Are you more interested in the landscapes, or the human form?" She leaned forward, angling her cleavage.

The last shred of patience Rowen had evaporated. He cleared his throat, stepping in front of the woman. "What we are most interested in right now is discovering how the paintings I purchased arrived at this gallery."

Her attention snapped to Rowen. "Mr. Peters, did I not explain that we do not discuss the origin of the artwork in this gallery? That we are discreet in both the origin and the sale?"

"Yes, you did explain that sufficiently the other day, Miss Daven, but I am now asking you very directly as to where my paintings came from. A name. And I do expect an answer."

The smile left her face.

"A name, Miss Daven."

She shook her head. "I do not know where your paintings came from, Mr. Peters."

"You are lying."

Her hand came up, flattening against her chest. "No, sir, I do not know."

Rowen stepped closer. "You do know, and you will tell me now."

She slipped a foot backward, and Rowen pounced, his hand around her neck as he shoved her backward. She ran into the wall, paintings falling around her.

"Tell me, woman. Tell me now, or god help you."

Hands clawing at his arm, she tried to pull away from his grip. Rowen tightened his hold.

"Rowe—enough." Luhaunt grabbed his shoulders, pulling him off the woman.

Rowen tried to shake Luhaunt off, but then he loosened his hold, dropping his hand from her neck. "She knows, Seb. She knows."

The woman's hands splayed up her neck, desperate to protect it from another attack. "No, I do not know. I swear. I just sell them. The owner is the only one who would know. And so many come through that are suspect, obtained by unscrupulous means—he does not ask either."

"Who is the owner?" Luhaunt asked.

She shook her head, mouth closed, tears streaming.

Rowen leaned over her, his face in hers. "Who is the owner?" The threat in his voice gave her no option to stay silent.

"He will kill me." Her eyes went to the ceiling. "It is Red. Red Bastnum."

"Of the rookeries?" Luhaunt asked.

She nodded.

Rowen took a step back, his eyes still narrowed at her. "If you are lying, woman…"

"I am not. I swear. If anyone knows, it is Red Bastnum."

Luhaunt's hand clamped down on Rowen's shoulder. "Come, Rowe. It is a lead. It is all we need."

A look at Luhaunt over his shoulder, and Rowen spun, stomping out of the gallery.

~~~

She would die before she lifted a brush for that man.

Sitting, leaning against the wall, Wynne stared at the easel across the room. The angle of the light into the room told her it was midday, and that she had lost time—a whole night.

She drew a shaky breath, her heart tightening. She should be married by now. And by now, Rowen would be questioning where she was. And livid. And probably in the thick of it with the duchess.

Her head dropped, a tear slipping. He would never know what happened to her. And she knew him—he would be questioning his own worth. Questioning why she had deserted him. Blaming himself.

And it was all her own damn fault. She never should have gone near that shop. Near that street. Rowen had been right. She had been in danger she didn't understand. So now she was trapped and all she wanted was to get back to him. To marry him. To pretend this never happened.

Wynne's fingers rubbed the chains, as they had done a thousand times in the last few hours, looking for a weak link in the iron. Her eyes drifted upward to the canvas again.

The man thought he could kidnap her, hold her captive, and she would paint for him? It was almost so ridiculous that it was laughable. Almost.

Her swollen lip, the cut dried with blood, was an aching reminder of how not-ridiculous this situation truly was. She hadn't fought at all the last time he came into the room. The shard of wood was in her hand but a moment before she dropped it and crumpled up.

She would do better next time.

She would at least try. Hopefully, he kept a key for the lock on his body, and if she could fight him, knock him out—something—she could get out of here. It really was her only option. For she would never paint for him.

Never.

He was going to kill her eventually—that she was sure of, for he certainly wasn't about to set her free now—so Wynne wasn't about to reward him with any paintings before that happened.

Her eyes whipped to the door as the knob turned. She scrambled forward, dragging the chain as she dove after her sturdiest brush. The only possible weapon in the room. She had picked at the end of it, forging it into a poker. If she could stick it in his eye, in his throat, then maybe, maybe she had a chance.

Wynne buried her hand holding the brush in her skirts.

The man stepped into the room carrying a bowl. He set it down by the door and Wynne could see that it held a spoon and something white.

He glanced around the room, his eyes resting on the blank canvas. "You have not started painting. Unfortunate."

Wynne did not let the threat in his voice quell her. She stood. "Where am I?"

He glanced at her sharply, instantly irritated. "Here."

"Where is here?" she asked, her voice stronger.

He stomped over to her, fist in the air. "We can do this again, if that is what you wish. Again and again until you do what I want. I do not tire of it."

Her eyes narrowed at him. "I will never paint for you."

A smile, evil, carved into his face. "We will see."

His fist came at her head.

Wynne was ready this time and dodged out of the way. A second swing came at her. Wynne ducked, and it only brushed the top of her scalp.

Her grip tightened around the brush, poker end out, and she lunged, hacking it at his left eye.

He shifted and it hit his forehead, scraping along his skin to his temple. Bloody. But a minor wound. Nothing more. Nothing to slow him.

With a growl, his next fist made contact with Wynne's left eye and sent her flying backward.

She landed hard, the wind knocked out of her. He followed her and stepped on her hand, grinding it with his boot heel until her hold on the brush fell apart. Brush on the floor, he kicked the stick across the room.

Wynne yanked her crushed hand into her belly, sheltering it.

"Are you ready to paint?"

Pain deep in her face, she opened her eyes to find she could only see out of one of them. But that one eye found his face. "I will never paint for you."

The words weren't out before he was on her. Fists so fast at her face that Wynne's arms flew up to cover her head.

She kicked at him, a wildcat, both fighting and trying to escape at the same time.

But then a crunch.

A scream, and the instant pain up her leg told her he had broken at least one, maybe two toes with his hard heel.

He took a step back, and Wynne curled into herself, trying to make herself invisible. Walking around her, he blasted one last kick into the back of her ribs, sending her screaming, arching against the pain.

He bent down, balancing on his toes as he propped his forearms on his knees.

"Take care, Miss Theaton, or you will need to learn to paint while lying on the floor." He leaned closer, his sticky breath invading her ear. "Are you ready to paint?"

Wynne had no breath, no way to speak through the vicious pain that consumed her body.

But she could shake her head.

"Unfortunate." He stood.

Wynne tried to brace herself for another kick into her side, but could not control her muscles enough for even that.

His footsteps went around her head, stopping in front of her. "Then I will have to try a different way to persuade you."

Cracking her one eye open far enough to see, she watched his boots retreat out of the room.

Her body went limp, defeated.

So that was what fighting got her.

She wasn't given but two minutes of reprieve before the door opened again, his boots clicking on the wood floor. Wynne opened her right eye.

This time, he was not alone.

A skirt followed his boots, slippered feet jutting out from the folds. They both walked in, stopping in the middle of the floor.

Wynne followed the skirt upward, wondering what new torture a woman could bring her. Her eye landed on the woman's face.

Shock so deep it froze time.

Froze Wynne to the point she could hear the blood pounding in her ears, feel her eyelid blink, hear the wood plank creak under her.

Her mother.

A gasp broke free from Wynne's chest and ripped her from her shock. She jerked, finding the strength to sit upright. Not able to believe the sight in her one good eye. Not able to believe she wasn't hallucinating.

Her mother. Her nose crooked. Gaunt. Pale. But her mother.

Wynne mouthed a "mother," but no sound escaped.

Her mother's eyes were on the window, glassy, unfocused. A soft smile played on her lips.

Wynne realized then that the man was holding her mother up, holding her steady.

Why would her mother need to be held up?

Why was her mother alive?

Words weren't possible, so Wynne grunted. Grunted just enough to get her mother's attention. It took eons, but her mother's eyes left the window, drifting down to Wynne.

Still glassy. Still unfocused.

Her mother stared right at her, but it was as though she looked at air. No recognition of Wynne. No recognition that anything other than dust floated in front of her. Glassy eyes and a soft smile.

Her mother looked from Wynne to the man. "Dream?" Her voice, gentle as ever, floated to Wynne's ears.

Wynne realized in that moment that her mother was drugged. Drugged to the state of incomprehension.

Dragging herself forward, trying to gain her feet, Wynne heaved an attempt to get sound out of her lungs.

The man's hands moved up, and her mother swayed. The swaying stopped the second his hands went around her neck. Tighter. Tighter.

Wynne found her feet, stumbling forward, and then fell.

"Stop." A word finally formed.

She fought to her feet again, watching her mother's face turn purple.

Her mother didn't struggle. The smile stayed on her lips, even as life was being choked out of her.

Wynne gained another step forward before dropping to her knees again. Her hand went up, pleading. "Stop, please."

Trying to clear her mouth, Wynne gulped blood, clearing a path from her lungs. "Stop—let her go—I will paint."

He did not loosen his hold. A vein on her mother's forehead bulged.

"I swear I will paint." Desperate words tumbled, almost incoherent. "I swear—I swear I will paint. Just let her go."

His hold loosened, and he looked down at Wynne.

"I imagined you would say that."

One hand going around her mother's shoulders, the man leaned forward.

"For my trouble," he said, and smacked his fist across her face. A crunch vibrated up from her nose, the pain overwhelming as she fell to the floor.

"I expect to see progress soon."

Wynne could only watch through one foggy eye, stuck in a limp puddle, as the man guided her mother out of the room. The door clicked closed behind them.

Unable to move, Wynne lay on her side, her temple on the floor. Her brain was spinning in her head, creating a fog she could not see through.

Maybe it was time to die. She had always been a fighter. But this pain—it was too much. Maybe it was time. Just close her one good eye and let it all drift away.

Slowly, her lashes collapsed.

Darkness took over, and Wynne welcomed it.

But the pain remained.

She opened the one eye she could see out of.

"Not so easy to let it go, little bear?" Her grandfather sat on his heels in front of her, his arms resting on his knees, his beard as long as ever. He had a wood carving in one hand, a small knife in the other. He looked down at the piece, flecking free a chip of wood with the tip of the knife.

Wynne's fingers twitched in his direction. This was either the afterlife, or she was hallucinating. She couldn't be sure which world she was in.

"It appears you can do one of two things, little bear." He looked from the wooden figure to her. "The first, is fight to survive. Fight to free your mother—to get back to those you love. The second, is to lie down and die at the hands of the devil."

His voice, gravelly, weathered but gentle, filled her head. The voice she missed so much. The voice that had been her guide for so long.

He pointed at her with the tip of his knife. "The granddaughter I know would never let the devil win. Never."

She nodded, her cheek scraping against the floor. It tore at her throat, blood trickling from her lips, but she forced words. "I know. But I…I hurt. I fought, but he…he is too strong."

"You are right, little bear." A smile split his haphazard grey beard and he whittled a few more shavings from the wooden figure. "You cannot win this fight with your strength. This is a fight you have to win with your hands, your brush."

He moved forward, bending on one knee. He set the wooden figure onto the floor and tapped her forehead with his forefinger. "This is how you win this fight. With your mind. You know how to get out of this, little bear."

"How?"

"You only need to trust in the one that you have sworn to trust."

In that instant, he started to fade, his body shifting into smoke. Wynne reached out, trying to catch him before he left her.

"Grandpapa—how? How? Do not leave. How?"

He smiled, full with a twinkle in his eye as he inclined his head and pointed. Wynne followed his crooked finger downward, only to see the wooden figure he had set on the floor in front of her.

The start of a horse. The nose, the head, the mane, appearing out of the block of wood. Beauty out of nothing.

Her eye went back up. He was gone.

Only dust hung in room, floating in the light.

She looked down. The figure was gone as well.

Shutting her right eye, she tried to quiet her mind against the pain racking her body. She had to think.

Trust in the one I have sworn to trust. What the hell did that mean?

Irritation began to replace the pain in her gut. Since her grandfather had bothered to appear in the first place, he could have been a lot more specific about what she needed to do.

She latched onto a deep breath.

Sworn to trust.

Rowen.

If she could reach him, send him a message—he would come for her. He had to. He would not abandon her again. She had to trust that.

He knew where the shop was. He had to be searching for her. And he could find her. She just had to find a way to reach him. Send him a message.

He could find her.

Grimacing against the pain, Wynne crawled over to the easel, foot dragging the chain. She lifted the lid on the wooden crate.

Paints. Good.

She needed to get started.

{ CHAPTER 26 }

Rowen stared at the hanging jowls of the man behind the sleek mahogany desk. The man's elbows sat propped on the desk, and he did not look up at Rowen and Luhaunt for several minutes, instead, staring at a fat stack of papers bound in leather. A ledger, from what Rowen could see at his angle.

In the back of the rookery tavern, the Flashing Crow, Rowen resisted the urge to cover his nose—the stench of sweat and rotten ale and sewage and decomposition overwhelmed him the second they stepped into the dingy room.

But there sat the gleaming desk in the middle of the room, proud against the surrounding squalor. Red Bastnum leaned backward, and his bright red overcoat, trimmed in gold, stretched against his weight as his elbows left the desk. He clasped his hands over the mound of his belly.

"Ye wants to know about me paintin' shop? Where the art be comin' about from?"

"Yes." Rowen refused to let his hand clench into a fist. They had already been through this conversation twice with Red, and had been interrupted twice by a squirrelly little man poking his head into Red's ear.

"Ye be diggin' in things ye no business to be diggin' in."

Rowen could feel the four thugs behind him and Luhaunt take a step inward, collapsing on them.

They had come into the Flashing Crow undermanned, with no alternate plan. But Rowen was desperate. And Luhaunt, to his credit, had not let Rowen come here alone.

"I will pay," Rowen said, his voice even.

"Ye, ain't be payin' me 'nough to ruin me right business. Me reputation. Ye ain't 'nough even for proper clothes."

Both Rowen and Luhaunt had changed into rags of clothes so as to not draw attention in this part of town. They had both learned to play the part of nondescript drunkards during the war—and to great accomplishment.

But right now, that facade was hindering Rowen's progress with Red. Rowen wasn't about to tell Red his identity—he liked his own life too much and he knew the dowager would happily refuse to pay a ransom for his safety—but he needed to impress upon Red that he did have the means.

"I can assure you, sir, I have the funds. And I will be willing to pay a more than generous amount for the information."

Red's eyes narrowed at Rowen. "Ye got the funds, then ye got a noose for me as well. Yer language be too fancy for me establishment." His forefinger sprung from his belly, and he swished it at the four thugs.

Blast it.

The tip of a blade poked into Rowen's back. He could feel cloth tearing as the blade dug in. His hands flew up. A clear signal to Luhaunt they weren't going to fight.

They normally would in this situation, but he wasn't about to chance his only lead to Wynne.

"We are leaving," Rowen said.

"Aye. And they be makin' sure of it." Red nodded to his thugs.

Seconds later, a foot went into Rowen's back and he joined Luhaunt splayed out in the muck by the tavern's back door.

Rowen sat up. Again to his credit, Luhaunt just looked at Rowen and laughed, shaking his head.

"It has been far too long since this particular scene has played out." Luhaunt's thumb jutted at the tavern. "Fond memories, my friend."

"You regard this scene with much more humility than you would have in the past, Seb."

"A man can mature, Rowe." Luhaunt got to his feet, his hand extending down to Rowen. "Besides, a foot in the back is a gift compared to how that could have ended."

"We are rusty." Rowen grabbed his hand. "That is not the confidence I am accustomed to from you."

Luhaunt chuckled, hauling Rowen to his feet. "Of course we would have fought them and been successful—it is just the aches and bruises along the way that I am happy to avoid. I do not recover like I did years ago."

"Next you will be telling me how you are going to settle down with a wife and babes."

"Do not go drastic on me—I only said I like to avoid fists to my face." Luhaunt brushed his chest and chunks of mud flew off. "The ladies do not like the bruises. That is the extent of my settling down."

Walking out to the main thoroughfare, Luhaunt surveyed the night traffic. Drunks and whores and thieves. He looked at Rowen. "So what is the plan now?"

Rowen shrugged. "Patience. Like always in this situation. I follow him. For his instant refusal of my money, there is something he knows. He will slip up. He has to."

"He will." Luhaunt clamped his hand on Rowen's shoulder. "And I will keep watch on the docks and the leaving ships, just in case."

"Thank you."

"We will find her, Rowe. I have never known you to fail on a mission. And I do not believe you will start with this one."

Rowen nodded, mouth grim.

"It is good to see you like this."

"Like what?"

"Torn up. In angst. I saw it at Notlund, but this is different. You have come to terms with how much you need this woman. It is good to see the passion in your eyes."

Rowen sighed, not answering.

He did need Wynne.

And while Luhaunt saw some of it, he had no idea the depths to which Rowen truly needed Wynne.

No idea at all.

~~~

Five days, and no leads.

Rowen had camped himself outside of the Flashing Crow, following Red Bastnum to and from his business in the rookeries—whorehouses, gaming hells, thieves' dens—the man had his thumb in any and every business that would make him a coin.

But not once did Red venture to the gallery. Not once had someone with a painting walked into the Flashing Crow. Rowen had fed Luhaunt every location that Red visited, so Luhaunt could dig deeper, particularly in the gaming hells, but to no avail.

Of the bits and pieces they did uncover, they were quickly finding out that there was a web of illicit artwork trading that most did not know of, and those that did, dared not to speak of.

Rowen took a sip of brandy from his tarnished flask, picking at the threadbare trousers he wore. He looked the part of the drunk, wedged into a sitting spot under some stairs a half block from Red's tavern. Clothes that weren't fit for a mudlark. Cap pulled down, almost over his eyes.

No one had noticed him, save for the pity glances, which was how he needed it. Following Red around was much easier this way. But Rowen was sick of sitting in this hovel. Sick of the cold. Sick of smelling like a drunk. Sick of not finding Wynne. Sick of imagining what had happened to her.

Endless hours spent staring at the battered black tavern door had given him too much time to think, too much time to dwell on what his life had almost been—a life with Wynne.

The way her hazel eyes lit up when she saw him. How she adored him without judgment, without asking for anything from him save for his love.

It was all she ever wanted from him, and he had been so close to making her his. So close to a life—a true life with a family, with children. With the hole that had always been in his soul, filled.

Five days, but Rowen wasn't about to give up on finding
Wynne. Wasn't about to bow to the demons in his head. Demons
telling him she was gone. Telling him too many days had passed.
That she was not coming back to him.

Rowen refused to entertain those demons, not even for a
second.

He took another sip of brandy, stretching out his legs as he
glanced at the tavern in the early morning light. Red had been in
there for hours, and Rowen had watched as the lanterns on the
level two floors above the bar went out. For once, Red was in bed
before dawn.

Rowen hadn't been by the art gallery in two days. After he
had broken into it to look through paperwork and then found
nothing, he had Luhaunt keep an eye on it and the clerk. But
there had been nothing unusual to report.

Rowen looked up at Red's windows again. All was quiet
there and on the street. It was a good time to check the gallery for
himself.

To his feet, Rowen hurried west past Charing Cross, and was
soon walking along the street of the art gallery.

Before he reached the front window of the gallery, he could
see several of the empty spots from the other day were now filled.
The first two new paintings were pedestrian, the usual gardens.
Rowen slowed his gait, now before the shop's windows. At that
moment, his eyes caught sight of the painting on the far right.

Rowen sprang before it.

Phalos.

It was unmistakable. A dark horse. Haunted. Dramatic. Eyes
that told of greatness. The odd ring of white around his left ear.
Phalos.

Just the stallion's head, filling the canvas, larger than life.

Rowen looked in the bottom left corner. An odd splotch of
black paint cut across the corner where Wynne would usually sign
her work with a humble "WT." But Rowen knew it was hers. He
knew it was Phalos.

Blood pounding in his veins, Rowen resisted the urge to smash the glass and grab the portrait. He had to be smart.

Wynne could not be sending him a clearer message than if she were standing in front of him, yelling his name.

But what was the message? She sent him Phalos. There were no words on the canvas, no scenes buried in the peripheral as she liked to do. Just Phalos.

He had to get his hands on the painting, but he also knew he couldn't just walk in and buy the painting after the other day. And neither could Luhaunt.

Loathing to turn from the painting, Rowen ripped his eyes away and spun on his heel, taking off down the street.

If he was going to be smart, he needed someone he could trust.

At least as far as Wynne was concerned.

~ ~ ~

Wynne shot upright, eyes open and the blanket falling from her chest. The creek of the door now instantly sent her body on guard, even from the deepest sleep.

She had orientated herself before the door fully opened. By the light in the window, it was early morning, much earlier than the man usually appeared.

He carried the usual bowl of porridge, setting it within her reach.

Her eyes fell to the floor, docile.

"It sold," he said, walking further into the room.

"What?" She couldn't control her head from jerking up to look at him.

"It sold. It was not there but a day, and it sold for a tidy sum."

Wynne dropped her head, collapsing inward on her excitement. She couldn't let him see it. Couldn't let him see the smile on her face.

"You will paint more. And you will paint faster."

Wynne kept her head down, wrapping her arms around her ribs, trying to control her breathing.

"Do not look so distraught," he said. "This is a good life. You can paint. You are fed."

I am a prisoner. She swallowed the words, instead, nodding her head, but refusing to let him see her face. No reason to poke the devil. Not when she had hope. Not when the painting had sold so quickly.

It had to be Rowen. It had to be.

"The woman that bought it liked the horse. She is a collector and wealthy. She asked if there were more like it. And it was promised to her."

A woman? Maybe someone had bought it for Rowen? Or maybe it had been random. Either way, she needed to send him another painting.

Her excitement tempered, Wynne looked up at the man. The swelling around her left eye had gone down enough that she could see out of both eyes again. There had been no more beatings. As long as she was painting, he let her be.

He brought in porridge. Tea. Replenished the paints. But Wynne moved very lightly around him, not looking him directly in the eye. She wasn't about to give him reason for another beating. Reason to hurt her mother.

But now she needed something more. She needed to know something about this man. If Rowen knew she was alive, she now needed to somehow let him know where she was.

The problem was, she had no idea of her location. The only thing she could see out of the window was sky. She heard things—carriages, horses, people—so she guessed she was still in the city or maybe in a nearby town. He could not have brought her far.

But still, she had not a clue where she was, and she couldn't very well paint the man into the portrait—too obvious and it would only result in fists to her face.

"I will do the horse again." Wynne forced her voice to its softest. "But please, let me see my mother. I paint faster when I have someone to talk to."

His chin jutted out, clucking his tongue as he stared at her.

"Please. I worry for her, and it slows me. I can work faster when worry does not bog down my mind."

He gave an exaggerated sigh. "Start. If I see progress, I will allow it for a short time."

Wynne nodded, bowing her head. "Thank you."

Hours later, Wynne had much of Phalos done. She had set the horse—this time in his full form, but much smaller—off to the left of the canvas. She didn't know what she was going to do with the rest of the scene—she would have to figure that out after she talked to her mother.

The door opened, and Wynne stepped back from the canvas. The man came in, leading her mother.

In a simple peach muslin dress, her mother looked about the room, her lazy hazel eyes stopping on Wynne. She looked more lucid than the other day, but still slightly out-of-focus, like she was stumbling out of a yearlong daze.

She smiled upon finding Wynne's face.

Wynne glanced at the man. "May she have a chair?"

He looked down at Wynne's mother. At that moment her mother swayed. It was enough to convince him. "Yes." He moved her mother's hand from his forearm to Wynne's hand.

The man left, shutting the door behind him.

Wynne grabbed both of her mother's hands. What she wanted to do was to hug her, cradle her, but she didn't know if she would get this chance alone with her mother again.

She squeezed her mother's hands, searching her glassy eyes. "The man. Who is he?"

"Who?" Her mother's stupefied smile was still on her face.

"The man who walked you in here. What do you call him?"

"Vutton?"

"Vutton, what? Is that his Christian name? His family name?"

Her mother wedged a hand free, placing it on Wynne's cheek. "My daughter?"

"Yes. It is me, mother, Wynne."

"You left me?"

Instant tears sprang to Wynne's eyes. She nodded. "Yes. I did. I was afraid."

Her mother's smile did not fade. "You were right to leave. I was afraid for you."

Damn. There was so very much to say. Wynne took a deep breath. She had to stay focused. "Mother, do you know where we are?"

"We are here, dear. At home, Wynne." Her mother brushed a tendril of hair from Wynne's forehead. "Home."

Wynne swallowed a scream. She didn't want to agitate her mother, but she needed real information—details.

"No, mother. Where is this house? Where—"

The door opened, cutting Wynne's words short. The man walked in, carrying a simple wooden chair.

Her mother turned to him. "Where are we? Wynne was just asking."

Instant rage flashed in his eyes. Rage directed at Wynne. "She was?"

Her mother nodded, the soft smile still on her face.

The man's focus shifted from Wynne to her mother. He grabbed her arms, pulling her from Wynne. "Come, let us get you back to bed. This must be overwhelming."

Docile kitten, her mother nodded, following him out the door.

Wynne's eyes closed, her throat collapsing on her. She couldn't take another beating. Not now. Not when she had something tangible in hand. A name. It was little, but it was something.

She didn't have to wait in agony for long. Within minutes, the door opened, and she widened her stance, bracing herself. She knew if she fell to the floor, he would kick her. And the kicking— the toe of his boot—was the worst. Her ribs still pained her with every brush stroke, and she couldn't slow down because of the pain—not now.

The rage in the man's eyes had not waned. He advanced on her, and Wynne's head went down.

He stopped in front of her, grabbing her chin and forcing her face up to him. "Do not test me again. You know very well how that will end," he seethed. "You are lucky that I have another engagement to attend to and have little time. Now get back to work. You have a painting to finish."

He shoved her chin, and Wynne had to take a step backward to catch her balance, the chain clanking across the floor and almost tripping her.

The door closed, and he was gone by the time she looked up.

Her body shaking, Wynne exhaled all of her held breath, collapsing to the floor. It took long minutes for the shaking to subside, for her mind to start working again past the immediate threat of pain.

She looked up to the canvas, staring at the empty area. His name. What had her mother said? Vutton. Why did she know that name?

The white of the canvas stared back at her, taunting.

She had to fill it with something, but what?

The name—she couldn't just paint it in. The man was too canny for that. And the retribution would be harsh.

Vutton. The name flashed in her mind once more, recognition hitting her like lightning.

Vutton—the man that had stolen Rowen's almost-fiancée.

Wynne's mind swirled. It couldn't be. It couldn't be the same man. Could it? Rowen had said he had shown up in the area of Notlund and stolen Victoria from him. And Notlund was fairly close to Tanloon.

She fought to calm her excitement. It could very well just be a coincidence. Vutton could be the man's Christian name, for all she knew.

But it was information. True information she needed to get to Rowen.

Wynne got to her feet, contemplating the canvas. She needed to get this right.

Hands heavy, she picked up her palette and brush.

{ CHAPTER 27 }

Four days had passed since the painting of Phalos had appeared, and Rowen was still stuck in the mud in his under-the-stairs hovel. His patience whittled down to a tiny shred.

He sighed as an enormous black carriage stopped on the street right between him and the Flashing Crow, blocking his sight line.

When the carriage stayed stubbornly in place, Rowen actually took a moment to look at it.

"Damn," he muttered to himself, getting to his feet. The Letson family crest on the carriage door stared at him. The duchess.

He hurried to the coach's door, letting himself in before one of the liveried footmen could let down the stairs.

He opened the flap in the roof to the driver. "Go. Fast."

He sat, heavy, opposite the duchess, shaking his head. "Pure idiocy. You should not be in an area such as this."

"And you should not be gracing my carriage with the filth on your person. Is this some sort of penance for losing Wynne, L.B.?" She wrinkled her nose. "Your friend, Lord Luhaunt told me where to find you."

"What are you doing here, Duchess?"

"The next painting has appeared."

Rowen near jumped to his feet, but had to settle for moving forward to balance on the edge of the bench. "It has?"

"Yes, I received notice this morning. I have already purchased it."

"Is it hers? Are you sure?"

"It is, as far as I can tell. Like the last, it does not bear her mark. But it does look like her style, and your horse appears in it again."

"Where is it?"

"Your residence. It came to my home first, and then I had my men deliver it."

Rowen settled back on the bench. "I assume that is where we are going?"

She gave him a pinched smile. "It is."

Rowen looked out the side window. They were almost out of the rookeries. "What is it of?"

"It is a scene with people. Your horse is oddly off to the side." She flickered her white-gloved fingers in the air. "I can make nothing of it. You will hopefully see something I cannot."

Rowen nodded.

They rode in silence, Rowen's leg tapping. Flecks of dirt fell off his ragged trousers, dropping to the carriage floor. Rowen saw the dowager's face twist in disgust, but she said not a word.

Near his townhouse, the duchess cleared her throat. "I have been thinking, L.B., on these paintings from Wynne. The colors do not seem as vibrant. Not her usual paints. You had bought her the best at Notlund. Here in London, she also had access to the best."

"Yes?"

"So how many sellers of paint are there? Many, I imagine. But then again, maybe not so many." The duchess leaned forward. "Someone has to be buying the paints for Wynne."

The carriage stopped. They were in front of Rowen's townhouse.

A smile spread across Rowen's face. He stood and bent over, his hands capturing the dowager's cheeks. "Genius." He kissed her forehead. "Genius."

She bristled under him, appalled or shocked, Rowen could not tell. It didn't matter. The dowager had just delivered him not just one lead, but two. He would kiss the devil himself if it meant a way to Wynne.

"Thank you, Duchess." He opened the carriage door. "I will keep you apprised of the progress."

"Please do so," she said as Rowen jumped from the carriage.

Bounding up the stairs, Rowen was into his study in seconds, his heels skidding to a stop when he saw the painting. Propped on the floor, it was Wynne's—he could see that immediately.

He quickly went to the sideboard, moving the brandy and crystal-cut glasses to his desk. After checking the back of the canvas and any nooks that could possible hold a hidden clue, he set the painting atop the sideboard, leaning it to the wall.

He sat on the edge of his desk, staring at the scene. What was Wynne telling him?

The canvas captured an outdoor view, Phalos on the left. The back of a man was next to Phalos. Dressed in tall black boots, buckskin breeches, and a loose white shirt, the man had dark hair and a hand possessively on Phalos's neck.

Clearly, that was him.

The slight profile Wynne gave Rowen in the painting showed that he was looking at the two figures on the right of the canvas. Both of them also faced away.

That was where the mystery came in. And that was where Rowen knew the message was.

A woman and a man, her gloved hand nestled into the crook of his arm. The woman had on a gown, emerald, bold and expensive. A necklace, gaudy and fat, even on the back side, graced her neck.

The man was dressed in finery as well, tail coat, cravat, trousers. In his hand opposite the woman, he held a riding crop.

Above them, further away in perspective, a brown mare stood, head hanging.

He scanned the rest of the painting. A forest, and the moors—a bog—rounded out the landscape. She had located him and Phalos near Notlund.

Rowen looked back at the rendering of himself. His fist was clenched, but other than that, he could see no emotion on the figure. So, he was mad and near Notlund. Nothing unusual there.

His eyes traced a path around the painting, again and again. What was Wynne trying to tell him?

A half hour of staring at the painting passed, and Rowen rubbed his shriveled eyes, turning to the brandy next to him and pouring a dram. He was still chilled to the core.

"You have not changed your clothes."

Rowen tossed back the amber liquid, eyes going to the door of the study. Luhaunt walked in, stopping next to him to take in the painting.

"This is it—the latest?" Luhaunt asked.

"Yes."

Luhaunt took a side-step away from Rowen, his eyes on the painting. "And you still smell."

"I am aware."

"Beautiful—she is talented. But other than Phalos—and I am guessing that is you beside him—I do not understand it." Luhaunt looked from the painting to Rowen. "Do you?"

Shaking his head, Rowen sighed. "No. But I did not expect this to be easy. Wherever she is, she cannot just write a note with her location into the painting. But it does reinforce that she is trying to reach me. Trying to tell me something in the only way she can."

"Reassuring." Luhaunt clamped his hand on Rowen's shoulder. "I had thought at the start of this that we would have little chance of finding her. But you kept faith, and it was warranted."

"Do you have news?" Rowen asked, looking to his friend.

"I have a list."

"Of?"

"The duchess found me this morning and set me to discovering all the proprietors of paint in London."

Rowen rolled his eyes. "Of course she did. I apologize for her presumption." The duchess wasn't about to wait for Rowen's approval in sending his friend to do her bidding. But since it was for Wynne, Rowen gave pardon to her audacity. He turned to his desk and poured a glass of brandy for Luhaunt.

"She thought it may help in finding who has purchased a full set of lower-quality paints recently." Luhaunt took a swallow.

"I agreed with her idea. Painters go through different colors at different speeds, so are more apt to buy one or two colors at a time. But to buy a complete set at once—it would not happen that often and it would narrow the search."

"True."

"I plan on visiting the names on the list—but I stopped here to pick up the Phalos painting. I am under the understanding that paints can be very different, and if I show them the painting, they may be able to tell me if it was done with their paints or not."

"It is yours." Rowen motioned with his head to the Phalos painting behind them. "That was the herald." He pointed to the painting in front of them. "This is the message. Keep me posted."

"Of course."

Luhaunt gathered the portrait of Phalos, dropping a sheet around it before carrying it out of the study. Taking another sip of the brandy, Rowen's eyes went to Wynne's latest painting.

He studied his own figure in the painting. He was mad and looking at the couple, so his anger must be directed at them. His eyes went to the couple.

Rowen jumped to his feet, launching himself at the painting, his nose nearly touching the canvas.

Was that blood on the riding crop?

It was slight. Three red drips falling from the crop in the man's hand.

Rowen's eyes went up to the beautiful mare, cocoa colored. This time he saw it. Also slight, red lines mixed with the brown coat on the mare's rump.

The man had just beaten his horse.

Rowen's heart stilled.

Vutton.

He looked at the woman in the painting. Red hair. Victoria.

Victoria was dead, so this was about Vutton.

He shook his head.

Impossible.

Rowen's eyes went through and traced every stroke on the painting. He had missed nothing else.

Vutton was the message.

Rowen straightened, stepping back from the painting, frozen in shock for a long moment.

And then he broke free, running from the study, taking the stairs three at a time to get up to his room.

He had to change and catch up with Luhaunt.

~ ~ ~

"Are you ready?"

Luhaunt nodded, half of his face shadowed from the light of the carriage lantern. "Two pistols at the ready and two knives should they be needed. Which is less than what you have on your body, I am sure. But you always liked to be more prepared than I."

Rowen gave him a grim smile. It was true he had three knives strapped to his body. But it wouldn't be the first time he had to toss Luhaunt an extra weapon. "It has saved your hide on more than one occasion."

"That is why I stick with two—I trust that you have me covered."

A dark fog cocooned their carriage, and Rowen leaned forward, pulling the curtain to look across the street at Vutton's front door. The heavy fog combined with the night to make it hazy from this distance, but he could see several lights lit on the main floor.

"Remember, we have no proof, only suspicion." Rowen's eyes stayed on the townhouse. "This could very well just be a lead that Wynne gave me, and not the actual end game. If it is he, we cannot act until we know where Wynne is. We may need to string him along, shadow him until we find the paint origins. Until he leads us to her."

Luhaunt nodded. "It is a shame he has no servants in the house. It would have been nice to pay one of them for information on what we are going into."

"But it also makes him even more suspicious." Rowen's jaw set hard. "And now that we know his lands butted up to Tanloon, his involvement with Wynne's mother would make sense."

"'Lose the teat and there will be hell to pay'?" Luhaunt quoted from the drunk in Tanloon.

"Exactly. Vutton may very well have run that town."

Rowen ran through the list in his mind of what they had found out about Vutton that day.

The man had several sizable debts at three gaming hells, and had recently paid off another debt at a fourth. His finances in disarray, he had managed to keep up appearances in the ton by attending several key events in the past weeks. And word was that he was searching for a bride attached to a sizable dowry.

Rowen had also learned Vutton had been quietly selling all of the land that wasn't entailed in his estate. He kept no servants, other than a cook that delivered food twice a day. The man's finances were dire. That much was obvious.

A minute later, Rowen and Luhaunt were through the fog and at Vutton's door, clanking the heavy brass knocker.

They had to clank it three more times before the door moved. Not surprising, Vutton, instead of a proper butler, cracked the door, eyes squinting as he looked at Rowen and Luhaunt. "May I help you?"

They had only crossed paths that once when Rowen tried to buy his horse, but Vutton clearly did not remember Rowen from those many years ago.

"Your lordship, we apologize for the intrusion on your evening," Luhaunt said. "I am Lord Luhaunt. We have not met, but I believe you chatted with my sister at the Vaudhill ball two nights ago, a Miss Emily Rallager?"

Vutton shook his head, slightly confused. He refused to open the door more than a crack. "Miss Rallager? I am not sure."

Luhaunt feigned embarrassment. "Oh, I apologize. My sister led me to believe there was a deeper connection between the two of you. But I understand there was quite the crush there and you may not remember her. In which case, that answers my question."

Vutton slipped the door a bit more open. "Possibly. Possibly I remember our conversation. What was it you wanted to speak with me about?"

Rowen hid a smirk. Luhaunt's imaginary sister had come in handy more than once throughout the years. And she was still as useful as always.

"Frankly, Lord Vutton, I am here to appraise you. My sister is attached to an enviable dowry, and I am very protective of her. There have been attempts to compromise her by some unscrupulous men, so I am here to judge your worth. My sister can be...flighty in her choice of men." Luhaunt solemnly shook his head. "But I fear if you do not even recall her I am wasting your time. I apologize for the disruption. But as an honorable man of society, I am sure you can understand my concern over my sister. Good eve."

Luhaunt nodded to Rowen, and they both turned to the stairs.

The door swung open. "Please, Lord Luhaunt, wait. I do recall your sister, and I will be happy to answer your questions. I apologize that it took me a moment to remember her. There was indeed, quite the crush there. She is rather charming, if I remember correctly?"

Luhaunt turned back to Vutton, wry smile on his face. "She is indeed." He motioned to Rowen. "This is Mr. Hallton. We were on our way to the club and he graciously agreed to stop off on this meeting with me."

"Of course, enter." Vutton stepped back into the entryway, ushering them in. "I apologize for the unusual welcome. I gave the staff the night off, as I was not expecting visitors this eve. Let us go to the drawing room."

Vutton showed them into the dark room, quickly fluttering about to light several lamps. There was little furniture—a sofa, a wingback chair, and a sideboard hosting a set of short glasses and a carafe. "Brandy?"

"No, that will not be necessary," Luhaunt said. "We do not have a great amount of time. A few quick questions should do."

"Please, sit," Vutton said. "What is it you would like to know of me?"

Rowen and Luhaunt sat on the sofa as Vutton went to the chair, perched on the edge in uncontrolled eagerness.

"I will ask it outright, Lord Vutton," Luhaunt said. "First, your estate, is it self-supporting, or are you in the market for an infusion of money by way of a wife?"

Vutton coughed, stumbling at the question as he looked quickly back and forth between the two men. "The estate...the estate is self-supporting. The land does that."

Luhaunt gave him a reassuring smile. "Excellent. And you, would there be any untoward passions that you indulge in? Wine, women, gaming?"

Vutton waved his hands exuberantly in front of him. "No, no. Nothing like that. I live a quiet life."

Luhaunt nodded, satisfied. "My sister, she said she spoke to you of art and you were very knowledgeable. It is a passion of hers." Luhaunt made a show of looking around the room at the empty walls. "But I see no art here. Are you a collector?"

"Art? Oh, why yes—"

Vutton stopped as a woman in a simple dress, dazed, appeared in the doorway of the study. He jumped to his feet, going to her.

"Vutton, I heard voices," the woman said, her eyes focusing on Vutton.

Rowen stood.

The woman looked just like Wynne.

Rowen moved to the side to gain a view of her past Vutton's back.

It was unmistakable. Wynne, twenty years from now.

"Just some visitors." Vutton grabbed the woman's elbow, guiding her into the hallway. "Go upstairs and wait, and I will be up shortly."

Shock waning, Rowen followed them. The woman had turned, walking away to the stairs.

Vutton looked at Rowen, a pitying look on his face. "You must forgive my cousin; she is slightly addled."

Rowen pushed past him. "Violet?"

The woman stopped, turning to Rowen. It took a moment for her glassy eyes to focus on him.

"Violet?" Rowen asked again.

She nodded, a sweet smile on her face. "I am Violet."

A hard board slammed into the back of Rowen's head, sending him sprawling, hitting the wall below the staircase. He slid down the wall, hearing a scream and a sudden scuffle.

Forcing his eyes open against the sucking blackness, Rowen fought to keep consciousness. Landing on the floor, he managed to turn, only to see Luhaunt struggling against Vutton in the drawing room. Blades were flashing, and Rowen could not tell which blade belonged to which hand.

Scampering forward into the room, Rowen grabbed Vutton's ankle, yanking it and sending Vutton flailing. Through the blackness still threatening to overtake him, Rowen saw a blade slice through Luhaunt's arm. Luhaunt unfurled a string of expletives.

Vutton hit the floor, and Luhaunt's fist flew into his face, knocking him out cold before Rowen could find his own feet.

Luhaunt stepped over Vutton, getting to Rowen in the doorway and grabbing his arm.

"Are you going down?" Luhaunt asked.

Bent over, hands on his knees, Rowen lifted his fingers to the back of his bloody head. "No, it was hard, but not that hard. I will be fine now that I am upright." Rowen nodded to Luhaunt's bloody forearm. "Is that deep?"

"No. Rope? You have this while I find some?"

"I do." Rowen nodded, looking into the drawing room. "Shit—no."

Violet was standing over Vutton's head, lit oil lamp clasped in her hands. She lifted the lamp up above her forehead, same sweet smile on her face.

Seeing her intention, Rowen started toward her, but before he even got a step, Violet smashed the lamp down onto Vutton's head.

Flames exploded.

Rowen skirted the blazes coming from the scattered oil, grabbing and dragging Violet out of the room. He got her to the front door while Luhaunt pounded out the flames on her skirt.

The sweet smile remained on her face, eyes vacant.

Rowen grabbed her shoulders, shaking her. "Violet. Listen to me. Wynne—your daughter—is she here?"

Violet's eyes drifted up to Rowen's face. "Wynne?"

"Yes. Wynne. Is she here?"

For a second, it did not look like Violet understood a word Rowen was saying. But then she nodded. "Yes."

Rowen sucked in air, relieved, only to have to cough out the smoke that came in with it. The drawing room was quickly going up in flames. "Where? Where? I need to know right now."

She nodded again. "Upstairs. It is locked."

Rowen passed Violet to Luhaunt. "Get her out of here. Keep her safe from the house."

Luhaunt grabbed Violet around the waist. "Be quick. This place will not last long."

Rowen was bounding up the stairs before Luhaunt finished his words.

The second level, Rowen tore through. Five rooms, all empty. And the smoke thickened in the hall.

Seconds later, he kicked in door after door on the third level, all of them locked. Empty.

That only left the servants' quarters.

Up a skinny staircase, his eyes stinging, the smoke was even thicker on this level. Rowen pulled his linen shirt up over his nose. The first door he got to was locked, and Rowen braced himself on the opposite wall, kicking it in.

He dove forward, bending down below the cover of smoke to see into the room. Only slight light from the street lamps made it in through the window.

Movement.

He ran forward. "Wynne."

She sat in a huddle on the floor, her head coming up at his voice.

"Rowe?"

"Wynne, come. We have to get out of here." He grabbed her arm, pulling her to her feet.

"Rowe. Oh, God, Rowe. No." Her hands clamped onto his arm. "I can't. I can't get out of here. It is a fire? You have to go. You have to leave me."

"What?" He dragged her toward the doorway, ignoring her words.

A sudden painful scream, and she yanked from his hand, dropping.

He flew back to her, sliding to his knees and gripping her shoulders. "Wynne? What? What is it?"

"I am chained to the floor." She coughed. "You have to go. You have to get out of here."

Rowen's hands went down her body, down her legs to her ankles. His fingers found the cold metal clamping her in place. Quickly, he followed the heavy chain to the plate bolted to the floor.

"Fuck." His hand slammed onto the floor.

Flames were starting to lick the hallway wall opposite the door.

Rowen ran to the opening, slamming the door shut. Ducking the smoke, he ran back to the plate on the floor, pulling a blade.

Wynne grabbed his upper arm, tugging.

"Rowe. Please. You need to go. This place is burning. You need to get out of here."

"Hell, no, Wynne."

He slid to his knees by the plate on the floor, digging the blade into the wood next to it. He tried to wedge the plate upward. It didn't move.

"Fuck."

"Rowe—go. Leave, dammit. Go."

Tip of the steel digging in, he started scraping his way through the wooden plank, tearing it, splinter by splinter.

Wynne crawled across the room away from him, coughing. "Rowe, you need to get out of here." She dragged herself back to him, holding a glass jar. Stopping next to him, she smashed the glass on the floor. Hacking from the smoke, she picked up a chunk of glass and started to saw the best she could on the wood intersecting the line Rowen worked on.

The glass squeezed out from Wynne's hand several times, too slippery with blood and paint to hold.

"Dammit, Wynne." Rowen stopped his sawing for a moment, pulling out another knife and putting it in her hand.

Both sawed at the wood, desperate.

The thick smoke closed in on them, suffocating them closer to the floor.

Furiously, they both hacked at the wooden planks, trying to break the plate free. But it was going too slow.

"Rowe, you have to go." Wynne's sobs and coughing overtook her words. "Please. Do not die here. Do not die because of me."

Rowen grabbed her face, yelling over the crackling wood, the heat around them. "I am not leaving you, Wynne. Never. Do not waste your breath."

He dropped his hands, going back to the floor.

Sawing. His muscles ripping. And then he felt the tip of his blade clear the plank.

Covering his face with his shirt, Rowen stood, kicking downward with all his strength. The plank loosened, wood tearing.

He dropped back to the floor. Wynne had collapsed, prone on the floor next to the plate, knife still in her hand.

Dammit.

He went to the next plank of wood. Sawing with a fury.

With what Wynne had started, he got through the skinnier plank in short order.

Standing, he kicked at it, and it broke free. Rowen went to his knees, wedging his hands under the wood attached to the plate, and yanked the planks, twisting them upward.

Finally, luck. The wood, brittle, tore. Within a minute, he worked loose the clump of the two planks attached to the iron plate.

Wynne free, Rowen looped the chain and plate over his arm and picked her up. The flames from the hall had already engulfed the door.

He spun, going to the window. Shifting Wynne into one arm, he took his elbow to the window, breaking through the glass and middle pane. Tucking Wynne along his body, he ducked through the opening, landing on the slight slope of the roof.

It took him precious seconds to orientate himself in the fog-smothered smoke that enveloped the house. He edged along cautiously, Wynne in his arms.

Vutton's house was on the corner, but Rowen knew it butted up tightly to the next townhouse on the block. He could tell by the dip when he got to the edge.

Throwing Wynne over his shoulder, he jumped to the next roof. Feet sliding, he caught himself once his hand hit the roof's clay tiles. He moved up to the nearest window, kicking it in.

Within seconds, Rowen had Wynne down through the adjoining house and to the sidewalk by his carriage.

Rowen laid her on the ground, stretching her flat on her back in the light of the flames consuming Vutton's house. She was still limp.

"Wynne, wake up." Both of his hands went to her face, slapping her cheeks. It did nothing. "Wake up, Wynne. Wake up."

His hands ran down her body, desperate, checking for injuries he didn't know of. Other than her bloody hand, she wasn't bleeding anywhere else.

Hell.

He went back up to her head, capturing her face in his hands, pulling her limp body from the ground. "God—do not leave me, Wynne. Do not. You swore you never would. So wake the hell up, Wynne. Wake up."

Luhaunt's hand landed on Rowen's back, his voice soft. "Rowe. The smoke—it happens. I think...I think she is gone."

Hands shaking, Rowen set her head gently back to the ground, turning to slap Luhaunt's hand away. "Shut the hell up—she's not gone, Seb. She is not gone."

Luhaunt took a step backward.

Rowen's head went on Wynne's chest, searching for a heartbeat. "Just wake the hell up, Wynne. Wake up. Please." His voice cracked, broken. "You cannot leave me now, Wynne. Not when I just found you. I need you to wake up, Wynne."

"He is right."

Rowen looked up.

Violet knelt, looking at Rowen, her hand going to Wynne's forehead. "You are right. My daughter is not gone. Not yet. She will fight. She has always known how to fight, this one. She has her grandfather's spirit."

The same smile as earlier still lined Violet's face. But her eyes looked focused.

Violet stood, looking down at her daughter's prone body. "She will fight. She just needs a guide."

Rowen dragged his mouth to Wynne's ear, his hand cradling her head as he pulled her up from the ground, crushing her to him. His voice went harsh, demanding. "Listen to me, Wynne, listen. You can do this. Just follow my voice. I am right here. Wake the hell up, Wynne. Take a breath. It does not need to be big. Small. Just a little breath. Tiny. That is all."

His palm pushed on her back. Hit her lungs. "Get these working. You can do this. Just a little breath, Wynne. One to start with. Just one. And then you can open your eyes."

Hand moving between them to her heart, Rowen pressed. "Your heart will beat. Your breath will come. Just fight it, Wynne,

fight it. You can do this. You need to come back to me. You need
to fight for me."

Rowen gripped her body even harder. "God, Wynne, please.
You need to be in this life. You need to come back to me. To
marry me. To bear our children. To die when we are old and you
are in my arms. Not now, Wynne. God, not now. You need to
do all of that in this life. This is where you need to do it, Wynne.
This life. This one."

The tiniest shudder.

He felt the breath start before Wynne's body jerked. She
sucked in air over his shoulder, only to be consumed by a fit of
vicious coughing.

It racked her body, her spasms fighting Rowen until he set
her on the ground. She curled onto her side. For every breath she
gasped, five soot-filled coughs heaved back out of her body.

Minutes went on, but Rowen didn't care. Wynne was
moving. Her body convulsing in pain against the suffocating
smoke in her lungs. But moving. Alive.

Rowen patted her back through it, one hand on her shoulder,
holding her as steady as he could against her body jerking to clear
her lungs.

When the hacking eased, her breath raspy, Rowen pulled
her torso upright. Holding her shoulders for stability, he went in
front of her to see her face.

Still fighting against the wheeze in her breath, Wynne
cracked her eyes at him. The whites of her eyes were stark against
the soot covering her face.

"My mother?"

"She is here. Safe."

It took her dazed look several seconds to focus on Rowen.

"You found me." She had to hack the stilted words out.

Rowen's face broke into a wide smile. "I did. I got your
message."

"You should have—" Her words stopped, her head dropping
as a set of coughs overwhelmed. When she caught her breath, she
looked up at him. "You should have left."

"I could not." He slipped one arm around her back to hold her up, moving the other to her face. His thumb dragged across her cheek, smearing a clear line through the black soot. "Life or death, I am not leaving your side, Wynne."

She stared at him a long moment. So long, that fear suddenly clamped onto Rowen's chest. What if she would not have him? What if he was too late? Her eyes—he could always read what was in her mind, her heart, but in that moment, he saw nothing. Could read nothing.

The yelling, the fire across the street drew her attention, and her head swung, looking past the carriage at the fiery destruction. The fire now consumed the adjacent house as well.

Her eyes went to her leg with the shackle. "The clamp…off."

Rowen's head fell. "Yes. We need to leave this place." He picked her up, going to the carriage.

Luhaunt and Violet followed.

{ CHAPTER 28 }

The dowager had made a huge fuss, demanding Wynne get into a bath—even before Rowen had a chance to get the clamp off her ankle.

So Wynne was dunked, clamp and all, into a tub. Rowen hadn't had the energy to fight the duchess, even though he knew Wynne needed the clamp off her leg.

Waiting in the hallway, leaning on the wall, Rowen had heard her coughing through the ordeal, still hacking out all of the soot in her lungs. He had taken a moment to wash his own face and arms at a basin in the room across the hall, and had poked around until he found a simple white linen shirt to change into. As long as he heard Wynne's coughs, he wasn't overly worried.

The dowager stepped out of Wynne's room, followed by two maids. The maids disappeared down the hallway.

"How is she?" Rowen asked.

"She is doing well. I have her in bed." The duchess pointed at the tools in Rowen's hand. "She is rather annoyed at me. She wants the shackle off. Can you do so with those?"

"It is what I have been waiting for."

The dowager harrumphed. "Fine. I will go to oversee her mother." The duchess moved down the hall.

"Duchess."

She turned back to Rowen.

"Thank you."

She nodded, a tight smile on her face. With a swish of her black skirts, she continued on.

Rowen opened the door, poking his head into the room.

Wynne was on the bed in a chemise, propped up by pillows with the coverlet half covering her body. Blond hair still wet, it was pulled over her right shoulder. Her clamped left leg sat out on the spread, the chain and plate piled neatly on a rag next to it.

"May I come in?"

She smiled when she saw him, her hand outstretched. "Yes, please, and tell me you can get this shackle off."

"With luck." Rowen breathed a sigh of relief. Her smile was a good sign. He grabbed a wooden chair and brought it next to the bed, setting it by Wynne's leg. "First, how is your hand?"

Wynne lifted her bandaged hand, white cloth wrapped thick around the palm. "It will survive. It will be a while before I can paint again."

Rowen nodded, setting the few surgeon tools Luhaunt had delivered to him onto the bed. Long and skinny, the two silver probes would hopefully be enough to pop the lock on the clamp.

"May I grab your leg?" There was a time when he would have just picked up her leg without asking—Wynne was his and there was no other possibility in his mind. But right now, he needed to be extra cautious.

"Yes." The smile on her face wavered.

Rowen's hand went under her chemise and slid around her shin, lifting her leg and setting it in his lap. He spun the metal around her ankle to get the lock on top. It had a fat keyhole, and Rowen slipped both of the probes into the lock, digging for the pins.

He worked in silence for a few minutes, poking around. He could feel Wynne's eyes on him the entire time.

"I did not know you possessed such a nefarious skill."

Rowen had one probe on a pin and didn't want to lose it, so he kept his eyes on the lock. "I have had the occasion to learn."

"You are not going to tell me when that was, are you?"

"No."

"Rowe, is my nose crooked?"

"What?" He didn't look up.

"My nose—the duchess would not let me look at it. But I think it broke and it is crooked now. It is hard to see my own nose without a mirror."

Rowen looked up, scanning her features.

He hadn't noticed it before—there was too much soot on her face and his eyes had been downcast since coming into the room. Whereas once the bridge of her nose had been perfectly straight, there was now a slight bump.

His stomach churned.

Slowly his eyes met hers. "Will it bother you if it is?"

"Does it bother you?"

"Yes."

"Oh." Her head fell, crestfallen.

Rowen would be smiling at the simple fact that he could read her again—would be, except he realized he had just inadvertently hurt her.

"Wynne, I am bothered because I am sitting here, working on a damn lock that held you captive, looking at a bump in your nose that could have only gotten there with a great amount of pain." His voice shook. "So yes, I am bothered by it. Furious that I did not save you from that. But it does not mar your beauty— your beauty does not come from a straight nose—it never did. If anything, it gives you character."

She looked up at him, eyes shining. "Character?"

Rowen went back to finagling the lock. "Yes. Character."

The lock sprung free. Rowen quickly threaded out the lock from the clamp, opening the shackle. The raw, red skin beneath it made him pause, and he touched her ankle lightly.

Wynne laughed, lifting her leg and flexing her foot. The laughing turned into a cough that took a few moments to control. "Rowe, this is—I had thought never to get rid of it."

Rowen gathered up the shackle, chain, plate, and wood shards and went to the door, throwing them into the hallway.

Wynne leaned forward, rubbing the rough area on her ankle. "Rowe, are you leaving?"

He turned to her, standing in the doorway. "Do you want me to?"

"No. But you have barely looked at me." She sank back onto the pillows. "You are mad at me?"

Rowen walked to the bed, sitting heavily into the chair. "I am not mad at you, Wynne. Far from it. But there are things we need to discuss that I am trying to avoid."

Her face went somber. "Such as?"

Rowen leaned forward in the chair, his forearms resting on his knees. He had to say it, get it out before he could not utter the words. "Wynne, if you want to stay here and live with the duchess. Not marry me. I would understand."

She jerked upright. "What are you talking about? You no longer want me?"

"God, no, Wynne." He grabbed her unbandaged hand. "It is me. I am not...deserving of you. I sent you into this. And you have paid a terrible price."

"Ridiculous. How did you send me into this?"

Rowen shook his head. He didn't want to dredge this into the light, but he truly had no choice. "Wynne, after you found me here in London...I had finally started to believe—believe that fate had decided I had suffered enough. That I was actually worthy of your love, your trust. But then the second I came to accept that belief, fate took you away."

Her hand turned in his, clasping his fingers. "You had nothing to do with Vutton taking me, Rowe."

"No—but I did not know how to protect you. So instead of doing just that, I drove you away. I let you leave my house. And then I followed you for days—and you did not go near the shop, so I thought you had dropped the matter. Left it to me." He sighed. "Fate tested me, and I failed. The second I stopped watching was the moment you decided to go there. And then you were gone."

Her head shook against his words. "I was stupid, Rowe. You told me to stay away from the gallery, and I did not listen. That is not your fault."

"No, it is, Wynne. I should have told you the full danger. Everything I suspected. I did not trust you with that."

"It does not mean I would have listened."

"The fact remains, Wynne, that I let you go. I let you take that first step away from me. And then I was too late—I failed you. I could not save you in time." His hand went to her ankle, tracing the red ring around her skin. "That I let this happen to you."

His thumb went to her face, gentle on the bump in her nose. "And this. You sent me the signs, and it took me too damn long."

His hand dropped from her face. "You deserve a better man than me. A man that never would have let this happen to you."

"Rowen, stop. You found me. You saved my mother—and me." Wynne scooted forward on the bed, pulling her hand from his fingers and settling it on his neck. "Through all of what happened to me, I trusted in you—you, Rowe. I trusted that you would find me. That you were looking for me."

Rowen's eyes fell closed, his head shaking. "What you had to go through."

"Rowe, look at me."

He opened his eyes, only to see the flecks of blue in her hazel eyes glowing bright.

"You are worth whatever it took—fighting the devil himself—to get back to. You are the one that kept me strong. That I stayed alive for. You. You do not know how badly I wanted to just shut my eyes and slip away. How I almost did."

Her hand moved up, cupping his jaw, fingers curling against the dark stubble on his skin. "But then I knew—deep, in my soul—that you were coming for me. That you were looking for me. That I could not disappoint you. You are worth everything I have in this life—and any other. You, Rowen."

The weight of a thousand stones lifted from his chest. Wynne's words were secondary to the love that shone in her eyes.

His hands cradled her face, thumbs catching the few tears slipping down her cheeks. "So you will marry me? Birth our children? I will get to experience every day the magic that you create in the world?"

Wynne nodded. "I want nothing more than to marry you, Rowe. Carry your babies. Wake with you. Wrinkle with you."

"I was hoping you would say that. I—"

A short knock on the door interrupted his words. The dowager opened the door, walking into the room.

Rowen dropped his hands from Wynne's face, but he grabbed her unbandaged hand again, capturing it between his palms.

"You will need to leave now, L.B. Wynne needs to rest."

"Duchess, while I agree Wynne does need to rest, I have a differing plan."

The dowager stepped closer, facing Rowen and wedging herself the best she could between them. "I do not care what has transpired, L.B. I will not allow you to stay in this room with Wynne overnight. She is an unmarried woman under my eye. You are a fool to think I would allow it."

"I would never ask you to bend your morals, Duchess," Rowen said dryly. "Has Lord Luhaunt returned?"

"Your friend? No, I do not think so."

"Did I hear my name?" Luhaunt appeared in the doorway. "I apologize for just coming up, but know that your butler did his best to dissuade me, your grace."

The dowager's eyes narrowed at Luhaunt. "He clearly did not do his best."

Luhaunt shrugged. "Rowe, I arranged what you asked for."

"Excellent."

"It will be exorbitant," Luhaunt said. "If we wait until morning, only slightly exorbitant."

"We do it now," Rowen said and leaned sideways to see past the duchess's skirts, finding Wynne's face. He squeezed her hand. "Marry me? Right now? I do not want another hour to pass where you are not my wife."

A moment of shock crossed Wynne's face, only to be replaced by a smile that went impossibly wide. "Yes."

"No." The duchess threw her hands between them. "This is not at all proper, L.B. It is the middle of the night. I will not allow it. There is not even a proper license."

"You do not get a say in the matter, Duchess. Lord Luhaunt has roused the clergy at the church a block away. And I do have the license. I had it weeks ago." Rowen didn't take his eyes off of Wynne. "I do thank you, though, for the proper bath Wynne got in preparation."

"No, no." She stomped her foot. "I will not allow it."

"Then you can stay here, Duchess." His eyes left Wynne to look up at the dowager. "But I do believe Wynne would want you to witness this, as her friend."

Rowen stood. "And I would like you to witness this, as not only the dowager duchess, but as my lone relative."

The duchess's gaping mouth closed, silenced. She took an uneasy step away from the bed, nodding.

Rowen tilted his head to the duchess. "Thank you."

Wynne squeezed his hand and he looked down at her, his head tilted to the door. "We can leave this second—you will need a dress, of course. Are you ready? I will carry you so it is no extra strain on your lungs."

A twinkle appeared in Wynne's eye. "You will carry me with the proper care?"

Rowen smirked. "Only the most proper, Wynne."

She nodded, her face reflecting his mirth. "You are the one beyond compare, Rowe. Yes. A thousand times over. Yes."

Heart bursting, Rowen looked down at his almost-wife. Sudden disbelief that he had actually arrived at this moment shook through his body.

Fate had finally done it.

Finally shown him exactly what his life should be.

Finally given him exactly what he needed.

Finally decided he was worthy of this woman.

And he could now spend a lifetime proving it.

{ EPILOGUE }

Wynne sat in the rocking chair, eyes on the bright green vistas of the Notlund pastures. A warm breeze tickled the hair on her forehead. Spring was upon them, and Wynne was lost in the calmness of the moment, eyes half-closed, both wanting Rowen to finish quickly with the horses, and wanting him to take his time.

She looked over at the painting, just started, under the wide roof of the porch. It had been days since she had worked on it—the luminous greens of the spring leaves and grass were too gorgeous not to paint—but seeing the dowager married and packed had been far more important.

Rowen had the small building up the hill from the stables built for Wynne soon after they arrived back at Notlund. He wanted her to have a painting studio close to the stables, as she had once too often dragged her painting supplies through the woods to the area.

Large and cozy, even in the winter, her studio had soon become her favorite spot at Notlund. She could paint inside or outside, and could easily access her horse to go exploring. Plus, seeing her husband throughout the day was a delightful bonus.

Rowen walked out of the stables, his dark hair mussed and white shirt dirty. An instant smile came to his face when he noticed her up the hill. Wynne's breath caught. He still did it to her, still made her heart speed when she saw him.

"You look peaceful," Rowen said, halfway up the hill. "I almost do not want to disturb you."

"I am." Wynne smiled. "But you can always disturb me, my husband."

"I missed you this morning." He went to the matching rocking chair, grabbing her hand and pulling her up as he sat.

Tugging her down, he nestled her sideways onto his lap, his arms wrapping around her. His nose nuzzled into her neck. "I want some of your peace after the last few days."

Wynne chuckled. "Did you think marrying off the duchess was going to be an easy affair?"

"No. It went as well as I suspected it would. Is she ready?"

"She is, finally." Wynne curled her fingers along his ribcage, tucking her head on his shoulder. "It is why I came down here, and then I found myself sidetracked with sitting here."

"So what were you thinking about that produced such peacefulness in your eyes?"

"The mountain."

"Do you want to go there soon? We can. Anytime you want." His fingers danced lightly up and down her spine.

"Yes, I do want to go back, someday, and my mother would like that as well, I think. But not soon."

"No?"

"That was what I was thinking on—about my life on the mountain, about what I still believed my life was in those first hours when I met you in the forest. My grandfather was alive, my mother was happy, we lived on the mountain. I painted. I was at peace, utterly content. Happy."

"And then you saw Notlund." She could feel Rowen tense underneath her.

"I did. And I lost everything—my grandfather, my mother, my home, my life—I thought never to have happiness again."

Wynne leaned away from Rowen so she could see the silver in his dark eyes. "Except that you were there. You were by my side. My life had been completely dismantled. But then you happened."

He relaxed under her, his hand coming from her waist to rest along the lines of her neck.

She shook her head. "That I am here today—it is impossible—more than I ever could have hoped for in those days. I never could have even dreamed of this happiness."

Her hand swept around them. "You gave me this. A completely different world from what I knew, but I am more content now—happier in this moment than I have ever been." She settled her palm on his cheek, the dark scruff prickling her skin. "You gave me you. You are the reason."

"No, Wynne." He turned his head to kiss her palm. "You did this for yourself."

A soft smile touched her lips. "Since I have had enough drama in the past few days, I will avoid the argument. Shall we just say we did it together?"

"We can do that. It sounds remarkably fair." He gave her a tight squeeze. "And speaking of the drama, we should get up to the castle."

"Yes." Wynne sighed, swinging her legs off his lap. "Plus, I have something to show you."

"I do hope it is something in my rooms. Something without clothes on." Rowen stood, smirking and settling an arm around her shoulders as they walked.

"You will have to wait and see." She slipped her arm behind his waist. "Did you decide on the horses—they are set?"

"Yes. I picked out several of the best mares for his stable— it should make a nice parting gift for Lord Wilmington. He is taking on the dowager, after all."

"Stop." Wynne swatted Rowen's chest.

"The man did not know what he was getting into when he first came here to check out that Arabian he bought." He sighed. "Is the dowager truly ready this time? We thought she was yesterday."

"Yes. I do hope so. There have been no last minute requests that will take a day to arrange."

Several minutes later, Wynne was leading Rowen into Notlund's main hall. Sunlight streamed in as they walked past the long row of paintings of Rowen's ancestors. At the end, Wynne stopped, turning Rowen to the wall.

He started shaking his head before Wynne even got a word out.

"No." Wynne interrupted what she knew would be his refusal. "You will not fight me on this. It is up and hanging in its rightful place."

She stepped forward, grabbing the bottom of the white sheet that hung in front of the newest painting on the wall. Turning back to him, she dangled the carrot she knew she had. "Plus, do you not want to see it after all this time?"

Arms crossed over his chest, Rowen stared at her.

She stared back, her sweetest smile in place.

Moments slipped by, and then he finally relented with a curt nod.

Eyes on Rowen, Wynne yanked on the sheet. It dropped, pooling to the ground.

His gaze swept over it, dropping quickly to Wynne.

"No background?" he asked, left eyebrow raised.

"No."

He looked up at it again, longer this time, taking it in, before pinning Wynne with his eyes. "But all of the time we spent sitting for this. What were you doing in all of those sessions? I saw you painting."

Wynne stepped from under the painting to stand next to Rowen. She looked up at her painting of him, not at all worried about her skill in catching his likeness. Rowen and nothing else. Just his face. His face on a black background. Of all the paintings she had ever done, she knew, down to her soul, that this was her best work.

She looked at him, meeting Rowen's eyes. "I have been painting black. There have to be thirty layers on there by now."

"Rapscallion." His fingers went under arms, tickling her ribs.

She squealed, jumping away until his hands dropped. Stepping close to him, she slid her arms around his waist, setting her chin on his shoulder.

"But what about Phalos? He gets no place in it?"

"He has his own portrait. And you hung that one in here months ago." She rounded him so she could look up him. "Everything I know of you—your history—it is mine. For all the other people, the other paintings, who they were was not mine to hold. But yours—your history, your mind, your heart—all of it is mine to hold—all of it makes you. So all of it must live in my heart, my soul, since that is where you are. Nowhere else."

Wrapping his arms around her, Rowen smiled down at her. The easy smile, the one only she was blessed with. The one she loved the most. "So you will not share me?"

"I will not share you." She nodded backward to the painting with her head. "Only this. And only because it is in its rightful place."

Rowen's dark eyes drifted up to the portrait, staring at it. Long seconds passed, but Wynne could see that Rowen was not fighting it, merely coming to terms with it. He gave one long nod.

And then his head came down, his lips finding hers. The heat of him filled her, taking over her senses, owning her every thought, every nerve.

He broke contact for just a breath, his words thick. "Thank you, Wynne. It means more than you know."

She went to her toes, not letting him escape her lips so easily.

"Here you are." The duchess's voice echoed along the hall.

Eyes closed, Rowen groaned, pulling slowly away from Wynne. They both turned to the dowager duchess, Rowen tucking Wynne under his arm.

"We are prepared to leave." The dowager walked toward them, her boot heels clicking on the stone floors. "But there is one last matter I need to take care of here at Notlund."

Rowen heaved a sigh. Wynne dug her elbow into his ribs, trying to silence his exasperation.

"We will see you as soon as you return from your tour, Duchess?" Wynne asked.

"Of course, dear." The dowager stopped in front of Wynne, her gloved hand cupping Wynne's cheek. "I have already said goodbye to your mother. I will miss her. I will miss you."

Wynne stepped from Rowen's arm, grasping the duchess in a tight hug. For a second, the dowager was stiff, but then her arms came up, returning Wynne's squeeze.

"And I will miss you, Duchess. My mother will miss you as well. You have been a godsend to her," Wynne said. "Though I am so happy for you and the baron."

The dowager nodded, dropping her arms and smoothing her skirts after Wynne released her. "I had once been like you, Wynne. Young and fanciful and not going to let the world tell me how to live my life. That did not work out for me, not until today. Not until the baron."

The duchess swept a lock of hair from Wynne's temple into her upsweep. "Though I am happy, dear, that it worked out for you. Perhaps you have a purer heart than I did. Or perhaps fate just wanted me to wait until this day. Regardless, you gave me the courage to live beyond what the truth of my world had become, Wynne. I am forever in your debt."

Before Wynne could even reply, the duchess turned to Rowen, her manner instantly brisk. "The last matter I have here at Notlund. Please, follow me."

The duchess spun and retraced her steps to the middle of the hall. In front of the portrait of the sixth Duke of Letson, she stopped. She went to the tall painting, lifting the bottom of the thick frame from the wall. "Please, Letson, hold this."

A quick questioning look to Wynne, and Rowen grabbed the gilded frame, holding it away from the wall.

The duchess ducked behind the painting and started to wedge free a stone from the wall. Setting the heavy grey stone to the floor, she went to the cavity in the wall, pulling out a wooden box.

Swiping the dust from the top of the box, she waited for Rowen to set the painting back in place and turn to her. "The baron has made me a better person. I recognize that, and as part of asking me to marry him, he demanded that I let go of all the past. I do not intend on disappointing him. So to stay true to that, I need to give you this."

She held out the box to Rowen. He took it, eyes perplexed.

"It was to be passed on to my son, the next in line after my husband died." She smacked her hands together, clearing the dust from them. "I discovered it after they died. And I kept it. You will find the contents interesting, I am sure."

"What is in it?" Rowen asked.

"It is unbecoming to speak of the past, so I will not." She shook her head. "But know that I have let my anger free. I harbor no ill will to you, Letson. And I give to you now, the last of the secrets I have been forced to harbor for this duchy. I want them all removed from my life. Plus, I believe it is time to intervene. And you are the one to do so. So the box, its contents are yours. Yours to do with what you will."

Rowen inclined his head to her. "Thank you, Duchess, for the trust."

"I am also sure that you will be the one to do right by the contents, your grace." She winked at him.

Clearing her throat, the duchess stepped away from Rowen, her eyes going down the wall and resting on Rowen's newly placed portrait. She paused for a long moment, and then the smallest smile touched her lips.

"It is fitting." Her eyes dropped to Wynne. "Well done, my dear. Well done."

With a swish of her bright red skirts, the dowager duchess walked out of the great hall.

Still dumbstruck at the entire scene, Wynne turned slowly to Rowen.

"Did the duchess truly just wink at you, my husband?"

Rowen nodded, eyes wide. "I believe she did."

"What is in the box?"

Rowen flipped the latch on the simple wooden box. A stack of papers, some scrolled, sat inside. Handing Wynne the box, Rowen pulled out the top piece of thick vellum, scanning the writing.

Wynne watched Rowen's eyes flip from curiosity to hardness. She set the box on the floor, grabbing his forearm. "What is written?"

His eyes stayed on the paper. "It says there are more."

"More?"

Rowen looked up to her, dark eyes in shock. "More of me. More children."

"What? More children?"

"I am not the only by-blow." His head shook, stunned. "I have sisters, Wynne, sisters."

~ ABOUT THE AUTHOR ~

K.J. Jackson is the author of *The Hold Your Breath Series,*
The Lords of Fate Series, and *The Flame Moon Series.*

She specializes in historical and paranormal romance,
will work for travel, and is a sucker for a good story in any genre.
She lives in Minnesota with her husband, two children,
and a dog who has taken the sport of
bed-hogging to new heights.

Visit her at www.kjjackson.com

~ Author's Note ~

Thank you so much for taking a trip back in time with me. The next book in the *Lords of Fate* series will debut in Fall 2015.

If you missed the *Hold Your Breath* series, be sure to check out these historical romances: ***Stone Devil Duke, Unmasking the Marquess, and My Captain, My Earl***.

Be sure to sign up for news of my next releases at **www.KJJackson.com** (email addresses are precious, so out of respect, you'll only hear from me when I actually have real news).

Interested in Paranormal Romance?
In the meantime, if you want to switch genres and check out my Flame Moon paranormal romance series, ***Flame Moon #1***, the first book in the series, is currently free (ebook) at all stores. ***Flame Moon*** is a stand-alone story, so no worries on getting sucked into a cliffhanger. But number two in the series, ***Triple Infinity***, ends with a fun cliff, so be forewarned. Number three in the series, ***Flux Flame***, ties up that portion of the series.

As always, I love to connect with my readers, you can reach me at:

www.KJJackson.com

https://www.facebook.com/kjjacksonauthor

Twitter: @K_J_Jackson

Thank you for allowing my stories into your life
and time—it is an honor!
~ K.J. Jackson

CPSIA information can be obtained
at www.ICGtesting.com
Printed in the USA
BVHW031716061020
590428BV00001B/7